THE LITTLE AMBULANCE WAR OF WINCHESTER COUNTY

A Trowbridge Vermont Novel

A Novel by
I. M. AIKEN

Published by Flare Books,
an imprint of Catalyst Press, El Paso, Texas

9781963511024 paperback $19.95
9781963511079 ebook $12.95
9781963511086 audiobook $9.95

For further information, write info@catalystpress.org
In North America, this book is distributed by
Consortium Book Sales & Distribution, a division of Ingram.
Phone: 612/746-2600
cbsdinfo@ingramcontent.com
www.cbsd.com

In South Africa, Namibia, and Botswana,
this book is distributed by Protea Distribution.
For information, email orders@proteadistribution.co.za.

LCCN number: 2024936188

To
All of those who walk, or run, towards danger

THE LITTLE AMBULANCE WAR OF WINCHESTER COUNTY

A Trowbridge Vermont Novel

A Novel by
I. M. AIKEN

Prologue - 2022

I left public service several years ago. Yet with the perversity of the Fates, I still find myself standing next to dead bodies for hours. I still find myself driving to car wrecks. And like yesterday, standing in a house being destroyed by violence, fear, alcohol, and incurable illnesses. The events echo a life's work. Someone dials 911, and then I walk in.

My desire to dash about in a big ambulance with lights and sirens came from the television shows of my youth. In my office, I have a few notable uniform patches displayed on a cork board. The yellow and red "County of Los Angeles Fire Department Paramedic" patch hangs there. I hung it in tribute to the show that introduced us all to paramedics. On that same board, I have pinned a 250 dinar note from Iraq, the shoulder patch of the Boston Fire Department and Boston Police Department, and the shoulder patches of towns with names similar to Trowbridge. The collection also includes two patches from New York City: New York Task Force 1—the urban search and rescue team—and NYC Office of Emergency Management. My father's shadowbox hangs with honor, each of his rank insignia and awards displayed neatly against a red velvet background. We both entered public safety at the age of twenty. Different uniforms. Different cities. I also have a photograph of my father in a custom dark-blue double-breasted suit leading a mother duck and her ducklings on a path in Boston Common. Built from similar foundations, my life diverged from my father's before I left university.

Bea, a near neighbor, called my mobile phone at three in the afternoon on the Wednesday before Christmas Eve in 2022. I drove to her. My vehicles used to have radios and emergency lights just like my father's city-owned cars. No longer. I no longer carry radios on my hip nor mounted in my truck. My truck no longer cries into these hills with its siren. My truck no longer ignites the forest with red and white strobe lights. I no longer carry a medical kit, or crime scene tape, or any of the other accoutrements of the EMS chief that I once was. Regardless, I can still drive fast. I learned that skill young. I followed my own property boundary, and I passed exactly one home, the home belonging to Bea. The rest of the drive involved hard-frozen dirt roads in a heavily forested and mountainous region of northern Appalachia. Later in the evening, when debriefing a friend after the crisis, she asked, "What did you think you were heading to?"

The answer was obvious: Someone was dead, and the other family member—in full panic—called for help. I am expert at that call. My words and actions no longer carry legal significance. I am no longer a paramedic, no longer a firefighter. I stepped, or got stepped, back to the humble rank of civilian. Following my years in public safety, the world kept changing on me, on us all. We faced international and domestic terrorism, two wars, a global pandemic, and the political landscape of our Earth wobbled on its axis. I carry only seasoned skills.

My neighbor, Bea, stood in the driveway. I climbed out donning gloves. Bea said, "Nobody's dead." She added that Mrs. Stein was drunk and beating on Mr. Stein. Frankly, Death makes a better guest than what I will find in my next steps. One ought to avoid Death's comradeship. We, Death and I, still meet at the threshold with solemnity and respect. Sometimes when people don't know how to greet Death, I get called. And why? Because official help comes from a far distance out here—if it comes at all. I live in a region of the United States where people tend not to rely on outside help. If a house slips from a jack while someone worked on a foundation crushing a thumb, you wrap it tightly with a towel, and then ask one of the kids to drive you to the hospital in the farm truck. It is easier to clean and superglue a wound at home or at a skilled neighbor's house than it is to waste a day in an emergency room an hour away.

While Bea informed me that Death had not yet arrived, I wondered what was beyond the closed door. With caution, I stated, "Domestic violence is the most dangerous call we face."

Bea said, "I called 911 and the state police are coming," a statement that eventually proved false—twice. I love Bea's optimism, an optimism born of city and suburban life where systems work. Once upon a time, I served as a member of a team that required us to respond to every 911 call within seven minutes. In this state, at this time, there is no requirement for the police or anyone to respond to a 911 call. I shared Bea's optimism, expecting the state police to arrive within forty-five minutes. That may seem like a long time, but given the distances, road conditions, and the scarcity of cops, I have waited an hour or more for help from the police.

I entered the house slowly. I have known Mr. and Mrs. Stein for over a decade, and I know their medical histories well. I knew that Mr. Stein used to love shooting clay pigeons with his shotguns. Therefore, I knew guns were in this house. He was on hospice. Mrs. Stein had been possessed by a kaleidoscope of mental health issues plus severe medical conditions. She approached her own end crabwise given that any of her three chronic medical conditions might kill her with a sneeze. After three years of declining health during the Covid pandemic, they deliberately and loudly shuttered the door against Death. She believed that the weight of the door would prevent that virus, any virus from sneaking into their sanctuary. Believed that door would keep Death at bay. Ironically, three years of isolation provided a trail for Death to follow.

Early partners trained me on scene evaluation and personal safety. Walking into yet-another-scene of violence, I assessed the setting, looking for guns, knives, axes, sticks, and fists. I walked past the suicide note Mrs. Stein had written on the plaster wall in pen. She had signed it by smearing the wall and words with blood. I missed the note the first time. Primarily, I did not see it because the note did not threaten me. Mrs. Stein's suicide note could not animate itself. Her note could not bludgeon me from behind.

Yet, the note on the wall shall haunt me during some future

night. It shall join the other images, demons, and ghosts I still carry. Alone with my thoughts, these letters would animate themselves. They became creatures with reticulated legs formed of brittle oak twigs. The blood's near-black color reverted to the living glossy red liquid I knew too well. When the note manifested into a clicking spider, it would not hurt me in the same way a kitchen knife pierced my skin. Knives, bottles, guns, chairs, and sticks would leave physical scars. Perhaps the creepy clicking spider image of her suicide note would climb free of the wall, carving a deep scar.

I feared the full bottle of amber-colored booze between me and Mrs. Stein. A bottle makes a perfect cudgel. The wine Mrs. Stein had already spilled on the floor turned into a sticky purple dye. The purple stains on the wall demonstrated both high-speed and low-speed splatter patterns. Clearly wine and not blood. While I knew Mr. Stein owned firearms, I spied none. The suicide note demonstrated the depth of their crisis.

I placed Mrs. Stein in her tattered recliner and escorted Mr. Stein to a back room. I counted on her inebriation and exhaustion. I gambled on his desire to live. Instead, like two mean old cats, they sought battle.

There I stood at parade rest. Any noise could cause a flare-up between these two combatants. Mr. Stein would move. Mrs. Stein would then discover a path for attack. Mrs. Stein maintained a cat-like posture in her recliner. She appeared to have passed out, but one eye remained ajar and alert. Mean old cats? No. I recognized Mrs. Stein as a human spider. Quiet, still, patient until she strikes.

I held twenty-one feet, six-and-a-half meters, as the magic distance. I learned this during firearms training. I did not have a weapon with me at this scene; I preferred not to have a weapon. I made that decision long ago: no weapons on routine medical calls. During firearms training, the instructors drilled us on the relationship between time and distance. The closer someone is to you (or you to them), the less time you have to react. At twenty feet, a fleet-footed fighter can strike an armed person faster than the brain can tell the finger to pull the trigger. The process of pulling the trigger involves our brain deciding to aim and then aiming, followed by our brain deciding to pull the trigger, and then pulling the trigger. Most people cannot pull the trigger or react fast enough to stop someone who is closer than twenty feet away. The reaction time between the eyes, the brain, and our ability to pull a trigger takes measurable time. I wanted twenty feet between me and the two people in this small house. I believed that I could still maneuver faster than two people who were each in their seventh decade, yet there I stood, feeling all of my five decades. My days of climbing towers and running mountains with heavy packs had faded. Both Mr. and Mrs. Stein qualified for hospice. I expected them to be slower than the military-aged men and women that I have faced over the decades, but I could only react if I could see them both. I clung to the idea that without me, these two people would kill each other. If I turned my back, I would die.

Maintaining control over the scene required understanding my limits. I was alone. All but one phone line in the house had been cut into multiple pieces. The cord from the wall to the phones had been severed into short pieces. The curly cord from the phone base to the handsets had also been sliced into several small sections. My own mobile phone sat two kilometers away on my kitchen counter. Bea stood outside the door, but her default actions resembled those of a sparrow. She flittered and hid from trouble. I was a hawk.

Like the hawks of these woods, such as the broad winged who hunts the forest, and the red tailed who hunts the fields, I stood my perch unmoving, watching both Steins with a raptor's care. My duty at emergency scenes involved three objectives: first, live; second, protect my exit; third, minimize further damage. My duty ended when the cops arrived. At the sight of flashing blue lights, I expected to step away.

Teachers, my father among them, taught me to rank the people at emergency scenes. Number one at the top of the list is me, always me. Number two is my partner or partners. Number three are the bystanders. Number four are the patients. The bottom of that list is the aggressor. It is a dizzying calculus that plays out monthly here in the United States: the tiresome tally of the dead when, in fact, nobody escapes unharmed.

I spoke very little during those hours. In the beginning, I established boundaries: "Goal number one is that nobody dies today. Goal number two is that nobody gets hurt. Goal number three is that we find a way through this crisis." I had spoken these words aloud before. In the early years, I thought I would fight to keep others alive, as if Death were a distant and fierce adversary. As it turned out, I often struggled with goal number one. People die. Sometimes, they die minutes before I arrive. Sometimes while I am there. Standing for forty-five minutes, fifteen feet from Mr. Stein and fifteen feet from Mrs. Stein, I acknowledged I had no idea where Mr. Stein's firearms were stored. I had no idea if he had a pistol tucked in a drawer. In Trowbridge, there are more guns than people. Keeping the living alive remained paramount. If I failed at Goal Number One, then I would find a way to walk out of this house unharmed.

I stood in floppy plastic clogs, wearing purple nitrile gloves on my hands and a medical mask over my face. I wore my old EMS uniform trousers. Ironically, I also pulled on an old uniform T-shirt and a green hospital scrub top. Today, I wore these sturdy old trousers because I appreciated their warmth when doing farm stuff on a cold December afternoon. My uniform trousers had a small hole in the crotch. The pockets, once filled with the tools of my trade, flopped emptily against my thighs. In the plastic Crocs, my feet sweated. My hands perspired inside the gloves. After standing for a very long time, long enough for the standard forty-five-minute response from the state police, I dug through their home office to find the sole working phone. I dialed 911. I asked the 911 operator to dispatch Trowbridge Fire and our regional ambulance. I asked them to send, please send, the state police. I described a scene of violence. I described a profoundly intoxicated person. I informed the dispatcher of a suicide attempt and of ongoing suicidal ideations plus depression plus paranoia. I spoke professionally and used the uncool lingo of the trade, proving myself to be an insider. Domestic Violence becomes DV, drunk becomes ETOH, the chemical shorthand for ethyl alcohol. I acknowledged that I barely had control of the scene. To that point, I put down the phone to once again separate Mrs. Stein from Mr. Stein. I placed Missus back in her ancient recliner before returning to the 911 operator. I turned my back and the old lady spider danced across the web to strike her prey again. The operator never admitted that the initial call had been cancelled. Before I clicked off, she assured me that help was forthcoming.

When I was active with fire, rescue, and ambulance services, I was always prepared. At this scene, I had nothing except for the remaining landline. I appreciated that my neighbor Bea stood outside the house in remote support. I had no other resources. Achieving Goal Number One required my vigilance. If I spoke, they flared up. If I moved, she attacked. We three human beings formed a triangle. Mr. Stein shifted himself from the room I had put him in. He sat in his office guarding the last working phone behind the partially closed door. He sat slightly to my left. Mrs. Stein faked a benign and drunken stupor—her alert eyes flashed towards any movement. She sat in her sunken recliner against the back wall in front of me. I stood with my back to the exit hallway. Within a meter of my right shoulder, I noticed a block of kitchen knives. I knew that if I moved towards those knives, I would be in trouble. I could not protect myself from them, nor get them away from us. Instead, I shifted two dining chairs and placed them between Mr. and Mrs. Stein. Obstacles intended to give me one more second to act, or to retreat.

I learned how to knock on a door in Cambridge Massachusetts as a young EMT. The first time I stood as if at a friend's apartment. I faced the door with my full body. I got tugged away. "Don't stand there. You'll get shot." I learned that first day—never stand in front of the door. Why? Sometimes people shoot through the closed door. If I don't stand in front of the door, I am less likely to get shot. Back then in my Metro-days, I looked like a cop with blue-over-blue, lapel radio mic, badge, and the rest. Those were great days. We had such freedom. Furthermore, I was young and reckless. I was lean and fast. I followed an unseen path with my own fashions, my own way of playing, my own way of dating and my own way of enjoying life. Regrettably, I had to run away from Cambridge. Actually, I was driven away in my father's city-owned police car to the Appalachian Trail.

The battle that once awaited me in Cambridge eventually re-emerged in Winchester County, Vermont as another battle, a series of battles. I didn't win. Nobody won. I feel these losses with a dry throat and quiet anger.

In time, my former teammates arrived. I knew the trucks instantly. I knew their body shapes. Having shared over a decade of trauma, drama, and car wrecks, little needs to be said among us. Jay walked into the house. I provided him with a scene assessment and the immediate needs. I spoke in a whisper. Jay whispered back.

Suddenly Mrs. Stein shrieked out that we were conspiring against her.

Jay told me that Vermont State Police decided not to respond to the original DV call, the call Bea made. I would have stood there for hours believing help was coming from the police, yet they were not coming. The police told no one about their revised plan. Jay says they also declined to respond to the call I made from the house phone.

Jay told me that Robby was in the dooryard, yelling at the police dispatcher. Without a look, a touch, or a word, I felt love and respect from both Robby and Jay. Robby got confirmation that the State Police again cancelled their response after rescue and fire rolled to the scene. The Vermont State Police dispatcher told Captain Robby of the fire department, the incident commander, that the VSP will not be able to help. Robby provided more details and I do believe that he stated that "one of his own" was in harm's way. He convinced them to send a trooper. By the time I left hours later, we had three troopers on scene with us.

Though my friend Jay did not feel safe nor able to maintain the peace in the house, he let me step out the door to brief the troopers. I had written a narrative of the battery and alcohol and suicide attempt on a piece of stained paper. I had handed that narrative out the door to command when Robbie arrived. But as the sole person in constant contact with the people and the crime scene, I needed to brief the troopers. Which I did: immediate history, long-term history, setting of the scene, risks/weapons on the scene. When done and re-masked, we entered the home again. I introduced one trooper to each subject. Here is Mrs. Stein. Here is Mr. Stein. Each in their little spaces separated by fifteen feet and an unclosed door.

After an hour or maybe longer, my role as peacekeeper had been turned over to two young men. Immediately, the senior trooper's actions brought relief and pleasure. The trooper squatted in front of Mrs. Stein to address her at her eye level. He asked open-ended questions using non-judgmental and non-threatening language. In a few minutes, Mrs. Stein admitted to battering Mr. Stein. She admitted to suicidal thoughts and actions. She admitted to long-term mental health issues as well a list of medical conditions that may yet prove fatal. Yes, she was a mess. The trooper walked through each issue, listening carefully and finding the crucial facts. On Christmas Eve day, the morning I wrote this, I sent a formal letter praising the actions of the senior trooper on scene.

He convinced Mrs. Stein to allow paramedics to get vital signs. I stepped outside to the awaiting ambulance. I briefed the two guys on the ambulance. I spoke more about hematocrit levels, aneurysms, and open-heart surgery than weapons and evidence of violence. I walked in with the paramedic. We did the introductions and I stepped back to my "duty station" as overwatch.

When I saw the ambulance arrive, I knew both men on the rig. I have known them through my EMS career in these hills. One is the least competent paramedic I have ever known. He hates the sight of blood and vomit. And I have known him to get car-sick in the back of an ambulance. He once got me suspended for three months for providing the right medical care in the right situation. His efforts to suspend me were seconded by the other gentleman on the ambulance. These two guys nearly ruined my career and destroyed my reputation. And yet we've done hundreds of calls together. I keep thinking I am done with him—done with both of those bastards. Then tragedy blossoms. They arrived in an ambulance. Ironically, the ambulance they arrived in had been bought by me. Later, I gave it away to another service. Now these two bastards have it parked up the road from the Steins' home.

I introduced them as "my friends" and said they were here to help. Both statements were false. The two guys from the ambulance had never been my friends. I doubted that anything we did could help the two Steins on this darkening winter's eve. Neither the paramedic nor the trooper convinced Mrs. Stein to seek medical help. In Vermont, if a patient refuses care, then EMS personnel cannot take them against their will. Exceptions exist for those who are unconscious or juvenile. We accept *implied consent* from these patients. From an alert woman who can retell the events of the last few days flawlessly and without slurring, the medical team cannot legally justify forcing her to go to the hospital. No consent, no transport. That's the law. In this case, the trooper then sought help through his chain of command and through the Vermont social services agency, Health Care and Rehabilitation Services, HCRS.

To digress, the laws in the Commonwealth of Massachusetts differ from those in Vermont. I trained and worked in Massachusetts as an EMT and then later as a paramedic. In Mass, EMTs and medics can be dispatched to a crisis with a "pink paper." The pink paper, also called a "Section 12," permits EMS folks to physically restrain a patient if "they are at risk of harm to self or others." Once hauled to an emergency department, patients can be held for seventy-two hours. Vermont has no such law. As a kid on an urban ambulance, I would have scooped one person into my rig, even if I had to use the handcuffs I wore tucked into the small of my back, clipped to my leather duty belt. We needed to resolve calls and get to the next one. Today, I comprehend that I once kidnapped a child from his family, denying rights in the spirit of public safety and public health. We were wrong then. I was wrong then. Conversely, I do not believe today's laws bring us closer to what's right or to justice.

In some places, police use "protective custody" as a means to de-escalate a crisis between two or more people. Protective custody involves cuffing people and stuffing them into the back of a police cruiser or ambulance—but without the legal formalities of an arrest. The hope is that this technique reduces the immediate risk to life and limb. Vermont police do not have the option to use "protective custody."

Some states have a "pro-arrest" law when police encounter domestic violence. In those jurisdictions, police are required to remove one party. One person always got arrested and removed. Sometimes both. Occasionally, the arrests got reversed when people sobered up and investigations commenced. Pro-arrest laws strive to prevent immediate death or serious injury to both parties in a domestic violence scene.

Not here. Not in Vermont. The freedom of the individual remains paramount. The "Live Free or Die" state fits snuggly on the entire eastern border of Vermont. Vermont lawmakers enshrined that same *Live Free or Die* mentality in our state laws.

The trooper heard first-hand about a woman battering her husband repeatedly during the day. He heard the story of her desire to kill herself, and her failed efforts to slice open her forearms. He had seen the suicide note written in large letters on the foyer wall covered in smeared blood, likely from her own forearm. My friend Bea provided a reliable third-party witness to the assault and the battery. And Mr. Stein provided a similar account to the trooper who interviewed him. On a TV show, the plot resolves at this point: cut to a scene exploring the hero's personal life and a sense of normalcy. I wish that were the case. Even arrests, transportation to the hospital, or a seventy-two-hour hold resolves nothing. Pulled by gravity, magnets, hope, loneliness, and desperation, these cycles cycle.

The senior trooper called up through his chain of command. The bosses informed him that the subject did not qualify for an arrest. Frankly, I never understood these thresholds. Last year, Captain Robby called the state police to arrest a subject at a traffic accident who assaulted a firefighter who was directing traffic. There were fists, shoves, and shouts. The guy, the bad guy, insisted he had to get to his ski condo to meet his wife for supper. The other guy was a uniformed Trowbridge firefighter maintaining public order and limiting access to a state highway shutdown due to a motor vehicle crash. The police did not even respond. Vermont has a criminal statute intended to protect public servants from assault. The statute has not yet been enforced in Trowbridge, Vermont. The decision not to send the police to arrest someone for assaulting a uniformed firefighter at an emergency scene means that the fellow from New York who struck another human being on a snowy highway had dinner with his wife and skied all weekend before returning to New York.

Our trooper worked through the HCRS organization begging for the authority to transport Mrs. Stein to a hospital for an involuntary psychiatric evaluation. We had a written suicide note, a trail of blood, an obvious suicide attempt, and a verbal admission to her efforts to kill herself. HCRS denied the authority to transport a patient against her will. She had to go willingly, or she was entitled to remain home.

Thus endeth the official efforts for a peaceful and legal resolution employing the standard tools afforded to public safety officers. The police were powerless. The ambulance crew were powerless. The fire crew were powerless. The civilian who stood between two warring people, me, started recognizing that I wasted my Wednesday afternoon. I ought to have stayed home cooking for the holiday.

We, the first responders, hatched Plan B through collaboration with relatives and friends of the parties involved. These people will remove Mr. Stein plus his medical oxygen, an overnight bag, and medications to their home. We invested another hour endeavoring to execute this plan. After initially agreeing, Mr. Stein then resolved to stay home. He said, "If I leave, she will destroy this house."

Yes, likely true.

Plan B failed. She might yet kill him, and then she would likely kill herself too. I had hoped that Plan B meant one of them would live through the night.

In the dooryard, I greeted other members of the Stein family.

I described how common this situation is, increasing the sense of frustration and futility felt by these well-meaning people.

Neither the police nor the State of Vermont has the authority nor resources to manage ongoing mental health crises. While Vermont has endured this situation for a long time, we've never fully funded public safety. We also never defunded the police. We opted to underfund all public safety since the founding of the Vermont Republic, which existed from 1777 to 1791. Over two hundred years later, we call the state police, and they cancel their own response. They do not have enough troopers to cover the two hundred plus towns. They do not have the funding to support these remote and isolated communities. Our town has approximately forty square miles of territory, roughly three times the size of Manhattan Island. Trowbridge hosts five hundred residents tucked into our forested mountains. Our firefighters volunteer their time without reward for the time or the expense. They face, we face, extreme hazards frequently.

I spoke to the family of Mr. and Mrs. Stein. They stood on the dirt road, staining hope with angry tears. I remained silent about my years of trying to help abused and neglected children in our hills. I did not speak of the years I spent trying to get help for the elderly rotting away in rotting houses with rotting food and no heat. Instead, I pointed my fingers at the political and the financial decisions being made by our lawmakers. The fact that this trooper does not have the authority to remove anyone from this scene stems from a lack of laws, a lack of funding, and a lack of resources. I suggested that if they wanted to solve this problem, they should call Uncle Bernie, our Senator; call the governor; and work with our local representatives. Nobody here has the money, resources, or authority to resolve this matter on a freezing December evening.

Before leaving, I offered verbal appreciation to the EMT and paramedic on the ambulance, both of whom have been terrible to me over the years. I thanked the firefighters from a department that once gave me the boot. I got a warm hug from my dearest friend in these hills, a man who once served as my assistant chief.

I then went to Bea's house. At her kitchen table, I briefed her on the status and outcome of this scene. My instructions involved not crossing the stonewall that serves as the border between the two properties. We could have a murder-suicide in that house during the holidays. If so, it would be the second suicide that week. On Monday, a human being who built a home about one mile south of my house accelerated a bullet through his head. Now, I stood a mile east of my house acknowledging Death might yet claim another—another one or another two. Death watches from near; this I know.

In Vermont, we faced long conflicts between the old ways and the new ways. Families that settled these lands before and after the American Revolution remain here in these hills. The Yankee spirit of self-reliance and community works only if there are resources in the community to care for those at the margins because of their age, health, or social status. So often the quiet arguments over money and priorities battled in marbled government buildings result in death, confusion, injury, and illness to our most vulnerable.

I miss the camaraderie of the fire department. There are times I think they hate me for the way it all ended. Then, when I was standing alone facing my fears, facing violence, and risking myself to prevent further injury, these teammates arrived to support me. They measured my fear. They weighed my exhaustion. When I climbed into Robby's truck for rest and warmth, we spoke only of his upcoming deer hunting trip, as if no time had passed between us. Jay and Robby had my back. We all gave up something. Both had children and wives at home on this holiday eve. They walked away from paying work to spend hours in the cold. They walked into the unknown, missing a meal with family during holidays. Together we tried. They stayed as long as they had because I needed them to stay. When it was evident that no amount of help from us could change the situation, we returned to our own homes.

I can confirm that Mr. and Mrs. Stein lived through the holidays. She sent me an email that sprayed venom into my eyes. I hoped this was the last of such notes. Some people do not want help. A few milliliters of mean only stings. The memory of that email will go into the leaky box where all of the screams go. I have been called a murderer—more than once. Words such as "You killed her!" haunt me during restless nights. People have occasionally decided to tell me to my face that they hate me. One person whispered, "Everyone here hates you." Regrettably, as dean of a community college, she pulled me from a practical skills exam to say these words to me. I cried. In revenge, I got the top marks. At one family home in Trowbridge, the family dialed 911 due to the normal mix of medical and mental health issues. Twice in the door yard, the missus-of-the-house screamed at me, "Why is it that *you* always come when I dial 911?" She totally hated me. She also hated the local ambulance service. When the calls came in, I went out.

I got called a thief. The Town of Langford's governing board called me a thief. When the local paper printed the comment, they sanitized the wording.

Intellectually, I acknowledge that my efforts earned more praise than venom. Far easier to remember the times someone calls you "murderer," "killer," "stormtrooper," "thief," and "fascist." Human memory avoids weighing the good against the bad. The brain, my brain, remembers the hurt significantly better. The hurt sits heavier. My father served the City of Boston as a hero cop, and a famous cop. During my university days, I jumped on urban ambulances. I learned lessons on those rigs that I brought with me to rural Vermont. I brought the good and the bad with me into these hills. What I did, what we did, as kids on the street, we did for the greater good. The Latin phrase is *pro bono publico*, for the public good. But was it? Did we serve the greater good? I do not know.

I killed the local ambulance service. I had said, in jest, that if you ever elect me chief of this service, I will kill it. Within three months, I had. The service quietly committed variations on the same crimes we committed in the city. In Vermont, the crimes served and benefited all. In Cambridge, less so.

When I put an end to it all, I became even more hated. In rural Winchester County, what we did on the ambulance saved lives and kept an historic and treasured ambulance service limping along. I killed it. I knew the rules. I always know the rules. Ironically, rules and laws may not agree. First, I followed the rules, then I followed the law. In the end, I strive to do what is right. I did that in my twenties, then again in my fifties.

A.F.

Part 1 | The 1980s

1 | Once Upon a Time in 1983

"Why didn't you tell me your name?"

"Well, sir, I thought I said, 'I am A. Flynn.'"

"Flynn?"

"Yes." I almost added Flynn yet again as we all may be confused by my last name. I did not spell "Flynn" for the boss. That seemed over-the-top. I told myself to be patient with the boss, as he attempted to divine whether I was one-of-us or one-of-them.

"As references, you listed two police officers from across the waters?"

As if Boston were farther than a short bridge over the Charles, a picture-perfect river lined with boat houses and park lands.

"I did."

"One of them is named William T.S. Flynn. Isn't he a captain?"

No, I had not provided his rank nor informed the boss that my father was a cop.

"He is."

My interviewer connected the dots yet again as he looked to the top of the job application form.

"And your name is Alexander Flynn?"

"Alexandra Flynn," putting a small emphasis on the last syllable.

The boss looked at me again. "Oh, right." As if confirming. He was still not certain if I was an "us" or a "them." What is an "us" to him? My father, the cop, fits squarely into that definition. Joining cops are firefighters, soldiers, and good local politicians. Us are people we trust. Us are people we know. Us are people like us. One can hear and see the differences between us and them. I believed I confused him.

"You could have saved us a lot of time if you'd introduced yourself."

And back to that name Flynn again. I stood offering my hand again to the boss. "Good to meet you, sir, I am Alexandra Flynn."

He shook my hand while seated. "Is Captain Flynn your father?"

"Has been all of my life."

"Well-cut suits? Irish brogue? Drinks tea?"

"He does seem to have a bit of an image," I agreed. The boss looked at my short hair and multiple earrings. He glanced over my haircut and the muscular shape of my shoulders and arms. His mind explored the heritability of us-ness. If my father is an "us," then the child ought to be an "us" as well. Or is it possible, Captain William Flynn had begotten a *one-of-them*. I admit I do look a bit like a "them." I let the boss struggle over the riddle. I love the freedom of youth.

"When can you start?" The easiest interview question ever. Also, the best interview question.

Minutes earlier we had been haggling over my lack of experience with ambulances. I took the EMT course on a lark at Northeastern University as a senior in high school. What can I say? I got bored. Now having completed my freshman year at university, I sought summer employment. I really wanted to join the Health and Hospital crew serving the City of Boston. Cool job, but not open to summer employment. Also, they wore brown uniforms like park rangers. On the other hand, Atlantic Ambulance was privately owned, owned by the boss asking me about my last name. I wanted to run a 911 ambulance within a city. If you are going to do this job, might as well do it right. Atlantic provides emergency services to the City of Cambridge. I couldn't work in the City of Boston without joining Health and Hospitals, or Health and Heroes, as they are called on the street. H&H is a civil service and career-only option. I couldn't dance in and out of their ranks as a college student. With a private service like Atlantic Ambulance, I could come and go during summers and holidays.

I did apply to services that were less urban and less focused on emergencies, which is where rookies ought to start. I had been told that most privately owned services will hire nearly anyone. Rumor was one just walks in with certifications and a pulse. With luck, you get put on the street with a sixty-thousand-dollar rig. Instead, all of the less urban services rejected me. Those bosses stated that I had no practical experience on an ambulance. I'll bet they each saw me as a "them" and not an "us." Hiring practice, in the early 1980s, fell within their own set of unspoken policies. One does not hire one of them, whichever of the numerous groups they are. The us group is always smaller.

In a metropolitan area filled with four centuries of immigration, I should have been yet another mick applying for a job. I should be an anonymous Flynn. Those other services turned me away due to my age. Maybe they turned me away because I looked like I belonged in a rowdy club. I had more ear piercings than most. My hair pushed the far edge of fashion for twenty-year-olds.

Walking into the station for Atlantic Ambulance, I removed three earrings. On the job application, I wrote the first name and family name of several Boston cops. I gave no ranks and no affiliation, just plain-Jane names. Not really name-dropping, is it? If you don't know those cops, then they are random Irish and Italian names written in a blue ballpoint pen. If you do know them, then you can connect the dots yourself. Which I watched the boss do, albeit slowly. Eventually, he put it together. That's what matters. And so, what if I did name drop my own father?

That was a bittersweet victory earned accidentally on the coat-tails of my father. My father had been a well-known cop for a long time. He was the guy the news crews from WBZ, WCVB, or WHDH wanted on camera. The talking-head said into their microphone: "We're standing outside of BPD headquarters with Captain Flynn." They loved that. William Tecumseh Sherman Flynn dressed every day for that fifteen second spot where he said: "I cannot really comment on an ongoing investigation." A no-comment from Captain Flynn commented on the importance and visibility of a case. He always answered with a knowing smile. He addressed the reporters warmly by name. While never winking, he appeared to wink for the camera. The corners of his eyes crinkled instantly. His big eyes embraced listeners with a hug.

Peter Clifton, the boss at Atlantic Ambulance, used the lower lids of his eyes as a measuring stick. He raised his lower lids, appraising me. The action enhanced the coolness of his personality. I handed him my EMT card, my Massachusetts driver's license, CPR card, and my real social security card. Some people have observed that the Commonwealth made a typo on my license. The social security number stamped above my name does not match the number of the official card. When asked about the disparity, I always expressed surprise at the error. I always affirmed that I would go fix that. Little lie, big lie. I displayed more interesting lies in plain sight. Explore it, baby. I don't wish anyone who looked at my driver's license to also get my social security number.

The boss sent me to a store in Inman Square called "The Haberdashery." I bought uniforms. I selected two pairs of triple-knit polyester police trousers with nine pockets. And I bought four shirts, all in the dark blue common to the fire and police departments nearby. My father once wore trousers like these, but not in decades. As a rookie cop, he walked into this store. I know that later in his career, he had all of his uniforms hand-made by an old Italian fellow in Revere. The fellow in Revere hand stitched the Captain's trousers in worsted merino wool. The trousers broke perfectly over his shoes. His blazers, double-breasted. Privately, I have wondered if my father learned of his tailor from one of the Boston capos he's busted. The tailor, a few blocks off of Revere Beach, served neutral ground for both cops and capos. That is the way of my Boston.

My father was the hero cop in *Make Way for Ducklings*, so my mother told me each time she read the book to me. I believed her. Sometimes, I still do. Except for two facts: first, the Captain would never permit a rounded belly or a fleshy face, as sported by the nice policeman in the book. Second, the book had been written at least one generation before my father was born. My father was too young to have served as a model for the drawings. Regardless of the visual differences, child-me saw my father leading ducklings to safety. My father earned a place within Boston's Holy Trinity:

The Pope, JFK, and a local hero.

I know now that my mother staged the photo of the Captain with the ducks on Boston Common. *The Boston Globe* published the picture on the front page above the fold. My father wore a blue double-breasted suit with a badge hanging from his breast pocket. The mother duck and ducklings waddled at his heels. It is a famous *Globe* picture. You can find this photo cut-out and framed at several bars in the city. In a lot of bars, you can find the picture of Bobby Orr flying horizontally over the ice, driving a puck into the net. Bobby Orr, Number Four, a hero of the Boston Garden and the Bruins. Then there is the picture of John F. Kennedy. Next to JFK hangs a picture of the Pope, again a cut-out from the *Globe* with the Pope standing in the damp on Boston Common.

Everyone in the city still remembered the day when John Paul II addressed 400,000 people who stood in the rain. Boston holds these mementos of recognition and victory with a firm grip.

Boston and its bars held my father in the same esteem reserved for other local heroes. That's good enough for a humble cop in an immaculately tailored suit. Therefore, it was good enough for me. I had sat in bars sipping a beer looking at the wall with clippings of my father, the Pope, and JFK watching over us all.

I never once had to point to the wall saying: "Hey stop it, that's my father there on the wall." I did not always avoid trouble, but I did tend to take care of myself when things got heated. I've got a smile and two rows of straight white teeth and my father's twinkling blue eyes. I have learned from him how to turn anger to humor with a word.

Years ago, when my father was a rookie cop, he stood in The Haberdashery, maybe talking to this same clerk ordering his first pair of uniform trousers. I doubted people in this store believed that I belonged in this store. I don't look the part of a cop or a firefighter or a construction worker. I'd guess that the Captain came out of Nana Flynn's loins looking like a young cop.

Me, on the other hand, I look like another-carefree-college-kid. Therefore, I heard the following phrase: "Come back tomorrow."

I paid while the clerk folded my clothes, placing them out of my reach. During the silence, he watched my face. "We will sew the patches on for you, unless you really want to do that yourself?" Oh, that does make sense. No doubt, the clerk will call Peter Clifton asking if he really hired me. I stood there at the counter, too young, too skinny, a mat of bleached hair bouncing over a bed of shorter darker hair. I had three small piercings in one ear and two in the other. Given it is Cambridge, I looked perfectly at home in Harvard Square sitting near the Out-of-Town News kiosk and riding on the Red Line. Our region is filled with invisible lines. Best and safest if one remains within established and familiar boundaries. A short decade after a violent crisis over bussing school children into different neighborhoods, wisdom suggests that people ought to honor the established structures. University students stay close to their campuses. Locals know to remain with their own folk. You know they are your people if the accents and family names are familiar. Everybody has their own definition of us and them. While in the streets of North Cambridge and Harvard Square, I was safer than when I walked through other neighborhoods.

I shook the clerk's hand. "Flynn, Alexandra Flynn."

"I'll remember." He winked, a real wink too. I suspected that within minutes, he called Atlantic Ambulance. By the end of the day, Captain Flynn will know that I bought a dark blue polyester uniform at the best-known uniform store in the area. I did not have to tell the Captain that I had been hired in Cambridge to work for Atlantic Ambulance.

I started the job on a Tuesday. I got off the Red Line and then walked from Porter Square south. I wiggled to Walden Street looking up Sherman Street in that moment after a May dawn. Those were my mother's streets: Sherman, Rindge, and Clay. She still has a great aunt living in a house on Magoun Street that has been in her family since the 1800s. My mother clearly sees ghosts of long-gone people and the black-and-white days. I do not see what she sees. That place owned by those great-grand-aunts looks tiny and run-down and cheaply built. I think my mother saw herself as a member of the Our Gang kids running wild with Spanky and Alfalfa. My mother roller skated and skipped rope on these streets. She used to walk to Porter Square for Saturday afternoon matinees at the movie theater. Throughout my childhood, she spoke of the car-barns which, with her accent "Kah-ban," didn't resemble any word I learned in school. Then I saw it, in my mind's eye. I envisioned the barns where the trolley cars parked and made their turnarounds. All gone by 1983. The iron-wheeled trolleys had been replaced with electric trolley buses. We also had very stinky buses that farted diesel fumes out the back.

Walking these roads in the stillness of an early summer dawn, remnants of the 1940s and 1950s hide in the shadows. I don't have her memories; I do have her stories. The 1940s and 1950s look shabby and worn when compared to the neighborhoods closer to Brattle Street and the university.

I arrived at the ambulance station, which was a cinder-block garage built into a formerly something-else building. I walked in wearing a mildly damp white T-shirt tucked neatly into the polyester uniform trousers. The trousers hung heavily from my waist. The T-shirt clung a bit and showed dampness along my spine and under my arms. I didn't think I would work up a sweat during the mile-and-a-half walk from the Porter Square T-station. I stepped through the garage to the bathroom at the back. I stripped my white undershirt off. I splashed with cool water, mopped dry with a spare undershirt (yes, thank you, Captain, I did carry two uniforms), then I dressed neatly. I gave the damp shirt a sniff before draping it neatly on top of my backpack. I arrived forty-five minutes before my shift, looking at a bay filled with ambulances. The overhead lights were off and the bay hummed quietly, echoing hidden equipment.

How should I introduce myself to others? Who was I? I had been inconsistent about showing myself to others. I have called myself Alex, Sandy, X, Lex and nearly every other variation of my name. My mother, when fussed, yells Alexandra. The name gave me freedom. I decided that for this job my name will be Lexi. It is cute, mildly feminine, and suits me fine. I tended to use both Alex and

Sandy at clubs, names I silently preferred over both Alexandra and Lexi. Lexi would help me fit in better.

Stepping upstairs, I met the dispatcher, Denny. The normal start of an introduction includes three questions: "What is your name?;" "Where are you from?;" and "Who is your father?" When asked where you are from, you answer with a neighborhood and street. When you tell people which neighborhood you are from, you are helping them shape their understanding of your background, your family, your lineage. Accent and name provide some help as well.

I added, "My mother grew up off of Rindge Ave and went to Ellis School."

Denny asked, "Is your father Captain Flynn?"

Instead of the boring yes, I said, "He told me that this job could get a bit messy. He suggested I carry an extra uniform." I decided to make it personal. After all, Captain Flynn was a father who gave good advice. Who knew that I would sweat through the T-shirt just walking from Mass Ave? My father did.

As Denny and I got to know each other, the station woke. Sleepy-faced guys came from the bunk rooms. Fresh-faced guys wandered upstairs carrying coffee. Dennis said, "We're going to put you with Bobby Clifton."

"Clifton? Seems familiar."

"Nephew."

Bobby Clifton landed solidly in the "us" column at this job.

"You guys will be in 25."

Thus began a routine of nearly a lifetime. Bobby, a bit too fat and a bit too stupid to serve as a good training officer and mentor, showed me how to check a rig. His answer to the daily inventory checklist: look for the stuff you need, ignore the rest. If the rig missed something then, he instructed that we replace it when on the road. My first lesson on an ambulance was "don't take supplies from the station's cabinet when you can steal them from a hospital." His daily checklist contained an irregular straight line down the "yes" column in blue pen. "It's all here. I was in this rig yesterday; it was perfect then." He appeared lazy and listless while executing the first duty of the day. When it came to washing the rig, Bobby displayed fastidious patience. Using a clean, dry towel, he polished the chrome and mirrors. He then erased every water spot on the rig. He polished the region under the driver's side window where "Bobby Clifton" had been painted in cursive gold letters. Clearly nobody touched Bobby's rig. He was, we were, the first to leave the station. And Bobby's rookie, me, hoped for the first emergency call of the shift. I wanted to start my career with a bang.

As Denny closed the big garage door behind our exiting rig, we got our first instructions. Using the radio, Denny said, "25, Purple Chicken for a quart-a-cow, then Double-D."

Bobby, the permanent driver for Unit 25, clicked the mic twice in acknowledgement. Our route of travel reversed my own walking path back to Porter Square. We made a stop at the White Hen Pantry for whole milk, the "quart-of-cow" from the "Purple Chicken." I bought a bottle of seltzer water. I picked it from the near-bottom shelf. We then drove the ambulance across the street to the Dunkin Donuts. Bobby bought coffees for the office team and a dozen doughnuts. I remained in the rig watching Bobby through the windows until I recognized that I must help him carry coffee and open doors.

After handing breakfast to Denny, he ordered us to post at Harvard Square. Within ten minutes, we sat at the curb on Waterhouse Street next to Cambridge Common. We parked facing north, leaving me a perfect view of the Common. Bobby turned up the FM radio so we could both listen to the oldies crap on WROR. Not my station. While I did once say that I hated disco, I secretly admit to dancing to it often and loving it in the clubs that I went to. Hating disco was the fashion of the time. Therefore, I lied when I said *I hate disco*. During the day, I'd preferred listening to Charles in the Morning on WBCN. Instead, we listened to WROR. As Bobby increased the volume, I pulled out a book, opening *Early Autumn* written by Robert B. Parker. I borrowed the signed copy from my father's library. I read about Spenser and Hawk while sitting in an emergency vehicle waiting for a 911 call. Spenser and Hawk were two fictional private detectives based in the Boston area. With the training of a book-loving father, I neatly removed the paper dust jacket. Tearing a book jacket or defacing a book stands in the top five sins for our family. Not honoring my mother leaps to the top. Never lie sits on number two. Although, that "never lie" business came with a lot of exceptions. In truth, the rule was "Never lie to the Captain." I never got in trouble when lying to others. And the few times that I fibbed to my mother, I did so out of love and an effort to protect her. The Captain knew that I had fibbed, and no trouble followed.

Opening the book invited Bobby to question me. He started with stupid questions like, Why do you have so many piercings in your ears? And which clubs do you go to? I offered few answers as some dude sang about sailing away on the FM radio. I closed the book cover on my thumb, making believe I cared about our conversation. I listened to the constant chatter on the dispatch radio. "22 meet the PD." "21 head to Fresh Pond Circle for an MVA." Our first call came about only a few minutes later. "25, Stillman." Bobby picked up the mic: "Firm"—a lazy shorthand for *confirm*. He hit the lights before putting the rig in drive for the short loop around the square to the Stillman Infirmary, which served as the medical clinic for Harvard University students.

I lasted a week with Bobby, my supposed training officer, before getting shuffled to a new partner. Bobby did the basics. He taught me how to knock on a door: stand away so that when the asshole inside blasts with a shot gun, you may live. He taught me how to avoid calls with a crackly radio. He taught me how to slow-roll in the Cambridge City ER to avoid yet more calls. He showed me how he flirted with nurses in the hospitals. He told me on day two what he would do when he won the lottery: he would hold his winning ticket then smash his uncle's ambulance into a concrete wall. This ambulance, the one with his name lettered in gold.

While we often posted near Harvard Square and Cambridge Common, Bobby's duties expanded my understanding of an EMT's job. Denny would call, "25 *RTB*," recalling us to the base. He handed

Bobby a box with envelopes and papers. Bobby handed them to me. We drove the streets of Cambridge slowly. He would stop in the middle of the road, flip on all of the emergency lights, then tell me to get out. He grabbed one envelope, then walked to the front door. Standing there in a uniform nearly indistinguishable from that of a police officer, he demanded payment. Bobby gave gruff-facial expressions, kept a thumb in his duty belt, and informed a former patient that they must pay their bill. He resembled a cop with his blue uniform shirt with a badge, name plate, and label mic clipped to his right epaulette. His belly pushed his uniform trousers and belts to the limit. Parts of the black leather had been tugged and strained by his belly. Parts of the belt reverted to natural brown. In the small of his back, he carried handcuffs in a leather holster. On his right hip, he hung his Motorola radio and below that, a four-D-cell aluminum flashlight. The flashlight deliberately resembled a night stick. On the other hip, he wore a heavy leather holster with various EMS tools. Most seeing the uniform and leather duty belt assumed that holster included a pistol, an image that Bobby promoted.

Bobby Clifton collected five- and ten-dollar bills from these former patients. An installment plan, he called it. The bills stacked up; they got rolled up. Some people met him at the door with their installment. Others begged for more time. *Capos and cops.* While Bobby fit in neither column, he borrowed heavily from the playbook of each team in the street game. Look like a cop then threaten like a capo. With Bobby's size, the gold lettering on the door, the flashing lights, and radio, he served Atlantic Ambulance as our debt collector. Peter Clifton bypassed the normal costs of hiring a firm to harass patients with letters and phone calls.

Then in a quick twist, we would pull into a neighborhood pizza joint. He ordered five pizzas, paying with the cash he'd collected. We then delivered these pizzas to the Mount Auburn Hospital emergency room. He put advertising magnets up while handing out Atlantic Ambulance pens. Everything included the phone number for dispatch. He handed out pizzas and pens while flirting badly with the women we met. During the week, we delivered over fifty pizzas to various hospital floors, clinics, ERs, and any place where people might need an ambulance. We walked into nursing homes with pizza and pens, sometimes coming out with a patient. We hauled off some little-old-lady, the original LOL, wheezing and rasping for breath. We dropped her at the ER, flirted, gave pens, promised pizza, and left.

We stacked warm pizzas on the cot then wheeled through the halls. Bobby had a kind and flirtatious word for each female nurse. They humored him by listening and laughing with him. He left magnets advertising Atlantic Ambulance, sticking them on filing cabinets, desks, and metal window trim. He drooled over the small fleet of young nurses that had been imported from Ireland. "God, don't you love their accent?" Pizzas, magnets, pens, and favors guaranteed that Denny's phone rang all day long. A ringing phone meant revenue for us. Nurses called to send patients home or send them to care facilities or send them to other hospitals.

While we occasionally delivered pizzas to hospitals in Boston and Brighton, we tried to recognize the boundaries of the Kingdom of Cambridge and recognize the cultural boundaries within the region. Marketing too aggressively in Boston will cause fights. EMTs had been known to key the paint of ambulances that too flagrantly violated the turf rules. Bobby did love bounding to Saint Elizabeth's with his oversized enthusiasm. He set a course for a specific sweetie or a honey or a darlin'. Then failed at finding her again. Bobby's imagined tally-sheet never matched the reality of his efforts.

Releasing Bobby to the streets and hallways proved beneficial for Atlantic Ambulance. Denny's phone rang. Ambulances got dispatched. Crews transported patients back home, to nursing facilities, to other hospitals for treatment. Bobby stole the advertising magnets, pens, and pads of paper handed out by Brewster Ambulance and Cataldo Ambulance, and O'Brien Ambulance. As he put their marketing swag into his pockets, he muttered: Fucking Wasps (when touching Brewster's swag) or Fucking Ginneas (when touching Cataldo's swag). He didn't disparage the Irish O'Brien, of course, because they were Irish. "The Irish have to stick together," he said while also stealing their pens and magnets. His definition of sticking together did not mean letting them sell to staff on our turf. Sticking together meant sticking together in fights against the others—the non-Irish, of course. Privately, Bobby Clifton would fight with anyone, including the Irish. He stole as quickly from the Irish as anyone in the same moment when he said: "We're in this together."

Bobby had earned the neat gold lettering on Unit 25's door. He made sure that Denny's phone rang and chased the money we were due. I did very few emergency calls during my training week with Bobby. I learned the administrative side of running an urban ambulance. I learned the fracture points and fault-lines in a city I thought I knew intimately. Haitians had staked a new claim in a few blocks between Harvard and MIT. The old Irish in North Cambridge faced pressures from both Greeks and wealthier folks wanting to be closer to the university campuses. Pockets of Armenians set up in neighborhoods near the Watertown line.

Unlike Bobby, I did get phone numbers and arrange dates. Bobby bounded into a flock of beautiful people with his immature woofing. I stood back, like a hawk. I watched him. He faced women, standing a bit too close. He towered over them. He tried all of the flirty words. He barked out line after line. My partner, the Saint Bernard.

I knew I was the better predator, and at twenty, I saw myself that way. Someone would step in next to me. We'd smile at each other, studying how Bobby worked his pens, paper pads, and pizza. I scored nearly every day with a staff member who stepped away from Bobby's antics. I would typically earn one or two new phone numbers each day. On a good day, I would arrange for a dinner or a glass of wine after shift. Poor Bobby, he never knew. He was good for me and my dating. Bobby never suspected that while he harrumphed in full voice, I whispered and passed notes silently behind his back with sexy hospital staff.

When I arrived at the station for my first Monday shift, that second week, I started running my checklist on ol' ambulance number

25, leaving the gold lettering and mirrors to Bobby. After four days of partnership, we had our routines. I did the real work. He drove. I did the real paperwork. He collected cash and handed out gifts. In four days on the job, I had not yet saved a life. I had not yet helped give birth to a baby. I had not yet responded to a gunshot or a stabbing. I had wheeled a lot of old people from one facility to another facility then back again. Run patients over to Mass General Hospital's big oven for radiation treatment behind foot-thick walls of lead. Down a back alley to the first MRI unit in Boston. We taxied the old and the ill between facilities.

Denny, watching from video cameras at his desk, used the overhead speaker to call me upstairs.

"Lexi," he said, "you normally come say good morning to your Uncle Dennis."

I smiled at the camera saying: "I am so sorry, Denny." When did he become my Uncle Dennis?

I legged it up the stairs. "Good morning, Uncle Denny," I lilted at him.

"I am going to put Adam on with Bobby today." Adam had joined a few weeks before me. He resembled Danny DeVito except the actor stood taller and looked more fit than Adam. With the cruelty of our streets, one of the boys taped wooden blocks to the gas and brake pedals on the old piece-of-shit Dodge ambulance. This stunt intended to reinforce that Adam was just too short to be an EMT. This hideous rig looked like it came from a 1970s movie with two glass emergency lights that rotated embarrassingly slowly, the sort of ambulance that might be used to buzz a coven of nuns. We all knew that if you ran this rig on Storrow Drive, you would shave the light bar from the roof with any of the numerous underpasses. You had to scoot up, around, then over every underpass. Storrow Drive has a long history of shearing the tops of tall vehicles off, described locally as being *Storrowed*. It was faster to cross the river or use the city streets than let a bridge remove emergency lights from the roof. The piece-of-shit Dodge served the company as the rig of last resort. Denny and Peter put crews in it for punishment or other reasons. And later, when the firm hired its first black EMT, it became his daily ride. Boston and Cambridge failed to realize the imagery of a melting pot. Except for elite university campuses, we sucked. Even at the elite schools, we still sucked.

I stood before Denny, waiting. Admittedly, I was glad not to be assigned Adam while feeling uncertain of Denny's next words. And Denny, now my Uncle Denny, decided to toy with me. He didn't answer until Aaron stood at the dispatch station next to me.

"I now pronounce you Aaron and Lexi, husband and wife. Lexi meet Aaron." I looked at a man taller than me but more fit. His cordovan-colored eyes smiled under command. He turned to shake my hand. I had seen him around the station but not yet as a regular on the day shift. Denny continued, "You'll be in 26."

At first glance, this guy looked like a friend of my father's, a young author from Montana named James Grady. Jim had arrived at our house to stay for a few days, driving a silver Porsche 911. Before he came, everyone in the house read his book *Six Days of the Condor*, which later became the movie *Three Days of the Condor*. We then rented the movie.

Unlike Jim, Aaron had a golden flake in one eye.

And Unit 26 was the newest rig in the fleet. 26 was the best rig. We had done something right in the eyes of Denny and the boss.

We washed and checked the rig with professional speed. Not in any of my four days on the job had anyone helped me with these duties the way Aaron did. When done, he hopped into the passenger's seat. In a week on the job, I had not yet driven the ambulance during any shift. Bobby felt propriety over the gold letter on his door and position as the rig's driver. You felt the "no trespassing" warning with every look.

Aaron swung up into the passenger's seat. He did look like James Grady, yes, but maybe more like Gary Cooper, another man from Montana.

I climbed up, checked sightlines, asking for Aaron's assistance adjusting mirrors. I made sure that I could see the back corner of the ambulance, a hint of our rear wheels, and anyone trying to pass us.

I drove out of the dark garage and onto the streets of Cambridge. Aaron watched me occasionally through his mirror, gauging my distance between the parked cars and the edge of the ambulance. I kept it tight and moved us in a straight line.

I did not need to tell Aaron that driving these streets fell neatly into the domain of acceptable conversations at our dining tables and family stoups. My family discussed roads and traffic the way some families talk about the Red Sox and the Celtics. Uncle Franny, a real uncle, owned Delany Brothers' Movers. It was a small moving company with red trucks lettered in gold, of course. While they did move people's possessions from one place to another, they specialized in moving art and valuables for Harvard University. Uncle Franny and his boys talked about nipping pedestrians with truck mirrors and hitting puddles just to splash expensively suited men. They assigned points to their shenanigans and games they played on these narrow and twisted streets. Dumb games given your family name shimmered on the sides of each truck. My family regards driving aggressively in Boston as sport.

I know driving skills are not inherited, especially from stupid cousins. I did learn to drive on these streets of Boston, Newton, Watertown, and Cambridge. At sixteen, the Captain took me to Mount Auburn Cemetery for driving lessons. His daily driver, the one issued by the City of Boston, had emergency lights and radio consoles mounted to the dashboard. I grew up hearing the chatter of the Boston Police Radio, and occasionally the Boston Fire Department. I got to drive James Grady's Porsche fast while he taught me how to accelerate through corners and keep my RPMs up. Part of my driving lessons came from tearing up dirt tracks at Stephen King's lakefront place in Maine.

My family stakes family honor on our ability to manage these streets. I showed no fear during my first hours driving the ambulance.

Our day started as we approached Fresh Pond Circle. Denny's voice cracked over a quiet radio: "26, MVA Route 2 at Alewife."

"Inbound or outbound?" I asked over the radio.

Denny replied, "Tell me when you get there." Fine! Not helpful at all.

The flow of cars got sticky as we approached the numerous traffic lights. With a judicious use of the siren, showing off my ability to invent new burping and whelping sounds from the controller, I pushed through the traffic, sped up to Lake Street, banged the U-turn, then returned to the scene. We beat Cambridge Fire there. We were met by two *staties* and one Cambridge Cop. We would have taken both drivers except that they were screaming at each other. The language, remaining vibrant and ethnically descriptive, suggested that neither driver needed medical attention. Except that the guy in the more expensive car, the guy that got rear-ended, suddenly remembered the cringing and crippling pain in his neck.

Aaron accepted a sign-off from the driver of the BMW and I walked the driver of the Mercedes to the back of our rig. Once in, I took vital signs, assessed for head trauma, and placed him into a neck collar. Aaron hopped into the driver's seat. With a quick turn over his shoulder, he made eye contact. Asking aloud, "Ready?" I responded, "Ready!"

Aaron burped the siren, easing cars from our path as he vectored towards Mount Auburn Hospital. My patient, our patient, when sensing our turn on to Mount Auburn Street, started complaining. He had to go to Mass General Hospital. He started refusing to go to Mount Auburn. And he kept complaining as Aaron backed up to the hospital's ambulance door. As calmly as if in a polite dinner conversation, Aaron said, "I am sorry. The protocol states that we must take you to the nearest appropriate hospital. And MGH is about three times as far and is out of our jurisdiction." Did that end the conversation? Not really, our guy complained to the first nurse we met. We scooped him to a hospital bed then walked away. With a soft tone, I briefed a nurse who spoke with a melodic accent that she carried from the Caribbean. She thanked me, thanked us just as Denny yelled for Unit 26 again. I had collected the patient's IDs. I scribbled down his social security number from his Mass driver's license and dug through his wallet to get his Blue Cross card. When

I needed his signature, the patient had already begun his bitching. Therefore, I used one of Bobby's multi-color pens then signed the patient's name for him in a maneuver demonstrated by Bobby. I could get the patient to sign if I had the time to wade through the bitching. We were already late for our next 911 call. Blue ink, ball point pen, and my right hand with the paper set to a funny angle. Every signature unique. That's the promise.

With Bobby, the 911 calls seemed to slip away as if his radio had been coated in Teflon. Aaron and I found ourselves in the hot rig chasing emergency calls minute-to-minute.

I was happy to be assigned to a new rig and a new partner. We ran ten-hour shifts, often longer. Aaron and I, now formally part of the day crew, did not get to quit until the chaos of the day concluded. During a busy day, we could run thirty calls. Atlantic, in the name of Peter Clifton, promised the City of Cambridge that we would not take more than seven minutes to respond to any address.

Cambridge City Hospital sat between Harvard Square and Inman Square. To our west, near the Watertown line, we had Mount Auburn Hospital. Then across the river we had easy access to Mass General Hospital, and the hospitals on Longwood Ave, then back to the west a bit sat Saint Elizabeth's Hospital, Saint Es. We provided little care in the rigs, we buzzed everywhere with lights and sirens. Our paperwork for each run involved scribbling a few notes on a single sheet of paper.

Denny taught us the three things that matter the most. First, always copy everything from their driver's license plus their medical insurance cards. I spent hours per day writing social security numbers down on my run reports. All of the insurance companies, starting from Medicare and Medicaid through to Blue Cross, used a person's social security number for everything. "Copy it all down." Lesson number two, we were instructed to never write the mileage on the documents. The third lesson involved signatures. We required the patient's signature. We are to tell them it is a consent to treat. They normally signed. Most of the small-print language specified that the undersigned is responsible for paying the bill. Few read the small-print. Then we, the crew, must sign the document attesting to both completeness and accuracy.

As a cop's kid, I ought to be able to tell right from wrong. But in our city, politicians, cops, firefighters, building contractors, and ambulance services each followed their own unspoken rules. The patients who were hounded by Bobby to turn over a few bills couldn't call the Cambridge Police Department to complain. They owed the money they owed because they dialed 911. Calling 911 will likely make issues worse. As for forging paperwork, who is going to report that?

2 | Falling from the Sky

I never shied away from Aaron. I never ducked, evaded, fibbed, nor misdirected him about me and my life. He knew who I was. He saw me. He honestly didn't care who my father was. He didn't care which clubs I went to. He didn't care about the multiple piercings nor my hair color nor how I dressed. And he caught me scoring phone numbers and dates during our shifts. Some might have tapped me in the ribs acknowledging my scores, not Aaron. He saw the clandestine maneuvers then said nothing and did nothing.

I don't think I have secrets. I really don't. I just don't answer direct questions directly. I duck and evade nearly every effort to get to know me. I am none of their business. So maybe I do have secrets; maybe I have a few of them. If I don't acknowledge a secret, it does not exist, right? If I don't tell you something, then I am fine with that. Aaron always accepted me. He never felt the need to probe. In his stillness, he saw me honestly. Sometimes, I think he saw right through me. He confirmed, for me, that I have no secrets. If you see me, you see me. If you listen to me, you'll hear all I have to say.

Within two days, I learned that Aaron preferred posting on quiet side streets under the trees and on a hill if possible. While we parked with the engine running, I read novels. He studied nursing textbooks. He napped for a few minutes in the passenger's seat, a skill I never mastered. I observed that he never went for fast food nor a chocolate doughnut at the Double D. One day four, I learned the rumors were true.

You did not learn Aaron's secrets unless he decided to tell you. He did not have a Vietnam campaign ribbon stuck to his car. He wore his hair in a style that was neither that of an army guy nor the long hair of one rebelling against an army haircut. Aaron wore fitness casually. He never got winded running upstairs for sick patients, nor whining when carrying them down. Unlike the boss, Peter, and his nephew Bobby, Aaron wore a loose belt over a flat stomach. He never wore the heavy holster that so many other EMTs wear. He had handcuffs but he never showed them. He kept them in a bag. I wore mine in the small of my back in a hand-me-down pouch from the Captain. Following Aaron's lead, I moved my radio clip behind my hip. It made me look trimmer. Furthermore, I walked like a normal human. So many EMTs and cops adopted the John Wayne swagger with arms out wide. Some of the guys carried their arms nearly akimbo, ready for a quick draw.

Aaron moved like a marathon runner. I admired the simplicity and efficiency of his movements. When on-site, he offered patients trust and openness. Tell me anything, he communicated, without ever saying the words. His hands said it. When he touched a patient, he was purely clinical: not a caress, not gentle, not rough, not timid, not sexy, not flirty, not intimidating, not strong, and not weak. His hands were always just mildly cool and always the right kind of dry.

He shook people's hands. More correctly, Aaron held their hands. In one maneuver, he placed a forefinger at the wrist measuring the pulse. He felt your strength. He measured your pulse pressure. He learned the speed of your capillary refill. He knew your muscle tone. And he'd hold the patient's hand while talking with them. Again, he avoided the grandmother's softness and the overt manliness of a crushing handgrip. While holding Aaron's hand, patients involuntarily followed Aaron's careful breathing rate. In for a four count, hold for four, and out for four. Never ever did I hear Aaron ask anyone to calm down. He held their hand, took their pulse, measured their health, then controlled their breathing with his fingertips and those brown eyes.

There on Haskell Street under the leaves of a warm June day, Aaron took my hand in his, as if I were his patient. When done well and relaxed, he taught me his technique. I learned that I could also measure the patient's breathing rate. And brilliantly, I felt issues in the lungs. With practice, I learned to feel a wheeze, a wheeze that Aaron generated deep inside. I felt the purring rattle deep in his lungs. We let our clasped hands relax so that my hands touched Aaron's chest then stomach. I learned, from Aaron, that you can sometimes feel what you cannot hear.

Where did he learn this technique? We climbed into the back of the ambulance to continue our practice. He laid on the cot and I sat on the bench next to him. I practiced Aaron's clinical greeting until it felt familiar. First, I proved that I could feel the pulse rate and pulse pressure with ease. Then I learned to settle our entangled hands on his abdomen allowing me to feel his breathing and the pulse bouncing from his aorta through his tummy.

But why? Or rather, but how? I asked, "How did you learn this?"

"I learned it at 500 feet in a Huey helicopter."

I listened. He sat up, then spun while on the patient cot to face me. His heart rate trended around fifty beats per minute, and he breathed eight times each minute. I released his hand.

"Up there, just over the trees, I could hear nothing. Once I got some blood or plasma running through an IV and I sealed up the wounds the best I could, I never heard another blood pressure. My stethoscope was useless up there," he said, describing his time as a Vietnam-era combat medic. Except he never said, "I was a combat medic in Vietnam." He assumed everyone knew he went to 'Nam. Conversely, nothing about his affect confirmed these rumors. On that June day, he simply said, "I learned it flying at 500 feet in a Huey."

"Trust your hands, Alex." Yes, he called me Alex sometimes too, which I did like. He called me Lexi in front of folks from the station. As I said, he saw me for me.

"Ask yourself, what is your minimum blood pressure if you have a pulse at the wrist?"

In 1983, I did not know that answer. Once hearing it, I never forgot it. Roughly, the answer is 90. The magical thing about a blood pressure of 90-over-something is that 90-over-something is the minimum blood pressure that keeps the extremities perfused and the kidneys perfused. If you have a pulse at the wrist, you will live one minute longer. For every minute a pulse exists at the wrist, the patient will likely live one more minute. Losing the pulse at the wrist indicates bad things follow. When you lose the pulse at the wrist, you check the femoral at the groin. Losing that pulse is deeply worrying. Losing the carotid pulse at the neck precedes death by a few breaths. The body dies from the edges in.

"But why?" I asked Aaron. "Why did you learn this?"

"I couldn't hear shit. We often flew with doors open and door gunners spraying treetops with lead. Getting a soldier into bird then taking off was no guarantee that he lived. When I lost the pulse at the wrist, I moved my hand to his chest. When I lost that pulse, I would hold his hand again for a while. I then strapped both arms tight and shut down the IVs. There was no one to tell and no shouting to do. I would read their name tapes and read their first names from their dog tags. I never wanted the men to die without a name or to die alone. I put the IV bags on his chest then covered his face." Aaron's eyes lost focus on me and the rig. "I wished him peace. Then I made him as neat as I could."

On that day, he said, "Death can find us anywhere." Aaron never viewed Death as an adversary nor an enemy. Death, said Aaron, becomes a companion. That is what I learned under an ash tree on Haskell Street in Cambridge, Massachusetts. Instead of running away from Death and the horrors of Vietnam, he returned to the field first by earning his EMT then by starting nursing school.

We returned to the front seat, where I read a mystery written by one my father's friends. I read words written by man who went to Red Sox games with my father and mother. Meanwhile, Aaron sat next to me and studied anatomy, physiology, pathology, and pharmacology in the front seat of a Ford ambulance.

I thought of the crew in Unit 25. Bobby Clifton and Adam barely belonged in the same field as Aaron. Bobby used his uniform and size to bully people, demanding they pull cash from their nearly empty wallets. Bobby experienced confusion and even anger towards male nurses. It was an unnatural act, according to the Gospel of Bobby.

In the near quiet of the driver's seat, I reflected on the calls during the recent days riding with Aaron. Denny sent him, sent us, to calls related to veterans, regardless of where we posted in the city. It also meant that we got dispatched to calls involving street people. His hands and his recall of his time in Vietnam helped those who could barely be helped. Denny sent me to calls involving young people being victimized, abused, or just in the wrong place.

In four days, we earned a reputation as the hot rig. We sprinted from North Cambridge down to Kendal Square for a *111B*. "26, Respond to Mr. Lincoln and his cane." Mr. Lincoln was known to all crews. We told stories of how Mr. Lincoln swung his cane at people who were better off than him; or people who ignored him; or people who had paid attention to him. He stood in front of the big post office building threatening pedestrians and cars with his cane.

Mr. Lincoln, a Korean War vet, acknowledged Aaron as an army medic by using the honorific "doc."

Mr. Lincoln shared his remorse and shame with Aaron, "Doc, I am so sorry. I did it again, didn't I? What are they going to do with me?" Aaron flashed me hand signs. "Stay," "Ok," then after getting Mr. Lincoln to sit on the granite curb, Aaron flashed me the hand sign for five with all four fingers and the thumb spread wide. I knew the plan. I fetched Aaron's bag from between the seats. The five-sign stood for either "five" or "fifth," we were never particularly clear on that. Aaron's use of code "five" stepped beyond the boundaries of established, legal, protocols. It worked for Aaron. Even better, it worked for his patients.

I placed the bag between Aaron's feet. Aaron lifted a pack of cigarettes and a Zippo lighter. He shook one free, offering it to Mr. Lincoln. He then flipped the lighter open, igniting the cigarette behind the cupped hand of a combat veteran. An army's medical symbol, the caduceus, had been engraved into the stainless-steel Zippo plus the date: "1970."

"Thanks, Doc."

Aaron reached into his bag, where he had a plain Hershey's

chocolate bar. Aaron slowly unwrapped it, like a kid with a special treat. He moved deliberately while Mr. Lincoln puffed. He broke a piece off, eating it himself. He offered me a square, then carefully he offered Mr. Lincoln half of the bar. I sat on the curb next to Aaron. I'll admit the smell of folks who lived on the street proved challenging for me. My nose curled away from Mr. Lincoln.

We were three friends, three veterans sitting on a curb sharing chocolate and a smoke. Except neither Aaron nor I ever smoked. Nor was I a veteran. Mr. Lincoln enjoyed the smoke, stubbing the butt into the same street where he once swung his cane at people walking by.

"My friend, you might want to find another corner today. I don't think the PD needs to find you here today." Aaron stood, offering the old man a firm grip to help lift him to his feet. Once up, Aaron handed over the last two gifts. I'd seen him do this before. Aaron placed a fifth of gin wrapped in a five-dollar bill into Mr. Lincoln's hand. Aaron forged Mr. Lincoln's signature on the ambulance run form. He forged the signature again on the "Against Medical Advice" release form.

The first time I helped Aaron with a "Code Five," he said: "A drunk will die sober faster than he will die drunk." Geez, man, if anyone went through Aaron's bag during a shift, he'd get sacked in a second. You can't carry booze on an ambulance. And nobody would ever recommend giving a patient a cigarette, at least not since World War II.

To Aaron, his "Code Five" protocol had everything he needed. Nicotine to calm, chocolate to bring up blood sugar, and booze to lift a soul one fifth of a gallon. I should add that I had previously looked in Aaron's doctor bag. He carried a purple heart and his dog tags in there. He also had an old army shirt with rank, name tape, sweat stains, and a frayed neck collar. Aaron was always ready to treat and comfort one of his brothers. He spoke the right words and offered the right touch to bring peace with him, even if that peace meant passing a soul from his hands to Death's hands. Peace is peace. We all find peace where peace is offered.

When called to a 111B, a rowdy street drunk, Aaron gifted a fellow vet with one minute of calm; one minute of kindness; one minute of brotherly understanding; one minute of warmth—both men knowing the demons would return, for that is what demons do. Demons return. Unlike Death, demons prove themselves restless and furtive.

I did not yet know demons. I witnessed hints when they visited Aaron often enough. I suspected that the Captain had a few demons of his own. I had seen my father being haunted. I ought to amend my statement to say: I had not yet met my demons. Frankly, I never thought they'd come for me. At twenty, strong, healthy, educated, loved, and working a summer job while living with my family, I believed that I was not the person demons came for.

Aaron double parked at a CVS, hopping from the rig. Returning, he handed me a small jar of Vick's VapoRub. After handing me the white paper shopping bag, he said, "Learn to apply it just below your nose on the upper lip. Do it quickly and quietly."

Aaron said, without saying, "Never shy away from a patient again."

I heard that lesson. Instead of telling me to man-up and toughen-up, he offered me a trick he learned a decade ago. Aaron walked into the suck with a ramrod straight back and eyes opened for the hundreds of things that may kill him or kill me. Never wince, never look away. He did say, "Alex, it isn't your pain. It isn't your stink."

I knew cops sometimes dipped a bit of Vicks on their nose before walking into autopsies. But real cops had to tough it out at crime scenes. A rookie may be permitted one episode of vomiting on scene, but after that, one must "man up." Losing your breakfast at a crime scene can earn a cop a life-long reputation, often tangled with concepts of weakness, girlishness, and not being tough-enough for the job.

"You have a Purple Heart medal in your bag." I either asked a question as a statement or made a statement, expecting an answer.

"I do." The least satisfactory answer.

"Yours?"

"Yes. One of three." He figured out I was not letting go of the topic.

"Three?"

"One for each time I got shot out of the sky."

"You got shot three times?"

"No, my helicopter got shot three times. I crashed to the ground three times."

"Fuck."

"Yup, fuck."

So many other questions, but none of them mattered.

I wanted to ask: "Did men you flew with die?" I didn't have to ask. I knew the answer. Well, yes, of course they did. He's told me as much. You are on a medevac flight that gets shot down. That means you get medevac'd. The medic becomes the patient.

We vectored back to the tree-lined streets of North Cambridge, meaning it was nap time for the Hot Rig. This neighborhood served as Aaron's quiet place. I preferred the busyness of Memorial Drive and Harvard Square. These were the places I hung out when I was off work. I loved watching the people. Frankly, watching college students fed me like pretty candy. Except for the huge white ambulance and blue uniforms, Aaron and I blended well with the university crowd. Aaron needed a break from our calls and we both knew it.

I enjoyed finding PG-level entertainment along the river and in the crowded streets and squares of the city. That was my style. We were partners. I got my way sometimes and he got his. We silently crawled under Aaron's ash tree on Haskell. Aaron swapped seats with me. He closed his eyes. I listened to WBCN while reading my novel. WBCN celebrated local musicians: The Cars, Boston, J. Geiles Band, Aerosmith, and others.

It was from Aaron's napping position in North Cambridge that he heard, we both heard, a lot of sirens. To civilians, all sirens sounded the same. First responders learn to hear the difference between cops and fire trucks and ambulances. Cops move faster. They use their siren sparingly. Ambulances tend to flip the siren on from the moment of dispatch then let it blare all the way to the scene arrival. Fire trucks are heavy and slower moving. You often hear the heavy diesel and the hum of their big tires. Under that ash, we heard cops coming from every direction. We heard them coming from the east, aggregating on Mass Ave. We heard them coming in from the south.

Aaron sat up. "That sounds like an entire division of cops. Let's go!" The combat medic wanted out.

We rolled down the slight hill to Mass Ave. We were north of Porter Square. I took the easy right on to the busy road. The sirens, louder and ubiquitous, still vectored towards us. Aaron flipped on our lights. "Move it," he said to me, pointing south and east down Mass Ave. We looked over our left into the parking lot that served the Dunkin Donuts. We witnessed a ring of cruisers each with their doors open. The officers all had their pistols drawn, pointing at a dark blue Mercury that had crashed into a chain link fence at the back. This was the same parking lot that had once been home to the trolley barns—the car barns my mother spoke of. These were my mother's streets. This was where she played as a young girl.

One of the cops waved a stop motion from the middle of Mass Ave. He yelled "Stop" a few times, but Aaron had the lights running and the siren going. I slowed and lowered my window: "I am really sorry; we have a call. Someone is coming for you." Yes, a lie, the call had not even been dispatched. We cleared the traffic in front of us, driving with all urgency to Harvard Square. I cut right onto Chauncy Street while Aaron shut down the siren and lights. I wended my way towards Brattle Street then vectored towards the river.

Denny broke in: "26, what's your 20?"

Aaron grabbed the mic, "Putnam and Cambridge St near the river." He located us about two miles east of where we stood. A well-placed lie, setting us a goodly distance from a division of angry cops. The former combat medic and the cop's kid shared a common understanding of cops, drawn weapons, and open doors. Bad things happen when cops leave their doors open and run forward with pistols in hand. In fact, as a rule, if a cop runs, bad shit happens.

Denny dispatched Unit 25 to the scene in Porter Square, sending the boss's nephew Bobby and his partner the Danny DeVito clone, Adam, into the crisis. They were probably fetching coffee or milk in the area already. Or maybe shaking down some old couple for cash.

At the end of shift, we learned twice what happened. We heard the stories from Bobby and Adam as the first ambulance on scene. "We got there even before they had the guy cuffed." And we caught the story on Channel 4. Three fellows robbed the Harvard Trust Company that sat opposite the News of the World kiosk and the T station. The T station had a sign that read, "Rapid Transit 8 Minutes to Park St." These fellows banged a U-ey in their Mercury sedan driving away from Park Street. Within eight minutes, the blue dye canister exploded in their front seat. The get-away driver, with a face full of blue paint, stuck his head out of the window. The dye canister turned the windshield into an opaque mess. One guy used his ski mask to clear the blue while the driver felt the pressure of the pursuing police. An MBTA bus that came to a sudden stop forced the driver into the parking lot. Then the car discovered a rusty chain link fence by smashing into it.

The cops forced all three men to lay face down on the pavement which was when Bobby and Adam arrived. Had Aaron and I pulled over as instructed by the cop, we would have been a bit too early and a bit too close to an uncontrolled scene. Aaron would have said: "Call us when it is over." There was only so much that two unarmed EMTs can do.

Adam's hand was stained bank-robber blue. He was proud of it too. "I had to check for injuries," he said. "I helped wipe down their hands so that the cops could cuff them." That's right, Adam. Somehow, Adam, CPD knew that you would waste your time and towels stolen from the ER to clean up their prisoners for them. The cops would have left the crooks to bake in the afternoon sun. Let the sun dry the dye before placing them in their cruisers or the paddy wagon. Less to clean up. Less mess all around. Thankfully, Adam was there to save the cruisers from blue dye and to keep cops' hands clean.

WBZ carried an abbreviated version of the story. The TV story missed all of Adam's colorful commentary. The news crew did get live footage of the scene in Porter Square, complete with the Atlantic Ambulance boxed in by police cruisers. Adam and Bobby could not have left the scene if they wanted to. Like the idiots they were, they got their rig boxed in. If we needed them to respond to another scene, they could not have moved. Every cop that arrived after them parked higgledy-piggledy behind the big ambulance. They got themselves stuck beneath layers of cruisers.

How many times in a week do we all hear Denny yell, "Don't get blocked in!" Don't get blocked in by fire trucks and hoses. Don't get blocked in by anything. The ambulance's job is to scurry away to the hospital with haste.

Aaron and I had similar reactions to the story that Bobby and Adam told: "Wow, that must have been exciting." And "Boy, I wish we'd have been there." I said the words with my most sincere smile. When I thought of Bobby trying to flirt with the pretty news lady from WBZ, I did smile. I knew Bobby. I had seen him at work. Oh, and I did know her too, the pretty news lady. She used to smile at the Captain and flirt with him even when she saw him at a restaurant with my mother and me. She once flirted with me too. I was likely a bit too young for her. She may have looked twenty-five on the TV but up close, she had already eased past twenty-five and thirty. I appreciated her beauty; I'll give you that. I believed that she was closer to Aaron's age than mine. They were both at least ten years my senior. She was probably better suited for Aaron anyway. But I never minded the sporting flirt. All fun, no risk.

With three handcuffed bank robbers and an ambulance that got blocked in by the cops for two hours, Adam and Bobby were the heroes of the day. Their heroics required no paperwork. It involved treating no patients and demanded little of these two EMTs except that they had to stand in a sea of cops. I am pretty sure that after the bank robbers baked dry, the crooks got shipped to the station for processing.

I returned to Harvard Square after shift. I swapped out the triple-knit polyester police trousers for a properly fitted pair of jeans.

I wore my work T-shirt then covered that with a jean jacket. A bit warm for a June evening, but I looked good. I had agreed to meet a medical student intern at the chess boards. I couldn't remember who I was meeting nor if we agreed to dinner, drinks, or even a game of chess.

When someone did sit then speak to me, I assumed we knew each other. Therefore, I never let on that we did not. I remained open to the idea we may have met sometime, somewhere. Let the games begin. In the first round, neither of us moved as we watched people in silence, an experience similar to sitting with Aaron. We enjoyed a richly colorful silence. In time, we both invented a story around one curious young woman we spied across the street. She looked at the big iron gates that stood between the sidewalk and Harvard Yard. In she went, then out. In again as if expecting something to be different or a person to magically appear. We both added her internal dialogue, narrating her erratic movements.

I liked hooking up with medical students, interns, nurses, and other professionals in the field. It saved us the awkwardness of explaining what you do. What does one talk about at the end of a day on an ambulance? Rarely are these adventures suited for the dinner table nor discussions with a date.

"Hey honey, how was your day?"

"Good."

"What did you do today?"

"My partner and I ran away from bank robbers and carried a lady with a broken hip down three flights of stairs and treated an old vet with a chocolate bar and a fifth of gin."

"That's nice. Well, I lanced two boils, treated a bed sore, and stitched up a kid's lip."

To outsiders, civilians, such topics terminate any thoughts of cozy handholding or sweaty romping sex. We need to meet others who have breathed the same stink, slid in the same mess, seen the same dark part of humanity, then still want to play. I knew that the person who sat next to me, who helped me spin a tale about a confused civilian, was like me: someone who smelled the same smells and saw the insides of human beings.

I lost track of the number of calls by the end of the day. Up and down the streets, in and out of the various hospitals in the region. "26, since you're at MGH, run up to med-surg and take an LOL home." Out on the street, LOL meant "little old lady." The term LOL changed during my life. In the back of my head, it still means little old lady.

My mother learned how to greet my father long before I was born. She must have had the same problem when the Captain came home from a long shift. "William, how was your day?"

"Good."

"What did you do today?"

He could never answer well, completely, or honestly. A double murder in a Dorchester triple-decker. A kid pushed to the third rail because he was in the wrong neighborhood. Escorting city buses during the busing crisis a decade ago. That's my father's life. Now it is mine too. I worked ten-hour day shifts with but a few memories and a stack of billing forms for Denny.

The following morning, Aaron handed me a small plastic chicken that he attached to a white satin ribbon and a safety pin.

"By the powers vested to me by the League of Street Medics, I award you the Yellow Chicken first degree for your actions that involved fleeing from cops, guns, and bank robbers while lying to dispatch."

"I only did what you told me to do."

"You drove fast and hard. You didn't fuss. I figured a cop's kid would want to be in the middle of the action. I thank you, Alexi."

Alexi had become his private pet name for me. I could have kissed him at that moment. I had already understood that Aaron would face anything he needed to. Let's all admit that everything doesn't need Aaron's skills.

3 | June 1983

The boss announced that Atlantic expected to pay double-time to anyone who worked on the Fourth of July. My immediate thoughts were about hitting the double-time holiday rate while on overtime which pays time-and-a-half. If on overtime when the holiday hit, I would make three times the wages of any normal day.

I started planning my approach. First, I would take a full twenty-four-hour shift on Saturday, the second of July. Then take the Sunday day shift off, starting again with the overnight shift on Sunday. When the triple-time offer comes on, I will have logged thirty hours. I'll make ten hours wages at one-hundred-and-fifty percent of my normal rate. From ten o'clock on, I'll be on triple time. If done well, I could earn triple wages for that holiday Monday, the Fourth of July.

While I had worked shifts without Aaron, the shifts with Aaron were my norm. He had become my partner with Unit 26 serving as our rig. Shifts with Aaron were always better, calmer, and funnier than shifts without him. Additionally, Dennis, who sat at the dispatcher's desk, appeared to cherry pick calls for us. I might brag and say we did more miles in Unit 26 than any other crew. It wasn't true. Some crews got sent on long-distance transfers with psychiatric patients. One crew drove out to North Adams, Massachusetts at the far western edge of the Commonwealth. Nearly every week, crews ran to McLeans Hospital in Belmont. Most would not consider Belmont a long distance from Cambridge. We did because the trip was unusual. We did not get those trips, Aaron and me. We did not make the most calls in a day either. Some crews were just faster than we. It does not take long to run into a nursing home, scoop out a little old lady, then run the few blocks to the emergency room or a treatment facility. I acknowledge we did not log the most miles, nor did we crown the day with the highest number of calls. We got slowed down by some of our calls. Denny sent us anywhere in the city he wanted. "Unit 26 respond MIT for a psych emergency, PD on scene."

"Unit 26, meet fire on Dana Street south of Broad."

"Unit 26, meet HUPD at their station." HUPD meaning Harvard University Police Department.

We would pass other rigs who sat in the shade at their postings. We'd chirped the siren and wave to a crew watching us go by.

Unit 26 got sent into the shit more than any other day-time rig. We were the shit collectors. We became known as shit-magnets. Some individuals showed envy with me but when it came to partnering with me or partnering with Aaron, people declined. They did not like the way we worked, and I think they did not like the calls we got. I know we ran from a bank robbery. It was the last time we ever got to avoid unpleasant and risky calls.

I laid out my schema to hit triple time in a conversation with Aaron. We sat in queue to make the *Bay Run* on a mid-June Friday. Bobby Clifton was always first to announce: "Unit 25 Bay." In twenty-minute intervals, the rigs cycled through dispatch. One crew member would run upstairs fetching two paychecks, then the ambulance would ran to the BayBank in Porter Square. We each exchanged our light-blue check for hard currency. The company rules required that only one rig be at the bank at a time. Some crews, like Bobby in his gold-lettered truck, took a bit longer and got in early. After the bank, Bobby stopped at the Purple Chicken for lottery tickets and scratch-offs. Bobby stood proudly in the group of people who tear up losing scratch-offs before tossing the shreds to the pavement outside the store. He blamed the store for his losses. He blamed the store clerk for the losses. "It is their fucking fault I lost. That little…" I'll skip that phrase "… sold me a dud. He always does that to me."

I reviewed my triple-time scheme with Aaron, thinking that my older and wiser partner would see the financial advantage of triple time. I ran through the shifts, the hours, and the step from straight time to time-and-a-half to triple time.

I wanted to describe Aaron as laconic. He wasn't. He spoke directly to the point, wasted few words on the approach, and then listened well after finishing. Oops, maybe that was the definition of laconic. Aaron showed greater warmth and interest than the phrase allowed. He listened.

"Alex," Uh, oh, my ears told me a lesson was to follow. "My father taught me this lesson once." Thus, I was right, a lesson, but from him, always a good thing. He said, "These two bulls ambled up a hill. At the crest, the young one saw a herd of cows and heifers grazing down near a stream. The young bull, full of himself and shaking with excitement, says, 'Hey, Pops, let's run down and grab one.' The older bull says, 'Let's walk and take them all.'"

I missed the point. We talked about humans, dating, and sexuality while we studied people along Memorial Drive and the Charles River. I knew that I was the young bull in his story. Still baffled, he said, "Play the long game. It all comes to you if you work at it."

I had heard versions of this theme during our weeks together. One of his more common phrases was: "Sleep when you can. Shit when you see a toilet. And only drink if you know you can pee." I failed at that last lesson. Putting a liter of seltzer water in my belly before 9:00 a.m. makes me desperate for a toilet. I kept making that mistake. Dropping trou in a bathroom stall got awkward. The radio and handcuffs weighed down my trousers. I first had to unclip the lapel mic then clip it to the antenna of the portable radio. Then I uncinched the thick leather duty belt, which meant removing five leather *keepers* that link the duty belt to the trouser belt. I tried to hang that on the stall hook, that same hook used by others to hang a purse. Then I had to uncinch the inner belt and pull down the nine-pocket triple-knit polyester trousers, which on hot days clung to my skin. As soon as I sat, I would hear Denny's voice on my portable radio: "Unit 26, blah, blah blah." Suddenly, I faced pressure to pee. When done, I had to kit up again. Trousers up, belted. I fastened the duty belt on with keepers. I moved the lapel mic to my shoulder. I washed my hands thoroughly in warm water and then returned to the rig.

On the other hand, Aaron snuck into the toilet in various emergency rooms. With absolute honesty and grace, he said: "26 acknowledged. Finishing paperwork at Cambridge City." He had it easy.

Aaron said to me, "Look at your paycheck."

I opened the envelope. I studied it. It was exactly the same as it was last time and the time before. The check showed me I got my normal pay for a two-week period. Aaron saw me looking at the check.

"What do you see?"

Answering him, I said, "I see the same check I see on every payday."

Aaron answered, "I worked every shift with you Monday to Friday for two weeks."

Still looking at the check, I grunted: "Yup."

"How many hours did they pay you for?"

I studied it. "I got paid for eighty hours."

He paused, waiting for the young college student to catch on. I was stuck. I liked math. I liked my paycheck too.

"How many hours do you work each week?"

"Forty?"

"Really?" He had never considered me stupid. This is the first conversation where I hadn't picked up the message.

"How long is each shift?"

"Ten hours, but I tend to get in a little early."

He finished the thought for me. "Then you and I roll in a bit after 6:00 p.m. each evening. You and I are never sitting in the barn at the end of a shift, waiting for relief. How many days do you work each week?"

"Five." Oops, for weeks and weeks, I had been paid forty hours every week while working ten-hour shifts five days per week. I worked fifty hours and got paid for forty. Except for Memorial Day which was a Monday holiday. I got my overtime rate for those eight hours.

"How is that possible?" I asked him, suddenly gutted with this.

"Clifton claims he operates under rules used for tow truck operators and others who staff twenty-four-hour services. He deducts for meals and if you are on the overnight shift, he deducts for sleeping."

I returned to the math problem and the challenge of getting triple time on Monday the Fourth of July. If a ten-hour day shift got paid only for eight hours, then I did not know how much an overnight shift gets paid. It did not seem like I could hit the Monday holiday with forty hours on the clock.

"How much does Clifton pay for an overnight shift?"

"Normally eight hours. He considers it an eight-hour shift."

Out loud, I mumbled: "8:00 a.m. to 6:00 p.m. is the day shift. That is ten hours for which we get paid eight. Therefore, the night shift ran from 6:00 p.m. to 8:00 a.m. 6:00 to midnight is six and midnight to 8:00 is eight hours. That was a fourteen-hour shift! They get paid for eight?"

"Yes. That is why I don't work overnight shifts."

"No doubt!"

When I cashed my check at the BayBank, I held the cash in contempt. I stuffed the crisp bills into my wallet, feeling robbed.

I reviewed my scheme for triple time again while sipping my nearly frozen seltzer water. I learned which shelf at the White Hen Pantry kept the seltzer water at the right temperature. If I picked too high, the bottles were a bit warm. When I picked near the bottom, the entire bottle froze hard when I cracked the screw-top open. The bottle took most of the morning to thaw slowly. Each sip was fresh and cold. Not very bubbly, but the cool sips felt so good. If I worked the full weekend at the station starting at 8:00 a.m. on Saturday and finishing at 6:00 p.m. on Monday, I would be paid for forty hours, eight of which would be double my normal pay rate. I would be at the station or in the rig for fifty-eight hours in a row. For those fifty-eight hours, I would be paid for forty of those hours. I would have sold my time to Peter Clifton at a thirty-one percent discount.

I then evaluated my normal shift. I worked for ten hours and got paid for eight. So, every day I worked for Peter Clifton, I gave him a twenty-percent discount. I became interested in getting home to talk with the Captain about this situation.

Denny's voice cracked in: "26, construction accident."

We arrived at the same time as the first cop and before Cambridge Fire. Men in hard hats met us all talking, all of them giving instructions. I hopped from the driver's seat. The construction guys gathered around Aaron who appeared to listen to them all. Not me. If I were Aaron, I would have shouted out: Just one. That was a difference between him and me.

I swung around the back of the rig. I got our kit then I walked towards the steel frame of a new building. The men in hardhats swarmed Aaron, walking him towards a construction lift. Two men came from an office trailer with a harness. He looked up. He looked four stories up to naked steel I-beams. I saw the look. He was filled with dread. Aaron was a combat vet who had three choppers shot down while he was in them. The Young Bull charged forward, thinking I could manage this call on my own.

I stepped into the harness the guy was holding for Aaron. I had never put one on before. It seems obvious. Leg in, leg in; shoulder under, shoulder under; buckle and cinch. I lifted a hardhat from the ground, putting that on my head. I shouldered my medical bag and started walking to the lift. Aaron was still listening to the crowd of construction workers. The foreman and I got in the lift. He clipped in. Then he grabbed my clip snapping it to the basket.

I got to our patient. He was still breathing although my EMT book would call it ineffective. A few times after a shift with Atlantic Ambulance, I flipped through my EMT book. I studied from the Third Edition of a book first published in 1971. The book was called *Emergency Care and Transportation of the Sick and Injured*. It was produced by the American Academy of Orthopedic Surgeons. The Third Edition, my edition, was published in 1981. In four-hundred and forty-eight pages, the authors did not write a chapter on falling within a steel construction framework from fifty-feet above the ground. The topic never came up during my semester long class at

Northeastern. The class reviewed a chapter about rescuing people from vehicles. The class and the book contained lessons on recognizing a downed power line, not helpful here. Nothing in my book or my class prepared me for being lifted up a steel frame in a yellow basket suspended by a cable. Riding up, I closed my eyes, breathing, striving to visualize my actions when I met the patient.

Aaron's voice came into my head. "Treat what you see—A.B.C." I opened the patient's airway, recognizing I was shifting a broken jaw as I introduced an oral airway. I was in a harness clipped to a steel rope. My patient took up most of the small metal platform that served as a partial floor. The crew had bolted sheet metal to form a landing at each area where the lift stops. It was large enough for four men to stand. With my patient laying down and the foreman and one other construction guy, I found myself without a place to put my bag. I handed the bag off, saying: "*Ambu* bag please."

The guy handed my bag back. I returned it. "No, look inside for an Ambu bag." He stared at me and at the patient. "Hold it open." I stood, retrieving the Ambu bag from our medical kit. I fitted the mask over the nose and mouth. I got a good seal, then I started breathing for my patient. Each squeeze of the Ambu bag pushed air into the lungs, causing the chest to rise.

"We need to get down from here," I said aloud. The two construction guys watched me work.

I radioed down to Aaron. "Aaron, we need a plan to get down." His eyes had never left me. He gave me a thumbs up. He took his posse of construction guys back to the rig. Within seconds, men pushed our cot, carried our backboard. In the distance, I could hear Cambridge Fire coming with the older style mechanical siren and the heavy tire noise of a full-sized truck plowing its way through narrow Cambridge streets.

Deciding I was in charge, I said to the foreman, "Can you both go down? Then have only one of you come back up. Do what my partner says." At the count of every five, I breathed for my patient. My cool aviator sunglasses slipped down my sweaty face. They gradually slipped off my nose then tumbled to the ground.

My eyes followed them down. They kept falling and falling. While I thought I was only fifty feet from the ground, I found myself suspended about seventy or eighty feet. The building's frame stood over a naked foundation of concrete that had been dug deeply into the ground. I heard my glasses crash at the bottom.

My patient transitioned from ineffectual breathing to not-breathing. I checked his pulse. I laid my fingers on his neck. I repositioned my fingers once, then again. I breathed for the patient as my silent five-count hit five. I pulled my stethoscope out and listened carefully to his chest. Thinking that maybe I had gotten my lefts and rights reversed yet again, I checked both sides of his chest. I heard only silence.

I had done CPR once before in my brief career. Aaron and I had walked into a nursing home. The nurses met us at the door. One held it open, the other pointed. We gave a quick look at the elderly patient, gave a quick assessment, knowing the results ahead of time. It is a very odd thing to put a stethoscope on a human body then hear absolutely nothing. One hears the absence of a heartbeat, the absence of any lung sounds, the absence of movement. One might be placing a stethoscope on an empty cardboard box to hear the same nothingness you would hear in a dead body. On that day, Aaron started CPR and I breathed. We had a nurse help us wheel down the hallway. In the back of the rig, I did CPR alone while Aaron drove at a measured paced to Cambridge City Hospital.

Unlike an old person in a nursing home bed, this man had been breathing when I arrived. He was vigorous. He wore a yellow safety harness and a flannel shirt. His wedding ring provided proof of a family and love.

I repositioned myself. I folded one leg in close to me and extended the other leg forward under the patient's neck. Every five count, I breathed with the Ambu bag, then I started chest compressions at one per second. The book discusses the topics of CPR and rescue breathing clinically with monochromatic drawings. Neither the book, nor my teacher at Northeastern, made any mention of doing CPR while in a safety harness on a thin sheet of metal and having to transport the patient via a hoist down to the ground.

I did not have to call Aaron on the radio. He saw me, he always did. Regardless, my lapel mic had fallen off too. It bounced at the end of its curly cable. It bounced in the free air below the steel. As the crane hoisted the lift, I heard Aaron: "Lexi, shift to the other side."

Shit. That meant stepping over the patient. That was against the rules. The book said: "Never step over a patient." So many rules. It also meant hanging my backside in the ether with neither wall nor floor. Some part of me would be exposed to a great fall. I liked my position between the patient and the lift. I felt secure with a thin floor below my backside.

I listened. I pulled the patient towards me. Compressed the chest a few more times. Then I stepped over his body. This time, I kneeled with my body leaning over the patient. I was less effective at keeping the airway open. On the other hand, all of me felt secure. Aaron and the foreman pushed the backboard at the patient. I rolled the patient up onto my knees. I rolled the guy down onto the board then I pushed the patient so that he was roughly centered. Aaron and the foreman lifted the patient to the top yellow rung of the basket.

"Climb up."

"Climb?" I asked while doing it. I climbed up one rung then another. The foreman snapped my safety line in. Then the foreman grabbed my harness with his hands. I did my counting thing: One potato, two potato, three potato, four. With each potato, I pushed as hard and deeply on the patient's chest as possible. Then I gave another chest compression and tried to provide a rescue breath with the Ambu bag. Working alone meant that the Ambu bag lost its seal each time I did chest compressions. Putting the device over mouth and nose each time slowed the effort. The compressions were slower than the book called for. Air leaked a bit from the face mask as I forced air into the lungs.

Once on the ground, the construction crew lifted the patient to the cot. I got hoisted and placed on the cot where I pumped his chest. Aaron breathed for us all. Aaron and I shifted around in the rigs. As first in, I managed the airway. Aaron stepped in. He took up chest compressions. The ambulance moved backwards.

Aaron looked at me. "Call it in."

"Denny, 26 en route, CPR in progress." Without waiting for a reply, I clicked the radio to the medical channel: "Cambridge City Hospital, Atlantic 26 in bound, CPR in progress, accident at a construction site."

I breathed. Aaron counted potatoes. I leaned back at one point, finding that my lapel mic had been clipped to the center back of my construction harness. It felt like a stone on my spine when I leaned back.

"Four potato." I got a good seal on the mask. Aaron did compression number five. I forced in the breath. Aaron started with "one." Whoever was driving did well. The use of the siren was judicious. The speed felt comfortable. We did not roll and tumble in the back. Together Aaron and I did the pump-and-blow. Pump and blow. Together we worked at keeping oxygenated blood circulating through the patient's body.

The ambulance backed into the hospital bay. I looked up and saw it was Mount Auburn Hospital. *Oops.* With the radio, I called dispatch, "26, Mount Auburn."

Denny said, "26, code 55 when you can."

Yeah, no shit, boss, call the office. Two nickels, or a double nickel, buys three minutes on a public payphone. The ambulance doors opened. We got pulled from the rig by firefighters and hospital personnel. Two firefighters took over the pump-and-blow routine while we got stripped away.

I sat in a wheelchair for a few minutes, breathing and feeling the sweat drip.

Aaron placed his hand on my shoulder. "Helluva job, kid. Damn, that was impressive. You've been on the job less than two months." I think he lifted me from the wheelchair, pulling me into an embrace. With my face buried into his very sweaty arm pit, I cried. I don't know why I cried. He wrapped his arms fully around my back, feeling my sobs and exhaustion with his hands. Then he did that dude-thing with his hand on my shoulders. "Time to clean up. Go wash." I probably really stunk during our first hug.

He pushed me back a few inches then started undoing my harness. I had had a few thoughts of him undressing me. Why not? He has never said an unkind word to a patient. His style of American Hero resembled the gentility and soft-spoken nature of Gary Cooper, the movie star. My harness dropped to the ground taking my lapel mic with it. I un-did the leather keeps and dropped my duty belt to the floor as well. Walking into the bathroom, I had already started to unbutton my uniform shirt. I shut the door. Within a minute, I heard a knock.

"Occupied!" I shouted out.

"Lexi, it's me. I have towels for you."

Damn, he was good. I opened the door a crack for him. My white cotton T-shirt was off. I stood there in my bra and ugly police uniform pants. They hung a bit low on my hips. He didn't look. But he sees everything. I know he saw my sexist part: that paired indentation between the hip bone and the stomach muscles. On a fit person, like Aaron and me, the dark shadow and tunnel that only hinted. I love seeing that spot. I love touching that spot. I love being touched there.

I held my towels. I wet one, washing myself. I unzipped both boots and dropped my trousers. I washed everywhere. I did some sweating during the recent hour. My spine served as a canal for sweat that flowed from my head and my shoulders. It flowed down and down. Through my underwear, elsewhere, then to my inner thighs and down my legs.

As I washed, I looked at myself in the crappy yellow light of the hospital's bathroom. I liked what I saw. I felt sexy and in desperate need of a romp. I removed my bra which made all those feelings even more intense.

I had never thought of Aaron *in that way*. Ok, that is a lie. I tell myself he is off limits. I admit to being a hound dog in the hospital, in Harvard Square, in classroom, in clubs. But never Aaron. Aaron remained off limits, the way a super-hot cousin is off limits. I dried myself and re-dressed, leaving the cotton T-shirt off. I buttoned the blue unform shirt up. I tucked in the shirt tails. I gave myself a professional assessment in the mirror before stepping out with an armload of damp towels and one soaked T-shirt.

Our kit had all been cleaned up. One of the nurses came over to me.

"I heard you did an amazing job on that guy. Were you really hanging from a steel beam while doing CPR?"

"Of course not. I was kneeling on a steel plate seventy feet in the air doing CPR while clipped to an I-beam with a safety harness."

"The boys were all talking." She paused. "I am sorry that he didn't make it."

"I sort of knew that." Her words made it official. "He wasn't long for the world when I got to him."

"You tried." She kissed me on the cheek. After kissing me, she then looked around for witnesses. Seeing none, she kissed me on the lips, thereby intensifying my own fuck-me-now feeling.

I walked through the glass doors to the ambulance bay, holding my wet T-shirt.

The four firefighters greeted me first. They clapped me on the back and said words such as "Damn" and "You got balls" and "Well done." The last firefighter looked at me, giving me the brotherly tap on both shoulders like a teammate, then leaned in to say something. Then said nothing.

Our medical bag was intact and returned to the rig. Our two harnesses had been laid neatly on the bench seat.

Three of the four firefighters headed to their truck. The silent one hung back. He watched his mates leave, then came to me. Then he too kissed me—on the lips, just like the nurse did. He slipped me a piece of paper. "Damn, that was hot," he said with a wink. Then *sotto voce*, he added, "I had to try after seeing that nurse plant one on you."

Oooh. I was wicked glad he did. I wanted more, and immediately.

Aaron asked, "Alex, wanna drive?"

"Fuck no."

We returned to the construction site. We walked somberly. The foreman saw us, then the rest of the crew saw us. We passed on the sad news. The crew shook our hands. They expressed appreciation for our efforts and heroics.

"Station?"

"Oh shit, I forgot to call Denny."

"I did. He told us to return here and take our lunch break."

At the station, I swapped uniforms and underwear. Thanks, Dad. You are right. Always carry extras uniforms.

Denny asked, "Where are you guys going for lunch?"

I looked at Aaron, wondering if he had an answer. He made no movements or any sound.

"I feel like Greek food. There's that guy in Porter Square."

"Bring me something." He put a ten-dollar bill in my hand.

The Greek guy was one of several restaurants that provided free food to cops and EMTs. We offer money and he waves it away.

We ate rice, tzatziki sauce, and mystery meat from aluminum pie tins. I handed Denny back his ten spot.

"I got a call from Captain Mahoney about that call this morning. They are all talking about it."

To be a smartass, I said, "Talkin' about what?" I smiled. Denny smiled. Aaron took another bite. "I thought we'd get in trouble. I called the wrong hospital. That was embarrassing wheeling into Mount Auburn without notification."

"That's alright. Cambridge Fire sorted it out for you."

"Was it Fire who drove us?"

Aaron answered, "Yup. The young guy that gave you a kiss is the one who drove. He watched you working while driving. He was a bit gah-gah over you."

"The poor people at Cambridge City getting all ready for a nasty trauma code."

"They'll get over it."

"How was I to know where we were going?" We chatted a while. The pile of Greek food and the mounding salad with feta went into my empty belly with ease and speed.

After Aaron cleared the dispatch desk of our mess, Denny asked, "Want an easy one? I've got Mr. Goldstein in Brookline waiting for his ride to treatment at MGH."

The radiation treatment center at Mass General Hospital was deep in the basement. Each of the rooms had walls that were about a foot thick and lined with lead. You would wheel the patient in then lift them to the treatment bed. Then the staff used custom braces to hold the body part in place. They would line up the skin tattoo with the brace and the cross hairs from the machine. We would all leave the room. They would do the treatment. Then we would all go in, remove the hardware, put the patient back on our cot and wheel them home.

Running from Brookline to MGH took us out of the 911 call rotation for a couple of hours. We enjoyed an easy ride to Brookline. We walked up to the patient's door. Mr. Goldstein knew most of us. We secured him to our cot then made him comfortable. We all chatted casually. As we worked, Aaron told Mr. Goldstein a tame and edited version of our morning adventures. Aaron sat with Mr. Goldstein on the way into town. I sat with him on the way back.

On the ride home, he looked stoic and brave. In sympathy, I said, "That is a hard hit."

"I tell myself the treatment is saving me, but I dread the hours and days after treatment."

I asked Mr. Goldstein, "Want me to tip you back a bit?"

I tipped Mr. Goldstein back, then I held his bony hand.

He had been sitting nearly upright for the trip in as he and Aaron talked. Aaron told him of me and my Irish-cop father, the famous Captain Flynn. Mr. Goldstein related going to MGH to his days as a tail gunner in a B-17 over Europe during World War II. "You climb in never knowing."

At eighteen years old, Mr. Goldstein climbed to unshielded plastic bubble at the backside of an American bomber. At eighteen years old, my partner Aaron climbed into Huey Helicopters as a combat medic.

And today, I climbed up the steel latticework of an unfinished building while trying to save a life.

I thought about the phrase, "You climb in never knowing." As I held this old man's hands, I found myself leaking a few silent tears. I don't know why. The old man slept.

I placed my other hand on top of his, laying our hands together. I felt exhausted and ready for sleep myself. No day on an urban 911 ambulance achieves routine. Little patterns do appear within the battle rhythm. I know nothing about my day when I walk from the T-station to the ambulance station. Somehow sweating my ass off high up on a steel beam made me feel energized and as horny as I have ever felt. I wanted—no, I needed—passionate, out-of-control sex. I would have taken Aaron there in the bathroom, except he was off limits. Let's admit that sex in an ER bathroom seems a bit disgusting. But I would have taken the nurse had she kissed me in that bathroom behind a closed door. Then I started coming down from the high. Informing the construction crew of their friend's death made me feel like a failure. I could do nothing to help. I cycled through dark thoughts of my failure then to the sadness of our patient's family.

After eating lunch, I wanted to sleep alone in a dark room or listen to classical music with my eyes closed. This hit me like another cycle in my ten-hour day. I let my eyes drift closed, waking only when Aaron opened the rear door.

"Mr. Goldstein," I said, tapping his hand then shoulder, "we're home." We lifted the cot from the rig then wheeled him back into his place where we were met by Mrs. Goldstein.

Monday morning, I walked into the station with two chocolate doughnuts for Denny. I felt a bit sheepish. I did not look around. Denny accepted the paper bag of doughnuts then tapped the cork bulletin board with an Atlantic Ambulance pen.

Oh, damn. They saw it too. And Denny posted it.

Front page and above-the-fold the headline read, "All in the family." *The Boston Globe* had printed a photo of me trying to save a life in the unfinished steel building. The article started, "The child of Captain William T. S. Flynn follows in her father's footsteps.

Alexandra Flynn worked heroically to save the life of…" The article went on to identify the patient and document his career. In the last graph of the story, I got my second mention: "Alexandra Flynn works for Atlantic Ambulance of Cambridge." It was our rescue, me and Aaron. We both went up that building and hauled that fellow down. A family lost their father and husband. A crew lost their friend.

Who gets top billing in the *Globe's* article? My father. I find it funny. Aaron never got a mention. How did this happen? First, someone took the picture and sent it to the *Globe.* Second, the *Globe's* Metro desk did one minute of research to connect me to my father. Which means all of New England got to see a picture of me doing the one-potato-two-potato dance four stories up in the empty shell of a building.

"Alright, Denny, I have a serious question for you. How is it I work a ten-hour shift and get paid for eight?"

"That's easy. You work an eight-hour shift and get paid for eight hours. It is fair."

"But my shift starts at 8:00 a.m. and ends at 6:00 p.m. That's ten hours."

"And we give you sixty minutes for lunch. And you get four fifteen-minute coffee breaks during the day." The answer made some sense to me. Clearly, Denny had practice at saying these words. The word "but" pushed forward in my head repeatedly. I wasn't sure what my objection was.

Except that while we do have down time during the day, we never get a real break. We grab lunch on the go. We get breaks between calls. We are never allowed to leave the rig, drop our uniforms, or turn off the radios. If on a break and a call comes in, we must take it. If having lunch and a call comes in, then we must take the call, abandoning lunch. Walking away, I observed that nobody here punched a clock. We never provided timecards to anyone.

I returned to my Uncle Denny, who is not an uncle. I smiled. Then I asked, "Who reports our time for payroll?"

He said, "Either I do or whatever dispatcher is on duty. I think

Aaron just walked into the barn." Uncle Denny told me to go away and shut up.

Atlantic Ambulance managed our payroll the same way that they managed our insurance billing. We did the minimum needed on the street. We signed what we need to sign. We left the mileage blank. We used blue ballpoint pens on each paper, leaving a neat furrow created by the pen's nib. This furrow lent proof that the paperwork had been done by hand. We were never allowed to use felt-tip markers. And we were never allowed to use black. Xerox photocopiers can't reproduce the blue ink as blue. By writing in blue pen, we were proving that the document and our signatures are original and true. If we used black or felt-tip, someone could make a photocopy that may look as good as an original. Someone clearly needed to prove to the insurance companies, Medicare, and Medicaid that our work is original and free of fiddling, fudging, or fixes.

4 | The Fourth of July

Starting the ten-hour shift, I felt better about my pay. For the Fourth of July 1983, I will be paid twelve hours for the ten that I will put in. That is the way math works. Either I get paid one-hundred-and-fifty percent of my hourly rate, or I get my normal rate for one-hundred-and-fifty percent of the hours that I worked. Given my normal day was paid at eight hours, I expected to get paid for twelve just as I did on Memorial Day in May.

Peter Clifton and Denny re-arranged the posting for the day. They attempted to keep one ambulance in North Cambridge. We added two ambulances to help cover the river front. Aaron and I got assigned to the primo spot. We had been instructed to post at Kendall Square. The Longfellow Bridge with its Salt-and-Pepper Shakers provided quick access to the ER at Mass General Hospital. I wiggled my way through the MIT campus, pointing us towards the river on Wadsworth Street. We had three boat houses in sight. And directly across the Charles, we had a perfect view of the Charles River Esplanade where The Boston Pops were expected to perform in twelve hours. John Williams was to conduct. John Williams wrote the music for *Jaws*, a great movie about the beaches of Massachu-setts and filmed in the Commonwealth. Williams wrote music for other movies as well such as *Star Wars*, *ET*, and *Close Encounters*. Approximately six hours before John Williams and the Pops, the Red Sox were to play the Yankees in New York.

With temperatures vectoring towards one hundred Fahrenheit, it hinted at being a hot summer's day. I had been modifying my uni-form to find a better summer look and something cooler than the heavy polyester I bought at The Haberdasher. So far, neither Peter nor Denny had taken me to task with my lighter-weight uniform. I substituted the police trousers for lighter weight dark blue Dickey work trousers. These are not attractive, and they lack the nine pockets of uniform trousers. I gave up the standard white T-shirt for a ribbed wife-beater T-shirt under a lighter weight cotton uniform shirt. I also eschewed the classic zipped paratrooper boots for black sneakers. Aaron, with his experience from Vietnam, reminded me about other types of self-care. He knew something about how and where fungi grow and their favorite conditions. He discussed toes and other parts of the anatomy with clinical blandness.

At his coaching, we carried an ice chest with water. We carried a few damp hand towels we stole, or borrowed, from Cambridge City Hospital's ER. We carried a bit of food. We carried spare clothes, spare socks, spare underwear, and we each wore cotton ball caps. My hat displayed the Boston Red Sox logo. Aaron wore a cap with the caduceus and "U.S. Army" embroidered on it. It was the first time I had ever seen him wear anything that overtly affiliated him with Vietnam or the Army. The dog tags he carried in his pack seem to be there as talisman for him, just like the Zippo. I assumed that he wore an army hat in tribute to the Fourth of July.

Our plans for a fun day melted before our eyes. I love studying pretty people. I love watching them flirt and play on the grass. But that day, the morning runners avoided running. The few who ran along the banks appeared beaten by the heat. The dogs walked lethargically. Those who planned their day on the grass retreated after a few minutes in the sun. Everyone in Cambridge and Boston felt like me—irritable, sticky, and unpleasantly hot.

Unit 26, originally built by Ford before being converted to a big shiny ambulance, resembled a van. The tail end of the engine block stretches into the cab separating the driver from the passenger. The heat of the running engine acted like a furnace. On the other hand, many fire department ambulances and the rigs driven by Boston's Health and Heroes had been converted from truck chassis. On a truck chassis, a full and complete firewall separated the engine compartment from the cab. I think that ambulances on truck chassis are cooler in the summertime because they do not have the engine block sitting between the two EMTs. Regrettably, we cannot turn off the rig because we need electric power to run the radios and keep systems in the back operational. Every minute of every hour, the heat of the engine attacked our legs.

We kept the air conditioner running full tilt in the back, striving to keep our rig cool enough to resuscitate a patient suffering any of the heat ailments. Aaron and I kept our windows open because we preferred it that way. We both loved hearing the world. We both loved talking with people. With the windows open, people said, "Glad you are here." Or, "Hot enough for ya?" And once in while we got called to a crisis by shouts.

By 9:00 a.m., we rolled up the windows and increased the A/C in the cab. Denny had gone quiet too. We had no scheduled transfers. There were no routine medical treatments. No patients to haul to cancer treatments or dialysis.

By 9:30, I spied that the engine's temperature gauge had climbed up. Aaron, sitting next to me, was neither sleeping nor studying. We both felt susceptible to the heat. The sun moved to the southeast, hitting the nose of our rig. The sun threatened us with yet more heat.

"Should we move before we bake?"

"I guess so."

"Thermostat is climbing."

"Yeah, no shit, Alex."

"No, man," I pointed to the dash. "The rig's engine is getting hot." He leaned over and looked.

"Thoughts?"

"Run Mem drive?"

"Ok." We needed to get air flowing over the radiator. I shifted the lever down from P through R and N to D. I gave a little look through the mirrors, then eased forward on Wadsworth Street. We followed Mem Drive east along the river, crossing the Broad Canal Drawbridge and cruising down Cambridge Parkway. We banged a U-ey, returning on the Edwin H. Land Boulevard, named for the guy who invented the Polaroid. The street named for him sits here on the far eastern edge of the city. And the Polaroid Building sits miles to the west on the way to Watertown. I ran back to Mass Ave and Harvard Bridge. I banged another U-turn running east. On our third lap, the engine's thermostat shifted to the left slightly. Our efforts had cooled the engine effectively.

The fourth lap carried us away from the river. I ran Cambridge Street.

We found shade on the MIT campus. We parked on the north side of an ugly brick and concrete wall—contrary to our shared aesthetic. The Harvard Campus is simply prettier. Sorry, MIT.

The river front shimmered in relentless heat.

Using a Bugs Bunny-like voice, I said to Aaron, "We must have made a wrong turn at Alba-turkey."

"What?"

"This isn't my city. Like we're in the desert or something."

I expected Aaron to resist my comparison given his time in southeast Asia. He'd earned the right to compare this heat to the heat experienced in a Huey and on the ground while in uniform.

Most of eastern Cambridge opened their views to the river and trees. Which meant that two EMTs could not find a cool shady tree to hide under while parked on the road or in a parking lot. Everyone on this side of Cambridge planted the trees to the south of their buildings. The northside of the buildings offered us sheer vertical walls. We live and work in a northern city where the Charles freezes during good winters. Some years, people ski along the river. During the summer, the river fills with boats. Sailors sailing. Rowers rowing. Coaches in little power boats yelling. Gorgeous. Dogs and people frolic along the sunny banks. In most seasons, we open ourselves to warm in the southern sun. We shun the cold northern exposure with thick walls. Our city offered us no outdoor refuge from the climbing heat.

"Unit 26, man down near the MIT Sailing Pavilion."

Aaron clicked the mic twice in acknowledgement. He rolled down his window. I rolled down mine. We hit the lights and pushed our way back to the river. The traffic was light. We came down Ames Street. I chirped the siren a few times. Yes, I was cleaning the intersection as we rolled through. I also used the siren to announce our arrival. "Hello, we're here."

"Man down" ranks as the most curious dispatch message we get. It can be anything from yet-another 111B drunk and passed out on the curb, to someone beaten badly, to a heart attack, to absolutely nothing. The downed man may be a woman. Or the downed man may have stood up and walked away. In order to get a man-down call, two things must happen. First, someone must recognize that the "man down" is someone in need of help. Then they must walk to a phone booth to dial 911. While the call is free, many people think that they can't make the call if they don't have a dime in their pocket.

As a city, we were pretty foul about racism and discrimination when we made decisions about who needs help. Most residents and students here learned to step over and around the various drunks and street people as if they belonged in the landscape. If white people saw a black guy down or hurt, the white folks stepped across the street to avoid the trouble. Little old ladies and children caused the traffic to stop and people to come from their houses and offices to render aid. We, as a city, turn callous toward those in regular need of help. There was no crowd of people worrying and waving us down when the patient was one of the uncared for, or unkempt.

On the other hand, waving hands and yelling people helped us find our man-down.

Along the river, in this heat, we might find anything. I headed the wrong way up Mem Drive, parking immediately in front of the Charles River Sailing Academy. We got out. Aaron went east, I went west. We both yelled: "Ambulance is here. Did anyone call an ambulance?"

I went into each building: MIT's building and the community sailing center.

"Did someone call 911 for a man-down?" The young man in the MIT building said, "No." The young man at the sailing center said, "Yes."

"Do you know where he is?"

"No. Someone came in and asked that I call 911."

"Did you know the person who asked you to call?"

"No. they were just walking by."

"Which way did they come from?"

"That way." He pointed west.

"Which way were they going?"

Obviously, he pointed east.

"How long ago?"

"I dunno, maybe ten minutes ago."

"Can you describe the person who asked you to call?"

"White guy, running shorts. No shirt, could be a student." And finding a white guy in running shorts on a hot day in July in Cambridge. That's useless.

I keyed my mic. "Aaron, sounds like he is east of here."

I did not run, I walked east along the river. I circled around each tree and each park bench. Approaching Mass Ave and the bridge, I wandered away from the river, taking up my search in the parklands between the east and west-bound lanes. I looked behind things. I circled each tree. As I walked, I unbuttoned my shirt. First, I opened up around my neck. When I was spying up Killian Court, I unbuttoned even further, almost to my navel. Aaron was in my line of sight now. We shrugged at each other. He had removed his hat.

"Unit 26."

Neither of us answered initially.

"26?"

I keyed the mic. "26."

"Any joy?"

"Nada."

"Well then, I got another one for you. This call is from the yacht club."

"Got it."

Aaron turned back to the rig, walking with a bit of haste in his step. As I pushed along still looking for our guy, Aaron turned the rig so that it faced the right direction. He waited for me.

I keyed the mic. "You go. I'll walk. I'll search from here."

I added haste to my step. I didn't walk around each tree with care. Instead, I peeked this way and that. Once my search territory overlapped with Aaron's, I went back to the river's edge. Aaron tapped the siren as he parked. I guessed that he meant to tell me, "Hey, I found him."

Our patient was seated with her back against a maple tree just outside of the yacht club's door. By the time I arrived, Aaron had whisked her into the cool ambulance, stepping her in through the side door.

I called Denny, "26. On scene. One patient."

I joined them in the back of the rig. Aaron had the lady on the bench seat, sipping water. He had her hand in his. He looked at me. "She's dry."

I stepped out of the rig. Heat emergencies fall within a spectrum. We humans sweat to aid cooling. As we humans dehydrate, we stop sweating. At this point, the risks mount exponentially. Without sweat, we cannot cool ourselves. Our core body temperature rises. We lose more fluids. We approach several types of shock, including hypovolemia. With a low volume of fluid in our bodies, we may damage our kidneys. Heat kills humans. No amount of stopping and resting under a tree will save this lady's life. She needs fluids, likely IV fluids, and she needs to be cooled.

Aaron discussed the plan with his patient even as I dropped into gear. "26 en route the General with one heat."

I dialed Boston C-Med on our medical radio, making a brief notification to the ER. "Atlantic 26 inbound. Alert/conscious sixty-year-old female. Heat emergency." They did not answer, but the calls are recorded. I made the notification. I played the game by the rules, even if the hospital ignored us.

The lady in the back corrected Aaron about her age, thank you very much. And she just needed some help getting home.

Aaron asked, "Do you have air conditioning at home?"

"No."

"Ma'am, your body is telling you something. We should all listen to it." Yeah, her body had told her it ran out of fluids to sweat. Her ability to cool had quit. She needed cool air and fluids.

Over the dispatch radio, we heard a unit in north Cambridge that got sent to a welfare check on a four-story walk-up.

I had planned a day of great music. A bit of reggae, some local bands, and whooping it up along the river. I brought a cassette tape that had Wagner's *Ride of the Valkyries*. I envisioned us freewheeling down Mem Drive playing from the speaker mounted on the lightbar above, just like the scene from *Apocalypse Now*. After shift, I had planned to strip down to proper summer clothing then wend my way to the Pops Concert. That was my vision for this Fourth of July holiday.

Aaron walked the patient into the ER, encouraging her to drink from his water bottle.

I parked badly, then walked to the triage desk.

"Denny?"

"Yah?"

"It is Lexi. I think we need a lot more water and ice? Where can we get it? And also, our rig keeps trying to overheat."

"Return to base. Peter brought in a few coolers and just bought a dozen bags of ice."

When Aaron stepped from the bathroom, I made ready to leave with him at my side. Instead, he stood still. He pointed to the toilet. I shook my head.

He handed me a stolen water bottle. "Drink or die."

I drank. I chugged the half-liter in a few steps. I led him back to the truck which was hidden around a corner and next to a dumpster. We climbed in. He handed me another bottle of water. "Drink."

I did. "We're heading to base for more water and ice." I gulped at the water, leaving a few minutes between swallows.

"22… 333 Hurley Street, third floor. Heat."

Approaching the station, we heard Unit 22 call in. "PD to scene. No transport." And we crossed a threshold with the day's heat. People had started to die. That's what "PD to the scene, no transport" means to us.

Saving a life on the Fourth of July in 1983 became as easy as offering water and air conditioning.

When the shift ended, we were still running calls. Every few hours, we refilled with water and ice at base, then returned to the streets. Fire hydrants sprayed water in a few neighborhoods.

During one call, we encountered a patient along the river. I pulled off her shoes, putting her feet and ankles into the Charles River. She freaked out three times over. First, she didn't like going barefoot or letting people see her feet. Second, she was convinced that touching the Charles would result in cancer, leukemia, and immediate hair loss. Third, she insisted that she would be just fine, thank you very much. "I can take care of myself. I got my undergrad from BU and I am studying at the Div."

While she tried to prove she was not a stupid human being, she continued to act in ways that will result in death before the sun goes down. Harvard's Divinity School does not teach their students about anatomy, physiology, and pathology. They focus on religious studies. While possible that the gods may have looked after this idiot, it was as likely that the gods sent us in Unit 26 to cool her off and find her a safe place to be.

Our protocols morphed during the day. Unsanctioned and unofficial, the hospitals, and Denny, suggested that if we could get people to a cool place and get them hydrated, then we did not have to haul every living soul into the lobby of the area's hospitals. We dropped patients at community centers and in one case, Aaron and I dropped a mother and child at a movie theatre. We expressed confidence that we broke one of the numerous Mass General Laws in doing so. The hospitals could not handle the load.

At 3:00 p.m., I ran two calls wearing only my wife-beater T-shirt. We had already run up and down numerous stairs fetching people.

At 9:00 p.m., the evening dispatcher sent us to a stabbing at a bar near Davis Square. Regrettably, we arrived before the cops. Aaron knocked the knife-holding guy to the ground and cuffed him within a blink of an eye. I packed a massive trauma dressing on the patient's abdomen. The knife seemed to have gone through the part of the abdomen, then through the diaphragm. And given the difficulty breathing, I wondered if a lung was starting to collapse under my hands.

I yelled at two men at the bar who had turned to watch the action. The Boston Pops and fireworks were on one TV. On the other TV, they showed highlights from the Red Sox-Yankees game, during which the Yankees creamed Boston four-to-zero with Dave Righetti tossing a no-hitter. Not a good day in Metro Boston. Too much heat and the Red Sox had lost to the Yankees.

"You two. Go sit on that guy."

They literally sat on the guy that Aaron had pinned and cuffed, which was not my intent, although I did use those words. Aaron provided two seconds of coaching about minding the unofficial prisoner while not killing him. Aaron wheeled the cot into the bar.

As we lifted then wheeled the patient towards the door, two CPD cops walked in. We beat-feet to Cambridge City.

The heat dropped a bit, then returned with revenge mid-month. We got hit with six days of extreme heat. When I arrived for my shift at 7:30 on Monday July 18th, someone had left a brown box of body bags in the passageway between the cab and the back. Body bags normally sat ignored under the bench seat. Each morning, during the rig check, I made sure that our two obligatory body bags remain tucked away and hidden. The Commonwealth required that we carry them. Therefore, they were on the checklist. We never touched them. Simultaneously, the Commonwealth required we carry body bags while forbidding that ambulances transport dead bodies. Additionally, the cops do not want us messing up their crime scenes. They made a big show of most dead bodies with cameras and investigators. A dead body served as a *de facto* crime scene.

Peter came down from the office, calling the day crew around him.

"Folks, people are dropping dead in their overheated apartments, especially the old folks and sick people." Information that had not yet made the local news, but I knew it from my father. The Captain gave me a word of caution and encouragement before my shift.

"Rules are going to be a little different. You'll each carry a big cooler of ice. When you climb up into one of those apartments, use your brains, if you have one. If you have one or two dead bodies, put them in body bags and pack them in ice. Call it in to us from the patient's landline or use the radio. Tell us how many patients and tell us to send PD and no transport. Then you leave the scene. Slap some medical tape on the door and run to your next call." These modified protocols violate both state laws and daily practice. We had been taught by the cops to control a crime scene until they arrived. Closing the door and abandoning a dead body in a third-story or fourth-story apartment felt wrong.

Peter continued, "The weekend has been fucking hell. If you can't get here for ice, stop at one of the firehouses to refill or at one of the hospitals. Your need for ice is this city's top priority."

Adam asked the necessary but dumb question, "We're just leaving them?"

"Yes." Peter displayed impatience for the dumb question. Peter normally displays impatience at Adam.

"We don't wait for the police?" Adam continued.

"You can wait for the police if you think it is suspicious or there was violence. There is nothing anyone can do for these people. We need to focus on those we can help."

The battle rhythm was as grim. As predicted, the elderly, the impoverished, and the sick died in their homes. Our mantra matched the mood. Within a day, we all muttered: "Bag it, tag it, zip it, and ship it." Those are the motions of putting a body in a body bag. We prep the body for the bag. We prepare a tag with some patient demographics and our names plus our unit number. We would zip the bag shut. We, as EMTs on the city's emergency ambulance service, did not do the shipping. We neatened up the bodies. Lifted them to beds or someplace comfortable after we sealed them into black body bags. We stacked ice on them, then left hoping that someone else would come along after us. Most community centers and schools did not have air conditioning. We dropped people at Filenes and Jordan Marsh. We dropped people at movie theatres.

And we hauled people to the ERs. People lined the cool hallways, often sitting on the floor. Thankfully, Aaron and I only did two of the calls where we used precisely two body bags. We gathered the patient's medications and tried to confirm that they really did die of heat.

The city's attitude turned grim, and impatient. Minor car accidents resulted in punches being thrown. The violence in the city climbed with the heat.

One evening after my shift spanned into the evening hours, I called the Captain to fetch me home. He drove over to Cambridge in his city ride, a dark blue Crown Victoria with whippy antennas and emergency lights mounted in the windows.

I waited for my father sitting on the roof top with Peter and Denny. Peter had his white uniform shirt off. His well-tanned belly demonstrated he sat out here often. That belly of his was larger than a basketball. Rounded and firm and covered in a mixture of white and brown hairs. His stainless-steel pistol, named Roscoe, sat on folding camp table. I stripped off my unform shirt wearing my white tank-top style T-shirt. Peter reached over to me with a beer. Instead of the expected statement of welcome such as, "Here, have one," he looked at me and said, "I guess you really are a girl. You're skinny too."

I was so tempted to look back at him saying, *I guess you really are a dude. You're fat too.* Instead, I watched him shake salt on his hand, lick it, then pour beer down his throat. I saw my father's unmarked pull into the lot. I picked up my shirt, scampering back into the office then down the stairs.

As I got up to leave, Peter said, "Be sure to put your name on some of the training rosters." I walked by the two clipboards on Denny's desk. I signed in and out for a two-hour class on back boarding. I did the same for a class on airway management. We require training hours to keep our EMT certificates. With a set of signatures, I just completed four hours of training.

The Captain and I drove home telling edited versions of our day. Once home, he walked me upstairs to my bedroom. He opened the door, beaming at me. A cool wave of air rolled out. He pointed to the window, and the new air conditioner.

While unlikely he did the actual installation himself, I gave him full credit for the work and the loving thought. My father, deadly accurate with a pistol and a certified marksman, is less handy with a wrench. That's just not him. He's the guy that hires the guy that does that work. My father is the guy that hires the guy that needs the work or the money the most. He'll deliberately overpay for the work. Some young cop or young crook who needs the leg-up got it from the Captain. After the work, no doubt my father offered food and some other kindness. He keeps our house and gardens trim by overpaying a needy person to run a mower, plant bulbs, paint a door, or repair a fence.

I had never had air conditioning in my bedroom. On hot nights, I slept in the buff. I pulled a cotton sheet up between my legs. I used cool, damp towels on my wrists, then lay there praying for real sleep. I kissed the Captain, hugging him. The professional that he is, he did not wriggle his nose at my stink. I smelled like an underground subway stop on a muggy day. I had my own sweat, the stink of diesel, hints of urine and death clung to me. Yet, my father embraced me back.

When he left, I walked into the cool room. I stripped, showered, then laid down on cool clean cotton sheets.

5 | Life with The Captain

We both saw the Ford sedan smash into the rear of a small car from Ohio at the traffic light. The driver from Ohio came to a full stop after the green light turned yellow. The Ford clearly expected Ohio to roll through the yellow like every other Bostonian. Instead, he smashed into the little car's trunk. I keyed the mic, calling Denny: "Base? 26."

"26 Go."

"On-scene two car MVC. Mount Auburn and Putnam at the light."

"26. You're on scene."

A Boston police officer exited his car, stomping towards the poo-brown Datsun B210. He moved only slightly slower than a full-sized bull who had been stung by a hornet. I rekeyed the microphone. "Denny, send Cambridge PD, will ya?"

I heard two-clicks in confirmation and a clue that Denny was on the phone. Aaron and I watched the uniformed cop approach the driver. Aaron tapped me, pointing forward. I hustled around the passenger's side of the Datsun. The cop was in the process of demanding that the driver crank down her window. The cop yelled with the aggression typically used for drug runners, street thugs, and armed suspects. Instead, I saw a young woman with brown hair gripping the steering wheel with a pair of fists. The skin over her knuckles had been blanched white. The woman watched my approach while the cop continued yelling through the still-closed window.

"What the fuck are you doing? Are you fucking insane?" the cop yelled at the closed window.

I held my hands up. My right hand slightly higher than my left. The right hand communicated *peace* and *unarmed* the cop. My left hand communicated a small *hold* movement by waving my open palm. Aaron remained at the rear of the Datsun. He gave the cop sufficient distance so that we did not trap the raging bull in a too-small corral. I did not really have a plan. As he yelled, I read the name plate and memorized the cop's badge number.

"Sir, maybe we should examine her first? She could be hurt."

"Who the fuck stops on a green light?" Given we had seen the accident, I knew the light had flipped from green to yellow the second before the brown Datsun approached the crosswalk. The driver slowed then stopped without jerking movements or skidding. The cop following her had not been paying attention, slamming into the small Datsun with an unmarked Boston Police cruiser.

I chose not to correct the officer. How easily I could have said, "Sir, the woman stopped for a yellow light." Certainly, that was what I saw. She had been driving slowly in a car tagged with plates from Ohio. Aaron and I saw her feint to the right for a turn on Banks Street then observed it ran one-way towards that intersection. She moved through our streets with the slow and hesitant movement of a foreigner, a stranger to Boston and Cambridge. With schools such as BU, BC, Harvard, MIT, Berklee College of Music, and others, urban Boston draws tens of thousands of students to an already crowded and confusing city.

The Captain joked that Massachusetts' roads had been laid out by a drunken mule. Few streets met at right angles. We make navigation more difficult by setting some roads one-way and other streets too narrow for cars to pass on two-way streets. The chaos of our streets confers a cool greeting on a guest to our region.

I did speak aloud: "Sir, I am Alexandra Flynn. I am with Atlantic Ambulance. How about you let me check her out?" I easily dropped my full name for this aggressive cop. While Metro Boston may be filled anonymous Flynns, I am not anonymous. I approached the steaming cop, slowly putting my hands down. He may not recognize me nor register my name, but I offered loudly and clearly.

"Why don't I take a look at her first?" I looked back towards the cop's city-owned car. It had a stout fender and had been built as a police cruiser then painted dark blue. His cruiser sat at the intersection undamaged while nearly totaling the rear of the Datsun.

He walked backwards then turned about sharply. Aaron maintained an even posture now, leaning disinterestedly against the ambulance's hood. I opened the driver's door. With practiced softness, I said, "Hey, I am Lexi. Tough day?"

"Am I going to jail?"

"No way," I said all-too-quickly. "I am not a cop. I am an EMT with the City of Cambridge."

"I saw he was a cop. He was up my ass when I tried to turn right on that one-way."

"I know. We saw."

"Is he going to arrest me?"

"Who can tell? What is your name?"

"Betsy."

"Betsy, how do you feel? Any pain?"

"I am terrified about going to jail. I have never been arrested before."

I took her right hand into mine. Using Aaron's tricks, I assessed her pulse and pulse pressure, and listened to her talking. Within the realm of street medicine, her vital signs proved to be within normal limits. In the rig, I planned do an official job of recording her vital signs. She had a blood pressure that was more than 90-over-something. Her pulse pressure bounded under my finger. I held her eyes with my own eyes. The left eye appeared hazel while the right looked pale blue.

"Any pain in your neck or back?"

"No, I am more scared than anything."

"Well, as of now, you have wicked pain in your neck and your knee hurts from hitting the dashboard."

"I am fine." Bad moment for an honest human to be honest.

"Let me help you." I attempted to transmit my entire message silently with my eyes, or telepathy, or the Vulcan mind-meld. "Your neck hurts and you banged your knee on the dashboard."

"Really, I feel fine. He scared the piss out of me."

I stood. "Aaron!" I yelled. He made eye contact. I pointed at my neck with a single finger. He stepped around our rig, opening the doors on Unit 26.

"Let me get you out of here. We can figure the rest out at the hospital." I spoke explicitly to a woman who simultaneously recognized her jeopardy while denying the risks. Aaron wheeled the stretcher around the wrecked car. He handed me the collar. I gave a quick, professional feel of the woman's neck. We closed the door for a second, wheeled the stretcher, then re-opened the door. In a quick movement, we had her laying on the stretcher. I briefed Aaron in a voice louder than necessary.

"36-year-old female, complaining of neck pain with numbness in her right hand. She also states she has 8 on 10 knee pain after hitting the dashboard. I'll get that splinted in the back of the rig." Once out of the cop's eyeline, I winked at Betsy.

The cop came up to Aaron. "Where are you taking her?"

"We'll run up to Cambridge City?"

"You need to take her to Boston City?"

"We can't. We're Cambridge's official ambulance. We should stay in Cambridge."

"But she is my prisoner. I'll be putting her in custody."

Aaron answered easily, "Sir, I am certain that CPD offers you the same courtesies you offer them?" A marked Cambridge cruiser worked slowly through the traffic lights. We loaded Betsy into the back as the Cambridge cop parked. In the rig, I grabbed my metal clipboard. I drew a sketch of the accident scene then noted the Boston cop's last name and badge number. Through the open windows at the front, I heard Aaron tell both cops that we were headed to Cambridge City Hospital. He then hopped in the front.

He called to the rear: "You guys ready?"

"Yup."

He burped the siren pushing east through the traffic light then wiggled north. He turned off the red-and-white emergency lights. Then in the time I would expect us to arrive at the hospital, Aaron called Denny.

"Base, 26."

"26."

"26, en route Cambridge City with 1."

We continued west. In the few weeks at Atlantic Ambulance, I had endeavored to learn all 917 street names in our fair city. Aaron wended north of Harvard Square, drawing an indirect line towards Mount Auburn. I pulled the neck collar off then started scribbling the details for our run sheet. I wrote down all of the information from her Ohio driver's license and her medical insurance card from Tufts University.

"Listen, Betsy, I have some friends that work here. When you get settled, call a friend, and find a lawyer. The general rule of traffic accidents is that when you get rear-ended, the car behind is always at fault."

"Really?"

"Yes. Both Aaron and I saw that you stopped for a yellow light. That cop may tell you that it was green, but you stopped for a yellow light."

"I thought so. I knew he was a cop. I didn't want to get busted for running a red."

I responded by saying, "I don't think he was paying attention."

We wheeled into Mount Auburn hospital. The first nurse asked, "Did you call it in?"

"No, we forgot," Aaron lied.

One of the nurses that I had dated several times saw me. I winked at her then gave a wave that said both "hello" and "come please."

She smiled, pushing through a cluster by the nurse's station.

I stepped away from the cot.

"We've got a fugitive from Boston PD. One of the asshole cops rear-ended her little car from Ohio. Now I think he is out to bust her. He wanted her taken to Boston City. We told him we went to Cambridge City. Then we traveled here quietly. That's why we didn't call in. Can we sneak her into a curtained room? She should call a lawyer too."

"Anything wrong with her?"

"I told her she had neck pain and knee pain. It took her a minute to believe me."

"So, she's fine."

"She's fine until BPD catches her."

"Got it. Not a problem."

As I turned, I said, "You may want to run a full tox screen. I don't know what bullshit BPD will pull."

"Aren't you a cop's kid?"

"I am. My father is not an asshole that would jam up anyone for stopping at a yellow light. That guy was pure asshole."

"So, fuck him."

"Fuck all assholes."

"I've got you."

Then with a flirty wink, I said, "I do look forward to that?"

"Tonight?"

I looked around the room. "Absolutely."

"My place. 7:30."

"I have shift in the morning. I'll need to run home for a fresh uniform before morning." We returned to the patient. We wheeled to a waiting bed. Betsy shifted from our cot to their bed with a bounce. We pulled the curtain.

We wheeled the cot near the ER door. We stripped the linen and made it up again with fresh linens. Aaron held up two fingers meaning "Code 200." He stepped into the unisex bathroom near the ambulance door. I returned to the nurse's desk to make a Code 55. I called Denny explaining in the fewest possible words how we accidentally ended up at Mount Auburn Hospital. While lying to Denny, I explained that a moving truck blocked a road and Aaron turned towards Mount Auburn because it was faster than waiting.

I had lied to Denny. I knew it. Denny knew it. We both understand the rules of the street. Denny only has to ask himself why I lied to him. The options remain few: protect my partnership with Aaron; protect Denny and Peter from information they don't need; protect Atlantic Ambulance; or protect someone else. I served

Denny a lie he can sell to Cambridge PD, the mayor of Cambridge, and even Boston Police Department.

I then called the Captain. I bounced through the BPD operator. The final hop involved me saying, "Family matter, this is his kid Alexandra."

"Da," I spoke into the recorder, "I just transported a lady who was rear-ended by an unmarked BPD cruiser." I gave all of the details: the officer's last name, his badge number, location in Cambridge of the accident. Then I painted a verbal picture of the scene. While not explicitly stating that the cop was at fault, I proved it with a detailed witness statement. I also confessed to our game of hide-and-seek with our patient. I untangled my lies, telling my father the full and complete truth.

I snuck into the house during the minutes that tick midnight. I rode the T wearing pink scrubs that I borrowed from my date. I had rolled my blue uniform, messily stuffing it into my backpack. I'd have to wash these scrubs then arrange a date to return them.

The Captain and I sat at the breakfast table at dawn. He poured a second cup of Earl Grey tea sipping it with dry toast dipped into the crown of a soft-boiled egg. He read *The Boston Globe* while eating and enjoying his tea.

"Would you like to join me this evening?"

"Sure." I ate another bite of oatmeal. "What are we doing?"

"I am giving a talk to a local group of writers."

"Oh. That will be fun."

"No doubt there will be food and too many drinks after."

"No doubt." The Captain loves hanging with this crowd as much as they love counting a Boston Police captain among their ranks. "Da, what are you going to talk about?"

"I'll come up with something. Probably a few stories about real crimes."

"And dumb criminals?" I finished the thought for him. Captain Flynn can create a funny, suspenseful story from a random page torn from the phone book. Tear a page from either the yellow pages or the white pages, he didn't care. In front of award-winning novelists, he would cradle their souls in his hands as if a magic doll. When he wanted them to cry, he'd wring out a tear. When he wanted laughter, he'd tickle.

"Do you want a ride? I am a little early. I can drop you?"

"Sure."

"I'll pick you up after your tour. I'll aim for 18:15."

"I'll tell Denny and Aaron we need to be back before 6:00 p.m." Thinking that if we do run late, Denny will have to call the Captain's office at BPD. When I ask for that favor, Denny will post us to North Cambridge and Area 3 for the late afternoon.

My mother stirred upstairs as the Captain and I cleared away our dishes, placing them into the dishwasher. She met us at the bottom of the stairs, kissing my father tenderly on his lips. She caressed my left cheek while kissing my right cheek. I wonder if she reads quietly alone, listening to the Captain and I clank dishes. She could not hear more than muted mumbles. Standing on that bottom step, she kissed her hero cop husband who wore a small thirty-eight caliber pistol behind his right hip. Then she kissed her hero EMT kid wearing a blue-over-blue uniform and a metal badge that has my EMT number under the seal of the Commonwealth.

We climbed into my father's city-issued Ford sedan. My station is not on the way between the house and BPD headquarters. But like me, the moment he sat in the cruiser, he was on duty. The radios came alive when he turned the key in the ignition.

For the last call of the day, Aaron and I pushed Unit 26 through the city from Haskell Street near Porter Square to the big post office building. "26. 111B with a cane. Post Office."

"26. Responding for Mr. Lincoln."

Aaron dropped me at the light when I saw Mr. Lincoln. Aaron said that he would loop the block to find a safer place for the rig. I grabbed Aaron's Code 5 kit. I removed only the cigarettes and chocolate bar. I cannot get away with all of Aaron's tricks. I swiped Vick below my nostrils then exited the rig.

I walked Mr. Lincoln back to the demi-wall near the granite steps of the large post office building.

"Here, sit." I tapped the stone next to me. "What's going on today? Are you ok?"

Mr. Lincoln kept talking. He talked about the incurable rudeness of the people who walked by and those who stepped over him while he slept. I put a cigarette down on the granite. I also placed a plastic Bic lighter. He picked both up.

I put my hand on his back. I could feel emphysema or pneumonia crackling inside of his barrel-shaped chest. I watched his carotid artery pulse at his thin lizard-like neck. At a rate of one hundred, it ticked faster than it should. He demonstrated irritation. I don't know how his heart keeps beating week after week, month after month living on these streets.

After a few puffs, the rate of speech slowed. Speaking was a great vital sign, Aaron had said. It told me nearly everything. When speaking in complete flowing sentences, even when ranting insensibly, you know the A-B-Cs. Airway works. Breathing is happening. Circulation moves blood throughout the body. Short choppy sentences can foretell problems. One- or two-word sentences offered in a staccato rhythm between labored breaths indicates very real problems. And there was no reason to grab a wrist to take a pulse when you can see a carotid pulse bounding like Mr. Lincoln's. Without a BP cuff, I know that his blood pressure is at least 90-over-something. Given his medical history, his BP could be disastrously high, even lethal. There is nothing we can do about that. He won't remain in shelters for long. He never follows through on the required regimes of medications to keep himself healthier.

Aaron parked then joined us. He tore off a bite of Mr. Lincoln's chocolate.

"Tough day today?"

I walked to the ambulance. I grabbed the metal clipboard while the two vets talked; while Mr. Lincoln talked; while Aaron listened. I returned to the demi-wall, sat, then started completing our run form. There is not much to write for a fellow who lives on the street. I then prepared the AMA—the Against Medical Advice form. We use the AMA to demonstrate that that patient refused treatment and transportation. We do call it "against medical advice," knowing full well that we often recommend that people do not get transported and we suggest that they fill in the AMA.

"Mr. Lincoln?" I interrupt. "Would you like to go to Cambridge City or the VA today? We can take you?"

The abbreviated version of his answer was "no." The complete answer involved him cussing at the treatment from the staff at both the VA and Cambridge City. I filled in his AMA/no-transport form. I put a blue ballpoint pen and the clipboard in his hands. With barely a look, he scribbled loops through the middle of both pages. Which I hoped Denny would accept as a signature. If not, I could re-write the forms then forge a better signature before end of shift. From my thigh pocket, I pulled out my frozen bottle of seltzer. The water had been thawing at the margins, yielding cool sips.

We sat longer than Denny would have liked and shorter than Mr. Lincoln wanted. Aaron patted the man on the leg offering him a ride as a kindness. "We can take you to a shelter or another neighborhood if you'd like."

We crossed through Harvard Square before Uncle Denny squawked at us again.

"26, Fresh Pond Circle by the grocery store on the east side. Facial burns."

I clicked twice, acknowledging the call. Aaron turned on the siren and lights. I drove more aggressively than normal, impatient with cars who failed to pull right. We found one car with the hood up near an auto parts store in the old strip mall. A cluster of people stood around. Some waved their hands and arms in the air calling us towards them.

"Over here. Over here," they all yelled.

This time Aaron took the lead, walking directly to the patient. I went around to the back, grabbing our kits and pulling the cot out to the pavement. I pushed the cot with bags towards Aaron and the crowd.

Aaron started pouring his drinking water on the kid's face and hands. At my arrival, I stood stock still. I froze. The kid had the same button nose as me, eyes close together, brown hair, and blue eyes. He would have looked like my brother if I had one. He looked like half of my cousins. Looking at this red and blistering face felt like looking into the face of any of my own family or even my own face.

"Lexi?!"

Aaron had observed that I froze.

"I need sterile water and burn dressings." Crack. He got through.

I put the bag on the ground then lowered the stretcher to the height of a chair. Aaron walked our patient over while I opened packages of burn dressing. I wrapped each hand with dry dressing then loose gauze. The hand burns ranged from light first degree to deeply blistering second degree burns. The worst was a dark ring on the palm of his right hand. Aaron continued rinsing the face. He poked small holes through the cap of his water bottle, dripping water into the fellow's eyes and down his face.

We rotated our patient up on the cot. Wordlessly, we dropped the cot, then lifted the patient to the back. Closing the doors on Aaron, I said, "Mount Auburn?"

"No, let's run to Mass Gen, they have a better burn unit." He gave a knowing look to the right hand. Aaron leaned into his shift bag, the one where he kept his Code-5 materials, one of his three Purple Heart metals, and a ratty army shirt. He pulled out a clean one-liter bag of saline solution. He spiked the bag and hung it on the stretcher. As basic EMTs, the law prohibits us from setting IVs and using needles. Aaron, as a former combat medic, had tricks and training that I did not get in a classroom at Northeastern University.

Aaron took a real blood pressure and listened to the patient's lungs with his stethoscope. Then he asked for the history. The young man, not knowing what was wrong with his car, had opened the radiator cap. The cap burned his right hand; steam escaped, burning both his hands, parts of his forearms, and his face.

"Are you breathing ok?"

I heard the patient answering in full sentences. Aaron asked, "Can you open your mouth?" He turned to look at me briefly. "Lexi? Whip these ponies, will ya?"

Aaron obviously saw something he did not like in our patient.

I flipped the siren on. I bobbed and weaved through traffic. Not the way my father taught me to drive. He had encouraged me to let the lights and siren do the work. Let the cars sort themselves out. You drive a straight line. You, he said to me, be predictable.

I gave cars a second or two to move then I moved around them. I put two wheels up over a curb to wiggle through a traffic light.

"Call it in for me will you, kid?"

"Boston C-Med, Boston C-Med, Atlantic 26 with priority traffic."

"Aaron, airway?"

"Involved."

"Got it."

Once the hospital answered, I made my report: "Twenty-six-year-old male with first and second degree burns to the face and airway. Deep second degree burns to the right palm. Patient alert and conscious. Vital signs within normal limits. Airway presently open."

We did our hand-off to hospital staff in one of the larger trauma rooms. Aaron's IV bag continued to drip saline into the patient's eyes and face. Aaron briefed the medical staff while standing in the corner of the room. He employed an outdoor voice to speak to the room. He spoke loudly, clearly, enunciating each word. While he spoke, the doctor at the head of the patient called out orders: IVs, EKG, portable chest x-ray. We wheeled our now-empty stretcher from the trauma room.

Aaron sat in a wheelchair. I made the cot then sat next to him for a second.

Aaron controlled his breathing, actively stilling his heartbeat, working into his personal Zen space. Rarely did calls cause him to break that glass wall.

We sat in silence. Our portable radios belched out calls to others, both the routine and the emergent.

"20, Brookline for Mr. Goldstein."

"25, Area 3 posting please."

"27, man down…"

Aaron looked at me. He might have reached for my hand had we not been both sitting in cheap ER-style wheelchairs. "What hit you?" he asked.

I might have wanted to ask him the same question. I guessed at his answer. Our patient was the rare military-age male that Aaron would have once treated. I have met many of his demons. I have seen a few of their faces and brushed against a few of the ghosts that follow him.

"He looked like any number of my own family. He could have come off the streets of Dublin or Southie."

"That's scary, isn't it?"

Maybe, just maybe I met my first demon.

"Is he going to be ok?"

"I dunno. They will have to intubate him pretty quickly. I heard his airway swelling. If they wait too long, they'll have to do a trach." He debated whether the team would slide a plastic tube down his throat or make a small slice through his neck to introduce a plastic airway lower down.

"Circling the drain?" I asked.

"Circling fast!" He leaned back with his head against the plaster wall. I tapped him on his thigh then wheeled the stretcher back to the rig. When I came back in, I found a full saline bag and setup kit in the empty wheelchair. I put the equipment in my pocket, sneaking it out to Aaron's medical kit. I pulled the ambulance out of the bay, parking near a dumpster.

"26, 20?" Aaron's voice broke through on the radio, softly asking me where I was.

"Dumpsters to the right."

Click, click.

Then Denny called out. "26, status?"

"26 clearing MGH in a minute."

"Tell me when you are over the bridge."

"K!"

Aaron opened the door, climbing in.

Back on the Cambridge side of the Charles, I keyed the mic. "26."

"26. Area 3 for coverage. Unit 25, 26 is relieving you."

I guessed that Bobby had already bought his fill of losing lottery tickets and scratch-offs from the Purple Chicken, cussing out the clerk for selling crappy tickets to him. I drove slowly. Aaron had his head back, breathing. His fists clenched then unclenched rhythmically.

I do not know how or why this gentle man faced these traumas every day. While most of our work seemed as routine as driving a city cab, Denny blew up the routine with calls that trip every alarm bell in the human body. The body screamed, This is dangerous. The body screamed, You could die here now. The body screamed. Then the mind screamed. You either control it or you run away.

My training involved sitting in a classroom Monday and Wednesday nights for a semester. At the end of the training, I took a university exam earning an A-grade. Following the semester, I scheduled certification exams with the Commonwealth. First, I had to pass a practical exam that proved I could splint a long bone, apply a traction splint to a leg, and secure a patient to a backboard. I do not know Aaron's training. He had skills that paralleled paramedics'. In the army he set up IVs, gave blood, and did more invasive techniques. I am pretty sure that he carried morphine to help manage pain. Regrettably, the army training did not qualify him for any civilian certification nor license. Like me, he had to sit through an EMT course, listening to a civilian EMT discuss the horrors and tragedies of the streets. Aaron was likely older than other students and possessed all of the required skills. Like me, he had to step through each station at the state exam. Then like me, after passing scores at the practicum, he had to take a written exam.

During our summers together, he studied nursing at Northeastern. I hoped that he would get off the streets before it became too late. I don't know why he didn't get a job as a plumber, mechanic, or librarian. Or maybe I did know. We parked in Porter Square at 5:30.

The windows let the summer breeze blow through the cab. Aaron laid his head back. I pivoted in my seat to get my book. I spun the radio dial to land on WCRB, the classical music station. I opened the book.

"26." My heart dropped an inch. Then Denny said, "RTB."

I picked up the mic. "RTB," I said, parroting his call for us to return-to-base. I clipped the mic back. Set the dial back to WBCN, dropped my book, then shifted into drive. We parked our rig for the night, giving it a quick cleaning. I gathered our paperwork.

I took the stack of eleven run forms upstairs to Denny's desk. I showed him the documents from Mr. Lincoln with the blue circles scribbled on the pages.

"Denny, do you want me to re-do these?"

He looked at the mess. "Nah, don't worry about it. We can't bill anyone for it." The law states we can only invoice insurance if we transport a patient. When we got an AMA signed, we gave away our services for free. Or maybe the City of Cambridge paid us fees for these types of calls. Crews had spent entire days at fire scenes. And we had deployed crews for special events. Somehow, Peter Clifton and Atlantic Ambulance made money from these efforts.

Each form, except for Mr. Lincoln's, had names, addresses, social security numbers, and patient signatures. The boxes for recording mileage were all blank—as per our protocols.

Bobby came up the stairs as I finished. He turned in three run reports and two large manilla envelopes. I presume that each envelope had been filled with cash: fives, tens, and twenties. Bobby had his heavy mag light hanging from his well-strained belt.

Denny looked at the black-and-white television monitor on his desk. "Lexi, the cops are here for you." I glanced up at the wall clock. Not only was my father early, Denny had pulled me from the street on time.

I bounced down the stairway. I hopped into Aaron's arms for a quick hug. We don't normally hug at the end of a shift. Today seemed like a good day to bathe in his strong arms.

I started climbing into the Crown Victoria with my bag. My father took my bag, then handed me a WGBH tote bag. "Your mother dropped this off with me today."

I looked. She had packed me a linen skirt and peasant blouse.

When I stepped from the bathroom, several of the guys hooted. They had never seen me in a skirt. Dressing down for me was a pair of jeans and a T-shirt. I have worn a few white oxford button-down shirts. This evening, I walked across the garage floor wearing girl-clothes. The hooting stopped after exactly one whistle.

My father, the Captain, had stepped out of his unmarked police cruiser. He came around the door in an immaculately fitted grey double-breasted wool suit. That shut them all up. Every one of the boys cast their eyes from me to my father. A few said, "Have a good evening," with polite manners that we never heard at this station. All eyes watched me as I sat in the front seat of my father's car.

We arrived at the Parker House Hotel on School Street just off of Tremont Street. We had parked in a garage in the same block. We got directed to a private banquet room. Many of the faces in the room had been to our house for supper. Some of these authors had invited the Captain and our family to their homes. He walked in carrying the prestige of a famous guest of honor, yet the room included several award-winning authors, including writers recently presented Edgar Allan Poe statues from the Mystery Writers of America. This room included authors who had sold several million copies of their books. Authors seen occasionally on morning television shows. As we walked across the room, these famous people dropped their conversations to greet my father. Robert Parker sidled up next to me, dropping his arm around my shoulder. "Hey, kid."

"Mr. Parker," I said in greeting.

"Don't you think you're old enough to call me Robert. Nice pic in the *Globe* this summer." Yup, he saw it too: Cop's kid worked to save a life.

I answered, "All in the family," recalling the bold headline that morning.

"No doubt you have stories to tell."

"No doubt, but nobody wants me talking while they eat."

"That bad?"

"Well, not if you enjoy Stephen King." I pointed in Mr. King's direction.

"That scary?" Mr. Parker asked me.

"More *Firestarter* than *Cujo*. On a bad day, it is like creepy slasher movie. On a good day, it is only boring."

"Which do you like?"

"I want boring until I am bored. Then I want anything else."

"What did you do today?" the author of Spenser for Hire books asked me.

"You really don't want to know."

"I really do. I have an editor and a publisher pushing me for more books."

While I stalled for time, I waffled between telling him about Aaron, the Vietnam combat vet treating homeless vets in Cambridge, or telling him how a young man nearly died opening a car radiator. I flip-flopped, thinking of how and why my father is so popular in this room.

Captain Flynn did not tell a tragic story without a reason. Young innocent man opening a car radiator taking in sufficient hot and potentially toxic steam didn't have a point—no humor, no plot, no lesson. Instead, I told the novelist about my hero partner—three times shot from helicopters in 'Nam; attended nursing school; and our interaction with the street vets of Metro Boston. Hero—check. Tragedy—check. Call-to-Action—check. We all need to do more for our veterans. A couple of younger writers joined in, listening.

I looked around the room. Filled with professional story tellers, my father held a group of seven in a tight circle telling a story. Me, I came in second place with a group of five. He had Stephen King with him. I had Robert Parker. I do not have my father's lilt, although that switch toggles with one beer or one sip of good whiskey. He did teach me to tell stories.

The head table had four chairs, two place settings on each side of the lectern.

I segued into a story about Peter Clifton, the owner of Atlantic Ambulance and cousin to the mayor of Cambridge. I described him as intensely tanned under his white uniform shirt—or rather how he takes his white uniform shirt off in the afternoons while sipping beer with salt on the roof of the ambulance station. Then introduced my growing audience to Bobby Clifton, the nephew, who shook down patients at their homes for cash payments. Standing with this audience of crime writers, I explored what else might be going on at my station. We did dodgy paperwork, chased patients for cash, while getting paid for a fraction of the time we spent in our rigs out on the streets. Little lie, big lie. Maybe my father's line was "little crime, big crime." It worked either way.

People lie about stupid stuff. My father educated me that all suspects lie always. He added that most witnesses also lied. During my summer on emergency ambulances, I learned that all patients lie too. This lie protected that lie. That lie protected that crime. That crime obscured the next crime.

At the clink of a few glasses, the writers and their guests move towards seats. I stuck with Robert knowing that I did not have a seat on the dais with my father.

The Captain walked to the front table, taking a seat to the left of the podium.

I walked with Robert to a table at the front. I sat with my left shoulder pointing toward the speakers.

My father's voice spoke through the din. "Lexi, come join me."

I looked over. The dais now included five chairs. The Captain put his arm around the empty chair.

I shrugged at the others at the table. Like being called to play after taking a seat at Fenway Park. Nervously, I stepped up to the raised platform. I nodded to a few people. I was not the youngest in the room, but very close. Most seemed to approximate my father's age. One older lady in the room, Helen Dresser McCloy, published her first book in 1938. She took the prize for the most senior member of the audience.

I sat at my father's side. Others in the room sat. After a few introductory words, the salads arrived at each table. Each table had a basket of Parker House Rolls. Our dining selection included scrod.

Dessert included Boston Cream Pie, another classic dish attributed to this hotel, the Parker House Hotel.

After a brief, and unnecessary, introduction, the Captain stood. He raised his still full glass of whiskey.

"*Sláinte*, my friends. I am honored that you invited me back. I don't know what a street cop from Boston can tell an audience as prominent as the folks in the room. I don't think I could count the Edgars, Elleries, and Pulitzers collected by you all. I don't know what you ate, but I enjoyed that scrod." He looked around the room. "Do you know they invented the term 'scrod' in this building?" He waited a beat, smiling. His eyes crinkled just like they did when he was on television.

"Was it you, Robby? Or you, Toms, who told me about a flight to Chicago a few years ago? Nah, it was Robby, here up front. He flew to LA from Boston for a meeting. What was it? Maybe a movie? Or a television show? I still don't know; he won't tell me.

"He got into a black car at LAX. The chauffeur drove towards downtown LA. They passed the time chatting. It had been a long day for our friend Robert Parker. His belly rumbled. He had already commented to the driver that he hates being 3000 miles from the ocean. Then as they come downtown heading to the Hilton Hotel, Bobby says to the driver, 'Hey, where can a fellow get scrod in this town?'

"Well, the driver turns in his seat, 'Sir, that is the first time I heard the pluperfect of that verb.'"

Know your audience. A cop with an Irish lilt just cracked a grammar joke in a room full of writers.

My father then looked at Robert Parker. "I never did learn. Did you get fish or something else delivered to your room? Oh, don't answer that one. Remember, I am a cop.

"You guys all make crime pay. Well done. I have got to tell you that most of the guys we bust in Boston can't figure that part out. We bust some of the stupidest people. Maybe one of you should publish a crime handbook. Not for cops, but for crooks. Step number one, when out for a night of climbing through windows, do not put your wallet in the back pocket of your jeans. We picked it up right where it fell under the window. We wait an hour or so, then go knock on Joe Bad-Guy's door. 'Hey man you dropped this, and someone turned it in.'

"There was that guy who stole a sewing machine from a neighbor. His nana wanted to sew costumes for the grandbabies. The guy climbed down the fire escape. He lifted the Singer from the table then pushed it out the window. Then toted it up the iron fire escape stairs. With each step he took up, the red thread unspooled another foot or three. We followed that thread out one window into another. We found the sewing machine under a blanket on the living room floor..."

6 | Heroes on Film

School caused me to reduce my hours at Atlantic Ambulance. First, I dropped my weekday shifts as I prepared for school. Then, I informed Peter and Denny about my last day of work for the summer. We negotiated my departure. I said that I would remain available for shifts on the occasional weekend or holiday. In trade for my availability, I remained eligible to take free training at the Atlantic Ambulance station. As an EMT, the Commonwealth requires that I participate in continuing education to maintain my skills. I have to take the CPR class each year renewing that card. Some classes I attended but for other classes, I added my name to the paper roster. In each case, I signed in; I signed out; and I wrote my Massachusetts EMT number.

I worked my last shift with Aaron on a Friday. We embraced tenderly. We said our goodbyes, understanding that our partnership had closed. Aaron would be employed during the summer of 1984 as a registered nurse after completing his degree. My return to the streets after two semesters in the classroom would require that I find a new partner. We both made sincere promises of friendship and enduring contact.

I walked up to Porter Square, feeling that dreadful dry lump in my throat. I knew that Aaron and I would drift apart. Aaron had told me as much during the rare stories he shared from Vietnam. Men he served with and fought with made passionate claims of friendship and brotherhood that failed to sustain past the homecoming that the United States offered these soldiers. While it was unlikely that Aaron and I would follow the path taken by his peers, we both knew that we would drift apart.

I stepped onto the red line train heading towards Harvard Square then the eight-minute ride to Park Street. At least the Harvard Square kiosk informs all that the trip takes eight minutes. But that happens only when the trains run smoothly. My blue uniform trousers showed the abuse of spending fifty hours per week on urban ambulances. My white ribbed wife-beater T-shirt told a story of sweat and rents from a summer of violence, heat, and work. With my backpack sitting on my lap, I felt something new tucked within. On top of my two uniform shirts sat a standard white envelope with "A. Flynn" written in Aaron's handwriting.

I felt it, then opened it. On a beaded necklace of stainless steel, Aaron had hung two dog tags. Confused, thinking he would never give me his, I brought the embossed metal closer to my face. They read: Alexandra Flynn, 14 JULY 1964, O+. In lieu of my social security number or service number, I read my EMT number. I kissed each dog tag as if kissing Aaron, then I hung them around my neck.

I had crossed a threshold with my friend.

Changing to the Green Line at Park Street, I stepped into a busy car. After a summer of watching, I spied the interaction between two people near the middle door. A large man examined the neck and thus jewelry of a young woman seated on the plastic chair. She spied him obtusely. He spied her obtusely. At first, I thought I witnessed the opening moves of a tryst or flirtation. Instead of cooing at each other with warm eyes, they made furtive glances. Each tried to avoid detection by the other. As the train slowed for the station, the guy made a shuffling move. When the train stopped, he stumbled forward. He grabbed the woman's necklace then sprinted out the door. I immediately took chase. "Hey, stop." While not-a-cop, I was wearing police trousers, a white T-shirt, and grew up in the house of Boston's favorite police officer. The lady, seeing me charging forward, held out her hand to stop me. She silently shook her head. She then looked down at her own left hand, inviting me to look as well. She had stolen all of his jewelry. She handed it up to me. I hefted it. At least one piece that she grabbed felt as heavy as real gold. I returned the ill-gotten booty to her hands. I winked.

Another story for my father's repertoire of stupid criminals. Unlike his stories, mine were true, no matter how often my father swore to the veracity of his tales. Unsure of what to do with my own stories, I examined new scars on my body. Most obviously, I had a jagged cut near my right elbow where someone sitting in a car pushed my arm up and away. I had torn the skin on a metal shard. I dripped blood continuously while securing that patient to a backboard. I began to wonder if I had developed scars from the unseen cuts. I met Aaron's demons. I felt Aaron's fears. And ghosts from southeast Asian followed him home to Cambridge and Boston. Still uncertain why he would rise each morning to climb into a white Ford ambulance five days per week. Hadn't he done enough? Hadn't he seen enough? Hadn't he given enough?

When in the classroom starting the fall semester, I ignored changes within my own body. I could sit in a lecture hall of forty students paying attention to the professor, yet I felt and heard every movement from every other human being in the room. I pushed myself to sit in the front and center in the rooms. Within a few days, I migrated to the corner furthest from the door. I watched the door. I inventoried sounds I heard. I inventoried each movement I saw. I inventoried each distractive thought that crept into my head. As if Denny would crack through on the radio: "Unit 26."

I preferred small classrooms and quiet rooms. But I hated the library. Sitting at Cambridge Common, or along the river, or tucked into a corner of Harvard Square, Aaron and I watched the world. We did get in trouble with some agency. At Cambridge Common, we observed two men with button-down shirts and casual trousers with binoculars. They took turns studying windows in a brick building to the west. I moved the ambulance to obstruct their view. They were not watching birds. They had no dog. They were two professional men sitting on a park bench in the middle of a summer's day. They moved. After moving, they returned to their binoculars. I moved the rig again. That pissed them off. They yelled and badged us. We fled. Would I have seen these two in years past? Or did my months on an emergency ambulance change how I saw them? Did the calls and time on the streets change how I heard everything?

I hated the library because of the quiet. Our library was not silent. The hushed tones of whispers and gentle steps sounded like people wanting to be quiet. Yet that was the loudest possible sound. On the streets, each sound had a life cycle within a greater context. The sounds told a story. They filled the landscape: here a door closed; there a pigeon cooed; inside a house, a dog barked; that car had a failing muffler; that driver smoked a cigarette; an MBTA bus passed, leaving behind an odor of burnt diesel. Aaron and I parked with strong sightlines. He could never tolerate surprises. I now inherited a touch of his startle response.

I sat in the classroom on duty and alert for the next call, the next tragedy, the next violent act. I listened to the professors. I wrote my notes.

On a cool September afternoon, I returned home, finding a message in my mother's handwriting. "Call Denny at the station." I remembered the hundreds of times during the summer when I heard Denny's voice say: 26, code 55 soonest. Likely when he called me at home, he put on a polite voice, calling my mother Mrs. Flynn.

"Mrs. Flynn, can you have your Alexandra call me today?"

I dialed the phone.

"Uncle Denny?"

"Lexi. How are you? How is school?"

"I am fine. Things are good. Miss me?"

"Sort of. Sometimes. I have a mission for you and Aaron."

"As in, Unit 26 please respond to HUPD?"

"Sort of, but I have never said 'please' on the radio once in my life."

"No, you haven't."

"Never will either."

"What is the mission?" I asked the dispatcher at Atlantic Ambulance Service in Cambridge, Massachusetts.

"This one is easy. You and Aaron are going to take your rig to Hanscom Airfield for a movie shoot."

"You mean we'll be in a movie?"

"Fuck no. Nobody wants you in a movie. Maybe they'll take your partner, but you? You'll wreck it." I left the jabbing unanswered. I got more dates and romped around with more people during the summer than any other staff member at the station. Oh, and I got more press than anyone else too.

I asked, "When is this?"

Denny answered, "Next Wednesday."

I reviewed my schedule: An outline due to my international relations professor, a lecture on Russian history; and a Russian language course.

"I can do it."

I arrived at the station at 6:00 a.m. I pulled Unit 26 from its space. The current crew left an empty cooler and a backpack in the rig. I removed them, laying them near the stairs. I pulled the stretcher. Then I took my time with each element of the checklist. By the time I was done with the wall next to the cot, Aaron arrived. I leapt into his arms. I kissed him on his left cheek, then buried my face into his shoulder. He smelled so good. Damn if my ankle didn't kick up as if I were in a stupid rom-com. We hugged a bit longer then, after he let me go, I lifted my dog-tags from under my uniform shirt.

"They never leave me." Likely meaning something a bit more.

"I'll clean the front." He returned to the rig with a spray bottle of cleaner. Every surface of plastic, pleather, and glass got cleaned. I did the same in the back. I remade the cot, pulling everything army-tight and army-square. I strapped the pillow down. By 6:30, we were drying water spots from our rig. We stopped at the Purple Chicken in Area 3 for the day's snacks, water, and a second coffee for Aaron. I cracked the seltzer water open, watching the ice form instantly. Magical.

We drove out Route Two, climbing the hill through Arlington towards Bedford and Lincoln.

On Tuesday, I had my hair done. I had part of the left side shaved short plus a dramatic weight-line cut across the back. The top of the hair colored to a warm flaxen blonde. The under hairs remained neutral brown. I could see that Aaron had a neat trim as well. A faint line of pale skin traced his hairline from the left ear, down around the neck, then back to the right ear. He did wear a soft brown bomber jacket. The exact jacket I once imagined him wearing, a jacket I never knew he owned. The gate guards waved us through with impatience.

Aaron stopped. "I don't know where we are going."

They gave directions to the clinic with pointed hands.

"No, we are here for some movie and film set."

"Oh. That's out on the airfield. Drive towards the airfield then look for tents and trucks. You can't miss it."

Aaron mumbled, "Damn I hate it when people say, 'You can't miss it.'"

The gate guard was right. Finding an airstrip on an air force base proved easy. It is their reason for existence. Finding a pile of boxy tents and box trucks on a taxi way also proved easy. It looked entirely wrong and out of place.

We wheeled up. Looped slowly, parking, facing the exit. We climbed down from our rig. Aaron gave it a fresh wipe with a clean hospital towel. He dropped the towel inside the rear door.

"Should we see what this is about?" We walked towards the busiest cluster of people. Nobody paid any attention to us.

One open-walled tent had a table filled with breakfast snacks and urns of coffee. They had a table display of cold bottled water, both still and fizzy. We looped around again. Crews worked with cameras and other equipment. Other crews worked with portable lighting. We both spied a trailer that contained toilets and we also spotted a row of Johnny-on-the-Spot plastic poopers. Nobody cared about us.

We ambled back to our ambulance.

Aaron and I debated where and how to park. Denny's voice rang in our head: Don't get blocked in. As per our training and his words, we parked away from the action facing out. We both saw the logic placing the rig such that we could watch the film set. We did the right thing. We followed the rules. We positioned our rig ready for action. We climbed into the front seat. We looked out over a small suburban U.S. Air Force base.

"Any clue where the nearest hospital is?"

"No."

"We should probably find out, huh?"

"I guess so," I answered. "Isn't there a hospital a bit farther out on Route 2 in Concord? Emerson or something."

"Oh, there is. They have a pair of paramedics out there. I wonder why they don't have this duty. There are several services out here." He asked, "Think you could find it?"

"Sure, Route 2 west, follow the blue and white hospital signs until we find a red sign that says, 'Emergency.'"

"Works for me."

I asked, "Think the radio works?"

"No idea. Should we try?"

"Probably." I picked up the mic. "Base, 26."

"26, go ahead."

"On site for the detail. How is the signal?"

"Five-by-five."

"Any instructions for us?"

"Check in with AD."

"AD?"

"That's what my note says."

"Confirm."

We climbed down from the rig again. We walked towards the food service.

"We are looking for someone named *AD*?"

The first fellow said, "Which AD?"

"You have more than one?"

Impatiently, the fellow pointed towards a cluster of people walking away.

We approached that crowd. Aaron said, "Excuse us, we are looking for a fellow named AD, can anyone help us?"

Three people laughed.

One guy looked at us. "Which one? Are you guys talent? Crew?"

"I dunno," I answered. "We are the ambulance." I pointed at the white rig with Atlantic Ambulance painted in blue above an orange stripe. The three who laughed returned to their coffee and conversation.

A Jaguar XJ6 rolled past our ambulance. The jackass pulled in behind us, parking so close that we could barely open our rear doors. We both saw him turning at the same time. We opened our stride.

Aaron went to the driver's window, rapping on it. "Hey, you can't park there. That is an emergency vehicle. We need access. Can you park over there?"

Instead of moving away from our backdoor, he opened his door, climbing out.

"Eliot?" I asked.

The asshole in the Jag turned towards me. "Lexi. I knew if I found an ambulance, I'd find you."

"But did you have to park so close? What if we get a call? We need room to work."

"You won't get a call, I promise." Shit, famous last words.

"Aaron, this is a friend of my father's, Eliot Warren. He is a mystery writer. Eliot, this is my partner, Aaron."

The two men shook hands.

I asked, "Eliot, what are you doing here?"

"They are making my film."

"What?"

"Oh, yeah. Cool as shit, huh?"

"You didn't say anything at the meeting this summer."

"I thought everybody knew. Anyway, I barely talked with you. You were surrounded. You had Robert Parker on one side and a bunch of gah-gah baby writers on your other side. Then during dinner, your father pulled you up to the front."

"That was a nice night."

"Do you know why we are here? We were told to find someone named *AD*? We've asked around for him, but everyone laughs at us or points in random directions."

"You don't know why you are here?"

"No fucking clue. I assume that we are on standby as set medics. That's our best guess."

He laughed. "This was all your mom's doing."

"My mother?"

"Absolutely."

"What did she do?"

"When she heard we were filming a scene here, she told me that we needed to hire you and your partner for the scene."

"What scene?" Honestly, my question sounded more like "what the fuck" but I trimmed it back out of respect.

"A Learjet will arrive soon. Then you two and your ambulance will fetch out the mobster that the FBI are returning to the city for justice."

I looked at Aaron. Aaron looked at me.

"My mother?"

"Totally. Here, let me introduce you around."

Eliot walked us back to the food tent. People either parted, making way for the author, or they stepped up to him. "By the way, *AD* means assistant director," Eliot whispered.

We got introduced to the two assistant directors, the director, and others. We tailed Eliot around for a while, then we both started getting bored. I said, "We'll go sit in our office. Come find us if or when you need us."

We spun the ambulance around so that we faced the runway, the taxi way, and the entire film crew. Then, like being posted in a quiet corner in Cambridge, we read, studied, and listened to music. I listened to WBCN, studying the present tense of standard Russian verbs. Aaron reviewed flash cards, describing common dosages and the standard range of human biological function. Average urine production rate is 40 milliliters per hour.

The Learjet landed with a camera crew at the far end of the runway and a crew at the midpoint. The jet took off again then landed a second time. An hour later, camera crews had moved all of their equipment to a taxiway on the other side of the runway. They filmed the jet taxiing and turning; taxiing and turning; and taxiing and turning. I quizzed Aaron about various bodily fluids, liver function results, and blood chemistry tests. Aaron quizzed me about Russian.

Before noon, I climbed out. I walked towards the shiny white bathroom trailer. I let myself in. I peed quickly. I had none of the street crap on my hips. No cuffs. No duty belt. No heavy portable radio. I washed my hands in warm water. Then exited the trailer.

Somebody yelled at me, "Hey, that's for talent only. You need to use the blue ones in the back."

I ignored the voice, and I ignored the coaching. I did not even turn to look as I walked back to our ambulance. A guy in a dark blue Izod shirt wearing khaki trousers chased me down.

"Hey?"

I ignored him. But he kept chasing. I could hear his footsteps. This was not the same voice that yelled at me for peeing in a clean white toilet.

"Hey?" he yelled again.

"Yes?" I turned, stopping.

"Are you with the ambulance?"

"Yes."

"I am one of the set medics."

"Cool." I started walking again.

"What are you guys doing here?"

"I don't really know. They needed an ambulance for a scene or something."

"Are you medics?"

"No, we're both EMTs."

"So am I," he said.

"Where do you work?"

"Here."

"No, I mean for which ambulance service?"

"None. I just work special events and stuff." He walked alongside me. I wondered how someone could get enough experience without working for a busy service. I discovered that I lacked generosity and patience for this young man.

"Where do you work?"

"I work for Atlantic out of Cambridge. We do all of the 911 service there."

"Oh."

At Aaron's window, I said, "Aaron this is one of the set medics. Sorry, I didn't catch your name." I left the set medic at Aaron's window, climbing back into the driver's seat.

Aaron said, "This is pretty boring. Does anything happen?"

The young EMT started telling war stories to a former combat medic and veteran of an urban 911 service. I overheard stories of cuts, bruises, and electrical shock.

We watched the Lear taxi back across the quiet runway again. A self-important fellow wearing a headset and carrying a clipboard came towards us. Joe Clipboard looked at the set medic, which sent the kid scampering.

"I need you two to do some paperwork." Officious and curt, he added, "Go to the office trailer. They have forms for you to complete." Aaron and I both climbed down, following Joe Clipboard. He vectored towards the taxiway and the Lear.

With a bark, he said, "No. The office."

Aaron asked, "Where's that?"

"It is the white trailer."

We both turned, seeing a row of white trailers. He pointed towards all of the trailers.

We turned away from the Lear, walking towards the trailers. Aaron asked, "Where is the office trailer?"

The lady did not answer. Instead, she said, "Who are you?"

"I am Alexandra Flynn. This is my partner, Aaron."

"No, who are you?" It wasn't a question. It was a statement that we had somehow answered wrong.

"We're with the ambulance," Aaron pointed.

"Well, go back to the ambulance."

"Some guy with a headset and clipboard sent us to the office."

"It is over there." She pointed to the left half of trailers, then left us.

We continued farther. People proved little help to outsiders.

We knocked at the door that said, "Office."

"Come in."

"Some guy with a clipboard and headset sent us here."

"Who are you?"

"My name is Alexandra Flynn and this is my partner, Aaron."

"No, who are you? Are you cast, crew, cops, what?"

"We're with the ambulance," Aaron said. "I think you need the ambulance in a scene today or something."

"There is an ambulance here?"

"Has been since nearly dawn."

"You should have checked in immediately. We've been waiting for you." The lady reached for a folder. The tab read: Atlantic Ambulance. "You are Atlantic Ambulance?"

"Yes," Aaron and I said at the same time.

"I need you each to sign an insurance waiver. Then a waiver for the ambulance." She read the notes. "Are you members of SAG?"

"What is SAG?" Aaron asked.

But I knew. I had heard the phrase enough around my father's friends. "Screen Actors Guild. This is a union shoot."

"How do we join?" Aaron asked.

"You don't join, you have to qualify."

We each got a stack of papers and our own clipboards. We sat to fill them in. Each form seemed identical to the prior form. The last document was a SAG brochure about non-union background actors.

We returned to the desk with our clipboards. "You can work a maximum of three shoots without joining SAG. This is number one." She spun, making copies of some of the forms. "Keep these." She handed us a copy of some of the forms. She then handed us each a check plus a voucher. The value of my check was two hundred dollars. The voucher, I inferred, had something to do with the union process on a movie set.

"Which of you is the boss?" She looked at Aaron who is male. He was also taller and older than I.

My elbow tapped him in the ribs.

"I am," he answered.

"Then you need to sign a waiver for the ambulance."

Aaron made a show of pulling out his three-color Atlantic Ambulance pen. He clicked the blue ink down. Then with his left hand, he scribbled his name. A bit neater than Mr. Lincoln, but not as tidy as his own real signature.

Even EMTs and an emergency ambulance needed to sign waivers against injury and damage on a film set.

"Find the AD and tell him you're all set."

"The guy with the headset and clipboard?" Aaron asked.

"Yes." She appeared done with us.

We left the office looking for Joe Clipboard or Eliot.

Instead, they all found us. Suddenly, we were late. We were out of position. "What is the ambulance doing over there?"

I asked, "What would you like to do with the ambulance?"

"It needs to be over by the taxiway."

We both walked away towards our rig. "No, you can't drive it. That's not allowed."

"What?"

"Go get a driver."

"We can't let anyone else drive that ambulance."

"Well, who are you?"

"I am Alexandra Flynn."

"No, I mean who are you? Aren't you two extras?"

"I suppose so. But that is our ambulance." Some guy was now hustling towards our rig. He climbed in with a cigarette dangling from his lips.

I yelled across the hundred meters. "Put that out!"

Aaron took off in a run.

Joe Clipboard said, "That's ok. He is one of our drivers."

"He can't smoke in an ambulance. It is filled with oxygen." The guy opened the door climbing in. Aaron slowed to a jog, then to his fast walk.

Aaron approached the rig. Without hearing the words, I knew Aaron yelled about the cigarette, pointing out the numerous signs about no smoking and oxygen. The guy flicked the cigarette to the ground of a US Air Force Base. Aaron handed him the keys through the window.

Nothing happened. Aaron remained animated while talking

with the driver-guy. Aaron thumbed, "Out."

The guy jumped out. Aaron bent, turning the battery switch from off to dual. I did not see Aaron flip the switch, but I knew the movement. It was routine for us. Turn batteries on before starting the engine. Turn the batteries off after killing the engine.

Aaron negotiated his way out of the driver's seat, climbing into the passenger's seat. The set driver moved the ambulance a hundred meters then back towards the parked Learjet. I walked towards Aaron. Aaron had his keys again.

The next guy that came to us seemed super important. He had a bevy of people following. The camera crews moved cameras. The lighting crews moved lights. Aaron and I returned to our rig sitting on the rear step. Everybody ignored us as they hustled.

Eliot came over. "Isn't this exciting?"

"Absolutely. Totally exciting," I lied. "I still have no idea what we are doing here." My father's friend was clearly doing me a huge favor.

"You're in the movie."

We had both come to understand that.

He waved his arms around. "The FBI have a mobster like Whitey Bulger, Buddy McLean, or Howie Winter. I named my character, Simpson Whitman. He is played by Clyde Pritchard. Have you seen him around today?"

"Yes," I lied again. I wouldn't know Clyde Pritchard if he bit me on the ass. "So cool to be around all of these famous people. We really appreciate you inviting us out here today."

"Oh, let me go find him."

We three stood for a cheesy photo with our stretcher at knee height. Aaron and I flanked the world-famous actor. He looked like any of the mobster, or capos, from Southie or the Winter Hill Gang from Somerville.

Aaron and I returned to Cambridge well after dark. We hugged after parking the ambulance. We had been gone for over twelve hours and been on shift for over thirteen hours. In my little cubby-hole mailbox, I found an envelope. In the envelope, I found five one-hundred-dollar bills. I held my envelope up for Aaron as a question. He looked in his box. He found the same, nodding back to me. I don't know what he got paid and I never told him what I got. We closed the overhead garage door with a button on the wall then let ourselves out the man door.

"Can I drop you?"

"Sure. Porter Square is fine."

"Nah, I'll drive you home." He had never offered before.

Climbing from his car at the curb by my parent's house, I kissed him on the cheek as if I would see him tomorrow.

On Friday morning while getting ready for school, my mother handed me the *Boston Globe* Metro section. Above the fold stood a black-and-white photo of me, Aaron, and Clyde Pritchard. The story muddled the facts. The movie, based in Boston, written by an author who was raised and attended school in Boston, told a story of the Boston mob. Clyde Pritchard, who was educated in Boston after being raised in New Hampshire, starred in the film. I read the name Atlantic Ambulance across the top of my favorite rig, Unit 26. And yet, somehow the story was about my father, Captain William T. S. Flynn, and his child Alexandra. My mother beamed with pride. Maybe I misread the article. More likely, I picked up the wrong details. But for a guy who did not write the book, did not write the screen play, was not on the film set, my father got his name mentioned twice. Eliot got mentioned as the author and earned the photo credit in the lower right corner.

My father often said that the key difference between Leif Erikson discovering America and Christopher Columbus discovering America is that Columbus had a better press agent. I wonder who my father has as his press agent. He, or she, is the best.

By Monday, I returned to being another anonymous Flynn studying on a busy campus in Boston.

7 | 1985

Two years into my career as an EMT, the routine of school holidays knitted easily with the anti-routine of the shifts on the ambulance. Semesters plus their requisite exams ticked through the phases of the year as hands on a clock face. Summer and holiday work started and ended with the same regularity. Yet the days, nights, and weekends on the rigs spilt with messes across my life. I declined Denny and Peter access to my weekends after the first few horrors. I did believe that one could run a quick shift or two, study, rest, socialize, then return to the classroom unburdened. I had to accept that visions of a knife into a human belly does not erase with the ease of a blackboard. My growing library of images from the streets brought reality and color to the trials of Roman gods and Greek myths. I sat alone in a classroom of fourteen students discussing birds plucking body parts from humans and demi-gods. I alone had seen how ravens and rats pick apart rotting humans. While the faulty men of the myths faced the wrath of Olympus or the older Titans, I nurtured a few demons that seemed well homed in these ancient stories.

I returned to the streets for the summer of 1985 as I had done for the summer of 1984 and 1983 before that. But I discovered a lack of eagerness for the long hours. I faced shifts where, getting paid for a fraction of the time, I worked with anger. I blamed the hours and screwy pay arrangement for the creeping darkness. I failed, then, to understand the impact of looking for weapons, drugs, needles on each patient. Basic lessons emerged from the streets. Number one: violence begats violence. Number two: there are few innocents. Didactic analysis followed with axioms and corollaries. Each proving the point that if you land in my ambulance, then you are most likely the cause of your own troubles. The kid with the knife gets stabbed. The man with the gun gets shot. The man with a belly, cigarette, and no exercise gets the heart attack. The young people outside the gay bars get beaten. The bad drivers, timid drivers, and mean drivers get into wrecks. The gods listened and the gods punished.

I returned to the streets in 1985, having proven that patients cause their own injuries and illnesses. Certainly, not a one-hundred-percent proof as it did not apply to all. The crews progressively used terms like "No humans involved" as if the phrase were part of a fad like Punk Rock or Skateboarding. The crews would state, "This guy deserved it," or "This guy should know better than going to that sort of club." Some of the crews developed a warped sense of justice that modeled a bit too closely on the behavior of some of the worst cops. When with these guys, I missed Aaron the most.

In 1984, I often partnered with a tender soul named David. He and I responded to a man-down call near the big post office. David spoke his own name with an extra-ordinary soft "D" and an open soft "A," an accent not common to our streets. That he worked for a few months surprised me. That he drifted away did not.

A call came in for us. "Unit 23, respond near post office at Mass and Inman. Man down." I double keyed the mic in acknowledging the call from Denny. We wheeled east with the lights on. David chirped the siren at a few intersections.

One lady stepped into the road to wave. We parked between the two crosswalks and the two lights that pointed up Inman Street. People walked by. I did a quick scan to find my old friend Mr. Lincoln laying on the sidewalk next to a half-height wall made from granite. He had found a niche between the stairs and scrubs. Approaching, I swiped Vicks under each of my nostril, then leaned in. "Mr. Lincoln?" I tapped his shoulder. His response was slow and incomplete. People walked by. Some looked at what we were doing, some did not. I tried to roll him over to his back. He held himself in the curled position of a sleeping dog. I put on a pair of gloves while walking back to the rig.

"He's alive but not well. He is barely conscious."

"Drunk?"

"I don't know. Not sure I care. He's not well. Bring the stretcher. I'll see what I can find."

Mr. Lincoln resisted me. I tried to remind him of our past friendship. He yelled at me like he had yelled at many others while swinging that cane. I pulled and tugged him from the corner. I forced him to roll over. He remained balled up. Instead of fighting with him, I examined what I could. I pulled up three layers of shirts. The skin near his low back and along his spine looked faintly yellow. I pulled the shirt up, exposing his ribs. I observed profoundly deep and large bruising. The coloring informed me that he had been hurt the night before or the day before. My heart broke for the old vet.

One asshole in an expensive grey suit with a perfectly executed Windsor knot barked at us while we worked with Mr. Lincoln. He said, "An ambulance. Is that how the city removes trash these days?" I can confirm that the man's tie matched Harvard's crimson.

David pushed the stretcher in front of me, preventing me from chasing that bit of human scum. I listened to the unspoken words. Right. Aaron's voice came into my head. "Focus on the patient."

We lifted Mr. Lincoln to the cot. David withdrew himself and his nose, displaying the same rudeness that Aaron trained out of me. *I'll have to introduce him to Vicks VapoRub,* I thought. We loaded the patient then David returned to the front the second he got the cot locked. I was able to roll up Mr. Lincoln's shirt and see that he had been severely beaten, likely kicked, or stomped. David did not use the lights nor the siren en route to Cambridge City. We wheeled Mr. Lincoln into an ER that knew him well. They knew him by sight. They knew him by smell. The first nurse told us to leave him in the hallway. I briefed her once. Then I briefed her again. Her response each time was, "We'll get to him."

He lay there all day. In and out of the E.R., we found Mr. Lincoln curled under the same blankets we had covered him with. I went to one of the doctors to describe the bruising and beating that the patient endured. "I'll give him an exam."

Late in day, the evening shift informed me that he was just

sleeping it off and that when he waked, they'd street him. I again described the bruising and the injuries. I again heard, "We'll get to him soon."

On the way out, I walked up to the hospital bed that had been parked in the hallway for six hours. He smelled of old shit and new urine. He smelled of old urine as well. His odor resembled the smell of an underground T stop on a warm July day. Absolutely nobody had cared for this man during the hours. I touched him and felt nothing—no tension whatsoever. I pulled my stethoscope from my pocket and listened. First to his back as I could get to that easily. I then rolled him over. He rolled easily. His chest sounded as empty and hollow from the front as it did from the back. I looked up at the clock over the nurse's station: 15:23.

I returned to the young doctor. "Mr. Lincoln is dead. I think he died a few hours ago. I feel a rigor in his fingers and his cheeks." Mr. Lincoln's cheek held the flat impression of his hand and the wrinkles of the hospital bed.

Mr. Lincoln, a veteran of the Korean War, spanned the arch of my rookie year at Atlantic Ambulance Service. With his passing, I felt my soul shift. The next time we rolled in, the bit of wall where I had parked Mr. Lincoln for his last lonely moments was clear and open. Someone had wheeled Mr. Lincoln to the morgue. Unless he possessed VA paperwork, dog tags, or something that proved that he was an American soldier, he would be cremated as an indigent and a pauper.

Is it better to be ignored by the gods or hated by them. The ancient myths failed to answer that question for me.

My summer job influenced my courses. I thought I knew something about me and what I wanted to do. Then I added courses about Liberation Theology and the modern history of Central America. I added courses where I learned Spanish, while continuing to advance my Russian.

During that summer, I met then transported my first AIDS patient. We stupidly joked about hazardous duty pay. Upon our arrival at Mount Auburn Hospital, we were instructed to don a bunny suit that protected us head to toe. We wore medical face masks, a facial shield, and a double layer of gloves. The hospital staff similarly turned our human patient into a burrito with layers of wrappings. The patient also wore a surgical mask. We knew so little.

At Mass General Hospital, we delivered the patient via the never-used decontamination entrance. After dropping the patient on a bed, our linens went into a biohazard disposal bag for burning. As did our coveralls, gloves, and masks. In the decon entrance, we scrubbed every surface with harsh chemicals. The presence of AIDS in our fair city warped the bad attitude of cops and EMTs alike. Haitians, homosexuals, and homeless had been identified as the source of the disease without any understanding of how the disease transmitted from human to human. AIDS gave bigotry, hatred, and discrimination fresh legs and new justifications.

Every cop and every EMT, including me, feared touching any member of the H-H-h clade. The Irish, the Italians, the Greeks, the Portuguese, the WASPs seemed immune to the disease or so we thought during those early months.

The summer of 1985 meant walking from Porter Square to the station. Instead of my mother's sepia-toned stories of herself on roller skates, each block echoed my new stories. Here is the red light we roll at night instead of waiting for green. That's the after-two rule. Per the Atlantic crews, traffic lights after 2:00 a.m. serve in an advisory capacity. Here this lady had a stroke. In that house, we worked with a gardener who cut his palm with clippers. I had learned the 917 streets of Cambridge. Intersections, named squares, neighborhoods—each had a story of someone else's tragedy, horror, or humor. We occasionally got spill-over calls from Somerville, Boston, and Brighton and rushed into those cities as relief rigs, backup rigs, or when they were slammed.

On my walk from Porter Square with two chocolate doughnuts for Uncle Denny, I envisioned myself up on the white ambulance, running this road going northward back to Mass Ave with lights dancing off of the trees and houses. I walked recognizing the loss of eagerness and the loss of enthusiasm for this job that I once loved.

Who would I get as a partner? Would I be training some asshole rookie? Or would I be working with some crusty burned-out guy, putting in time waiting for his number to be called at an area police department? The ambulance services act as a holding place for people my age who had taken civil service exams. As their name gradually climbed up the list, they got less and less interested in being EMTs.

Would Denny and Peter put me in that old Dodge piece of shit as a welcome-back gift? Would I spend my days riding in the back with granny-poopy-pants running between this facility and that facility? On those days, I did read over two hundred pages in a novel.

I climbed the stairs to the dispatch office. I placed the bag of doughnuts in front of Denny. He stepped from behind his desk, first shaking my hand then giving me a dude-hug. Peter showed kindness with a rare handshake and morning greeting.

"Lexi," said Denny. "You'll be in 27 with Curtis Jackson."

"Do I know him?"

"No, he's new."

Peter interjected, "This will be his first day outside of the Dodge."

Oh, god, I thought. *I got some reject or fuck up.*

"Peter, you should sell that old piece of shit Dodge. Maybe to a museum," I offered.

I was wiping down the mirrors on Unit 27, which appeared to be newer than my favorite rig. Under the bench seat, I found the ancient unused gear that gets inspected and ignored during each morning's checklist. I found the one abused roll of silver duct tape. That roll was there in the event of an accident. Our instructions were to lay the silver tape over the company name before the news crews arrive. I used it once to tape a fellow's hands to the railing for the cot.

Curtis found me easily. "Lexi?" He stuck his hand out.

I shook. "Are you Curtis?"

We smiled at each other while I examined him from both sides of the Us and Them equation. Curtis did not look like anyone else in our station. To break the ice, I said, "A lot of people do not like riding with me."

"So I heard. But of course, I think I have the same problem."

During the winter, I let the left side of my hair grow long while having the right side shaved. At the winter holiday, I had it bleached a brassy blonde. I took a longer step towards a punk rock look. On Friday, knowing I was coming to this shift and might do CPR yet again, I cut the long hair short and cut the short hair shorter. I did not look like a magazine cover model. There were a crop of rockers and movie folks who sported a look like mine. At the clubs around Boston and Cambridge, I blended well. The rumors that I had kissed female nurses and female doctors circulated around the station. The rumors that I fucked Aaron in the back of Unit 26 also circulated.

Most of those rumors started with Bobby then spread via Adam's bizarre efforts to prove he was one-of-the-guys. Bobby was already polishing the gilt on his personalized door.

Curtis and I finished the morning routine, slipping out of the barn before Bobby.

"27, post at Area 2."

I clicked twice on the mic then made my way down to the river. I cruised slowly studying the familiar rowers on the river.

"27," Denny called out to us as I approached JFK street and the bridge. He sent us into a neighborhood where Haitian refugees had set themselves up. "Old man, unconscious but breathing." On went the lights and the siren. Curtis pulled out the map book to look up the address while I drove with confidence towards the apartment building. As a means of being helpful, Curtis informed me of the upcoming cross streets.

I wanted to reach over to touch his hand and the book. I didn't know him yet. I did not want to be rude to my new partner either. He wished to be helpful.

While wiggling around a car that did not pull to the right, I said, "This is my third summer on these streets working for Peter and Denny." Instead of touching my partner as I might have done once with Aaron, I pointed at the book. "I don't need that. Certainly, not in Cambridge."

He put the book back in the door pocket.

I regretted not having Curtis drive on his first day. Aaron extended me that courtesy. I ought to have done the same. I felt embarrassed for just hopping in.

We pulled up to the apartment building. I removed the keys from the rig then switched the batteries off. "Lock it, will you?"

We pulled out the stair chair and our medical bag. We kitted up with gloves and masks before making entry into the building. We then climbed three stories on narrow, steep wooden stairs. I dreaded the idea of pulling someone down from here. A large woman met us at the door.

"Hey, we are here with the ambulance."

She waved at us. The room was filled with people. Three, four, maybe five generations of families living in a small flat. We got escorted to the patient. With Aaron's magical grip, I took the old man's hand. His pulse was too fast. The pulse pressure seemed very low. His blood pressure, were I to take it, would barely register as 90-over-something. The sclera of his eyes shined orange, a blending of the yellow from a profound liver problem, plus red of leaking blood vessels.

"Unfold the stair chair."

Curtis did it with ease.

"Drape with a sheet the long way."

Curtis did that.

"Knees." I pointed.

I stepped back preparing to take the shoulders. "On my three."

Curtis nodded.

"One... two... three."

We swung the patient to the stair chair with easy comfort. Curtis wrapped him quickly in our hospital sheet. Then clipped the straps over his body.

I looked at the newbie. "Top or bottom?"

"Bottom, if you'd like?" He offered to go down the narrow

stairs first. He'd pretty much have to walk backwards down the painted, steep stairs.

The normal routine for a sick person at home was to ask family about past medical history, about current medications; to get information about their last meals, duration of symptoms, types of symptoms, and what allergies the patient may have. Our hostess spoke only Haitian patois. I had a few lines of classroom French such as, "Mon crayon rouge est dans le table." A sentence that fails all tests of communication.

We wheeled the old guy towards the door. I spied a very young child with stick-thin arms and rounded belly, the rounded belly that could hide a kitchen mixing bowl. The child looked like he belonged on a poster for saving starving children in Africa. He could stand on an Oxfam brochure.

"*Él también,*" I said in Spanish like an idiot. So, I dug through my brain for some hint of French. I tried "*Il aussi*," which was something like "he, also."

Curtis spoke up. "*L'enfant aussi.*" A phrase I did recognize: "The child too." As we walked out the door, Curtis said: "*Nous nous rendons au Cambridge City Hospital.*"

I scooped up the child with one arm. Then wheeled to the top of the stair. Curtis lifted the bottom rung of the chair with two hands, providing us the stability we needed. He stepped backwards down each step with minimal hesitation. Me, on the other hand, occasionally let the wheels drop to the wood. It jarred our patients.

At the bottom, Curtis took over the chair. He bumped and glided it down the stoop and the curb to the ambulance. We lifted the cot out. We laid out the old man, wrapping him tightly with blankets. I then swaddled the child in a cotton blanket.

"Know how to get to Cambridge City?" I asked Curtis.

"I think so."

"Well, take it easy on me." I had no identification for either patient. I had no names, no ages, no dates of birth. I started a run sheet for the old man only.

I never got a proper blood pressure on either of them. I did not want to unwrap them, nor did I want to decontaminate or trash our blood pressure cuff. We wheeled them into the ER. We got a cool reception from the staff. We offered no medical history and no summary of vital signs. Curtis and I performed the "scoop-and-run" technique of street medicine.

We decontaminated the cot, then made it up, neatly stacking two extra sheets and blankets. I washed my hands thoroughly with surgical soap pumped from a bottle near a sink in a treatment room.

Curtis handed me the key back. "Nah, you drive. You did great," I said in response. He missed a short cut opting for following well-known roads. He did not get lost. He drove at a comfortable speed.

"So, you speak French?"

"No, I am terrible."

"Why French?" I asked.

"My family came from Côte d'Ivoire. My mother required I take it all the way through high school."

"Well, you sounded good to me." But what I do I know? I spent three years studying Russian. Then I added Spanish to increase my street-creds.

"Why did you take that kid?" Curtis asked me.

"I don't really know. It felt instinctive. Did you see him?"

"Not initially. No."

"Did you see that belly on him and those arms? He has no flesh, except that belly stuck out there like a soccer ball. That's just not right."

"What if they don't get their kid back?"

"I don't know. But what if he died there?"

I thought about the scenario and the laws under which we practiced. Treatment and transportation require consent from the patient. In the case of juveniles, then consent comes from the parents or, in lieu of parents, we accept implied consent.

I had just removed a child from a family home without permission. The family did not dial 911 about him, but about the old man. I scooped up a child without consent from family because I had a feeling. I had no diagnostic proof. I never examined the boy; I think it was a boy. I took him. I took him up into my arms, walking out of their home.

Processes and procedures exist. I ought to have transported only the old man. The family pointed to him. His jaundiced eyes, thready pulse, and general look indicated he would be dying soon unless he got definitive medical care. If I had seen other issues in the apartment, I ought to have brought them to a nurse or social service person at Cambridge City Hospital. They would have investigated. They talk to a judge, get a warrant. Then they enter the apartment with police and legal authority to search and investigate.

I kidnapped a child from his parent.

Thankfully, I did no paperwork on the child. The immigrant family, fleeing the horrors of Haiti, would not trust the Cambridge Police nor authorities well enough to make a complaint. If they did, someone would justify my illegal actions.

As Aaron says, "Follow the rules, then follow the law. If those fail, do the right thing."

Who knows what the right things is? Had I committed a felony in the name of the public good? Or did I take a classic American solution to an ancient problem? I decided with a glance that I knew what was best for this family. I knew better than the mother and the grandmother.

Someday, someone might ask me difficult questions. "Have you ever committed a felony?" Or, "Have you ever killed anyone?" Or, "Have you ever done anything illegal?"

I have handcuffed people against their will. I have restrained people, tying them to my cot. I gave a drunk a drink and a patient a cigarette. I have ignored drug dealers and told people to run before cops arrive. People have died under my hands and today, I stole a child from his home.

At a minute before 6:00 p.m., Curtis and I wheeled back into the station. We cleaned our crap from the new ambulance. I ran our paperwork up to Denny. Denny asked obvious questions about Curtis.

"He drives really well. He is great with people. And he speaks

French. The Haitian folks understand him better than me." Also, I liked him, so I added, "I'll happily work with him tomorrow or whenever his next shift is."

Returning downstairs, I heard Bobby speaking not-softly-enough as he spewed hatred towards me and my new partner.

Those were the last words I heard on that Monday evening in May. I completed a ten-hour shift for which I would get paid for eight hours. During the last three years, I had been injured, jeered at, and committed numerous crimes, all for the privilege of being paid for eighty-percent of my work.

I walked up to the red line station in Porter Square, stewing over the assholes at the station and shit treatment. I sat on the subway, daring anyone to harass me. *Come steal my dog-tags. Come give me shit. I'll kick your fucking ass.*

I walked into my parent's house with the same meanness; the same level of hurt. Upstairs, I slammed my door before stripping off my polyester triple-knit nine-pocket police trousers, a pair I bought three years prior.

8 | The Rat

That was hard to face. The Captain, the one person I never lied to, sat me down. He identified the symptoms:

"Kid, there is no joy in you."

I nearly teared up, which meant my eyes got glossy. One small tear may have hung at the edge.

"What's going on?"

"There are parts of this job I love and stories that will last a life-time. I got to ride in the motorcade for a prince. Granted we were the last vehicle, and our secret service officer was really a postal inspector, that was cool. And I loved that day that Aaron and I spent on a movie set. It was boring while we were there, but that is a tick-in-a-box that few experience. So cool that you set that up."

He shook his head. "That was all your mother, by the way. She's the one behind the curtain with the levers and smoke."

I breathed. My eyes dried. "I struggle with the job these days. My current partner is ok. But the crews and bosses treat him like a total shithead. They are just racist fucks. I get tired of that. They rant on about gays, and Haitians, and everyone."

My father knew how to conduct an interview. And I had been interviewed by him enough during my twenty-plus years. If I held back, he probed. If I deflected, he forced me to dig deeper. I ran through his not-yet-asked questions in my head. I knew how to get information from people too. My father had trained me since I could write a full sentence on paper.

"I guess I am really tired of working fifty hours every week and getting paid for forty. I am tired of facing these hazards, dangers, and assholes without any real protection. We're pushed into the worst of what humans can do to each other, then I count the hours I work and the money I make. It makes me wicked resentful."

The Captain nodded. The cops in Massachusetts maintained strong unions. The young people who joined sought long-term financial stability while being a union employee of a municipality or state. Cops balanced this stability with the thrills and adventures of being a cop.

"My job is a job held between this and that. Between school and a slot to a police or fire academy; between under-grad and med school; a holding place while you go to nursing school. It isn't a real job. They treat me, all of us, that way.

"The city's plow drivers and trash haulers are treated better than we are. Those guys are not likely to get shot or fall from a building or get squished by a speeding car or thumped on the head during a domestic violence call."

I felt the tears in both eyes now. I thought I was doing better.

"I really, really hate that these guys steal our pay. The job is tough enough, then we're told: you don't get paid for lunch nor breaks. But how often am I eating in the rig while driving with lights-and-sirens to another scene? If you require that we remain in the rigs, in uniform, on the radio, then we should be paid for that time. It is the lying and the bullshit that I have grown to hate."

The Captain asked, "What are you going to do about it?"

What was I going to do about it? I had not thought about that question. "Quit?" I asked tentatively.

"Quit halfway through the summer? What then? Spend your days sailing on the Charles or running the Harvard Stadium?"

You're right, Da, Flynns don't quit. Certainly, we don't quit when stuff gets rough. I asked him, "What do you think I should do?"

He listened to my question in silence then thought. "What do you think is going on at Atlantic?"

"What do you mean?"

"Think about what angers you."

I ran through the death, the injuries, the treatment of vets, Haitians, AIDS patients, the violence, the meanness, and the rest of the nonsense. I thought about the hours, and the hospitals. Part of the job I did because I could do it. Parts of the job I did love. Day to day, the job had high points and low points. Somebody had to respond when people called for help and I had all of the skills. I did make things better for the minutes that I was with people and my patients. Many of my patients loved me. Some of my co-workers hated me. I didn't mind that they hated or resented me. I was different from them. These topics did not focus my anger.

As I explored my father's question, I recognized that I had ignored the fat fuck with an overly tanned belly who shook salt on his beer and played with his shiny pistol, little Roscoe. A guy who had important contacts with the City of Cambridge, a city run by his cousin, the mayor.

In answering the Captain, I possessed new clarity. "I am angry about the pay. I am angry about being shorted pay on every shift."

"Is that it?" the Captain asked.

I explored further. "The paperwork. It isn't right. I don't know what they are doing. I don't understand how an ambulance service does what we do. We have Bobby out there doing collections, intimidating poor people, elderly people, immigrants, and minorities for five- and ten-dollar bills. Peter is running a racket."

"Are you saying that to try it on? Or do you believe that is the case?"

A respected cop had just asked me if my employer operated a criminal enterprise. Boston knew corruption and favoritism. The "us" or "them" question boiled bigotry stirred with racism, classism, religious, and ethnic bias. True, but honestly, none of that mattered. But most important question was: "Can I trust you to play our game our way?" Those who are an "us" keep the right secrets in the right way. Those who are a "them" prove themselves as rats.

"Da," I answered, "there is a game."

He smiled. He waited while I thought. He sipped on his chamomile tea. My father, the hero cop, the face of Boston Police Department, the man who walked ducklings in Boston Common, waited for me to understand my own words and my own thoughts. My father, a man with a gentle Irish lilt, stood as the perfect definition of an "us." Captain William Flynn stood for the institutions.

After the Fourth of July, I acknowledged my anger at the world. I grew angry at myself for blaming victims. I read too many books during shifts. I blamed the streets for being streets. I blamed people for being people. I had not yet blamed Peter and Atlantic Ambulance.

As a college student, I didn't know that I had the standing to see Atlantic the way others did. I had it easy. My parents and scholarships paid for my university education. I lived at home where my mother had meals ready and kept food in the fridge.

Was I entitled to be pissed off at an employer shorting pay and such?

He asked, "Stinks a bit, doesn't it?"

I sniffed twice. "I think so."

He offered one of his lines: "Little lie, big lie."

Then I replied, "Little crime, big crime."

The little lies hide the big lie. The little crimes spill out around the big crime.

The Captain asked, "Do you think he needs to under-pay his staff?"

"Can he afford to pay us full wages?" I parroted back to him. "I think so. He buys a new Lincoln just about every year. He has a Ford 250 that he uses to haul boats. He's run up to the Wonderland dog track often enough." I tried exploring the math in my head. He ran an ambulance service around the clock using two shifts. He avoided all overtime. I added aloud, "If he staffed legally and properly, he would need three shifts." The same structure that hospitals and police departments use. I continued, "Three shifts require more people and runs into a chance of overtime for some."

My father added, "BPD runs three shifts around the clock plus some day shifts that start at 8:00 or 9:00 a.m., depending on the mission."

"And you pay overtime."

"We do."

"And you have benefits such as medical and dental and retirement."

"We do," the Captain answered. "Peter does not have those other expenses, does he?"

"I doubt it. Da, what do you think I should do?"

He answered, "What did Aaron say? 'Follow the rules, follow the law, then if all fails do what is right.'"

"What is right? How do I know?"

He sipped the last of his now-cool tea looking at me. That was a question he would not answer for me. He never had before.

A week later, after swapping a Wednesday shift for a Saturday shift, I walked into the Massachusetts Department of Labor Relations. I told myself that I needed answers. I told myself I was not here to rat out anyone. I had a job that paid me better than any other summer job that college students get. Furthermore, unlike nearly every other employee of Atlantic Ambulance Service, I did not need the money. I did not need the job. I was just an entitled brat working a summer job.

The counter was empty at ten o'clock in the morning. I expected this state office to resemble the Registry of Motor Vehicles. Getting anything done at the RMV required a day-long commitment. The Labor Relations team worked at metal, government-issued desks. One gentleman saw me approaching the counter.

He appraised me from top to bottom. I looked a bit punk with my bleached mop of hair over bits of shaved scalp. I had removed the safety pins that I kept in my ear lobes. In their place, I wore boring gold studs. My jeans were neat. I provided an introduction.

"Good morning, sir, I am Alexandra Flynn."

"How can I help?"

"I am asking for a friend who works for an ambulance service here in the Commonwealth."

"And you don't want me to ask which one?"

"Fair enough. I do not. I seek only information."

"Ask away." He smiled, going quiet.

"They had been told that ambulance services can use an old law that pays EMTs for the work that they do during a shift instead of the entire shift."

"Is that what they were told?" His broader smile clearly indicated that I ought to continue.

"This friend of mine works a ten-hour shift. He normally gets paid for about eight of those hours. And during the fourteen-hour overnight shift, he gets paid for eight hours."

"Ok." He wanted me to continue.

"My friend asked the big boss. The big boss said that the law helps small companies provide around the clock coverage without going broke. From the day shift, he deducts an hour for lunch and four fifteen-minute coffee breaks. And from the night shift, he deducts an hour each for dinner, a midnight meal, and breakfast. He deducts six hours for sleeping."

"And you think that your friend deserves better treatment?"

"No, my friend loves the job, and they make more money than most of our friends. They just asked me to look into it and see if that law is still valid."

"You can tell your friend that the statehouse repealed that law a long time ago."

I looked at him, not really surprised, although charmed by our mutual agreement to discuss a distant entity called "my friend."

Looking straight into my eyes, the way my father, the cop, does, he said, "Does your friend work for Peter Clifton of Atlantic Ambulance Service in Cambridge?"

He looked into my face. I was raised by a top investigator. I trained my face to yield nothing ever.

"I think they may," I answered blandly.

"Alexandra Flynn." The counter-guy leaned in close. "I have been trying to nail that son-of-a-bitch for years. But nobody has ever had the courage to turn him in."

And I could see why. If the stainless-steel pistol named Roscoe wasn't enough, then the deep connection with Cambridge City Hall and with the Cambridge Police Department ought to trigger fear. You did not pick a fight with Peter Clifton and win. A broken tail-light may result in death. He and his family have been woven tightly into the running of the city.

The counter-guy walked back to his desk. From a lower drawer, he pulled a clipboard and a short stack of papers.

"Are you willing to help me? The Commonwealth has been after him for a long time." I looked at the forms. "I have a few questions."

"Shoot."

"Do you ever get a set lunch break?"

"No, we grab lunch on the go." Yes, we both knew I was lying about *my friend*.

"Are you allowed to turn off your radios or step away from the ambulance during your shift?"

"Only when treating patients, or in the hospitals, or going to the bathroom."

"Are you allowed a bathroom break without your radio?"

"No, never. Pee when you can and always quickly."

"When working overnight, do you get a sleeping schedule?"

"No, you work when calls come in. If lucky, you might get a couple of hours of sleep, but…no. You don't really sleep."

I did want to ask, Is that wrong? But I knew the answers. I was standing at the Department of Labor Relations talking to a guy who had not only guessed the name of my employer but knew his first name and family name.

I picked up the first document, reading it in detail. The filing process required a lot of paperwork on my end, primarily paycheck stubs. The rest, I could not provide. I did not have the scheduling calendar nor any proof that my shifts lasted longer than the eight hours printed on my paychecks.

I breathed once through my nose, then again through my nose.

"Do you have a business card?"

"Yes." He returned to his desk. When he got back to the counter, I had already started the first form by filling in my name and my address. I grabbed the offered card.

"I'll mail you the evidence." I continued answering questions on the papers while standing there at the counter. "Hey, my employment dates are less clear."

"Do what you can."

"I worked some during winter breaks, I don't know those dates precisely."

"Know what…just put down your hire date from the first year. It sounds like they never dropped you from the payroll."

"Oh, right." I finished my story, handing him the stack of hand-written answers.

"You may not want to go to work again."

"I think you are right."

I took the T up to Cambridge then walked down to the ambulance station. I told Denny that I needed to look at the scheduling calendar. When he stepped away, I made photocopies of the recent and upcoming weeks. Each day showed that one crew worked from 8:00 a.m. to 6:00 p.m. and the next crew worked fourteen hours until the day crews returned. I copied evidence that supported some of what I claimed. I also copied several of my paycheck stubs showing weekly pay of forty hours.

On Wednesday evening when The Captain returned home from his shift, I briefed him. I showed him the evidence: my paystubs and the stolen calendars. I showed him the evidence while talking openly about the company and my experiences. We reviewed the evidence as I prepared to fold it into an envelope with a hand-written note to the investigator.

"We should make a copy of these documents before you send them. Let's run to the station." He clearly meant a Boston Police neighborhood district building and not my ambulance station in Cambridge.

We jumped into the city-owned Crown Victoria.

Walking into the nearest station, the cops greeted him with a mixture of humility and jocularity. He commanded their respect. Two senior guys made little jokes, probing their own familiarity with him. Except for one new cop who asked, "What did this one do? Lockin' her up?"

Captain Flynn stabbed the cop with an evil look. Another cop said, "That's his kid, you fuckin' idiot." The cop scurried away. We made photocopies of my documents. The originals were sealed into a Boston Police Department evidence bag that my father signed and dated.

We dropped the documents in a blue letter box outside at the curb.

After climbing into his city-ride, he looked at me. "I think you should run."

My father, Boston's famous cop, said, "I think you should run."

I agreed with him, entirely.

"Been thinking about that. What if I walked away?"

"What do you mean?"

"How about driving me out the Mass Pike to Lee and dumping me on the Appalachian Trail?"

He turned towards me. I read nothing from the skilled interrogator's face.

After shopping at Eastern Mountain Sports on Saturday and packing a bag, my father dropped me on the AT in Western Mass. I took cash, a checkbook, an ATM card and one credit card.

By the time I crossed the Vermont border heading north, I discovered that I traveled about one day behind Telemachus and the Snow King, trail names. They signed the guest books in the huts the day before I got there. The Snow King left a quickly sketched drawing of a snowman's face with a pointy crown. Telemachus wrote clean limericks in each book above his name.

I envied their candor on the trail. I read the names of fellow hikers at each hut. The first night, I signed the book as Lexi. The next night as "Alex." Then, desiring a better and more anonymous name, I wrote "Irish Hawk" at the huts for the rest of the summer.

The epilogue to this part of my story bifurcates. I came off the trail, returning home the day before my fall classes started. I started my final year at university with stories I could not share. Yes, I worked on ambulances. Yes, I walked the AT from Massachusetts to Maine. I let my hair grow to my shoulders. It started growing out while I hiked from Massachusetts towards Maine. I avoided driving through Cambridge for a full year. I feared some cop would smash my taillight, find weed in my glovebox, then haul me in where I'd get arrested and beaten.

The surprise came the following summer when *The Boston Globe* published an exposé on Peter Clifton and Atlantic Ambulance. Not only had he be screwing the employees out of wages for years, he had committed numerous counts of Medicare, Medicaid, and insurance fraud. He and his staff intimidated former patients while shaking them down for cash payment. A lot of the cash went to the Wonderland dog track. The insurance companies proved that Atlantic Ambulance fabricated the miles written on our patient reports, the root of felony insurance fraud. Insurance companies pay ambulances for the distance driven. In a small city with several hospitals nearby, we could hit hospitals within ten minutes from anywhere. To increase billings, Peter increased the paperwork miles we drove.

The next *Boston Globe* article published the following day detailed the legal troubles with the IRS for avoiding taxes and lying. The week after graduating, I got three large checks from the Commonwealth. One check paid for all my due overtime. One check paid me a portion of a civil award with penalties. The third check appeared to be a finder-fee for ratting out Atlantic Ambulance Service.

Had the Commonwealth looked deeper, they could have revoked all of our EMT certificates. Most of our training credits have been earned in empty classrooms. It seems stupid to practice skills we used all day long every day. What is the point of listening to someone teach a CPR class when you had done CPR twice already during your shift? All parts of the game, I suppose. We all fabricated training records, believing that the street was enough to reinforce our knowledge.

Unable to find an interesting job after graduating, I landed a new job as an EMT in eastern Massachusetts. I survived six months before getting fired, getting un-fired, then quitting. My shifts during that time ran from Friday evening to Sunday evening. I worked forty-eight hours on the clock with an eight-hour break sleeping in their station's bunk room. The Sunday day shift, often a quiet lazy day in front of the television, served as a normal overtime shift. I spent weeks seeking a replacement for my OT shift. No one wanted it. With tickets to Phil Collins at the Meadowlands in New Jersey, I walked out. The dispatcher told me repeatedly, "If you walk out, you are fired."

I felt ready to leave the world of EMS. I went to the concert in New Jersey. Once home, I carried my issued uniforms to the station. The owner's daughter scolded me up and down for abandoning a shift. I had to learn responsibility. She required that I learn the consequences of my decision making.

"Ma'am," I said, "I accept that I am fired. Here are the uniforms. I'll take my pay and go. No problem."

I placed the powder blue uniforms on her guest-chair.

"What are you doing?" she asked.

"I got fired. I am turning in my uniforms."

"Who fired you?"

"I got fired on Sunday. After weeks of begging someone to take my shift, I drove to New Jersey for a concert. I was told that if I left the building, I was fired."

"You can't leave in the middle of a shift. That is just wrong."

"I understand. I worked a forty-hour week. No one would cover my Sunday shift, which is OT for me. So I left. Here are my uniforms." I pointed to the stack of uniforms hanging neatly over her guest chair.

"You cannot leave in the middle of a shift. That is a very serious violation of our trust."

"I know and that is why I was fired."

"You need to be fired for what you did."

"I know and I did get fired."

But she kept on her path. "You need to learn responsibility. You're done with school. Employers cannot tolerate that kind of behavior."

"I understand. And that is why you guys fired me. Here are my uniforms."

We went around again. I stood there listening to her yell at me for my irresponsible behavior.

"Ma'am. You can't yell at me like this. I have been fired. I have returned the uniforms. You owe me my pay, then I go away. Done and dusted. We never have to see each other again."

"But that is not the point. You need to grow up."

God, like I was one of her wretched brats.

I turned my back. She started over, "That is not the point. When you are scheduled for a shift, you have to work that shift."

"I understand. I violated that rule."

"We need you here on Friday night." Ahh. There it was. If I could not fill my Sunday OT shift, it appeared unlikely that this ambulance service would be able to fill an entire weekend's worth of shifts. With a couple of years of experience and willing to work Friday night through the entire weekend, I filled shifts no one else would or could.

"I am not fired?"

"No. Be here on Friday."

"What about that extra OT shift on Sunday. I can't always work it. Why is it my responsibility to fill it? You pushed me on it. Therefore, I must find a way off of it. I'll only work here if you treat that Sunday day shift as optional. I'll work it as often as I can, but when I say no, you have to fill it."

I did not last too much longer after that. I got paid well working Friday nights through Sunday evening. I made as much as most of my newly graduated classmates.

I walked away from ambulances and EMS and my EMT certificate in 1987 for good.

I made a decision. *I am done with EMS.*

Part 2 | 2000s

9 | Into the breach

I returned to my native New England after two decades of travel and work. I could not afford to buy close to where I grew up in Boston. I could not afford a home in Metro Boston nor the suburbs. Instead of returning to the Commonwealth of Massachusetts, I bought a small farmstead in Trowbridge, Vermont. I could afford it. It appeared close to home. I bought it because I loved the property.

Boston lost its home feeling. My city changed with the Big Dig. Darkness, dripping rust, and meanness fell away as the region reached for the sun. The Combat Zone got plowed under. That region along Washington Street served the city as a place for peep shows, sex workers, drugs, and a familiar place for those who fell outside the lasso of normal. I missed the seediness for what it was. I missed the ugly steel structure that divided Faneuil Hall from the waterfront with the New England Aquarium. I never had the need for a peep show. No appeal for me but when I transited the Combat Zone as a kid, people greeted me; some people teased; others offered entreaties that caused me to laugh. I traveled to the nearby clubs. In those days, I landed on a spectrum between Boy George and Annie Lennox of Eurythmics. *Newsweek* ran them on the cover in January of 1984 in the middle of my university days. The headline read: "Britain Rocks America—Again". The photo informed the readers that some boys look like girls; some girls look like boys; and some people cut their own path. While glamour shots such as this cover hung near the supermarket checkout, on the streets Boy George and Annie Lennox hung at the outer edge of society. We were squeezed between the green of Boston Common and the tapestry of the Combat Zone. We lived, breathed, played, danced, and kissed in Harvard Square but not on Harvard Yard. When Joan Armatrading played in Boston, she filled an ancient theater that once opened to Washington Street in the Combat Zone. I sat in the Orpheum enjoying that concert with hundreds of like-minded people—a space that felt comfortable therefore felt safe.

My city teemed with accents and diversity; now lost. Someone cleaned this city, scrubbed the curbs, scrubbed the skyline. The once-upon-a-time Combat Zone of my lost youth had been converted to an outdoor walking district for shopping. I remember the pushcarts, and immigrants plying trade near Faneuil Hall, Haymarket, and the North End. The core of Faneuil Hall was once locals, people selling local wares to Bostonians. Suddenly, brand names and national stores replaced the old men and women. Similar exorcism occurred in the Combat Zone. Echoes of the ancient puritans who colonized this land from those whom they saw as other and less-than.

In the Combat Zone, the Pilgrim Theater awning advertised bawdy films. Next door, twenty-five cent "Live Nudes" and "Rap Booths." Boston Bunnies stood immediately adjacent to the Washington Street T entrance. The Pussy Cat remained my enduring icon for these lost blocks and lost days. Who laments the loss of prostitution and street-level crime? I should not. Neither should I lament the reduction in murders. Yet the Combat Zone served more than druggies and johns. For many like me and my kind, it was a place of personal exploration and finding like-minded people. These neighborhoods housed cheap theaters that hosted emerging bands and other performers seeking to follow the path laid out by David Bowie, Prince, Annie Lennox, and Boy George.

Boston remade itself respectable. John Winthrop stood on these streets in 1630 saying, "As a city upon a hill, the eyes of all people are upon us." My city underwent a Disney-like makeover. In the wake of AIDS, a disease associated with queers, prostitutes, immigrants, and gender-benders, the police pushed a big broom through the streets. In came the luxury high rises with big rent. Out you go, they cried to those deemed too low, too immoral, and too dirty. With rising buildings came rising rents and aggressive enforcement by the town criers. The town criers yelled: "Not here" and "Keep moving."

I loved the scalper's chorus once heard near North Station and the Boston Garden. Voices singing, "Gotta-Ticket? Want-ta Ticket? Gotta-Ticket? Want-ta Ticket?" Each scalper employed his own rhythm, his own melody. I even missed entrepreneurs hawking dime bags of marijuana and single joints.

In the old days, I felt the neighborhoods. I could hear the neighborhoods: Italian, Portuguese, Haitian, Black American English, Caribbean Spanish, South American Spanish, African accents, Irish lilts, and the tight-jawed English spoken by WASPs. Of course, we faced violence when these neighbors clashed, then they married begetting children of this city. In a neighborhood between Harvard University and MIT, I once stole a starving immigrant child from his home. I felt shame for poverty squeezed between the world-famous institutions. I loved the exposure to foods, words, and accents. Within a block, one enjoyed the r-dropping of my old Boston and the television-bland American accent. My father's friend Robert Parker's last name sounded just like a winter parka that one might need for walking in this city. The scientist might have called this the "Parka/Parker" merge. To me, those were the sounds of home. Cities fail at being cities if we don't have room for immigrants, poverty, and languages. That big broad broom pushed the color, flavor, and diversity of the city out.

Do clean streets equal clean government? I fled Cambridge after seeing the tangled corruption of the 911 system and EMS. Insurance fraud, shake downs, and shenanigans related to EMS continuing education. The city opened streets; cleaned the waterfront; and greened parks while whitewashing everything else. In my decades of work and travel, the city turned streets around, renamed streets, and rebuilt entire blocks.

On the ambulance, we found ways of slipping away from the Boston hospitals while lying to dispatch. We ran to Fish Pier then ate at a tiny fish restaurant that had no name. I learned to use the back door where you could see the massive pot of fish chowder they kept on the range top. We exchanged cash for a paper bowl of steaming chowder at the door, then sped back to Cambridge. When

I returned, I barely recognized the place. They had expanded their seating upstairs and pushed farther into their building. No longer could working stiffs queue at the back door for an amazing meal. The little restaurant had been officially named, "No Name." We all called it the *No Name*, but in my day, there was no sign that said, "No Name." Then suddenly, it was. It became a brand, a destination. A discovery for tourists.

The *No Name* went upscale, greeting guests with a maître d'. The backdoor access for working stiffs had been shuttered except for staff needing a smoke break.

I came home to New England seeking something called home. Yet I missed the old sites of overhead steel dripping oily rust on pedestrians. Seeing Boston without the Southeast Expressway showed me the damage a highway can do to a downtown area. It cleaved the city with a rusty knife. In the old days, families did not walk from Faneuil Hall to the Aquarium. Families and tourists took the T for two stations. The Orange Line ran them from Haymarket to State, then they changed to the Blue Line for one more stop to Aquarium. Some visitors took cabs instead of navigating the darkness below the Southeast Expressway. Modern visitors simply walk across the bright sunny street.

With the Big Dig, the scars disappeared, the dividing lines disappeared. I never wanted my Boston to be yet-another-shopping mall with national and international brand-named stores. You might as well be anywhere else.

My friend, Henry Longfellow, wrote:
> Often, I think of the beautiful town
> That is seated by the sea;
> Often in thought go up and down
> The pleasant streets of that dear old town,
> Any my youth comes back to me.
> And a verse of a Lapland song is haunting
>   my memory still:
> "A boy's will is the wind's will,
> And the thoughts of youth are long, long thoughts."

History marred my great-grandparent's decades with the destruction of cities. We blew them up during the twentieth century. During my lifetime, we hoisted cranes, poured concrete, moved streets, and shuffled people who proved inconvenient for our local governments or too poor for the owners of new high-rise apartments.

I did not want starve-to-death poverty anywhere on this globe. I felt shame for facing it here in my hometown. We did not solve the problem of crime, prostitution, drugs, poverty, and failing social institutions. We simply pushed them from sight. We pushed them from the stunning waterfront views.

My mother's stories had her seven-year-old self playing with an amorphic group of kids. They skated on metal wheels on the streets where Aaron and I napped in our ambulance. These young kids rode street trolleys to movie matinées. On the other hand, my stories include being offered concert tickets, drugs, and being solicited as a hooker while walking my streets of Boston. I felt nostalgic for those grimy days. But I danced with people who danced with me. I kissed people who enjoyed kissing me. I found my way to the bed of another like me then snuck home in someone else's borrowed clothes—sometimes a set of pink scrubs, other times an oversized white oxford shirt that fell nearly to my knees.

I could not move back to Metro Boston. It felt slightly foreign and a bit too shiny. I had just spent decades traveling the globe's cities where I worked at the seedy edges. Instead, upon my homecoming, I bought a small hillside farm two-hours-plus away in the hills of Vermont. Tired of top-down orders, airports, and the grind of my present life, I stopped—at least for a while. I left home with school-book Russian, a bit of street Spanish. I returned to New England with fluency in Russian, Spanish, and working skills in Arabic, French, and German.

Once home, I did not recognize my old hospital, Cambridge City Hospital—the one that I rolled into day after day. The squat four-story industrial building once clad in Boston brick had been brightened and freshened up, looking like a modern pastel confectionary. The main door once opened to the chaotic ER. If you followed an incline down to the left, you were welcomed at the psychiatric emergency room. As a city hospital, it provided services for all patients regardless of wealth, status, and language. Now, it is a teaching hospital associated with the world-famous medical schools in the area. Its primary role as a charity and public hospital folded neatly into the history books, then forgotten. The shiny new look came with a shiny new name. The non-profit public health mission replaced by the desire to train new physicians. They removed the psych ER during my decades away, removing a vital link between crisis and care.

Longfellow wrote:
> Strange to me are the forms I meet
> When I visit the dear old town;
> But the native air is pure and sweet,
> And the trees that o'ershadow each well-known street,
> As they balance up and down,
> Are singing the beautiful song,
> Are sighing and whispering still:
> "A boy's will is the wind's will,
> And the thoughts of youth are long, long thoughts."

I no longer fear being pulled over by Cambridge cops in retaliation for the demise of Atlantic Ambulance.

I seek still that old American spirit alive in days of Longfellow, Crispus Attucks, and Paul Revere. I seek the spirit we celebrate on Boston's Freedom Trail. In lieu of the theme park version of democracy, I stand on a wooded hillside in Trowbridge Vermont where Yankees yet meet on a March day to govern themselves. The New England town meeting remains the final last scrap of direct democracy. I romanticized my cities the same way that my mother had romanticized the Cambridge of her youth.

I set myself up in my farmhouse kitchen as a consultant, railing against terrible internet services, mud roads, and limited employment opportunities. For decades, I woke with:
> The sunrise gun, with its hollow roar,
> The drum-beat repeated o'er and o'er,

And the bugle wild and shrill.
And the music of that old song
Throb in my memory still…
"A boy's will is the wind's will,
And the thoughts of youth are long, long thoughts."

In 2008, determining that I found stability not previously known since my youth at home with my mother and the Captain, I drove down to the Trowbridge firehouse to offer my services as an able-bodied volunteer. Every day since I bought my first uniform at The Haberdashery in Cambridge, I maintained a life of humble public service to the people of our nation.

Thomas Reed, Trowbridge Vermont Fire Chief, looked me up and down. He did not see what Peter Clifton and Denny once saw. No longer the gangly kid wearing punk clothing, multicolored hair, and safety pins. Several of my ear piercings have sealed poorly. Now they erupt into small zits that I squeeze while watching evening television. Chief Reed saw a mature person with wisps of greying hair at the edge of a Red Sox ball cap.

"Hey, chief, I am Alex Flynn. I live up the hill a bit."

"I know where you live. How can I help you?"

"I'd like to volunteer for the fire department."

"We're all set for now." He did not know what I had to offer him nor the people of this town. Without a question, he said, "No." But the idea of sitting at home pushing paper, writing reports, and researching from the kitchen table seemed incomplete to me.

These New England towns once depended on militia as protection. Protection from the French, Native Americans, English, and, here in Vermont, one invasion from forces in New York. New England towns selected citizens to manage the daily affairs of the town. These selected people felt guided by the citizen's needs and desires as communicated during the annual town meeting, which served as the legislative process. These towns, founded during the reign of English kings, predated the founding of the nation. The town volunteer fire departments maintain this historical link to the ancient militias. Members meet, elect their officers, and govern with self-rule. Members respond to crises in town and when invited, they respond to neighboring towns. These members ready themselves to respond within a minute of the alarm sounding. Technology and time had replaced the musket with a pickup truck, the town bell with a fire radio.

The gravity of that mission motivated me. Also, I recognized that sitting at home writing reports, researching, and attending meetings would leave me feeling empty and disconnected. I still needed adventures even if unable to travel to remote places for missions.

Chief Reed said, "Maybe you want to ask over at the ambulance service." He pointed west towards the town of Langford. It took one look from the old man to evaluate my status as a "one-of-them." Peter Clifton of Atlantic Ambulance assessed me as "one-of-us." I now know that Peter Clifton wanted to know if I was a rat. Peter wanted to know if I could be trusted. And as a cop's child, he accepted me as an "us." Conversely, Chief Reed viewed me as a "them." I had not been raised in that house on the hill. I had not attended the local school. I had not been born to a mother or a father raised here in these hills. I was a "them," an outsider, an incomer, flatlander, a refugee of a foreign city. Thus, I met the first member of a group I later called the Green Mountain Mafia. Not for their criminal enterprise, as each member acted with personal and internal integrity. They earned the name for their tight internal bonds and rapid recognition of us and them. I am a them.

One week later, I drove to the Langford Firehouse. I acknowledged that if I joined the local ambulance, I would have to retake the EMT course. Then the various state and national examinations. Then for the next years, I would have to maintain my certification with training.

I parked my car, walking to the front door of the stationhouse. Through the firehouse window, I spied the hints of an electric light in the back. I walked around the station. In the back, I looked down at a pile of stubbed-out cigarette butts. I rattled at another locked door. Returning to the front, I banged a bit louder then waited.

I banged again, then waited again. I heard a gruff voice. A man came to the door, opening it only a few centimeters. I asked, "Is this the ambulance station?"

"Yes. But if you need the ambulance, you'll have to call 911." He nodded in the direction of a payphone across the street.

"I don't need an ambulance. This is not an emergency. I came to ask if you need volunteers."

"Who are you?" The door remained mostly closed.

"My name is Alex Flynn. I live over in Trowbridge."

"Unless you are an EMT already, our volunteers have to do a lot of training." The door remained mostly closed.

"I was an EMT for years and years. I let it lapse, but I do know the work," I said.

The door opened slightly. The fellow turned his back to me and to the door. I walked in following him.

"What was your name?"

"Alex."

We did not shake hands. My host sat down. I heard the familiar mumble of a public safety radio sending out fire and EMS crews to emergencies in the region.

"You live in Trowbridge?"

"Yes. On the hill above the village."

"How long have you been here?"

"I bought a couple of years ago. I live here full time now."

"Retired?"

"God no. I work. I am not old enough to retire."

"You were an EMT?" my unnamed host asked.

"I was. I worked inner-city rigs in Boston. I first got certified in 1982."

"If you join, you will have to take the course again." I did know that. I endeavored to keep my face blank. "I don't know when the next course is around here."

"There is one down the road in Mass starting in January."

"That's Mass."

"Right, but they use the national registry and so does Vermont, doesn't it?"

"Sort of. I think Vermont will require that you take the Vermont exam after your course."

"Do you guys pay for the course?"

"No. If you take it in Vermont, it is cheaper. We can reimburse you for some training if you pass all of the exams and remain with us for at least a year. Did you look at the Vermont EMS website?" I still did not know this guy's name while I sat in his office.

"I did. They listed a few courses for 2006 and a few for 2007 but nothing seemed local. And it is 2008."

"We can keep our ears open for a course. They come along. Usually about once per year either in Starkville or Warrenton," he said. These towns are each about an hour's drive. One is west. One is east.

"What do I need to do to join?"

The unnamed fellow reached into a desk drawer. He handed me a form that poorly blended the data needed for a job application with a membership form. The form said "Application for Membership" along the top. It asked for name, address, and contact person in case of emergencies. Unlike a job application, it did not ask for prior employment, credentials, or references. I completed the form in a thrice, masking my impatience at such a stupid form. I handed it back.

"Oh, you didn't have to do that now. You can take it home and fill it out there."

"It is done." I slid the clipboard back to him. Normally, when I fill out a document applying for an opportunity, it asked about my clearances, education, spoken languages, and work experience. Frankly, most of that information is buried deep in government databases, so I don't know why anyone asked that I handwrite anything on scraps of analog paper. The old employer had everything: a drop of blood for DNA comparisons, my fingerprints—several times over, my accreditations, awards, and missions. On some computer system, one could pull up my win/loss record. A few of my worst fuckups must be recorded somewhere. That's the old world. This is the new world in the hills of Vermont.

"What should I do next?"

"I guess you should come to our next meeting. We'll put your membership application to a preliminary vote."

By mid-December, the members elected me a probationary member of the Langford Rescue Squad. I stood before the membership who had gathered around the meeting table. Most failed to make eye contact. None of them introduced themselves. My application got passed hand-to-hand around the room. When the chair asked for a motion, it got offered by a deep voice who mumbled. When the membership voted, they made a grunting sound of cool approval. Mike Foote, the unnamed host to whom I handed my paperwork, issued me a fire pager with brief instructions at the close of the meeting. Not a single member offered me a hand or a chat after the meeting. I never heard the words, "Welcome to the team." I ought to have guessed at the problems to come.

Mike walked me into the garage bays. He said, "When the tones for Langford Rescue go off, come to the station." The orientation included how to mute the pager, how to keep it charged, and how to replay the last call. We explored their ancient ambulance. Like my old Unit 26, it had been built on a Ford van chassis. Familiar.

That's nostalgia. It trapped me. I chose to focus on the fun-filled days of people watching and buzzing around Cambridge in a new ambulance with great partners. We rolled red lights at 2:00 a.m. We pulled drunks from each other outside of bars. We raced wheelchairs in the ER and learned how to ride only on the rear two wheels. I remembered the boring days of sitting at the Harvard commencement, baking in the heat, and pulling people from car wrecks.

The memories improved with the decades. It was easy to forget Peter Clifton, Bobby Clifton, and their closeted criminal enterprise. It was easy to forget the other horrors that my time in Cambridge wrought.

After leaving home and starting my new career, I drove along a Roman road at twilight. I was twenty-eight years old. Suddenly, every traffic light and car light burst into a collage of fevered colors. I felt paralyzed from head-to-toe, even though the only pain came from my right elbow as I tried to shift the car into third gear. I pulled out of the traffic lane, laboring to breathe. I employed every trick Aaron taught me. I breathed. I put a bright lemon drop on my tongue. Progressively, during that year, I experienced new symptoms. The most upsetting came late at night. Laying in bed, not sleeping, I would suffer these loops of static images. They flashed behind my eyes, each image up for a millisecond or two: Faces of patients, scenes of twisted metal, a bloody knife on the ground, crime scene tape, dark city streets, and bodies. Like a slide show except banal images interjected with horror. The images clicked past faster than the speed of thought. Someone or something seized control of my mind. For the first time in my life, I could not tolerate the sounds of fireworks. I suddenly had to avoid large crowds.

Images from calls in the long past reappeared during these episodes. That Irish-faced kid with burns to his face after opening the radiator cap comes back. The process of digging through a hoarder's house. Our extrication of a six-hundred-pound man from his home. Moving nearly three-hundred kilos of human flesh required two ambulance crews and two fire crews for a total of ten people to cut a hole large enough at the front of the house. Firefighters cut the banisters from the stairs, so that we could use ropes to slide the still-living patient from the second floor. Merge that with the vision of a bullet's exit wound near the kidney, and a lower leg bent at ninety degrees—bent at a place where no human ought to bend.

Decades later, I decided that I ought to return to EMS. The conscious memory eschews the worst while clinging to the best. As an urban EMT, I had seen everything possible on the streets: walking into the bedroom of an obese fourteen-year-old girl who had never once experienced her menstrual cycle, then was surprised when I told her she was pregnant. The belly pains appeared at regular intervals.

As an urban EMT, I knew with certainty that rural EMTs were

under-trained, under-skilled, ran about like Keystone Cops. I had completed thousands of calls before my twenty-fifth birthday. Often, I completed eight to fifteen emergency calls during a ten-hour day shift. We did the worst paperwork, paperwork that resulted in fraud charges. Paperwork never slowed us down. Nor did pre-hospital treatment. The worse the patient, the faster we moved.

I chased my new ambulance pager for weeks and months. I worked with the pager clipped to my hip. When it blasted, I sprinted to my truck. I raced to the station three miles distant. As I came down the final incline, I would hear the ambulance leave the bay. Once I followed. Usually, I returned to the kitchen table and worked.

On a Saturday, I finally made it to the station before the ambulance disappeared. I climbed into the passenger seat. Gil Horne, the chief of the service, pulled us from the garage calling on the radio that we were responding: "15A1 on the air and responding."

On scene, Gil walked the patient to the waiting stretcher, laid him down on a plastic backboard. It was then that he applied the neck collar then strapped the patient down tightly. The fellow had pulled on to the state highway when a pickup truck clipped the front of his Jeep. He had been up and walking around for the twenty minutes before we got on scene. I drove to the hospital in Warrenton. I parked in the hospital's ambulance bay with the skill of someone who had backed an ambulance ten-thousand times. The gap between the loading dock and our bumper was barely big enough for my finger. I reviewed the accuracy with pride.

Gil paused for a cigarette before climbing back into the rig and our nearly silent trip to Langford. I offered to do the paperwork while Gil drove.

"No, you are not allowed to do the paperwork, you are not certified. And further, you haven't been trained on how to do it." He may think that he had chided me for my offer. Yet, I believe I knew the law better than he. We just ran an emergency call on an ambulance with exactly one certified person. Gil held a certificate as an advanced EMT in the State of Vermont. I sat in a classroom retaking the EMT class after a twenty-year hiatus. In a desk drawer at home, I had both a badge with my old Massachusetts EMT number and a set of dog tags presented to me by Aaron. These dog tags also displayed my EMT number. An old and expired EMT number means nothing. My once-upon-a-time certification does not allow the ambulance service to invoice insurance for our work. By law, the ambulance must have two certified people on board. We ran a patient to the hospital with one. Given what I know about ambulance paperwork, I was certain that my name as driver would be replaced by the name of someone who was certified. My first call with gray hair and I became an accomplice to yet-another felony. Fraud is fraud.

As we approached the station, he asked, "When are you going to come to a meeting again? The meetings are mandatory."

"I am sorry. I thought Mike told everyone. My classes are Tuesdays and Thursdays every week and most Saturdays." Squad meetings landed on the second Tuesday of each month. I had missed every meeting since the semester started. I explained to Gil, "My attendance is required for my EMT course as well."

With little irony or humor, he said, "You need to make an effort to come to our meetings. They are important."

I had little to worry about. I attended two meetings. During the training portion of the meeting, the instructor handed out a box of gloves for everyone. We donned them. Then he passed around an open tin of Hershey's chocolate syrup. Each member dutifully spilt chocolate from a hole in the lid. Spilt chocolate landed on our gloved hands, and some on the table.

The instructor showed us all how to remove gloves so that we kept the chocolate on the inside. Glove off, clean hands—that was the goal. The trick involved inverting the gloves while removing one, then the other. One glove goes inside the other, making a neat drip-free ball of purple nitrile. I not only did it faster but cleaner than anyone in the room. I walked to the trash can to dispose of my gloves. By the time I sat down, others were throwing their gloves towards the trash. Gloves hit the white-ish wall and the grey-brown carpet. Chocolate had dribbled on the conference table. It dribbled on the wall. And it dribbled on the carpet.

"Leon, you are a fat cow, why don't you go lick that up?" one of the assholes at the table said. Everyone else laughed. Everyone except me and Leon. Then Leon remembered that he was supposed to laugh so he offered a quick chuckle. Lizzie, one of the few women in the room, returned with a spray-can of window cleaner and a roll of paper towel.

Just like in the Atlantic Ambulance days, we all signed the roster. We attested to the fact that class started at six then ended at eight in the evening. Many of the attendees had headed home before seven, many saying that they had to get home for supper. Just like the Atlantic days, EMTs earned two hours of continuing ed credit for a few minutes of effort. We all ticked the box, declaring that we had done our annual training on bloodborne pathogens. I determined that I got more value from retaking my EMT class than wasting my time with purple gloves and Hershey's chocolate syrup.

Late on a Sunday in March, dispatch toned out Langford Ambulance for a call in Trowbridge. I hopped into my truck. I arrived at the closed dark station as dispatch toned the service a third time. The rule was that the ambulance never leaves the bay without a full and legal crew. After opening the door, I called, "15A1 on the air awaiting crew."

Dispatch hit the tones a fourth time, sending out a request for EMTs to respond to the station for a woman with a traumatic crush injury to her hand.

"15A1?"

"Go for 15A1."

"Have you heard from any other crew members?" the dispatcher asked me.

"No."

"Neither have we." I understood the implied question.

"Let's hand-off the call to someone else. 15A1 in station." Dispatch rolled the call to the nearest available ambulance service.

Within a minute, the dispatch transmitted tones for Trent River Ambulance.

"Trent River respond in Trowbridge for hand injury."

I returned to my car. I drove across Trowbridge from the west side to the east side, nearly an eight-mile drive on two-lane country roads. About half of the trip had me on gravel roads. I arrived at the patient's house about fifty minutes after the first tone for the ambulance. Likely an hour had elapsed since the patient called 911.

"I am with Langford Rescue, can I help?"

"Where is the ambulance?"

"It is coming." Lie? Not-a-lie?

I got escorted to the kitchen by a pre-teen boy. His mother sat holding a bag of peas to her hand. The finger appeared in immediate jeopardy.

I left the house then returned to the kitchen with my new medical bag—a bag I bought for myself, then stocked with my own equipment and supplies. I gloved up, then cut the ring from her finger. The top of her finger changed color immediately turning back to the pink and red of perfusing tissue. Even some of the swelling disappeared.

The patient sighed.

"Keep it on ice." I had so much more to say. "You should go to the hospital."

She said, "I can't drive with this."

"Maybe you can. Maybe he can help?" I pointed to the young kid. "But you do need to get to the hospital."

I pulled out an AMA—against medical advice form—then started filling it out. I asked for her name, date of birth, and mailing address. I had her sign it as a means of documenting that I had been at the house and suggested she go to the hospital. I placed the document back in my bag.

As I left, I said again, "You need to get to the hospital."

"Isn't there an ambulance coming?"

"I don't know. Regional dispatch has been calling for ambulances for nearly an hour. It doesn't seem like anyone is coming." I spoke too candidly.

Mike Foote called me into the office two weeks later. "Did you respond on your own to a call in Trowbridge?"

"Yes."

Thus endeth my career with Langford Rescue Squad. Within a day, I got put in front of a special meeting of the executive board. I stood at the front of the room as if looking at a panel of judges.

"You know you practiced medicine without a license?" The gravelly voice attempted to make a question of his accusation. The gravelly voice sitting at the far end of the table said, "You put the entire service at risk."

I said nothing in return. My inner voice chattered irreverently to the idiotic statements and accusation of these guys. I smiled wryly at my accusers because my brain warped their sentence around. I said to myself, "they are accusing me of practicing license without medicine." They decided to make a formal and awkward production out of this ordeal. Shit, I stand on record for having violated far more rules and laws than cutting a ring from a woman's finger.

"The state could have revoked our license were they to learn about your cowboying around our hills. It just is not done."

Only one gravelly voice spoke.

"As a probationary member, we have decided to end your probation and not invite you to become a member. Put your pager on the table."

When a citizen calls 911, the state requires that each agency protect the community by sending only trained and licensed people. I had a few weeks of my EMT class to complete. By July, I would be certified in Massachusetts and Vermont, plus hold a national registry card. I returned to my EMT class, never admitting that I got fired from an unpaid, volunteer position with an ambulance service that desperately needed new members. I got fired. I got fired for saving a finger when no one else chose to help.

Oh, the pride.

10 | Chief

Dispatch transmitted the tones for the newly formed Trowbridge EMS at one minute before eight in the morning. "Trowbridge Rescue respond for apparent untimely." I rapidly changed into my EMS trousers and pulled on my new sweatshirt, or work shirt, as they are called. The EMS trousers were so unlike the triple-knit polyester police trousers I once wore. These had been designed by EMTs for EMTs. Heavy cotton-blend fabric with reinforced knees and huge thigh pockets that provided ample storage for all of my kit. The trousers also included one pocket near each ankle, just like a pair of flight coveralls. This small pocket fitted a notepad perfectly. And it was right where you needed it.

The workshirt, also a newer invention, blended the best of cotton sweatshirts with denim at the elbows and collar. Designed as a uniform, the chest region provided surfaces for embroidery. Mine included the patch for Trowbridge Rescue and my name A. FLYNN done in yellow. Below my name, the word "CHIEF" had been stitched in the matching yellow. On my right shoulder, I wore an American flag. On my left shoulder, I wore the glittering golden patch of a nationally registered paramedic. Pinned through the denim collars, I wore the eagle insignia often associated with army colonels and navy captains.

In my thigh pockets, I carried a stethoscope, scissors, knife, pen, a tourniquet, and a few other tools of this trade.

I climbed into my truck. I pulled straight out of the driveway, flipping on my red-and-white strobe lights. I picked the mic from the dash of my truck. "Dispatch, 14RC1 responding." I had left my office, changed, then hopped into the truck within two minutes. I used the radio to let dispatch know that the rescue chief, "RC," from the new agency Trowbridge Rescue was responding.

Feeling lucky that I knew the road, I drove without consulting any maps. Once, I knew all 917 streets of my Cambridge, the Cambridge of my youth. Cambridge had about one-hundred thousand people huddled on the north shore of the Charles River. The city encompassed about six-and-a-half square miles of land. Conversely, Trowbridge's boundaries had been drawn on a map by old men who had never seen the terrain. They drew neat boxes on flat paper, each box with a six-mile edge, resulting in towns that hovered between thirty-six and forty square miles. Not every Vermont town shares this regularity. In some cases, rivers and state borders interfered. In one region of Vermont, the little boxes had been sketched askew. Near me, each town border traveled neatly south-to-north and east-to-west. Each corner met at precise ninety-degree angles with Roman accuracy and matching classical symmetry.

Leaving the driveway, I turned north while vectoring directly to a known address. It felt like one of many accomplishments. It proved that my investment learning the town's roads saved me a minute of time. I parked, informing dispatch that I was on scene.

"14RC1 on scene. 14RC1 establishing Trowbridge Command." The stylized process of using the format of the incident command system also felt new. It informed dispatch that I was the incident commander.

I knocked at the door, which had been left ajar, then stepped inside.

"Hello. Rescue is here."

A middle-aged woman, about my age, greeted me. A man sat on the sofa with his face buried in his hands. The woman walked me to a small bedroom off the kitchen.

"She is in here. My mother-in-law."

From the door, I realized that she had died quietly in the night. I walked in. I touched the cool skin. I felt quickly for the absent pulse at her neck.

"Ma'am, I am going to do a quick exam. Do you mind if I lift the blankets?"

The daughter-in-law silently shook her head, granting consent.

With the blankets lifted, I caught the expected odor. I lifted the night dress to her hip, then lowered her underwear to show me part of her buttocks. As expected, they were purple. I looked again at the body. I saw the same purple color at her elbow. I covered her back up. I wiggled her unmoving jaw. I then took my stethoscope out and my phone. With the stopwatch app, I listened to her silent chest for a full minute.

The daughter-in-law had left the room. I walked back to the living room. "I am very sorry for your loss. I think I can say confidently that she died peacefully in her sleep." That was the training. You must use the word "dead." The phrase lacks ambiguity. "I'll excuse myself for a minute." I turned, stepping away.

"Dispatch, Trowbridge Command."

"Trowbridge?"

"Trowbridge Command… Requesting Vermont State Police to the scene. Cancel the ambulance. No transport. Trowbridge rescue members not on scene, can return to quarters."

My phone buzzed. Looking I saw "Harry Grasser" appear on the display. Harry had been elected assistant chief after he nominated me for chief. That was the deal. He nominated me for chief and I nominated him for assistant chief.

"Need me?" he asked.

"Sure. Come."

"Woke up dead?" he asked, exploring the nature of the call.

"Yup." I confirmed that our patient had woken up dead.

Following the dictates of the incident command system, I had written protocols for each of the expected calls. With this type of call, our protocol described only two people on scene. Harry hung up.

I stepped into the old lady's room then shut the door. I surveyed the room, assessing the level of care, the number of medications, and other clues at my crime scene. I then called medical control at the hospital. I gave my name and the nature of the request. My observations and declaration were not legally binding until confirmed by a physician. Yes, I listened for a full minute, that I timed.

I confirmed dependent lividity and rigor mortis. I prattled off the list of medications: hypertension, statins, and a benzo for anxiety. The classic diet of the American elderly. We both recorded time-of-death at 08:11 hours, which was the time I noted when I completed my assessment.

The doc did not bust my chops on calling her ten minutes later than the observed time of death. Once done with the administration of death, I closed off the old lady's room.

I went to the living room.

"Again, I am very sorry for your loss. My name is Alex Flynn. I am the chief of Trowbridge Rescue and a paramedic. I have closed the door to your mother's room. Per protocol, I must seal off the area until the police arrive. If you guys want to go in and say goodbye, I can walk you both in." Awkward, offering to escort the family and homeowners into the room. It is their house after all.

They both looked at me. Neither moved.

"Ok. This will be a very difficult day for you. During the next four hours a lot of strangers will come through the door. First will be Harry. He is my partner. In about forty-five minutes, the state police will arrive. Then in about two hours, a pair of detectives will arrive. In about four hours, the funeral home will come."

I paused, letting the information absorb.

"If I may… I suggest that you both shower and take care of yourselves." Both people were still dressed in their pajamas and robes. "You've got time now that you will not have later."

My portable radio announced: "Trowbridge Command, 14RC2 on scene."

I clicked my mic twice, an old trick from the Cambridge days. A trick not used here. But I didn't want to answer. As a rookie chief, I could get away with a few mistakes.

"I'll leave you guys alone. Harry and I will be around and keep out of your way."

I met Harry at the door. "Mind pulling to the end of the road to mark it?" Harry's truck with his flashing lights would mark the turn thereby helping the state police find the place. We both knew that we would be there for hours.

"Dispatch, Trowbridge Command."

"Trowbridge?"

"VSP on scene." We let dispatch know that the state police arrived. This notification becomes part of the official recording for the call.

Harry stepped in while I stepped out to introduce myself to the two officers on scene. Like Harry, they parked on the larger road—opting not to turn into the small dead-end road. I briefed using notes written on cards stored in my ankle pocket. I didn't need the cards, but it made me look more professional. After the briefing, I said, "We'll leave you to it." Expecting to head home within the next few minutes.

"You should wait for the detectives to release you."

Defeated, I said, "Let me take you in. I can introduce you."

When Harry and I finally stepped outside again, one cop was photographing the old lady plus her room. The other cop interviewed the family. Harry and I sat on the bed of my Ford pickup truck waiting for detectives to arrive.

I learned at a young age where Ford put the various knobs and switches. Harry looked nothing like Aaron, but like Aaron, Harry spent time in Vietnam as a young man.

Harry, quick with a dad-joke, asked me, "What do you call twenty bunnies walking backwards?"

With a grimace, I said, "I dunno Harry, what do you call twenty bunnies walking backwards?"

"A receding hare line."

"Harry, that was horrible. But we do have something to celebrate. After two years of work, this is our first call. Number 1."

"Our response rate is one hundred percent," he answered.

"We were on time for our *untimely*." *Untimely*, the radio jargon used for people who die. Untimely had become the polite and secular term for passing on as if there were some superstition about saying the word Death on the radio. I touched the Vermont EMT patch Harry had sewn onto his uniform worksheet. Although he had spent time on ambulances in and around his time in Vietnam, I got the sense that the ambulance he drove looked more like a 1960s style hearse. He worked during the years the first EMT courses were being discussed. Three-plus decades later, he took the one semester EMT class in the middle of my two-year slog through my paramedic training. Being fired from Langford Ambulance caused me to push back at them.

"I kinda wanted to do this," Harry said.

"You mean sit in my truck outside the house of a dead lady waiting for detectives?" I paused. Of course, I knew what he meant. During the recent years, our conversations behaved like a bramble thicket. We pointed the chat then get snagged and pulled randomly. "I was nervous standing at town meeting. I didn't think we'd pull this off. I get very annoyed each time I hear someone say, 'Been doing it this way for a long time, don't know why we need to change.' It grinds at me. The sentiment informs me that this life, this town, this world is the best of all possible worlds."

"You mean it isn't?"

"I should like to live in a world where help comes when you call for it. People have food, y'know, the basics. Things do change, don't they?"

"No, not here, not if the old timers have their say." We were sitting on a dirt road in the ancient hills of the Appalachians in a town of dirt roads. Other towns have mayors and town councils. Not here. We stick to the old ways and the old terms. In the old days, people selected men to aid in governing the town during the fifty-one weeks between town meeting. Town meeting occurs on the first Tuesday in March. March, you ask? March is muddy. In March, the maple sugar season starts. Who starts the year in March? The answer includes the Romans and early America. We used to host the presidential inauguration in March. Nature regards the spring as the opening of the year too. Most of the world moved on.

Harry stood next to me when I spoke at town meeting, which serves as the town's annual legislative body. Each citizen gets a say, gets a vote, and spends a day discussing the town's road budget, the school budget, voting on random events and arguing over how much we ought to contribute to the tiny regional library in Langford. Direct democracy at work. It is inefficient, time consuming, slow, and time honored. It once served as my ideal for American democracy, until I recognized its failings.

"You did fine," Harry offered. He had said that before.

"How could we fail? We asked for nearly nothing and offered a new local rescue service. We promised education, opportunity for people, improved medical service, blah, blah, blah. And we checked a box."

Harry responded with "Martinelli said, 'I don't need some wanna be doc thinking they can help when they studied medicine from the back of a Cheerios box.'"

"He did say that didn't he. What a jackass. Did you know the family?"

"Martinelli? No, they came in from Connecticut."

"So did the Trowbridge family," I retorted.

"Different century."

Our nascent squad had discussed the process of presenting to the town's people. We were required, by the State of Vermont, to get the community's approval. An EMS agency in Vermont is required to serve an underserved community. Unlike Massachusetts, where an ambulance service can operate as a business seeking profit, Vermont considers EMS to be a local community thing. If your service has been voted in by all of required entities and you respond to your emergency calls, then of course you can also provide billable and mildly profitable interfacility transfers, taking folks between care home and hospitals, taking people to treatments, and other activities. But you can only engage in those services when your service also dedicates time and resources to the non-billable activities of supporting a town. With my background, I thought a presentation with images, plans, and budgets projected on the wall would be best. Bridget and Harry both said, "No." Too modern. Regina recommended a middle path using a flipboard and a few handouts. Bridget and Harry both said, "No." Too modern. In the end, we set up a small table at the back of the room with one poster. We displayed one medical kit and had one person sitting at the table. We were honored to be next to the school's bake sale, the busiest table. The library had a small display on the table next to us. Five ladies sat in the back row, chatting and clicking knitting needles. Harry and I sat in the middle of the room. As planned, we stood when called on by the moderator at the podium. Given we asked for a non-binding resolution, we waited through nearly the entire meeting. A lot of people left after voting on the town budget and arguing over a bridge repair on a town road that served only one family. More left after the school budget had been approved.

"Thank you. My name is Alex Flynn. We are asking for a non-binding resolution from you." I looked around the room. "We want to build then serve this town with a trained and licensed rescue squad. We will be dispatched to emergencies automatically. Our goal is to get to you within seven minutes if possible." Seven minutes felt like a realistic average. Several new squad members pointed out that one cannot drive end-to-end or corner-to-corner in less than thirty minutes. Trowbridge is slightly larger than Manhattan. We do not have a stop light. About ten percent of our eighty road miles are paved and most stop signs have bullet holes in them. My years in Cambridge gave me a clue that most calls would come from where the few houses were clustered.

I reviewed the plan that we had written. Frankly, I wrote most of it. It spewed out of me in a protracted period of simmering anger. I have written hundreds of mission plans. What does the community need? What can we, as a squad, measure? What was missing in Trowbridge? How do we find the resources? And how do we sustain the mission? The other members softened my tone. They also noted that I could not stand at Trowbridge town meeting while throwing fecal matter at Langford Ambulance. They told me I could not identify their failures. They told me I could not identify their lengthy history of responding to calls with crews that did not meet the legal minimums required by insurance companies and state law. They instructed me to praise Langford. I was to say, "We're only here to augment their services and get care to you faster."

So that is what I said to the citizenry. "We will respond first and faster to scenes. We will stabilize patients, provide treatment, and help coordinate getting an ambulance to the scene."

A hand went up. The moderator nodded silently. I remained standing but turned to face a man in his seventies standing. "As you know, I have had to call the ambulance a few times for my wife." He paused. The room offered silent sympathy for a widower. "They were amazing. They always came when we needed them. I don't see why creating something new is helpful. Why don't these people just go help the ambulance?"

Regina, who leapt at the chance to join another Vermont agency, had been fired from Langford Rescue two years before me. Harry lived in a far corner of the town outside of Langford's scope. He lived forty minutes from the ambulance station. I reminded myself of the purpose of the meeting. We needed a resolution from the town that we could submit to the State of Vermont and the regional EMS board. To build this squad, we needed this vote.

"I am sorry to hear of your wife's passing, sir. We offer help to you and to everyone in town," I offered. "They only have one ambulance and they are located over there in Langford. We're here in Trowbridge. Our members know this town. Many of you are related to our members. Our goal is to arrive first, provide care, and help get patients ready for the trip to town on their ambulance. And on those rare days when their ambulance is already out on a run, we can use our radios to bring in another ambulance."

The man, still standing, said: "And where does that come from?"

"Warrenton to the west; Starkville to the east; and/or any town in Massachusetts." I left out that we can call in helicopters. "We all have the same radio network." The widower sat.

Another hand went up. She waited for the moderator to acknowledge her. Of course, the moderator had stated that everyone was to use their full name and provide their street address when they spoke. The moderator enforced that rule for the first hour. He then enforced the rule for people new to town. As town meeting dragged on, the crowd thinned, leaving the older and familiar faces. The assumption was that everyone remaining knew everyone else in the room.

"What is this going to cost us?"

I had already covered that. I painted my face with stoic patience. "Initially, we ask that the town include us on the town's insurance policy. The law requires that we have worker's compensation. We are asking that the town add us to their policy with all of the other town volunteers. Second, we do have a few expenses. We will be asking for five thousand dollars next year. And of course, like the fire company, we will be seeking donations from people."

She opened her mouth to say something, then shut it. The moderator had lifted the gavel about one hand's width in warning. She sat.

Still standing, I decided to teach. "The modern goal of emergencies is that we need to provide real care within an hour. A lot has improved during the decades. You can thank the Korea War, the Vietnam war, the First Gulf War, the Iraq War, and the Afghanistan War for these advances. We humans must follow the Rule of Three. We can survive about three minutes without oxygen. We can survive about three days without water. We die after three weeks without food. If someone has a stroke or a heart attack, we have about one to two hours to get the patient to a hospital. With clot-busting drugs and surgical tricks, treatment is now possible. In my first go at EMS, the medical community had fewer tools for these problems. Even our techniques for managing traumatic injury have improved. We have dressings that promote clotting, even in the worse wound. We have improved methods to keep people breathing. Even the humble pulse oximeter informs us of the level of oxygen in the blood. We know when to use medical oxygen and not to use oxygen. Our crew with our kits, a tank of oxygen, and a portable radio can do a lot to help save a life, save a limb, and improve the outcome of a stroke or heart attack." Lesson over. I wanted to prove our skills to this gray-haired audience. Back before we had ready access to the pulse-ox machine, EKG machines, and other modern tools, we did treatments because they looked cool. Back in the day, we threw medical modalities at a patient with the phrase, "Might help, can't hurt, guaranteed to please a crowd." We had little insights beyond the few vital signs: heart rate, blood pressure, respiratory rate, and level of consciousness. All of these vital signs could be inferred from Aaron's handshake. With a finger on the wrist, he measured the heart rate, and pulse pressure. With a pulse at the wrist, he knew the BP was survivable. Now we can carry cardiac monitors that measure respiratory effectiveness. We can see what we had never before seen.

Even the process of giving CPR improved with years of evidence-based research. Today, the instruction is to beat hard-fast-and-deep while singing to the beat of the song "Staying Alive." Pump at one-hundred times per minute. This proved to be significantly better than my old slow song, "One-potato-two-potato." That slow rate of sixty beats per minute did not save many lives.

Inventing, creating, and building a new EMS agency in Vermont required following a recipe proscribed by the State of Vermont. The process illustrates Vermont's treatment of EMS, EMTs and paramedics. First, there is no law in Vermont that requires any town to have emergency medical services. In that same vein, there is no law that requires a Vermont town to have police nor fire services. Most towns do, but they are not required by law. For example, Trowbridge contracts with the Vermont State Police. During the town meeting, all voted "aye" for the eight thousand dollars we give to the state police for patrolling ten hours per month.

I looked around the room then to the moderator. Wordlessly, I sat.

The moderator straightened up. "All those in favor of supporting the foundation of Trowbridge Rescue through a non-binding resolution signify by saying 'aye.'"

There was sufficient mumbling to infer that the vote took place.

"All those opposed." The school gymnasium remained silent.

"Motion passed." The moderator touched his podium with the gavel.

I sat down next to Harry. My palms had sweated while I stood and spoke. I felt ridiculous for the feeling. I had presented to all sorts during my career. While not allowed to admit it aloud, I had presented to national leaders, regional leaders, city leaders overseas. I had presented to generals and senators in our country. Yet I sweated like a schoolkid in front of sixty old people who sat in wooden folding chairs. It felt like my carotid pulse was bounding. I felt my own pulse go thumpity-thump.

Harry and I departed from that town meeting together twenty minutes later. Now on the day of our first official call as a new service, we sat in the front seat of my truck listening to both the FM radio and the fire/EMS radio. I had parked under a maple tree on a side road on a hill in Trowbridge. Creating a rescue squad required one check in each of three official boxes. Before presenting to town meeting, we paid for and placed a legal notice in the Trent Valley newspaper. The notice invited anyone to comment on the proposed new service in Trowbridge. People had sixty days to write to the state EMS office in Burlington, two-and-half hours to the north. The third official duty involved taking our roster, plan, agency application, and non-binding resolution to the district EMS board.

"Why didn't you come with me to the district board?" I asked Harry again. Last time we discussed it, he said something vague like, "Let someone else go, share the experiences around." A noble sentiment from the new assistant chief. But I trusted Harry and I liked his fellowship. He had a vague understanding of my career. At one point, he said, "I consider you a veteran," which from a veteran told me he accepted me as one-of-us. Still technically not a veteran. I never went to boot camp.

"I did not think you needed me in the room. You know Nick?"

"The new chief of Starkville EMS?"

"Yes. I'd be a target for him."

"Oh, why?" Harry can be a divisive person, but most people adore him. He doesn't tend to instantly split a room like I can.

"I liked and respected the former chief. Nick pushed him out and hard. It was like watching a respected and good person being kicked in the nuts. I don't get what he is planning. I just don't trust him. I think his mother is a horrible person. She had horses taken from her farm after neglecting them."

"You know she is on his board of directors now?"

"That will be worth watching," he said with no irony. "How long before she seizes control as the chair?"

"I won't vote for her." I had been appointed to the board for the ambulance service as the representative from Trowbridge. Stark EMS covered the eastern reaches of our town. Each town in their coverage area got to appoint one representative to the Stark EMS board.

"Just wait and watch, Alex. Wait and watch."

We listened to a fire department get toned to a vehicle fire with possible involvement of a garage. The FM radio played songs from my school days.

"I really don't get the district board," I said aloud.

"How so?" We were still waiting for detectives to travel down here. People, when I say that I live in Vermont, often tell me how far away it is, how beautiful it is. Don't you just love Stowe? they ask me. It is so hard to get to. I don't correct them. I don't offer that I can be in Massachusetts in under fifteen minutes and that I listen to Boston radio stations in my home and my truck. Vermont's state services sometimes forget that we too are part of Vermont.

"Look, Nick took over Stark EMS, right?" I didn't wait. "So now he is the chair of the state's EMS district board."

"Ok," Harry offered, following my thoughts.

"Nick runs the only paid EMS agency in our district." I built another stepping stone in my syllogism. "Therefore, Nick is the actual boss of every paid EMT and paramedic in the area except for the few who work for Trent Valley Rescue. Trent Valley is in Winchester County but oddly landed in a different EMS district."

"Ok," Harry said again.

"Who is on the EMS district board?"

"Representatives of each agency in the district," Harry answered.

"Right. So, these representatives are likely senior members of their own service or even chief. Check?"

"Check."

"They each need training and more time on ambulances so they either volunteer for or get a paying job with Stark EMS. Who does the hiring? Who does the firing? Who does the annual reviews? Nick."

"Yeah?"

"Nick is the district chair and the actual boss of most of the board members. There is no independent thinking. The board has six or seven employees of Stark EMS, each representing who? Their own agency or Stark EMS? Can they honestly do both?"

"But does it matter?"

"I don't know, but we can't call that fair. There is one voting bloc led by Nick."

"I dunno," he offered with a meek shrug of resignation. I could imagine his own inner voice: "Alex, you are still thinking with a city brain." He pivoted. "You and Bridget got the votes we needed."

"We did. True."

We had earned the third check on our list. With a license in hand, we designed patches for our uniforms and coordinated adding our new agency to the regional dispatch service.

I observed this power bloc as a cozy means of running a state agency. While it honored the long-held tradition of direct democracy, it also faced the long-observed problems with direct democracy. It tended towards insular. It tended towards decisions that were minority controlled. It tended towards inefficiency. It fostered clan-like behavior, attitudes, and decisions. In my time in Vermont, I had gotten damn tired of hearing, "Been doin' it this way for a long time. Don't see the need to change." With that phrase in my head, I asked, "Did I tell you how one state employee takes credit for preventing Enron from taking over the state's electrical grid? He's damn proud of that story."

I did not wait for the no or the yes. I started, "I met with this fellow for my current work. He was sitting behind his desk with jeans and a fleece vest. He informed me of a day when a team of two men in expensive business suits arrived at the state office in Montpelier. These two flatlanders, out-of-staters, two of them advocated for the elimination of Vermont's rural electricity cooperatives in lieu of improved services from a larger multi-service energy company. My fellow with the State of Vermont did not trust a word his guests said. Was it because of their suits? Was it because of their instances of moving towards modern ways? My fellow tells this story with pride because he effectively and single-handedly thwarted Enron's attempts to take over the Vermont electrical grid. Years later, Enron failed catastrophically. My guy, by distrusting foreigners and new stuff, saved Vermont and our grid." Then aloud I uttered, "Been doin' it this way for a long time. Don't see the need to change."

It is because of this attitude that I do not have good highspeed internet that I require for my work. The terrestrial internet service provided over the telephone lines lags behind nearly every other state. "Don't see the need to change." I have spent a lifetime promoting change.

We waited and talked for nearly two hours.

We both gave up paying work to sit waiting for the police. Vermont has another odd law, or at least a law different from Massachusetts. In Vermont, one cannot be an EMT unless affiliated with a Vermont-based EMS agency. In Massachusetts, an EMT certificate is a personal credential. You earned it. You own it. Like being a licensed plumber or licensed electrician, you can take your certification to any employer. Not Vermont. Your certification appears to be held jointly between your EMS agency and the individual. You cannot take an EMT class unless you are affiliated. You cannot take an EMT exam, unless affiliated. If you lose your affiliation, then you are no longer an EMT. In states such as Massachusetts, the EMT courses get offered at universities. The job serves as a gateway to a paid and professional career.

By keeping EMS agencies and EMTs focused on providing services to remote and isolated communities, they appeared to require that EMTs work for free. For the most part, towns cannot afford to pay EMTs and paramedics. Some agencies may offer a stipend for each call worked, like ten dollars per ambulance run. The state does not fund EMS. It does not fund EMS training. I believed that if Vermont required towns to have EMS agencies, then the state would be required to provide funding for that mandate. If we, as Vermonters, keep that requirement off of the lawbooks, then we as a state do not have to fund the mission.

These were my thoughts waiting for police officers to arrive in a state-owned vehicle, police officers who drew a salary and benefits while caring for the people of Vermont. Not very charitable of me. Our squad wrote our own bylaws. We raised funds pleading with neighbors for money. We had enough interest to trigger our own EMT course. Regrettably, the instructors refused to travel to Trowbridge with their kit. So instead, our squad members each drove the hour over to Warrenton. We had to pay the instructor, the material costs, and for books. The volunteers paid for their own gas. While we prepared our new agency, I trained as a paramedic in Massachusetts.

"Did I tell you that everyone in my paramedic class hated me?" I likely already had. I probably called him the next morning with the story. "Remember I said that the dean told me that I did not possess the requisite experience, right? She told me that I would slow the program down and hold other students back." Her preference, she told me as she accepted me into the program, was that an EMT spent a year or five as an EMT before even attempting a paramedic class. No matter how often I cited my experiences in Metro Boston, she did not count that as real experience.

What was the difference between a paramedic and an EMT? An EMT took a one-semester course. A basic level EMT cannot perform any medical services that are invasive and, for the most part, they could not administer any medications. A paramedic took a two-year course of study akin to a registered nursing program. It included courses on anatomy, physiology, pharmacology, pathophysiology, and others. During the program, the student must perform hundreds of skills. We started hundreds of IVs. We learned to read electrocardiograms, then spent hours in clinical settings evaluating EKGs. We delivered some number of babies and logged each birth. We intubated a number of patients either in an ER or during planned surgical procedures. We practiced sticking needles into chests to release trapped air or trapped blood. Once licensed, I could provide up to fifty-five medications.

I continued telling a familiar and hurtful story. "During this one practical exam called the *megacode*, she pulled me aside. We had full-sized medical manikins that groaned and had fake pulses, if you could find the right place on their plastic wrists. We had to evaluate our plastic dummy, assess the causes, then treat. They design the megacode to be like the Kobayashi Maru. No matter what actions I took, or any student took, it resulted in failure and death. The lesson reinforced the concept that sometimes people die no matter what you do.

"Yeah, no shit. I had learned that lesson decades ago. During that practical exam, the dean pulled me aside to say: 'You know everyone here hates you.'"

Harry responded with, "She sounds horrible."

I did not admit to Harry that the dean made me cry. I was so angry and so frustrated at her. I wanted to hate this woman. I did at that moment. I still do not know what caused her to pull me from an exam to say this to me. My revenge came easily.

Bragging now, I said, "I made top marks and earned a spot on the school's dean's list. Yeah, so screw her."

Of course, I got my Massachusetts paramedic license easily and quickly. But not in Vermont. I can only be a licensed paramedic if I am affiliated with an agency that is licensed at the paramedic level. Trowbridge was licensed at the EMT-Basic level. In an ironic twist, I wore the patch I earned. My Trowbridge uniform sported the glimmering gold patches of a paramedic. But I could only operate as a basic EMT, two certification steps lower than my training.

Finally, a plain-looking sedan came down the road. It was smaller and cheaper than any of the city-owned vehicles Boston supplied to my father. Two detectives stepped from the vehicle. We stepped from my truck. We formally shook hands on the walkway to the house. They walked through the door, we returned to my truck.

One came out after a minute. "Do you mind talking with the medical examiner?"

Harry and I re-entered the house, offering our condolences yet again. The family had showered and gotten dressed. They looked marginally better. I spoke with the associate medical examiner via the family's home phone. The *ME*'s questions mimicked the questions asked by the medical control doctor. Harry and I stepped back outside.

"Dispatch, Trowbridge Command."

"Trowbridge."

"Trowbridge Command terminated. All units in service and in quarters." At the minute before eight a.m., I left my office and my billable work. I returned home at eleven thirty.

I ate lunch, wondering if this call would be memorable or forgotten. I thought about the thousands of other calls and the hundreds of days I had already spent on ambulances.

Like an aging racehorse, I acknowledged eagerness to return to the track. Forget the pain, forget the personal drama, I had the skills. Given what I have experienced in my youth and later in life, what more damage can a few calls a month do to me? Since that summer's day in Rome, I endured the cycles of personalized malaria. My disease had been acquired slowly during years on the streets of Cambridge. Then, like malaria, symptoms return. Occasionally mild, occasionally crippling. I do not call it malaria for fear of being misunderstood for being literal. I named it *tinea mentis*, a fungal infection of the mind. A name coined from the skin-flaking itchiness between several of my toes. When quiet and ignored, it grows symptom free. Then I must address it. Often too late. I feel the symptoms coming, returning. First mild and easy to ignore. Then of course, I am too busy and in the wrong place to face it. I lock it off to protect myself. Finding I only incubated the disease.

Was it a disease?

I can go into supermarkets. I can ride the T today. I can look calm doing it. I can act supremely confident. In any crowd, I am on duty, alert, and ready for action. That's how I survive the crowds, the lights, the noises. I am on duty. I picture myself at the edge of the crowd, under cover and ready. I can walk the aisles of a busy supermarket. The defenses do not last long unless I make it feel familiar, comfortable, and find a way to make the store my friend and ally. Do not play music at me. Do not track my every movement with your cameras. Do not approach me from behind. Do not ask me an unexpected question. I am on guard constantly. Surprises still cause reactions that I sometimes cannot control.

Most days, I try not to push myself to these limits. That is why I got off the airplanes and escaped foreign cities. Do you know what it is like to be in a place where nothing works, nothing is right, and you don't speak the language? I called back to the boss, fighting tears: there was no car, there was no meet up, I landed in the wrong city, the hotels are full, my documents got rejected. Trapped, isolated, alone in my own mind, every other drama revisits.

I get visits from Aaron's demons from his time flying nap-of-the-earth over Vietnam with injured soldiers in the back of his Huey helicopter. Not my war, not my patients, not my experience. When he handed me the dog tags and his illegal "Code 5" street treatment, a few of his demons transferred with that last hug. I did get to ride once in a Huey. The Huey was the helicopter that Aaron worked out of in Vietnam. My one trip was a quick up and down. I sat on the deck with my legs hanging over the open air. Unlike Aaron, I had no risk of being shot by people on the ground. Normally when Aaron's demons visit me, I know that all of the images had been sourced from movies. They are not my demons. Yet demons don't discriminate. They visit because they can.

Aaron's demons visit because they traveled with my own host of demons.

America once held high the virtue of civic responsibility embodied in the phrase "if you can, you must." While we drafted young people to fight in World War I and II and Vietnam, millions of others volunteered because "they could therefore they must."

No amount of reticulated fungal growth sneaking around in my mind has yet inhibited my duties. "As long as I can, I shall." Honestly, what was a few calls a month after my career and those heady young days on the street?

Too young to retire, too worn out to return to my career as it once was, I envisioned a life at home. Me, a few chickens, a garden, working at the kitchen table via an internet connection. Perfection. As chief of an EMS, I still get that sense of urgency and importance when I fly out of my driveway with my emergency lights flashing. I needed that hit, just like the street druggies I once knew.

11 | Skirmishes

When I saw his piece-of-shit Jeep tear down my road, turning into my drive with two wheels nearly lifting, I began to worry. I stood in my yard with a chainsaw, watching the Jeep approach. Clipped to the orange safety chaps, I had my fire/EMS radio. I wore the required hard-hat, face mask, and hearing protection as I cut a spruce down. I recognized my neighbor and occasional friend Loony Larry. I turned off the chainsaw. Dropped my helmet, striding towards him.

"You didn't answer your phone," he yelled at me. True, I hadn't heard a phone ring while I cut down a tree. I regarded my neighbor. He was naked from the belt up. His eyebrows were gone. His chest hair appeared absent. He seemed the sort of hairy fellow that had chest hair. Unlike the kids of my clubbing days, who shaved leg and chest hair, Larry generally seemed too slovenly for these grooming practices.

"Larry, did you call 911?"

"No. I called your phone."

"Just call 911. I can get to you faster than you can get to me. What if I wasn't here?" I stopped chiding him, altering my posture to guide him from the Jeep. "What happened?" I asked like a para-medic ought to.

"It blew up."

"What blew up?"

"The furnace." I scanned my mental map of the property where he worked. They had an outdoor wood burning furnace that heated outbuildings.

"And you were standing at it when it went up?"

"Yes."

I spoke to the radio mounted on my shoulder. "Dispatch, 14RC1."

"14RC1," they answered.

"Dispatch, I have two related incidents. First, tone out Trowbridge fire for an investigation of a reported furnace explosion." I provided that address. "Second, tone Langford Ambulance to my location," thus giving dispatch my address. "40-something-year-old male with first and second degree burns on his upper torso."

Within a minute, the tones tripped my radio into making the loud alert it had been programmed to do. Furthermore, the fire pager on my hip vibrated. These were my primary and secondary methods of making sure I got notified of 911 calls when working outside.

I stood with Larry at my sink using the sink hose to rinse his face, eyes, arms, and chest with cool well water. With a little coaching, I got him to keep wetting and cooling his own skin. I then pulled an IV bag from my medical kit. I hung it from a nail that I use for drying herbs. I spiked the bag, then with a bit of fiddling, connected the line to a nasal cannula typically used for supplying oxygen under a patient's nose. Instead, I used it to drip cool sterile saline over the bridge of his nose into both eyes then down his face. I checked his airway repeatedly, convincing myself that he likely kept his mouth shut when the furnace went up. When we breathe hot gases, we can burn the inside of our mouth and throat. Following the burns, the body triggers a swelling response. Sadly, that can kill people. His throat and mouth appeared unburned. Although the smell of booze, cigarette smoke, and dirty teeth nearly made me dive for my Vicks.

Instead of offering the polite and non-judgmental care that Aaron once did, I offered an opinion.

"Man, you should brush more. Then quit smoking. It will kill you."

Of course, exploding furnaces kill too.

"So, what happened?" I asked. Furnaces do not just happen to blow up. And given the position of the injuries, I could tell he faced the open door of the wood burning furnace when it went up.

"I poured used hydraulic oil in."

"And you were wearing a shirt, I assume?"

"I was," he answered humbly.

"Where is the shirt?"

"It was that fleece stuff. I pulled it off immediately."

Yes, American's favorite outdoor fabric melts and burns with tremendous ease.

"You got it off in time, I see." Had he left it on long, surgeons would be picking bits of melted plastic from scorched skin.

"I had a cotton tee under that."

I said, "May have saved your life or at least the skin on your chest."

"More ground rules," I added. "One, don't pour oil into a wood burning furnace that way again. Two, please don't wear synthetic fibers when working near heat and flame. That stuff is terrible." Easy to give advice to a man who won't listen: quit smoking; brush teeth; don't wear plastic fleece; and don't pour flammable oil on a fire in an enclosed furnace.

His burns were not that bad. Had he been a part of my family, I would have treated him at home. He remained an occasional friend with his own suite of issues. I was not going to provide at-home care for this neighbor. Regrettably, the ambulance stopped halfway down the drive. It could not advance past Larry's Jeep. The ambulance stood about fifty meters from the door.

My radio informed me: "15A1 on scene."

A lady walked into my kitchen where I still wore orange chainsaw chaps with a radio clipped to the belt. She assessed my kitchen as the incident scene. A well-trained EMT would be asking herself: Where is the fire? What here can hurt me? What caused the issue? What is the mechanism of injury? How is the patient?

Instead, she looked at the wet mess around my kitchen sink. The first words she chose to say were: "You can't do that!" She used a loud, commanding tone, a perfect tone for an incident commander assessing hazards.

"Do what?" I asked.

"You can't use IVs," she yelled at me, pointing.

"Maybe I should introduce myself to you?"

"I know who you are," she retorted with aggression.

I ignored the comment. "I am Alex Flynn, paramedic and chief of Trowbridge EMS." I got no reply. "Can I ask your name and certification level?"

"My name is Jules. I am a nurse." That is a funny and nebulous term in pre-hospital care. First, nurses are not licensed to perform care outside of a clinical setting. Typically, when nurses work on ambulances, they also get their EMT or paramedic so that they can protect their nursing license. Second, people toss the term "nurse" around loosely. A nurse can be a licensed nursing assistant, a limited practical nurse, a registered nurse, all the way up to a nurse practitioner. That range covers skills from being certified to wipe an ass up through the authority to diagnose illness and write prescriptions. Arriving on site with an ambulance saying, "I am a nurse," gave me several hints. First, not an EMT. Second, not a registered nurse. Most of those would say, "RN" as in "I am an RN."

I surmised that Jules was not certified for prehospital care. If Jules provided nursing care, it was at the lower end of the nursing spectrum—aiding with bathing and changing linens.

"Do you have a stretcher? And do you have an EMT on board?"

"Someone parked a Jeep in our way. He's trying to push the cot around."

"That someone with the Jeep is our patient, this guy. And his name is Larry. Larry, this is Jules. She is with the ambulance. Larry has first degree burns on his chest and face. Vital signs are all normal. So far, we have been treating with cool water."

"Please step aside. I am in charge now."

Regrettably, those were the words Jules said aloud.

"I will be very happy to hand over care of the patient. But we will comply with the common courtesies and the law both. I must hand over care to someone who is at least an EMT." The law stated that I must hand over care to someone of equal or higher certification level. The practicality of that rule is absurd. While I assessed the patient with the training and skills of a paramedic, I can hand the care off to an EMT because I did not engage in any treatment beyond the EMT level.

"You'll have to terminate the IV. We cannot do IVs."

"Jules, I did not do an IV. What you see is sterile saline that is dripped in the eyes and down the face."

The skirmish had begun.

"Jules," I kept using her name, "why don't you go outside and tell your EMT partner that I will walk the patient to the rig then do the hand off there."

Yes, I had to hear another round of "I am the ambulance, I am in charge." Which I ignored.

Jules walked to the patient's left, gripping his red and burned arm as if the patient were either a prisoner at risk of fleeing or someone with walking problems. Larry looked repeatedly at the squeezing hand, deciding to remain quiet. I might have yelled, "Let my fucking arm go, it is burned, you bitch." Not my arm. And Larry opted not to yell those words.

I briefed the guy at the ambulance. This guy was the same guy who performed the bloodborne pathogen class—the class where nine people spilt chocolate sauce on purple nitrile gloves then threw chocolate-covered gloves across the room. His name was Gary Healy, a paramedic with a region-wide reputation. I greeted him warmly as if he hadn't just told his wife to charge into my house and take control of the patient. He helped Larry into the rig. Gary Healy, paramedic, then laid a plastic blood pressure cuff on first-degree burns. I turned around before he hit the green button to inflate the cuff. I did not need to see that, nor hear that. Jules Healy climbed in the side door of the ambulance.

Walking back to the house, I looked in the Jeep for keys. As expected, they remained in the ignition, a courtesy extended to people on farms and large properties. Vehicles have to be moved: tractors need to pass, trucks make deliveries, etc.

I keyed my microphone. "Dispatch. Trowbridge Command."

"Trowbridge."

"Trowbridge command terminated. Patient with the ambulance.

All units in service, in quarters." Rather appropriate as I walked through my front door, stepping into my quarters. From the dining room window, I observed Gary, the licensed paramedic, climb from the back, then climb into the front. With a clear and masculine voice, I heard him announce: "15A1 en route to Winchester Memorial with 1."

I witnessed a paramedic leave the care of a mildly burned patient to his uncertified wife. Not only an illegal crew, but in terms of fudging around the law, the sole licensed person hopped behind the steering wheel for the forty-five-minute-long drive to the hospital. Any call billed to insurance, especially Medicare and Medicaid, must have two licensed people on board. Each patient in the back must be, or should be, attended by a certified person.

Skirmishes, unlike battles, fail to identify a winner. Loony Larry got the care he needed at the hospital. The ambulance service billed Larry's insurance for the full value of the trip. The dust-up in the kitchen and the rest should all be forgotten, forgiven, then ignored.

Months later, Larry rolled an ATV, or quadbike, in the orchard. I got there within five minutes. The unofficial assessment involved me silently repeating the phrase that the gods protect drunks and fools. No helmet, of course, left him with abrasions on his head and face and right arm. His arm had been mildly crushed, but no obvious diagnoseable fractures. He had full range of motion in his arms and neck. Larry had been up and pacing before my arrival, likely yelling at the same gods who protected him. My rapid assessment included a process called *clearing the cervical spine*. Back in my early days, any crash like this would prompt us to strap the patient tightly to a backboard and immobilize the head and neck. We basically splinted the entire body from the scalp to the soles of the feet. The dreaded fear of any EMT going through state and national exams involved seeing a patient slide a few centimeters. The examiners loved to test the tightness of a backboarding effort by tipping the board with its patient to its side. Fail that, a candidate must redo the station or possibly take the entire exam again. The exam reinforced the requirement to strap patients tightly. Which of course is horribly uncomfortable and possibly damaging. Laying that flat while tied down can cause sores. It often causes pain, and even more pain to patients with curvy spines: scoliosis or lordosis. In my later cycles through the training, I found that laying flat on a board messed up my own blood pressure then caused an extremely crippling headache. It became so bad that I could not volunteer as a test-dummy for any classmate.

EMTs, medics, doctors, nurses—we are all taught to diagnose based on evidence, then treat what we can the best we can and work within scope. Except when backboarding a patient. In this case, we strap a patient to a two-meter-long flat board because of what-might-have-happened and what-could-be-wrong. We had been required to do it if there was a remote possibility of actual injury. With evidence-based medicine, you treat based on signs, symptoms, and findings during an examination. Slapping a human on a backboard, then strapping them tightly, immobilizing the person from skull to feet was done on the presumption that falling from a two-meter high has been presumed to cause harm, regardless of what an exam determined.

Eventually, some were taught how to identify potential injuries though a process called *clearing the c-spine*. Using guided movements, we ask the patient to make precise movements: up, down, left, right. We palpate the neck and head for actual pain and other symptoms such as broken bony bits. We only immobilize the neck if we find evidence of injury, or we believe the risk of injury is greater without immobilizing.

Here was Larry pacing around his tipped over four-wheeler. No helmet present. Scratches and bumps. I did a complete c-spine assessment per the book. Then the ambulance arrived from Langford. Four guys got off of the rig. Yellow backboard in tow, two medical bags, a blue-and-white cervical collar. One poor bastard trying to push the cot through the rows of apple trees.

Without a word, the lead ambulance guy came up behind Larry, grabbing his head in a death grip. "We need to get you immobilized," he yelled into Larry's ear. "Stop moving."

Larry did stand still because two strong hands pinched his head between his own ears. "We're going to get a collar on you."

Larry yelled. He yelled loudly and broke free, stepping towards me. I put up my hands, telling the ambulance crew to slow down and even calm down. People never calm down when they are told to calm down. They also do not respond well to the hand gestures indicating that they ought to slow down and ease up. Larry used a goodly amount of Anglo-Saxon profanity as he broke free and chastised anyone for grabbing someone's head from behind. "You could have unscrewed my head." My occasional friend Loony Larry had long ago been diagnosed with a suite of mental health issues, some of which were treated with medications. Larry treated the remaining symptoms with a toxic combination of cigarettes, marijuana, and a lot of booze. The occasionality of our friendship happened mid-swing for him between the dark and the light. I avoided his extremes.

I introduced myself to this crew. "Good afternoon. I am Alex, a paramedic and chief of the EMS team here in Trowbridge. I have already cleared Larry's c-spine."

"You are not allowed to do that." Aggression and anger at the start.

"Can I suggest that you do not touch a patient nor my friend Larry without talking to him or asking his permission?" Another classroom lesson. Touching a patient without permission is criminal battery, or criminal assault depending on your state. In Vermont, it is assault. I opted to keep the law lessons to myself.

"Larry is doing pretty well. A few bumps and bruises. He was up and walking when I got here. He said that he never lost consciousness." The stretcher finally arrived. The ambulance crew lowered it to knee height, swept the pillows and blankets to the ground, then put the yellow backboard down on the cot.

"Sir, you need to sit here." A fellow pointed to the hard plastic board. As per the training from a decade ago, they remained insistent that Larry lay down on the board to be strapped like an unruly psych patient. They wanted to…they believed that were required to physically restrain this patient with six wide nylon straps. I feared Larry had been restrained in his past. He never admitted to all of his meds. As I learned young, "All patients lie." I think Larry obscured how deeply his history with mental illness went. I did not need to pry, and I did not require facts to honor his history.

"Guys, I am still in charge until I hand the patient over to you. And I am going to walk him to your ambulance. Then please do not restrain him to a backboard. I'll call medical control on your behalf telling them that I cleared his c-spine."

I heard and ignored the choruses of "you can't do that." And "stop" and such. Some guy grabbed my arm. I broke free of that grip.

"Don't touch me," I said calmly and quietly.

I got grabbed again. I turned rapidly. I had my right foot behind the fellow's ankle. I thought of pushing him over so that I put his ass on the orchard grass.

With an attempt at sincerity, I apologized. "That was a reflexive action. I am sorry. Please never grab or touch me again." I turned towards the ambulance with Larry at my side.

Our two squads had drawn formal battle lines. Different color uniforms stood facing each other on a New England hill, ready to fight. We looked like soldiers on Bunker Hill or Breed's Hill near Boston or the solders who stood their ground in the hills near Bennington. New England hills know the trauma of battles. We looked like the Minutemen facing off against the British.

After I got Larry to the rig and settled, Regina, a fellow Bostonian, informed me that as close as I came to punching a fellow, someone was about to push me from behind. With pride, Regina observed that all of our team were ready to drop their medical kits to brawl on that hill.

I asked Regina about the Langford crew. She was a fellow refugee of Langford Ambulance and a current resident of that town. She narrated while pointing at the only certified Langford person at the scene. Regina pointed to the next fellow, identifying him as a firefighter.

Then she said, "Those two, they are both perpetual EMT students. They keep taking the class over and over."

I interpreted that as they took the Vermont EMT or Vermont first responder class then either failed the exams or did not attempt the exams. Yet, again, an illegal crew took an ambulance to an emergency scene without meeting the minimum crew requirements for billing nor state law. State law does permit ambulances to respond with an EMT and one first responder. The first responder takes the state-recognized advanced first aid class. Then after the class, the candidate must pass a state exams. Even when a crew meets the state's legal minimum, they may fall short of the federal requirement to bill for the service.

Larry did ask me to ride with him. I explained that with four on the rig, I couldn't go.

My crew, our crew, each showed up wearing our uniform. Each shirt with embroidered names, each shoulder with a state or national certification patch. We looked like a professional crew.

We stood our ground on this hillside. We had three paramedics and one EMT. They had one EMT and three *JAFOs*—a military term meaning: Just Another Fucking Observer. If you aren't licensed as a first responder, EMT or paramedic, then you are just an observer.

As a reminder, I got shit-canned from Langford Rescue for cutting a ring from a grossly swollen finger. I saved a finger while attending EMT school for the second time. Yet on this hillside, I got yelled at by non-licensed idiots who arrived to provide medical care to my patient.

I called Harry at the end of the day, painting a picture of our crew standing in a loose formation in new uniform shirts. We had our backs to the sun. Langford's ratty-looking crew approaching us from the north and slightly downhill. Unlike the Boston Massacre of 1770 or the battle of Lexington Green of 1775, nobody fired a shot. The scene did not erupt into violence. I asked my assistant chief that evening if I could be liable, given I handed our patient to an incomplete crew.

"Alex, they had the ambulance. They responded with a crew of four. I heard them over the radio. Their own rules state that they never leave the barn without a full crew. Therefore, if they left their station in their ambulance then they had a full legal crew."

"And how was I to know otherwise?"

"Right. Did you see patches?"

"No. But they were not wearing uniforms. Mainly jeans and T-shirts."

"That's what goes in your report. You handed a patient over to a crew that reported themselves as a full crew over the airwaves."

"When I sit for the interrogation, I raise my eyebrows saying, 'Shocked, shocked, gambling at Rick's?'"

"That's it. Pure innocence."

"Sure. I am the picture of innocence."

"I did not say that, Alex. I know you better than that." His tone pointed towards humor.

Weeks later, dispatch alerted me to a motorcycle accident on the state highway. I did not know if the scene was in Trowbridge or Langford. I was visiting a friend nearby. I grabbed him. "Let's go."

Ok, he was not certified and never before expressed interest in 911 services. I thought I could leverage his time with the army and his sense of nostalgia. *Maybe,* I thought, *Al is an EMT in the making.*

A fast three-minute drive found us parking in the middle of the two-lane paved highway. I cocked the vehicle, creating a barrier across the paved two-lane road. The vehicle crash site and the patient sat one-hundred meters on our side of the Trowbridge line. This was my show in my town. The patient's riding companion showed me a belt he had placed around the leg.

"Al, come here." I barked at my recruit. "We need a tourniquet. For now, pull this belt as tight as you can." He held the end of the belt while standing. I smiled at this veteran. "Sorry, my friend, you'll need to get a bit dirtier than that." I positioned him on the ground. One hand on the thigh at the belt's buckle. It was then that I noticed the nine-millimeter semiautomatic clipped to his right hip. The other hand pulling the belt tight with all he had. I cut the leather legging free of the human leg below. Most of the people standing on the highway stepped back. I examined the parts of the leg.

I walked to my truck for more equipment and a moment to think.

"Dispatch, Trowbridge Command."

"Trowbridge."

"Start a helicopter to the scene for ninety percent traumatic amputation above the left knee. More to follow. Please request medics to the scene for pain control." Given Trowbridge has several medics, the state refused to grant the agency a paramedic license. We were licensed at the Advanced EMT level. Without the paramedic license, we could not carry narcotics for pain control.

I returned with a large trauma bag. I laid in a modern military-style tourniquet using the small black stick as a windless. I cranked until most of the blood stopped. The audience, as I came to think of the looky-loos, grimaced and groaned. Those that still watched.

"A-One, help me roll her up." The fact that Al's lunch and breakfast remained in his belly proved he may yet make a good EMT or medic. "Let's get her on a blanket." I laid out a cheap wool blanket next to the patient, scrunching about half next to her body. We rolled her. I got part of the blanket under half of her. She groaned from her barely conscious state. She now lay on a crumpled pile of wool. We rolled her the other way, again inflicting a lot of pain. I rapidly pulled the blanket up and around. We now had a means of lifting her and carrying her. The wool blanket under her and wrapped around her permitted us to keep her warmer than she would be in open air laying on pavement. I loosely draped large trauma dressings around the flesh and visible bone.

I took a clinical set of vital signs and noted the time of the tourniquet. I opened the blanket. I cut up the arm of her leather jacket, then her cotton shirt. I sunk a large-bore IV needle into one elbow, started an IV. Al, now dubbed "A-One," held the IV bag for me. I scampered around to the other side. I put another IV into the forearm on the other side after cutting the sleeves off. I covered her top again. Then scampered to her feet. I removed the leather riding boot from her good foot quickly. I pulled the sock down. I cut right up the outside of her leathers. Then made another cut up her jeans, right through the waistband.

On the left side, I cut the boot free. I cut the sock free. I cut all denim and leather I could find free of the lower portion of the leg, throwing the debris to the pavement. I had the looky-loos in full revolt at this time. Some nauseated. Some complained of my harsh and rapid movements. Some complained of the pain the unconscious patient must be feeling. I then cut up the outer seam of the leathers on the upper leg, then the denim. The leather and jeans lay passively on top of her body. I repeated the same with the torso. The clothing remained to provide warmth and afford a bit of modesty. In our game, especially with trauma, we adhere to the old saying: "EMS means *everyone must strip*."

Once, working as an EMT at a motorcycle race, I responded to a fellow with several broken bones in his leg. He threatened to kill me if I cut his leathers. "The goddamn bones will heal, and they are insured. I can't afford more leather." He proved to me he would wiggle out of his leather pants with multiple fractures in his leg. He was a tough bastard, thoroughly conscious, and committed to his sport. This woman seemed rather like a weekend warrior with expensive gear. I destroyed her leathers in an effort to keep as much of her alive as I could.

Gary Healy, the medic with Langford Ambulance, had been standing silently by. It took me a minute to recognize him in the crowd. Al served as my helper. Gary watched like the rest of the looky-loos. Like others in the audience, he appeared rather green. I made eye contact, then nodded to him. I looked up. The ambulance was also there.

I tried to send mental messages about fetching the cot and doing something useful. I nodded my head towards the rig.

"Gary, let's get the cot and wheel her to the ambulance."

Gary wheeled the cot back. He had the yellow backboard laying on the empty cot. They lowered it. Four of us hoisted the patient to the cot. Several of the looky-loos grabbed corners of the cot, pushing it rapidly to the ambulance.

"A-One, pick up all my medical crap and bring it to the rig. Leave the trash."

I climbed in the rig before the patient, getting the EKG machine and oxygen and airway stuff prepared. Gary stood on the ground and the other fellow climbed in.

"You out," I barked at the unlicensed JAFO. "Gary. Come through the side door. Can you do airway and EKG? I'll do the rest."

I had heard the rumors about Gary Healy and how he responded to blood and smells. I gave him the easy job. "Don't worry," I reiterated, "I'll take care of the leg." I shifted to the side bench. Al tossed my kits in after me. The fact that this woman had a blood pressure of 110 over 60 impressed me. It impressed me about the human body. Arteries, which carry blood away from the heart, have muscles. During trauma, they can recoil and close themselves off, especially with clean cuts.

I leaned to the radio console next to Gary. "Dispatch, Trowbridge. Status of the bird?"

"15A1, airborne. ETA thirty-minutes." The radios, especially the higher-powered radios mounted in vehicles, transmit a hidden code that splashes the unit number on the dispatcher's console.

We can make any of three hospitals in about forty-five minutes from this location. We had a decision to make. Do we leave this area racing to meet the helicopter at a hospital or do we stay? The drive requires crossing a mountain pass east if we go east, or a mountain pass west if we go west.

As a courtesy to Gary, the man in charge of the ambulance, I say, "What do you think about the elementary school as a landing zone?"

He looked at me oddly. "Sure?"

Using the radio, "Dispatch Trowbridge Command."

"Trowbridge."

"Tone Langford fire, request an LZ at their elementary school. We'll be enroute there in a bit. And maybe tone Trowbridge fire to manage the scene on the highway."

Al banged on the side door, then opened it.

"What would you like me to do?"

"Follow us in my truck, if you don't mind. There is a bottle of alcohol hand cleaner in the driver's side door pocket. Maybe clean your hands a bit before climbing in." Like me, he had a lot of blood from his elbows down.

"Gary, can you tell your guy to get us moving?"

I felt the truck shift gears. On went the siren, then I felt the peddle slam to the floor. I shouted aggressively to the front. "Slow down. We have twenty minutes to drive two miles. You can travel at a walking pace. We need it smooth and slow."

I emplaced a cervical collar on the unconscious patient. I debated splinting the leg. It seemed useless. First the flight medics would need to see the injury after they fully stripped her. Second, there was not much left to splint.

In a black sharpie, I wrote a "T" plus the time on her forehead. This is an old school trick showed to me by Aaron, a Vietnam combat medic. Anyone assessing this patient will know that a tourniquet had been applied and know the time. I cut the rest of her clothing free. On her right chest, I wrote my initial vital signs in black marker with the time. I pulled the remainder of the shirt and leather jacket from under her body. I then worked to free the remaining elements of the jeans and leathers from her bottom half.

"Dispatch 15A1."

"15A1," they answered.

"15A1, can you ask someone at the scene to bring her companion to the LZ. We need a name, DOB, medical history."

"15A1 requests personal data from the scene."

Gone are the days of Denny making an informal pair of clicks in acknowledgement.

I examined the patient as we bumped into the ballfields behind the elementary school. I asked myself, "Is there anything else that I can do?" The answer was no. She needed a surgeon.

Gary and I performed a professional handoff to the flight crew. I briefed, while we swung a naked trauma patient with two IVs from one cot to another. I pulled our EKG tabs as they put on their EKG tabs. I tapped the unconscious woman on the shoulder, silently wishing her luck.

Gary thanked me for my help.

I thanked him for his help.

Finally, détente.

Within two days, Harry and I were back calling each other when Langford Rescue missed a call after dispatch toned them three times. We kept a tally sheet of missed calls.

Missed calls, we assumed, resulted from an insufficient number of volunteers, or poor planning for volunteer shifts.

12 | Détente

In the spirit of détente, I attended a fire company meeting. The Trowbridge Fire Company, like Trowbridge EMS, is a non-profit corporation separate from the Town of Trowbridge. Each agency asks the town for funding at town meeting while denying the town's government authority over the agencies. The relationship comes from the olden days. Some modern towns reserve the right to appoint the chief fire officer. Other towns have folded their fire services into the town's dominion.

I attended the meetings to build relationships in our shared mission. Fire and EMS often respond together then work together.

"Hey," I waved, "I am Alex. As you guys know, I am a paramedic. I thought that since we will often be responding together, I thought maybe…" I trailed off, not knowing how to finish that statement. Frankly, I still wanted to join the fire company. I might not even be a paramedic, nor chief of an EMS agency, had I joined the fire company that first time I tried. Now I sat in a meeting room holding the proverbial olive branch. After two meetings, I headed to my first non-medical fire calls: downed power lines during a thunderstorm.

It was four months of meetings and responding to calls before the men of the fire company voted me into their ranks. I think their vote superseded the fire chief's desires. Chief Thomas Reed demonstrated that he wanted little to do with me. Given this organization operated more like a club, federal and state employment laws are not applicable. You get nominated to the company by one or more members. Another member seconds the motion. The company votes. Nobody gets paid; therefore, the common usage of employment does not apply. In a tip-of-the-hat at the twenty-first century, firefighters got worker's compensation through the town, thereby achieving a tentative balance between independent club and an employer. As a club, the fire company voted to determine membership and elected its own officers without interference from the town's select board. As an employer, each member had insurance against injury at emergency scenes.

I learned that I enjoyed standing at the edge of a road with a stop/slow paddle chatting with drivers. I rushed to the scene. I assessed patients. Then, when I handed them off to the ambulance, I directed traffic instead of returning home.

People invited our EMS squad to standby at town events. We edged our way into the monthly senior meals where we tested blood pressures and blood sugar levels.

One of my quiet pleasures involved being flagged down by a local fellow. I was certain he should not be driving at all. During recent years, he had already bumped into several trees and stones. Thankfully, he drives slowly. Harry and I have discussed the possibility of issuing Trowbridge driver's licenses—a license that is good enough only to pass through the village to the post office and back. It is hard to live here without a vehicle. You can't get mail. You can't get food. You can't get toiletries without a car. This ancient fellow in a less ancient truck waved me to a stop. In an accent that even I had trouble understanding, he asked me for a *physick*.

"Got a physick?"

At first, I could not discern the words. He repeated himself: "Got a physick?"

"I don't think so. Are you having troubles?"

Maybe I heard *collywobbles* and something about gas. Hard to know. The accent might be a bit strong. The missing teeth exacerbated the communications.

"If you do need anything, you know how to reach me. Just dial 911, I'll be there." I called Harry from home. His answer confirmed that I had been asked for something that settles the stomach. "Like what, Alka-Seltzer?"

"Maybe. Or sodium bicarb, more likely. Or a Tums. Who knows."

"Not in the protocol."

In truth some of what I do fell beyond the limits of our protocols. I decided to prevent a few 911 calls by visiting with people. I checked blood sugars at kitchen tables and reviewed medications. I checked blood pressures. We're likely not supposed to check on patients before they call 911.

Maybe I chased one lovely lady from town entirely, like an old-timey sheriff.

She took a small one room cottage the size of Manhattan efficiency. She suffered from post-polio syndrome. She called 911 when in pain. She called 911 when needing help getting from the bed. She called 911 when she had fallen. She called 911 when stuck on the pot. When she had been the only person to call 911 in a week and done it four times, I endeavored to explain how our services work.

The first eight times, I walked in with a smile. I assisted her back to her bed and comfort. On the eleventh visit in one month, I endeavored to find a gentle tone for a harsh message.

I said, "We get no state funding. We are unpaid volunteers. When I respond to a 911 call, I give up paying work in order to come help. When anyone responds to calls, we give something up. We give up pay. We give up labor we planned for our properties. We give up time with family. We give up leisure time. The town paid us five thousand dollars a year which goes to resupplying medical equipment, paying for fuel, and helping offset the cost of continuing education." She called four more times. Twice I basically forced her to be transported by Langford's ambulance. Finally, she recognized the challenge of being forty-five to sixty minutes from a community hospital.

After she left, I believed I behaved like a sheriff from a quiet western town out beyond the dusty plains. "Well, ma'am, we can't have any of your sort in town. You need to move on." Maybe I did. Where is the balance? The town did not elect to fund a proper public health agency. We do not have a town nurse and the town does not provide personal care attendants.

How would Aaron have handled this situation? The man found ways of providing people what they needed in their deepest moments of need. Instead of acting with his grace, I behaved like the village bully. I valued my time and my income over the needs of a woman who wanted to live in beautiful Trowbridge. There are times that I wanted to talk with Aaron. Sometimes only just to show off my accomplishments. I remember that he soothed the roar others silently heard in their heads. I wished he could do the same for me now, today. Yet, chatting with Harry in the early morning helped.

I had tried to find Aaron on social media. I lost track of his last name. No doubt my mother stored his contacts in her little black book. Most internet records do not stretch into the early 1980s. I now see my own youth through a grainy and fuzzy veneer similar to my mother's own childhood in North Cambridge. Aaron No-Last-Name, EMT for Atlantic Ambulance and registered nurse, cannot be found without more details. Nearly no one puts Atlantic Ambulance on their digital resume. Without more data, I could not triangulate him better.

I should have looked harder for my mother's little black book before I moved her into an independent living place. My mother, ever a force, packed herself and cleaned her own house before we toted a few boxes and three suitcases from my childhood home for the last time. The next time I got rolled in a wave of nostalgia, I had no one to ask. Both of my parents had passed on.

Brighid Doran followed me home one day after a call to assist with a diabetic emergency. The call was easy. Brighid did an expert job with her patient assessment and checking blood sugars. Instead of opening the plastic squeeze tube of glucose the squad had issued to everyone, she went to the refrigerator. She returned with a metal container of maple syrup and small cup designed for a toddler. She poured about thirty milliliters, two tablespoons worth, into the cup, roughly the same dosage recommended by our protocols. The patient's blood sugars came up followed by an unprovoked rant on the part of the male homeowner. Brie and I had parked our trucks on his lawn. Brie and I had both commented on the Connecticut plates on the very high-end SUV.

Brie plunked down in my office chair. She was new to EMS, like so many of our recruits. She did well through the EMT class, exhibiting a familiar determination and precision.

"Why do they do that?"

I didn't have an answer. I had heard the aggression too. After ranting about having to walk up his own driveway, which he had paved thank you very much, he actually said, "I pay your salary." That carried his rant a bit further, then he actually yelled, "Hey, I know the governor." Frankly, I was bored listening to this second homeowner here on vacation. While I had not come far from my own urban roots, at least I tried to feel the rhythms of Trowbridge. We both walked out while he continued his rant.

"What do I do about this guy if I go back?"

"You go back. And maybe we both apologize for his lawn." Yeah, ok, we both backed our trucks around his sports car and left tire impressions on his overly manicured lawn.

"Seriously, Alex."

"I am serious. You'll be sitting in that chair again talking about death and horror. You'll be rattled to your core after you see your first suicide and you will forget this asshat. Me, I think you are asking the wrong question."

She looked at me oddly with a half-cocked face resembling a cute pup expressing confusion and question.

"I think the question is what are we doing wrong?"

"We did everything right?"

"No, not about the call. You were perfect, but I do think that the syrup was a gift for someone back home. Who buys syrup in containers that small? That wasn't enough for five cups of tea or one stack of waffles. Stupid." I paused. In these hills, people bake with maple syrup and put it on morning oatmeal. "I think I learned that we are failing to get our message transmitted correctly."

I felt like Aaron putting down his nursing book in the front seat of Unit 26, offering the young me a lesson. Brie was a decade or more younger than I. She looked a vaguely like one of the classic women of Hollywood's golden age, except more fit and more athletic.

"Maybe we should communicate our funding needs better, somehow. Nobody knows that we are working for actual free. We respond to your house because you are a neighbor who needed help."

"Even if we were paid, we should be treated better." The statement came close to a whine from a woman who does not seem to be a whiner.

I let silence have a moment.

"You came in from California?" I asked Brie.

Brie responds, "Yeah. But I lived all over before that. Sam has been here all of her life and our house has been in her family for two centuries."

"That is a stunning house." Brie smiled at my comment. I continued, "In LA county, they have three thousand firefighters and ten helicopters that are all paid with pensions. In New York state, volunteers slowly buy their way into the state's pension system. Nobody sees that the taxes they pay in Vermont fall short of the expenses required to keep Vermont open."

I'd never said that aloud before. We both heard the sentence as it faded away.

"It's true," Brie responded.

"Our town budget balances every year at town meeting like magic. Any surplus goes towards reducing taxes. If we ran short, we increase taxes for a year. Tax revenue and expenses have remained balanced for three hundred years. But we never tally the stuff that doesn't get tallied."

She added, "Like my time, like your time."

"Like the cash donations to EMS and fire and the libraries and the hospice programs and rest. All of that accounting is off-book."

"Each May, we all spent a Saturday picking up trash after the winter's snow," Brighid started the thought.

I finished, "A hundred people give three or four hours. Say four hundred hours at ten dollars an hour, for easy math. That is four-thousand dollars. It might be better if we accounted for that time. The town's people pay one way or the other. Either cash or labor."

Her turn to interrupt the flow. "Except for the jackass with blue plates. He only sees his tax bill for the house he and the family visits twice a year. He gets to say 'I pay my taxes and you work for me.' So we need to account for the unaccounted."

"Or we need to show the imbalance," I said with imperial wisdom.

"How?" Brighid asked, deflating me.

Yeah, how? That does appear to be the question. These tiny towns, like Trowbridge and Langford, attract both retiring people and wealthy people from other states. Vermont's taxes appear high. Yet, the taxes for folks moving in from out-of-state and the taxes for people with vacation homes are supplemented by locals who volunteer their time to provide services. In Vermont, a fire company may tax the fire district for its services. In Trowbridge, Chief Reed, who hates all taxes and most all governments, refuses to tax the citizens for providing a qualified firefighting agency with modern and safe equipment. Instead, he adheres to the old tradition of soliciting donations.

Fire departments in New York, Connecticut, and New Jersey all ask for donations. Yet, those departments are taxpayer funded. The state regulates the training and equipment for the members. In Trowbridge, Vermont, people transplanted from other states believe that Vermont operates the same way as their home state. The logic goes thus: We pay taxes. The taxes fund services. The services we get were paid by taxes. We broke that logic by asking healthy adults to volunteer their time to pick up trash, to respond to emergency calls, and sit on town committees. The time and money donated by locals got obscured with very public financial bookkeeping. Let's admit that five grand per year does not fund a rescue squad. When we ask for donations, these families often state that they paid their taxes.

To Brie, I said, "How indeed. I am tired of hearing the phrase: 'Why should I donate, I already pay my taxes.' And 'You were just sitting in an empty station waiting for a call to come in. I did you a favor in this sleepy town.'"

"I've heard it too. I've actually heard it from my own mother. Why are you doing this for free, you could get killed, she said to me last year when I told her I joined the squad."

"Brighid, no doubt you walked away from billable work today for this call?"

"Yes. You?"

"Of course," I answered. Thankfully neither of us fled back to our desks. "I am thinking of taking some shifts with Stark EMS?"

"Really. What will that pay?"

"They start medics at $14.50 per hour."

Brie and I both worked as consultants, selling our time to clients. I basically worked for Uncle Sam, but my hours got paid by whichever defense contractor had the current contract. Brie did research and wrote reports for corporate clients often related to mergers and acquisitions. From my observations, she dug through the darker side of people, companies, and their activities. Her wife, Sam, served as a military intelligence officer in the U.S. Army reserves, except she appeared to work full time in that capacity. Brie and I likely billed about the same for our time. Maybe Brie with her corporate clients got a bit more than I.

"You can afford that?" The question was sincere.

"I'll do a few weekend shifts, just to keep my skills up."

"I've heard your opinion of Nick."

"No, you haven't." I smiled when I said it.

"Ok, maybe you haven't said it, but… I think I know your opinion of Nick. Didn't he install his own mother as the chair of the board of trustees?"

"Yes?" I furrowed my brows in mock questioning. I had not said any of this aloud to Brighid Doran. I had said similar words to Harry.

"Didn't he take control of the EMS district board?"

"He did." Again, watching a woman whose facts echoed mine.

"And now you'll take a job as his employee?"

"I was thinking about it," I answered.

"Ok."

I had decided to take a paying job with Stark EMS and accept Nick as my boss. The station was twenty-five miles from my house. As a board member, I still had to apply for employment. I handed over my credentials. They ran a background check and validated my Vermont paramedic license, which I did not have. The state records my license as an Advanced EMT. But I am certified in Massachusetts and nationally as a paramedic. Somehow, I now faced the need to challenge the state's paramedic exam. I was not afforded automatic reciprocity. Bureaucracy.

"Frankly, I thought I'd get more experience and have my Vermont certificate upgraded to paramedic."

"You are already a paramedic."

"Only in Mass and nationally."

Home Depot and McDonalds would both pay me more for doing less.

Brighid looked at me like we'd been friends for decades. Yet, this was her second time in my house and we'd met one year prior. Her look challenged me.

"What if I forget how to differentiate cardiac rhythms? It has been two years since seeing first-, second-, and third-degree AV blocks."

As an urban EMT, I spent minutes with a patient. We raced time.

As a rural medic, we raced time, but it often got measured in hours. Rural medics occasionally work through each step in an expansive protocol. We attempted mechanical fixes using our hands. Then we attempted medications, often stepping through several tiers of doses and combinations.

I added, "I think I need to push myself and get the most out of my education."

She looked at me, saying nothing.

Never in Cambridge did I deal with a nearly amputated leg. If I did, I would have scooped up the patient then been at a trauma center in a few minutes. Scoop and run. Later, we referred to this as providing a *bolus of diesel*. The term means a dose of a drug given via an IV. But when everything is failing, the solution may require burning more diesel as the team pushes the ambulance to the limits. A few hours per month in a paramedic ambulance would remind me of the skills I was not using in Trowbridge. Part of my frustration was that I had been trained as a medic. I ran a rescue squad with more medics than most first responder agencies, yet the district prevented us from upgrading our agency license beyond the advanced EMT level.

I did join Stark EMS wishing later that I had listened to Brighid. It felt like the old days spending weekends in someone else's bunk room with someone else's fouled up sense of corporate culture. Within months of my joining Stark EMS, several other members of Trowbridge EMS joined as well, including two of my fellow paramedics. About that time, Trowbridge EMS got our first mutual aid call from Langford.

I had heard dispatch tone Langford Ambulance once, then twice, looking for crew. Their one full-time guy sat on the air in a running ambulance waiting. Then I heard it on my radio: "15A1 requesting mutual aid from Trowbridge for 1 EMT."

In a split second, I keyed my mic. "Dispatch, 14RC1 responding to Langford Station."

I jumped into my EMT uniform trousers, pulled on a hospital scrub shirt, then started speeding to the station. "14RC1, head to the scene. Meet you there."

Mike bypassed radio etiquette.

"Dispatch 14RC1."

"RC1."

"Direct to scene."

Our détente reached a new level. Someone at Langford Rescue decided that they could tone Trowbridge to augment their crews.

I got a text from Erik Mason. "Can we meet?"

"Sure."

He gave me the address for a sawmill. "7:00 a.m. tomorrow?"

"See you there."

I arrived with a mug of home-brewed iced tea.

We sat at a wooden cable spool that served as a table. Short logs had been sculpted into chairs.

He stuck out his hand in greeting. A rare occurrence in these hills. "Thank you for responding the other day."

"Hey, no problem. I was pleased to be asked."

"Can I get you coffee?"

"No, I have tea in the truck. I'll get it, if you want to get yourself a coffee?"

We sat at the improveded blue table. "I am going to run for chief of Langford Ambulance." I looked at this young man in his twenties. "I work full time as an advanced EMT for Warrenton Ambulance."

"I heard. Nice job getting your *A*." The advanced EMT, or *A*, takes one or two more semesters after the initial EMT basic course, which is about one semester. Not as lengthy as a paramedic, but hard work.

"I moved back home to help my mother. I can't take what is going on with Langford. The old guys can't do much about me given my family has been here for a couple of centuries. They are not doing their training. A lot of the old guys keep their memberships while letting their first responder or EMT cards lapse. I think we need some new blood and new ideas."

"Been thinking that for a long time," I answered. "Harry, my assistant chief, and I keep a score card of calls responded and calls missed each week. It is getting bad." I left out my knowledge of their frequent use of incomplete and illegal crews. For each run they make with an illegal crew, they face a dilemma: do they commit fraud by placing a certified person on the call's paperwork? Or, do they skip the fraud, thus digging a deeper financial hole? I would likely commit a bit of light-weight fraud. How does patient care get affected by the certification of the person driving the ambulance?

"If I am elected, can we keep talking? Could we find a way through this?"

I see his plan. "If you are elected, you'd like us to join you?"

"No. I can't do that. But maybe we work out a deal for mutual aid. If we need someone, we tone Trowbridge."

"And if we have people free, they will respond to help your ambulance?" I finished the thought for him.

"That's the basic idea."

A lot of rural yards use wire spools as tables and yard furniture. This spool would stand as tall as me if it were upright. I looked around the log yard and sawmill for another artifact. I wanted to brand our agreement. Will it be the "Wire Spool Accords" or "Timberyard Agreement?"

I stuck my hand out. Erik embraced it. We shook, deliberately acknowledging a new level of commitment between the two agencies. We both hoped that the feuding would stop.

The chat ended when dispatch toned Langford Ambulance and Trowbridge EMS to respond in Trowbridge.

"See you there."

"I can't go. I have to work here today. This is the family business."

I hopped into the truck hoping that Mike, the day-shift-guy, would respond. Dispatch toned Langford twice more while Mike waited for a crew to arrive.

"Dispatch, 15A1, can you ask if Trowbridge can supply crew for transport?" I heard the ambulance call. I answered in the affirmative then sprinted off with lights and siren.

I was second on the scene. Regina, a fellow paramedic with both Trowbridge and Stark EMS, arrived minutes before me. We walked up to the house together. "I just met with Erik. We came to some accord. He wants to run for chief of Langford Ambulance."

"Huh, interesting. I wonder how that will go."

We stood at the door of a newish house. It was only twenty or thirty years old, unlike so many of the homes here that had been built in the late 1700s and early 1800s. We knocked. "Rescue!"

"Hello? Rescue is here."

"Did anyone call 911?"

We heard yelling from upstairs. We looked at each other,

shrugged then let ourselves in. We both yelled "Rescue" a lot and "Hello" a lot.

Entering the upstairs bedroom, we encountered a man with no trousers. He paced the room, yelling at the unseen. Fecal matter sat on the floor and the bed and in a dried trail from the adjoining bathroom. Regina and I both spied the rifle leaning against the wall under the picture window. Our patient paced, muttered, and yelled. We looked at a rifle.

I tried my telepathy with Regina. I eyed the rifle. My silent message was: "call him to you. I'll walk to the wall." For the first time in decades, someone understood. Regina coaxed the patient toward her. The patient responded by shuffling. While she distracted him, I stepped toward the rifle. In a smooth move, I opened the bolt, caught the chambered round as it fell. I released the bolt. I leaned the rifle back where it was. One bullet and one bolt tucked neatly into my thigh pocket. I debated opening the bedside drawers looking for loaded pistols. I thought the movement and noise may escalate the situation. If there were one or more loaded pistols in the drawer, then they would stay there.

Regina said, "Let's go downstairs," guiding our patient towards the ground floor. I found a clean-ish pair of shorts hanging from a drawer front. I grabbed them as the three of us stepped carefully down the stairs. I scooted around the house, carrying a kitchen chair into the foyer. We sat our patient. Regina took vital signs and asked the normal medical questions of a patient: recent medical history, recent meals, allergies, medications, and the rest. Meanwhile, I did a bit of sleuthing: first upstairs in the bathroom for medications, prescribed and other. I bagged those in a small red biohazard bag. I searched in the kitchen looking for the M-T-W-T-F-S-S container that held pills for each day of the week. I opened the fridge, gaining a better understanding of our patient's illness. The Vicks under my nose barely protected me from the smell. I caught sour milk plus something truly gone off.

I returned to the foyer to check on Regina and the patient.

"I am going to do a little clearing out in the fridge. And whatever is going on, we can't rule out food poisoning as well."

I found a trash bag. With little fanfare, I hoisted most of what was in the fridge into the bag. I closed it with an overhand knot, then placed it a goodly distance from the rear door. Some critter will revel in what reviled me.

When I returned to the foyer, Mike and Regina were preparing our patient for being wheeled to the ambulance. I had a handful of meds, each with Russell Southworth written on the bottles. I carried medications for high blood pressure, anxiety, mood stabilizers, gastric reflux, and enough narcotics to kill several human beings. None of the meds explained the current situation. Narcotics tend to trigger constipation. We have a patient walking about his house dribbling from his backside. The patient's answers to our questions make little sense. The most difficult diagnosis involves two disease processes interacting with each other. Changes to metabolic chemistry and an infectious process can alter the mental state of a patient. My classic memory aid comes from the number of times I thought I witnessed a stroke in an elderly female patient who had a urinary tract infection. Clear up the UTI then the mental acuity returns to her prior baseline. Mr. Southworth endured an altered mental state. It might be triggered by an infection. Or the altered mental state could be the result of his failure to comply with other medications. This provided a pathway for an infection like clostridium difficile.

I spied the ambulance, 15A1, turned around and ready to load. Then I returned to the kitchen. I cleaned a bit of the sink then washed with hot water and soap from elbows down. I grabbed an unopened roll of paper towels, tore the plastic off. Washed again, then dried with towels. I gloved up again. I then carried the clean towels to the foyer.

"Regina, these towels are clean. Water in kitchen is hot. This could be c-diff." And left out, it could be Hepatitis A, or salmonella, or pretty much anything. She peeled off her gloves, dropping them on the foyer's floor. Mike and I wheeled the patient out.

Regina came out carrying the clean roll of paper towel. Her hands were ungloved. She looked at me, "So who is going with Mike?"

I looked at her bare hands. "I'll shoot you for it. Odds or evens?"

"Evens."

"One. Two. Three." Instead of the classic display of fingers, Regina pointed at me and my thumb pointed at me.

"I guess that is me," I said. I reached into the compartment by the door. I handed a small red biohazard bag to Regina, indicating she gets to pick up dirty gloves and such. I stripped my gloves off, then handed Regina the rifle bolt and bullet.

"I'll drive, if you like?"

I stepped to the front. I climbed in then washed again with an alcohol mix. Of course, this is when my nose gets itchy. My fingers have some nasty bug swimming at the tips. Every bug wants to find a way to my gut. Therefore, the bugs on my fingers tell my nose it is itchy. I'll scratch. In a few days, I'll be as inside-out as this guy is. While educated enough about anatomy and physiology to discount worries and fabricated stories, I did have an itchy nose made worse by requiring I not itch it.

Mike and I washed down the cot, the back of the ambulance, the front of the ambulance, and especially the steering wheel after we dropped the patient into a private room in the ER. The team immediately hung isolation warning signs, then placed a cart with yellow gowns and gloves at the patient's door.

With the rig bathed, I washed my hands, arms, and face in the ER with warm water and their harsh soaps. Sitting in the rig next to Mike, I felt my face and hands dry, getting itchier.

Mike and I enjoyed a casual and wandering conversation on the way home. He asked me questions about the old days in Cambridge. I told him how I nearly failed my first CPR class because I did compressions slightly faster than the required sixty-beats-per-minute. What was once a point of failure, even shame, is now established practice. Today, we are supposed to do CPR at one-hundred beats per minute with the mantra "hard, fast, and deep."

Mike dropped me back at my truck. We enjoyed a polite conversational argument. I suggested he drop me on the paved road then I would walk up to the patient's house and my truck. Mike insisted on driving me up the small hill and performing another tight turn-around. Mike won, of course. He held the steering wheel; therefore, he could do as he wanted. Also, he scored a fair point about personal safety. Given that we didn't know what was going on with the property and who else was around, it was best that we stuck together until I was in my truck where I had my radios and a means of fleeing.

Mike made the u-turn, dropped me off, and I watched the old ambulance bounce down the road.

The next time I saw Mike, he came up behind me. I had been on scene for twenty minutes. I could see a body laying on the ground through the floor-to-ceiling picture window. The body's chest rose and settled with each slow breath. I could see shadows cast from a few veins. The patient had a vein that would normally travel vertically down his forehead. Except his forehead was on the wood floor and the vein shadow ran left to right pointing to one closed eye.

I had circled the house once slowly looking for any path in: an open window, an unlocked door.

When Mike found me, I stood at the front door. I spied a dead-bolt lock in the normal place that held the door extremely tightly. Like a complete idiot, I tried to smash the glass with my portable radio. It bounced badly as I hit the bullet-proof polycarbonate window. I need a Halligan bar or a firefighting axe.

Mike picked up a rock from the edge of the road. He stepped in. The window caused the rock to bounce.

"Any other way?" he asked in a pleading voice.

"I walked around and tried every window. This guy has some real paranoia going on."

"Or maybe they really are after him."

We stepped around to the big windows. I tapped it with my now-broken portable radio. The window did not tink, clink, or have that snappy sound of normal glass. It sounded like hitting plastic with something hard.

"Dispatch, Trowbridge Command," I called. When they answered, I said, "Can you tone Trowbridge Fire to bring a set of irons to the scene to assist with forcing an entry." The combination of the Halligan tool plus the heavy fire axe is called the "irons." Within a few minutes, Robby came up the road with the tools in his personal truck.

With a helmet on, he confidently slipped the teeth of the Halligan between the door and door jam. He forced the necessary gap, but we could not free the door. He stepped back to his truck, donned his turnout coat, and grabbed gloves. He gave the window a mighty overhead swing with the pointiest tip that his heavy axe offered. Then again, then again. Like shattering a car's windshield, the window yielded only a bit at a time. With a hole big enough, Robby reached through to unlock the door.

We all tried the now unlocked door again. We all failed.

Robby then beat the living shit out of the window, removing it from the frame. Mike and I boosted him through the window. Robby rolled when he hit the ground. Looking back at the door, he said, "There is a metal bar that spans the entire length."

Robby opened the door.

We got to the patient. His breathing rate had dropped below ten per minute. The pupils of both eyes appeared pinpoint in shape. "Anybody got Narcan in their pockets?"

Mike said, "I'll go get some."

I yelled out, "Bring an IV kit too."

Mike squirted Narcan into a nostril while I started an IV after cutting the guy's shirt up the arm. Robby positioned the ambulance and prepped the stretcher at the bottom of the short stairway. He came in with a white cotton hospital blanket and a white sheet.

We rolled the fellow over, placing him onto the blanket/sheet combo. We picked him up. I took the legs. Mike and Robby each grabbed near the head and shoulders. The patient started coming to as we stepped towards the mess of the front door. He yelled a bit and complained as we placed him on the cot. I placed the rarely used shoulder straps on the patient, then cinched them tight with the chest strap. Mike pulled the waist strap extra tight. Robby strapped the feet down tightly as well.

The Narcan counteracts the effect of narcotics. Narcotics reduce the drive to breathe, and they make the pupils constrict. Narcotics kill by causing the patient to stop breathing. When these patients wake fully, they can be angry, combative, or otherwise difficult to manage.

Mike and I looked at each other. We did not have the familiarity of true partners, but we had done a few calls together. He looked at me with my glittering gold paramedic patch on my shoulder, then said, "All yours."

We three lifted the patient into the back of the rig. I shouted my thanks to Robby as he closed the rear door. I cut the rest of the patient's shirt off. I emplaced the EKG leads: "White, right. Smoke over fire." I saw a normal sinus rhythm. The pulse oximeter showed me that the patient was sitting at eight-five percent oxygen saturation on room air. I put a nasal oxygen cannula on. In a minute, the oxygen level perked up to ninety-five percent. I attached a 500-milliliter bag of saline. I assessed the patient's eyeballs and breathing rate again. While not fully conscious, he was slightly responsive. His eyeballs were slightly less constricted. His respiratory rate hovered at twelve and the oxygen saturation level in his blood appeared tolerable. I opened the med kit, taking out two more doses of Narcan.

Narcan displaces opioids from their receptors in the human body. Narcan's half-life is about forty-five minutes. Regrettably, the half-life of opioids can be four hours. As we travel, the Narcan will wear off and the opioids floating in the blood stream will re-affix to their receptors. The patient's breathing rate will drop, and the eyes will constrict again.

If I give another full dose of Narcan now, the patient may fully revive. Suddenly, I am in the back of an ambulance with a patient who could be combative. Maybe we ruined his best high. Maybe he attempted suicide. Maybe he likes the feeling of narcotics on his brain.

I certainly do not need that fight while traveling terrible roads over mountainous terrain in the back of this rig.

As we descended the hills towards Starkville, I eased a few ccs of Narcan into the IV line. During the thirty minutes, I witnessed the Narcan reduce its effectiveness. Approaching the hospital, I delivered the last drops of the second dose.

We wheeled a patient through the door who was breathing on his own and responded slightly to stimulus. In my brief, I stated that we gave two full doses of Narcan during the recent hour.

After leaving the E.R., Mike said, "As an A-EMT, I can only give full doses and I have to give it via the nose. The state is talking about having us do it via IV." Almost an apology, but an unnecessary one.

"As a medic, I am supposed to give full doses. And I did." To myself, I added the phrase *just at my own pace*. "Did you look at the medication bottles?"

"No. Not really. I scooped them up. Most were painkillers."

I added, "All were signed by Doctor Kantel."

"Not surprised."

"Yeah, but every OD? Doesn't it get obvious?"

"He isn't very good with diagnosing anything. That is why they call him Doctor Kantel-death. He couldn't diagnose a dead body in a casket. Running a pill-mill helps pay the mortgage."

"Seems stupid." The thought of ratting out Old Doc Kantel-death to the DEA crossed my mind. I have been a rat before. Maybe I should do it again?

By the end of the summer, Erik Mason had worked himself into the chief slot. He found the section of the bylaws that required each elected officer must hold a valid EMS certificate. A painless coup d'état. Within a month, he passed a new set of bylaws that granted voting rights to members who were duly licensed by the State of Vermont. A generation of older volunteers stopped attending the meetings including Gil Horne, the former chief of Langford Rescue. While seated at our blue electrical wire spool, Erik said that Gil decided to let his EMT certification lapse.

At the table were Erik, me, Regina, and Robby. We discussed the future.

In Trowbridge, we have a crew of nine members, five of whom have paramedic-level certifications. In Langford, they have six members with current certifications.

We asked ourselves, is it possible to run an ambulance and EMS squad with fifteen people and cover eighty square miles of sparsely populated hilly terrain served primarily with gravel roads?

13 | Pig Roast

With five years of operational success, Harry and I decided we ought to celebrate. We had started an EMS agency. In five years, we had never missed a call. Furthermore, we discovered peace with our neighbors in Langford.

We dreamed up a party. I described a sit-down affair in the town's community hall. I suggested that we hire someone to prepare a meal. Then from a podium, we present awards and give speeches. As a high school athlete, I felt comfortable with the format. Each year with each team, we had awards dinners. The format also reminded me of the dinners with my father, Captain Flynn, where he spoke in front of famous people.

Harry, my assistant chief, identified the flaw in my thinking. Our crew, our crews if we include the Langford team, were too restless to sit still. In fact, he described himself in that characterization. He also pointed out that the community hall prohibits any booze. No booze, no party. Even if we implemented the rule of no booze, people would sip from mason jars regardless.

He waved his arms about at his farm with chickens, guineas, ducks, and geese strutting about the open yards. "We need this." He pointed to his farm. "Imagine people with jars of white lightning, bottles of beer, and a pile of food," he said. "People will lean on their trucks, sit on their trucks, and chat."

I thought of our people in neat uniforms with linen napkins. Harry envisioned our people standing in jeans over open fires, or boiling water. Of course, Harry won the argument. Within a week, we found a local farmer who pulled a smoker behind his truck. The trailer can smoke or barbeque anything. The same guy from Rowanhill Farm provided a pig, the equipment, and a cook. We needed to provide the field and the crowd.

Awkwardly, each squad held their own monthly meetings separately. Each squad held their own training sessions, separately. Each squad passed awkwardly phrased statements of mutual aid. Langford passed a rule that members of Trowbridge Rescue may retrieve Langford's ambulance and operate it without Langford members present. Our squad passed a similar motion permitting Langford folks to attend our training and respond with us in Trowbridge. We had better training.

Regina held firm that she would never rejoin Langford Ambulance. "No." She did welcome them into our training and meetings.

In years past, Regina and I both got fired from Langford Ambulance. We both grew to hate them. We both spent years keeping tallies of their foul-ups. We ticked off the missed calls. We measured the long delays in getting crews out the door. We scored the frequency of having Trent Valley Rescue come to the area with their ambulances to cover calls missed by Langford.

I listened to Regina, now a friend, and her firm no. "I am not joining them. I will never join them. And I will never go to a meeting over there again." Shame and humiliation leave deep scares.

My firm "no" started softening from that meeting with Erik. *What if... What if*, I asked.

It was like dating. Not the rash crazy dating I did as a kid sneaking home wearing someone else's clothing. Back then in Cambridge and Boston, I would make eye contact with a fellow human being, then a drink, a dance, then a roll or romp. Sometimes we stood. Sometimes, we made it to an apartment. Then AIDS. AIDS changed the clubs, and the landscape.

The flirtation with Langford Ambulance resembled two mature people, each stinging from their pasts, deciding to have supper together. Both teams moved slowly. We'd both been hurt before. We both acknowledged risks. I am older now. As a kid, I looked like the actor Mary Stuart Masterson. Especially in the movie *Some Kind of Wonderful*. My jaw presented more squarely; my face a bit wider; my shoulders, bigger; and my eyebrows, darker. Furthermore, my nose is softer, squishy, and rounded. I love the aquiline nature of Mary

Stuart Masterson's nose. Me, I got the button nose of my ancestors. Between watching friends catch AIDS, then die from AIDS and simply aging, my dating matured. If I were out looking for dates these days, I would approach dating the way Trowbridge and Langford have flirted. Iced tea at a make-shift table in a lumber yard, followed by a few adventures outside—that seems like a modern approach to dating especially after your fortieth birthday. Or am I approaching my fiftieth?

Wallowing in blood to the elbows might not resemble a modern dating activity. For this crowd, it works. You see the mettle of a person during these times of stress. You measure how well people react and move. You measure how people deal with stress. Once upon a time, my dating criteria involved fitness, tight skin, and that thing that made me ready-to-go. Today, if I were dating, my criteria include riding in a truck together, talking slowly, and dealing with the stressful matters of family, aging, and rural and farm life.

I see the world through the same eyes I had at twenty, twenty-one, and twenty-two on the streets of Cambridge and Boston. People do not see me the way they once saw me, as if I have changed. At the core, I am the same person who I was then. I get confused when driving in Cambridge. Then I get confused about being confused. Why do I fumble and feel lost on the streets of my own cities? Is it me? Am I changing? Maybe both of us aged and changed? The cities changed in hundreds or thousands of ways. I regret forgetting the names of the people I once had sex with. Yet, honestly, I did not know every name. I regret forgetting the names of people I once cherished. I lost track of Aaron the moment I put my feet on the Appalachian Trail. Within a few years, I forgot his last name, but never once did I forget the gold flecks in his leather-brown eyes. The dog tags that he made for me still hang in my office as yet another keepsake. I've got that board of shoulder patches and foreign currency. I see the dog tags with my old EMT number.

I approach my own maudlin thoughts by telling the fire radio to send me to a call: a fast drive, a bit of fun, something to do other than paperwork for four hours, then home to settle back into a bucolic life and a small flock of birds pecking through my yards.

Looking at my yard, I saw the possibility of a party. Compared to Harry's farm, my place has flat spots near the house and drive. I envisioned a pickup truck with a long black trailer roasting a pig over Vermont hardwoods. I can put a few portable toilets at the edge of the forest. I texted Harry: "This could work!"

He texted back, "What would?" Honestly, he texted a question mark.

I replied, "We could host the event at my house. Pig roast."

The challenge with Harry's place is that one faces uphill or downhill or one can stand sideways to the hill, feeling a bit unstable.

Standing at his place, he once said, "I kept trying to breed sheep with two long left legs and two shorter right legs."

"So, what happened?"

"I'd get one generation going pretty well, then I got lambs with long legs on their right side. And on the third generation, they accidentally bred with each other. Then I had sheep that could either go up a hill but not down it or go down a hill but not up it. Either their front legs were too long, or their rear legs were too long."

Looking around my flat-ish property, I envisioned a bluegrass band playing for the crews and their families, chickens running around, geese threatening children, ducks waddling with utter sincerity.

In a few phone calls and a few days of effort, I booked the pig roaster from Rowanhill Farm. I hired a local band and arranged for blue poopers to be delivered. I called Trent Valley Rescue, informing them that every EMT and paramedic in Langford and Trowbridge would be comfortably sloshed by 2:00 p.m. on the longest day of the year, a Saturday. I called dispatch arranging for Trent Valley Rescue to be toned automatically to every call in our jurisdiction. With the approaching summer, Harry, Regina, and I printed up a few award certificates and ordered presentation gifts. We invited the selectboards from both towns. We invited our local state representative. I even invited Thomas Reed, Trowbridge's fire chief.

Following a small car in Snelland, I got intensely frustrated with the slow rate of travel and the hesitation at each turn: here's a drive, let's look. Here's a farm field, is this the turn? I felt like that jack-booted Boston cop who once rear-ended a brown Datsun. The road curved as all Vermont roads do: left, right, up, down. Sometimes up and right, down and left. I could not find a legal way around this poke with a pale blue Connecticut license plate.

Finally, saved by the tones:

"Trowbridge Fire, Rescue, Langford Ambulance, respond in Trowbridge for a two car *MVC* with injuries."

Someone up there listened to me. I hit the emergency lights then blasted on the siren en route to a motor vehicle crash. The driver came to a full and abrupt stop in the middle of the road. I accelerated around her, then looked back once before she disappeared behind the green forest. I was gone in a second.

I understand the randomness of 911 calls. I acknowledge that no gods dedicate time to listening for my pleas. I'll beg for no calls. I'll beg for a call. Yet, out of respect, I'll never utter, nor think that a day is "quiet." The gods do turn their ears towards that hubris. A call is random. My thoughts are random. Calls come when I do not want them. Calls come when I do want them.

At the scene, I got yelled at by a sergeant from the Vermont State Police.

"You parked on critical evidence," he barked.

"In fact, I did not, Sergeant. Those tire tracks are perfectly preserved." I pointed to the dirt. I saw what he saw, except I saw it thirty minutes earlier. The dusty edge of the road had perfectly formed tire tracks with deep groves preserved in the loose gravel. I had spent thirty minutes telling people to not step on those tracks.

"Look how close you parked."

"I did park close." The voice in my head finished the sentence, *to preserve the stupid track*. "I also have photos for you as a backup. And you know me."

We both looked at apparent evidence that the red BMW drove off the road then down the embankment without breaking. Had the driver applied the brakes or even turned, then the tracks would show that. These tracks begged the question, did the operator intend to drive off the road in a suicidal effort? Or was the driver asleep?

The sergeant then worked his way down the steep embankment. I think he yelled at me in an effort to avoid that climb. In the glove box, the sergeant found two pill bottles both containing prescription opioids. Both bottles had been prescribed by my favorite local physician, Doctor Kantel. This fellow can't tell fakers from whiners. Like the old mantra from Boston Garden, he likely mumbled: *Need a pill, gotta pill.*

"Where's the patient?" the cop asked.

"Winchester Memorial."

"How is the patient?"

"Mostly asleep, or mostly passed out."

"Drunk?"

"He was in an altered mental state," I answered professionally.

"Did you use Narcan on him?"

"We did not use any on scene."

"Drugs on board?" he asked.

I know that there is a mic running. When the little red light in the grill of their cruiser is lit, then their mics record everything they hear. Instead of answering, I pointed to the two bottles that the cop discovered in the glove box. I also pointed to the glass bottle on the floor below the passenger's seat.

"I did not look under the seat, but I heard one of the firefighters say something." The cop opened the damaged passenger door, turned on a flashlight.

"Got a glove?"

In fact, I held a pair for him. When he asked, I put them in his hands. He retrieved a Glock from under the seat. With two bottles of narcotics, an empty whisky bottle, and a pistol, the cop then looked up the steep incline back to the road.

"Some of the guys have been going that way." I pointed to a freshening path that ran parallel to the road.

"Thanks."

I walked back to the cruiser while he prepared an evidence bag and box. We occasionally know what happens before these crises. Sometimes people tell us stories. Within a few hours, the drama disappears into the wind as if beech leaves rustled. I used to wonder. Is this guy in jail? Was he arrested? Was he attempting suicide? Maybe he beat his spouse then fled. Maybe his lover left him for another? My life, our life, can be like walking through a movie theater for exactly one scene.

My parents once hired a babysitter for me on a Saturday night. They had plans for a fancy night, like a police function or maybe an evening with the local mystery writers. Instead of watching my normal kid-friendly shows, this babysitter insisted on *The Creature Double Feature* on WLVI, Channel 56 out of Boston. Hating the show, I walked out before it started. I hated the rubber monsters and phony vampires; women in gauze dresses screaming and bleeding. Regrettably, I walked in just as a pair of heads looked through a stormy window to find their two bodies laying there. Yes, of course, the heads talked. And moved. They had been searching for their bodies. I never knew how the movie started. I never knew how it ended. All of my life, I carried this image of bodyless heads seeking the rest of their corpses.

That's the life of a medic. You see only the middle. Often, you see only the worst. When the scene ends, the internal movie continues. Unlike the horrible movies on Channel 56, my own movies have no director, no plot, and no story other than a flow of unguided images.

I woke at the sound of the tones. I pivoted sitting at the edge of the bed, pulling on my EMT trousers and slipping into a hospital scrub shirt. I clipped the chattering radio to my belt. I peed hearing the nature of the call. The call arrived just as midnight approached. I knew the address. I knew the people that ran the camp site. I knew the property.

After flushing the toilet, I informed dispatch that I was responding.

I pushed the darkness out of the way as my headlights cast tree shadows on the forest wall. I came down the drive then pulled past the door. I was met by the owner.

"She is the bathroom."

Within two meters of me stood a bathroom door partly ajar. I dropped my kits and EKG machine on the floor. I walked in. A woman had fallen from the toilet. Her head wound did not bleed. I felt for a pulse at the carotid. In one movement, I pulled the woman from the bathroom to the hallway by her ankles. Her head bounced a bit over the threshold. I positioned the body in the middle of the hallway. I started CPR, pounding fast, deep, and hard. I paused occasionally during those initial minutes. I looked for blood pooling under the skin. I looked for rigor. I looked for any injury that would be *incompatible with life*. After five plus minutes of CPR, I paused long enough to set up my EKG machine and strip more clothing from my patient. Working alone, I stepped my way through each task described in the protocol. I established access with an intraosseous needle that I drilled into her leg. I started IV fluids and each required drug as described in the checklist. At twenty minutes, still alone on the scene, I stopped. I noted the time on my notecard. I noted all drugs I gave. I printed the EKG strip—a black flat line between my external CPR compressions. When I did nothing, the line did not waver.

I called dispatch informing them that they could cancel the ambulance. It had been at least forty-five minutes since we had all been toned out. I worked the code alone. With the radio notifications complete and written notes finalized, I called medical control at Winchester Memorial. We, the doctor and I, determined that time of death was at zero-zero-fifty-two, fifty-two minutes past midnight. Dispatch notified the Vermont State Police. Knowing that most VSP shifts end at 11:00 p.m., I expected it would be two hours before anyone else arrived.

To my surprise, the ambulance arrived at five minutes past one.

I met them at the door. While I assumed that I managed a "commode code," the slang term describing the process of having a heart attack while pooping, I had already pronounced and cancelled the ambulance. As incident commander, I had the responsibility of managing a potential crime scene.

At the door, I went for the tone of appreciation when I looked up at the name Langford Ambulance printed on the side of the rig. "Hey guys, thanks for coming out. Nothing we can do. I did cancel you."

Three guys climbed from the rig. One was a certified first responder. One was a firefighter. One was a fellow who takes the EMT class every couple of years, then fails the exam three times.

"You're not allowed to cancel us."

"There is nothing we can do. We have already pronounced. I am just waiting for VSP."

"You're not in charge. We are. We are the ambulance."

Oh damn, this crap again.

"I am sorry you feel that way. I am confident that we can sort this out with Erik Mason in the morning. I am sorry you guys came all this way."

"We need to come in."

"I am sorry. It is a crime scene now. Nothing I can do. Those are my instructions." As if someone gave me instructions. The three of them came at me as if acting out a scene from West Side Story. They screwed up their faces, giving me their best menacing look. One held a heavy flashlight.

I appreciated the owner stepping through the door at that moment. I had a witness.

"You are not allowed to call a code. You have to do CPR until we arrive."

"Oh man, that was so last century. And guys, we cannot stand at a scene and yell at each other. Please just go."

The three climbed into their rig. They drove off silently. They made no calls to dispatch.

I sat on the floor of the foyer for two hours. At one point, when the owner left me alone, I lay down with part of my EMT/trauma bag under my head. I did not really sleep. It is hard to sleep with a dead body a meter away. She needed nothing for me. And I could do nothing else except wait for the cops through the darkest part of the night.

I heard the crunch of gravel on the drive. Rising, I straightened myself out. I put on my uniform work shirt that included my name, rank insignia, and my certification patches. I opened the door as the cop climbed from his patrol car. His arms filled every millimeter of his short-sleeved shirt. The Kevlar vest and his pectorals strained the shirt's buttons. He looked like a Chippendale cop with the tear-away uniform.

"What the fuck are you doing?"

Oh no.

"The guys on the ambulance say you did not let them in and you did not treat the woman inside."

"I did treat the patient and followed the protocols." I did not know this cop. He had two gold stripes on his collar, informing me he was a corporal. I wore two eagles informing him that I was a chief. He had the yellow-and-green patch of the Vermont State Police. I wore the gold and blue patch of a nationally registered paramedic. He had cuffs, a pistol, and a taser. I had scissors, a stethoscope, and a small flashlight. We both had portable radios on our hips clipped to microphones hanging from our shoulders. His cop car has blue-and-white lights. My truck had red-and-white lights.

Me, I had a mobile phone sitting idle in my pocket. Suddenly, I wished I had turned it on to record audio.

"Should I take you inside?"

"No, you need to stand right here." I had an EKG and thousands of dollars of medical equipment and medications on the floor in there. I straightened it up some after stopping CPR, but my trainers informed me I could not remove my equipment from a crime scene until cleared by cops.

When he came outside, I had my mobile phone running on record mode. I also used it to call both Robby and Harry. "Come immediately."

The corporal asked me to sit in his squad car. I walked around to the passenger's side door.

"No, back here."

"Sorry, Corporal. I'll stand unless you are arresting me."

"You need to sit in the back." Sitting in the back of a police cruiser strides a line between detention and freedom. Most might recognize that when cops cuff people, they have been arrested or are about to be arrested. When a cop binds a person's hands, it means that the cop has seen enough to curtail freedom of movement. The less obvious maneuver involves inviting a civilian to sit in the back seat of a cop car. Look, no cuffs. They sat willingly. Until they look around. The back doors cannot be opened from the inside. The windows do not open. And there is a cage wall separating the back from the front. The backseat of a cop car is a portable jail cell.

"The back of your car has me locked in and detained. If you detain me, you must arrest me. If you arrest me, you'll need probable cause."

"What the fuck are you, some backwoods fucking lawyer?"

"No, Corporal, I am a cop's kid and I have been doing this for decades. We both respond to 911 calls. We can talk as peers, or you can arrest me." What charges might this VSP corporal be considering?

"You're not going anywhere." Words that sounded like verbal handcuffs, but I had the freedom to shuffle my feet and pace in circles.

He closed himself in his cruiser, using both his mobile phone and the radio.

I went to my truck. And that pissed him off. I dropped the tailgate of my truck. He climbed from the front seat of his cruiser, yelled at me a bit more, then retreated behind his steel-and-glass office.

Robby and Harry arrived within a minute of each other. They saw me standing by my truck with a cop's finger pointing and wagging in my face. "You are not allowed to quit CPR ever. That is the law. That is how I was trained and how everyone is trained."

"Corporal, your training is out of date."

Harry and Robby walked toward me and the cop, both wearing their uniforms. I felt relief. Alone in the woods, I feared the thoughts spinning through this cop's head. What could he arrest me for?

"Who the fuck are you two?"

"I called them. They are two officers on the squad."

"They can fucking leave the scene."

"Actually, no, I am still incident commander. I am in charge until I turn over command and there is no way I am handing it over to you."

"No, I am in charge. Don't move."

The cop returned to his cruiser.

Harry whispered, "The ambulance is blocking the driveway. We had to tear up some grass to get around them."

"Seriously?"

"Yup. What is going on here?"

"I did CPR for twenty minutes. I went through every step of the protocol, called med control, then this. The Langford guys told the cop that I am not allowed to pronounce nor stop CPR. They kept saying that they were in charge even though they arrived an hour later than I did—well, maybe forty-five minutes after me."

Robby said, "I never even heard them sign on."

I added, "And they never signed off on scene."

Harry asked, "Are they even certified?"

"One has his first aid card or something," I said, making light of the first responder certification. "They do not make a legal crew. That's for sure."

Robby asked, "What is the status?"

"My kit and EKG machine are inside."

Robby shook his head, then pointed his nose to the cop. Robby asked again, "What's going on with him?"

"At first, I didn't know. I believed that the Langford guys wound him up. Maybe he is considering criminal charges?" I answered.

Harry nodded. Robby studied the cop who was engaged in an

energetic conversation. His mouth moved. His hands provided emphasis. His eyes drilled through the glass.

Harry asked, "Murder?"

Robby looked. "He's working hard at convincing someone of something."

"Maybe I should have let him cuff-and-stuff me into the backseat, I'd know more." Instead of discussing the improbability of charging an experienced paramedic with homicide, I continued my brief to Robby and Harry. "It was a commode-code."

Robby did not know the term yet. I explained to him that the vagus nerve winds its way from the brain down the digestive tract, visits near the heart, and continues toward the rectum. When stimulated, the vagus nerve causes the body to slow down: heart rate slows and digestive juices flow. The vagus nerve shares responsibility for the parasympathetic response in the human body. After a good meal, the vagus nerve stimulates the rest-and-repose actions that aid in digestion. Straining at the toilet, or a large poop, can also stimulate this nerve. The phenomena occur frequently enough to have earned its own name—commode-code. "The dead lady is laying on the floor in the middle of the hallway."

We three sat on the tailgate of my truck. Robby on my left. Harry on my right. My thoughts got stuck within the sticky fabric of a web. The more I wiggled to get free, the worse the thoughts held on to my brain. Did he think that I killed her? I squirmed uncomfortably, desiring a different conclusion. The worst he could have said was that I had not followed the protocol. I debated recognizing that a cop could charge me with murder after failing to tick a box on an EMS checklist. *What if,* I asked myself, *he thought that I dropped her from the toilet, cracking her head on the tile floor?* That brings the accusation closer to murder. The gap between intention and manslaughter spanned the width of a single thought. I imagined the possible charges if this corporal thought that I had acted from malice or anger. My palms sweated. My heart rate accelerated.

Another uniformed cop arrived. Then nearly another hour later, a dark blue sedan arrived with two detectives in blue sport coats. I knew one, and maybe I knew the other. With so many crime scenes, I was not too sure. I pushed the anxiety I felt from my body following a lifetime of training and practice. I have faced worse and been in worse places.

We three got invited to sit at a picnic table. The detectives on one side. Me on the other. They pulled out a digital recorder. Harry and I both placed mobile phones on the table, making an additional two copies of the discussion. The detectives were purposefully calm.

"What happened tonight?"

I pulled my notepad from my lower leg pocket. A movement designed to demonstrate confidence and professionalism. I opened the notebook, pushing all doubt from my voice. I started with the text of the dispatch. I recounted each radio call with the time—yes, I called dispatch to get the detailed history. I read my notes informing them of each action I took.

"We were told that you dragged the patient from the bathroom."

"I did."

"Can you tell us why you moved the patient?"

"Because I cannot do CPR and give medications in a room that small."

"We understand that her head bounced."

"True. I dragged her by her heels. Her head traveled up then over the door's threshold."

"Shouldn't you have protected her head?"

"She was dead. Her head raised and lowered less than an inch. Did you look at the threshold?"

"We did. But what about the gash on her head?"

"As noted, that was there prior to my arrival."

"Ok continue, what did you do next?"

"I started CPR."

"Why? You just told us she was dead."

"Fair enough. She was not breathing, and she had no pulse. According to our protocols, that is treatable. I need more evidence prior to quitting or legally pronouncing her dead."

"Like what?"

"Like what?" These two cops had been to more crime scenes and dead body scenes than me. It seemed like a dumb question. I answered, "To start with, any sign of rigor mortis or dependent lividity. There are injuries we accept as *incompatible with life*. I think you both can picture that." Opting to remain polite, I did not ask them, *Do you want me to list those?*

"So, no obvious signs of death. Continue. What next?" The routine aspect of the questioning stilled the demons and monsters that expressed a desire to lash back.

"I started CPR, alone. I worked at that for a while, a few minutes. Then I took several five and ten second pauses to setup my EKG and other equipment. I got an IO started in leg below her knee."

"We saw that. What is that?"

"An intraosseous needle. I can drill them into a bone to establish access for fluids and medications." They looked at me blankly. "They were developed for combat medics."

"Doesn't that hurt?"

"She was dead. I needed access for fluids and medications."

They nodded, indicating that I ought to continue.

I walked through each step of the Advanced Cardiac Life Support protocol.

"How do you know all of this?"

"You mean what training did I have to become a paramedic? Or what? It is what I do."

"Can you show us this protocol?" one detective asked.

The other detective added, "Why don't you show us your IDs and credentials?"

"They are at home."

"Can you go home and get them?"

"Sure."

They looked at me.

"You mean now?"

"Yes," they answered. I climbed out of picnic table's middle seat, walking towards my truck.

"No, not that. They'll take you." Now the questions involved my qualification and legal status. I have worked at hundreds, if not thousands, of crime scenes. Never once has anyone asked me for identification beyond my uniform and my word.

Robby, Harry, and I drove silently back to my house. I grabbed my wallet, all of my certification cards, my various large format certifications. I grabbed the manual for advanced cardiac life support. Then I grabbed a printed copy of the Vermont EMS protocols.

On the silent but fast ride back to the scene, I re-read the protocols related to dead bodies and CPR. I easily put a check mark next to every required step.

Dawn broke with hints of purple in the east.

I spread my credentials and training materials on the table. My Vermont paramedic card. My national registry paramedic card. My ACLS certification card. My CPR certification card. The ACLS flip book. I opened the Vermont protocols to the required section.

The two detectives read through everything, snapping photos with a digital camera.

"I was also taught that we could never stop CPR," the older detective offered.

"Folks believed that and taught that for a while. The brain can go about three minutes without oxygen. CPR may be an effective stopgap measure or help restart a heart, but prolonged CPR has proven to be ineffectual. Frankly, guys, dead is dead."

The eastern sky lighted with greater speed.

At the table, the detectives called the associate medical examiner for the region, a man I have worked with for years.

"Do you have questions for Alex?"

The AME asked me a few softball questions about the scene as it was when I arrived. He asked about the duration of my travel and likely time span between the 911 call and my arrival on scene. I think he knew, as I did, that the patient was well dead before I even arrived. One hundred percent of my actions were a stage play honoring the protocols until all measures had been exhausted.

He asked me, "Were you alone?"

"I was."

"Was anyone else coming?"

"No one was on the radio network including the ambulance. In fact, I never even heard the ambulance sign on."

"Did their lack of response impact your care?"

"Sir, I followed the protocol to the letter."

By the time the interviews were done, and I had my documents back in my hands, the sun had risen above the pines, maples, and beeches.

The younger uniformed cop escorted Harry into the building. He gathered my equipment and tossed it on the back seat of my truck. I left the scene. I could see where the ambulance sat waiting. They left a few cigarette butts and two empty energy drinks cans. I drove home. In my rear view, I saw both Robby's truck and Harry's truck following me.

I seethed with anger.

Silently, we three walked into my kitchen. I paced. They sat.

"Why me?" Was I not the hero of my own story?

14 | Mushrooms

I regretted hosting the pig roast at my place. I regretted inviting a slappy-happy-shake-your-bottom bluegrass band. I regretted inviting Langford Ambulance to the affair. I dreaded going outside my own door to join the festivities. So did Regina. So did Robby. So did Harry. So did Al. So did Brighid.

Erik Mason, now chief of Langford Ambulance, attended with precisely two members of their agency—both Erik's friends, both Erik's allies. The former Langford chief Gil Horne skipped. Mike Foote, the full-time AEMT, proved to be a no-show. As did Gary and Jules Healy.

Tellingly, our own fire chief Thomas Reed begged off.

Erik, and his allies, spent the entire time apologizing for the behavior of their own crew. I expressed warmth and welcome. The warmth came from training at my mother's side. People invited to your home get a warm welcome—that's a rule. My father would invite overly enthusiastic young cops, youth offenders, tired worn-out old mobsters fresh from decades-long prison sentences. My mother endured murderers and thieves mowing her lawn and clearing her gutters while Boston's favorite cop sipped tea. If my mother can accept axe murders and rapists on her lawn, then I can accept a few well-meaning assholes on my lawn. If my mother ever said *no* to my father, my father would have stopped instantly. She never did.

I invited these people, all of these people, to witness my shame, and my humiliation.

While right, I faced off against a cop who would have arrested me within one heartbeat. I would have spent years clearing my name of the accusation. Had he locked me in the back of his cruiser, taken my phone, and cuffed my wrists, I would have never been able to stand strong again. The stink would have crept into my professional work. The stink would follow me through the grocery store. "There is that medic that killed a woman by dropping her on her head then faking CPR."

"Did you hear that the EMS chief in Trowbridge got off on a technicality?"

These phantoms joined the chorus of ghosts, demons, and other voices that ebb and flow with my case of *tinea mentis*. The mycelial tangles, triggered fresh, stirred the other hosts in the belfry. "You killed my aunt. I called for help then you killed her." The phantoms never bother with truth. In the light of day, I know the truth. In the light of day, I acknowledge the ghosts, demons, and phantoms of my nights. I should not be doing this work. I should not walk into someone else's crisis. That is their worst day. I am the guest character who walks into the horror show for one scene, then disappears. I barely get credit at the end of the movie. I am the Rosencrantz, or the Guildenstern, of someone else's play. I am the character who fusses over wounds and drags the dead off stage.

I smiled my mother's best smile. I told my father's best stories. I recounted the stupid, scary, brave, and ugly with my friends on my lawn eating moist pork that dripped fat onto my piles of rice with peas. Like everyone else at the party, I wore my radio on my hip. I looked around.

Was Harry hoping for a call too?

Was Robby?

Was Al? or Regina?

Was someone's car wreck, ATV crash, or house fire the only desired end to this party?

The moment the fiddler put his fiddle in the case, and the first amplifier turned off, people returned to their trucks. Some approached me to thank me and express pleasure at such a nice party. As if I failed to feel the irony. It was a dreadful party.

Harry, Robby, Al, Regina, and Brie appointed themselves to the clean up crew and cleaned up the yard quietly. We made a bonfire, set it, then passed a few jars of throat-burning crap. This crystal-clear liquid caused an instant headache. When it hit my stomach, I felt the immediate need to vomit. With my second jar of this shit, the vomit bubbled low in my esophagus. One of the many gooses in our bodies, the esophagus is. As an anatomy teacher once informed me, we are filled with gooses and ducks. We have the vay-goose nerve running from our brains to our assholes. We have the esopho-goose running from our mouths to our stomachs. The ducks outnumber the gooses. Starting with the tear ducks. I've got the bile duck now in rebellion over this mason jar drink. The pancreatic duck, the hepatic duck, and dozens of other ducks.

As the summer's evening dragged on, we sat at a smoldering fire. A few intrepid mosquitos found our alcohol-bathed blood.

How many times did civilians need to hear veterans' stories that begin with "remember…" I desired the blissful balance of never remembering the bad, while finding pride in the good and humor in the funny. It wasn't possible. When civilians heard me say, "When I was in the ER yesterday," they jumped in with, "Oh my god, I hope you are fine. What happened? You look ok." I then had to explain, I head to the ER several times a week. Car accidents and people falling from roofs just happened to me. Well, not that it just happens to me. People wrecked cars. People got sick. And people slipped on mountain trails. These five drunken people around this fire represent the thousands of humans who then answer other people's calls for help.

Al shot a burning log twice with his nine-millimeter pistol.

Regina, startled, yelled, "What the fuck are you doing?"

A-One answered, "I wanted to see the sparks."

Yes, it was dark enough now to see sparks launch skyward. "My fucking ears are ringing." Each of us sang a variation of the refrain. Harry said, "If you are going to shoot at a fire, then do it quietly." Harry slurred his words.

"How about not shooting at the fire? Do like a normal thirteen-year-old boy, poke at it with a stick."

Sam walked in from the darkness. She lifted Brighid's shoulders and torso then slid herself under wearing the inebriated woman as a lap blanket. She stroked her hair.

I did not sleep well that night. I never do after drinking. When I laid down on the sofa, it spun. When the sofa spun, my stomach spun. I retrieved the mop bucket from the mudroom. I laid on the sofa praying I would vomit; praying I would not vomit; praying I would sleep; praying I could sleep someday or some future night.

I had one emotion the next day. That emotion bounced off the walls within my brain. At first, that emotion was only sadness. Then it affirmed itself to me as anger. Then it informed me, the only emotion I felt was shame. Then the emotion declared itself to be disappointment. Over my breakfast tea, I saw Brie's truck still parked on the grass. Two hours later, it was gone. So, one guest demonstrated the wisdom to not wrap their drunken ass around a tree.

Two days later, I called Harry.

"We have a disciplinary issue we need to deal with," I said sternly.

"Yeah, who?"

"Me."

"You? What did you do this time?"

"I did CPR on a dead lady. I think I need time away. I am putting myself on suspension until I get rid of some of this anger."

"You think it will help?"

"It will help me. I'll head to DC for a week or so. Tag, you're it. Interim chief."

"Don't be out too long. Call me tomorrow."

I turned off all of the radios, scanners, pagers, and pulled the fuse for the truck-mounted radio. I drove to DC, setting up hotel rooms and meetings from the rest stops along the way. Everyone got an easy lie. I said to anyone and everyone, "I am in the area for a meeting." Then I set up meetings, lunches, and evening meals.

Harry texted me about each 911 call regardless of my desires to avoid them.

He, Regina, Brighid, Robby, Brie, A-One, and others decided to screw Langford. If they did not roll their ambulance within ten minutes, the crew started requesting alternate ambulances. They called Stark EMS, where Regina and I worked medic shifts. They called

Trent Valley Rescue with their ambulance. They started calling in mutual aid ambulances from Massachusetts as well. Each member of Trowbridge asserted their command over emergency scenes. Each member stood at the edge of a crisis saying: I am in charge. I'll find help.

I did not answer the phone when Erik Mason called. I texted one message that said: "In DC." I flipped another message that said: "Meetings." Then I stopped replying.

I returned home to Trowbridge ten days later. I did not inform Erik that I was home. I continued to ignore his calls although I read his email and his text messages. I did not respond, but I had read them.

It took three months of effort on Erik's part to get us to listen to him. As chief, he created a rule that only certified people could vote and only certified people could be officers. This immediately trimmed the size of a small ambulance service. While intended to protect me and others in Trowbridge from abuse, it meant that his service could not roll the ambulance out of the station reliably. The size and shape of Langford Ambulance kept morphing. As much as Erik wanted to rid the ambulance of not-certified people, we all understood the reality that one certified person in an ambulance can save a life, save a limb, or improve a life. One of theirs, one of ours, and an ambulance formed a legal and viable crew, if the two did not kill each other. Every time they responded to calls with one certified person, Erik faced a dilemma. Commit fraud or pay the bills. If the service adjusted the paperwork, then the insurance reimbursements would help pay for fuel, medical supplies, and Mike Foote's wages. If they did not adjust the paperwork, then the organization bled money. Erik faced a divergent path in a mountain wood: Provide care or commit felony fraud.

Stepping between the fraud charges and responding to 911 calls meant that Erik required a seasoned crew of certified people. Trowbridge had five times the number of paramedics Erik's Langford crew had. That's because he had exactly one. We had more EMTs than he had. If he could get us to respond from his station on his ambulance, then he could keep his agency afloat.

"Can we meet?"

"Sure," I texted back.

"Your kitchen table?"

Ugh. Really?

"Sure." I liked the kid, but I hated my history with his organization.

He sat down. I brewed chamomile tea, placing a mug and honey in front of him.

He started the conversation by saying, "We need to replace that old ambulance. Will you join a committee to help select, buy, and fund an ambulance?"

On another visit to my kitchen table, he sweetened the pot, "We'll add your unit patch to the back door and have 'serving Trowbridge and Langford' painted on both sides." He found my soft weakness. Ever since Bobby Clifton's custom paint job on his Unit 25 at Atlantic Ambulance, I wanted a touch of that. My own personal truck looks more like a professional rescue truck than a farm truck. I grew up in a house where the City of Boston bought my father a new car or SUV every few years. His shiny rides would be handed down to officers of lesser rank. It is a thing for me: I like a shiny, well-kept, modern emergency vehicle.

When the leaves hardened up and the children returned to school, I joined Erik's ad-hoc procurement committee. We selected a vendor for the ambulance. We scoured websites for grants. I called all over DC looking for funding. Erik and I started pledging real estate on the ambulance walls to donors just like a NASCAR team. Reed Family Trust would get a one-square-foot space on the left rear door. The Modise 9-11 Fund was granted an equivalent space on the right rear door.

Shortly after the regional ski areas opened for the winter season, we ordered the new rig. We still had a few months of fundraising and begging before we had to sign the finance papers. No, not me, I did not need to sign anything. Just Erik. Only the Langford chief signs the finance papers. The ambulance, for all the show of inclusion, would belong to Langford Rescue Squad, a non-profit ambulance service.

I returned from an EMS district meeting when the chair of the board and district doc both questioned Langford's decision to buy an ambulance.

Nick, the board chair and boss of Stark EMS, asked, "Why are they doing this?"

"The ambulance is twenty years old. Repair costs are climbing," I answered in defense.

"But they can't even staff it." So many more questions and thoughts whirled in Nick's brain. Was I sensing a paternal interest or worse, a self-interest that involved expanding his services footprint? Langford's failures and near death could not be a secret to anyone listening to the regional dispatch service. We all heard it over the dispatch radio: "Third tone for Langford Ambulance." Both Trent River Ambulance and Stark EMS placed crews in rigs ready to roll every time dispatch toned Langford. Sometimes, Stark started rolling a rig after Langford missed a tone or two. I know this from my occasional shifts there. We strutted towards an ambulance, confident that Langford would yet again miss a call. Nick finally asked, "Why are they buying an ambulance when they can't even staff one?"

"Without an ambulance," I answered, "they will miss one hundred percent of the calls."

"But the state requires staffing to cover all shifts," Nick said. He sat at the head of the conference table as chair of the committee. This district EMS board formed part of the state regulatory agency. He also acted as the chief of the largest regional ambulance service that relies on territory and volunteers as a pathway for revenue. He spoke as his interests were not compounded with the duality of his roles.

In January, I heard Regina responding to Langford station for the ambulance.

"Dispatch, 14RP3, responding to Langford Station," Regina called out. *RP* standing for rescue personnel.

From my radio, I said, "14RC1 responding direct to the scene." That marked her first time fetching the ambulance since they fired her. Leaving her house then heading to the station indicated progression towards the strategic merger that Erik Mason wanted and needed to keep Langford Ambulance operating.

By springtime, we learned to chat on the radio about someone remembering to fetch the ambulance. Often it was me as I lived close to the town line. Sometimes, it was Regina who lived in Langford.

"14RC1 responding to the station for the ambulance."

During one snowy night, I drove past the patient's house to retrieve the ambulance. I performed a controlled slide down the hill through the bumper-deep fresh snow. Pulling into the unplowed parking lot at the station, I called dispatch, asking for the Town of Langford to send out a plow. I drove the ambulance out of the garage. I scrapped a furrow through the snow. The furrow followed me to the state highway. I looked at the gentle incline. I saw only my wheel marks and the hints of my truck's undercarriage. The hill I needed to climb with this ambulance had about two feet of snow and in some places, the drifts brought the snow depth closer to a meter. I backed through a normally dangerous intersection, then with my on-spot chains flailing the chassis, I gave the engine all the diesel I could, sprinting toward the hill. I made it about halfway. I slid and backed down the incline. I backed through the intersection again setting up another running start. Striving to keep my wheels in the same ruts, I accelerated again.

On my third try, I notified dispatch that I could not get to the scene due to the snow. I turned the rig around. Then I tried climbing the hill backwards which proved difficult to control going up. Sliding downhill while facing downhill proved easier. At least I could see the road during the descent.

Robby's voice came through the radio: "We'll bring her down to you."

"Great."

I positioned the ambulance towards the paved highway and the nearest Vermont hospital.

We transferred the patient from Robbie's pickup truck. With me at the wheel and Regina in the back, I tried to climb up the unplowed state highway. I failed. "We're going to Mass!"

Returning from the hospital, we crossed the Vermont line from Mass on plowed roads. On the road home, we laughed. "The little squad that could," I said as we climbed a snowy hill. Our little rescue squad had commandeered an ambulance and ran a call in Langford for Langford. Of course, we did exactly what Erik had been asking for. We felt it was a coup on our part. Erik felt similar pride in manipulating us to help his squad survive.

In our hills, we see trailers that gradually transform themselves into wooden homes. The small mud room made of plywood becomes a new front porch, becomes a new front parlor with a spare room built off the back. The distinction between the mobile home and the wooden house blur. Our little squad of EMTs and paramedics, formed to improve the quality of life in Trowbridge, Vermont, blended with the local ambulance squad, possibly even taking over. It became difficult to draw a line between us and them. You sometimes see this in a forest too. A birch tree and a beech tree get their roots intertwined.

In June of that year, we got toned to a trail in the Green Mountain National Forest. These multiuse trails interlace with the Appalachian Trail, the Long Trail, and a network of snowmobile touring trails.

I sat on the tailgate of a small pickup truck following a parade of all-terrain vehicles towards our patients. Our caravan was met on scene by Langford firefighters who had scouted ahead finding the patients. Looking around I saw Gary Healy, the sole paramedic on the Langford squad.

"What do you know?"

"Not much. They say they ate mushrooms."

What I saw did not match what Gary, the medic, was telling me. One fellow, laying on soft green moss, shot nearly clear liquids from his bare ass. The woman next to him was vomiting profusely.

"What should we do?" I asked Gary. I gave him the courtesy as he was the ranking member of the Langford crew. Technically, I was the assistant because I responded as a mutual aid.

"Get them out?" he asked me.

"How about we get some fluid into them?" I asked back.

One member of the hiking party looked just-plain-sick. One member was kneeling at an ash tree, retching dryly. Two members laid on the ground.

I knew the answer to my next question. I hold Gary and his wife in so little regard, that I asked: "Which patients do you want?" He famously hates body fluids. He also gets car sick in the back of ambulances. As the lead medic, he ought to take the tougher and messier cases.

Looking at the four patients, he picked the two on the left. "I'll take those two." Of course, he picked the two healthier patients— the two with less vomit and less mess.

On the guy squirting liquid from his backside, I set two IVs and hung one liter of fluid. For the other patient, I started one IV and hung one liter of fluid. I attempted the standard medical mystery interview: What were you doing? What did you eat? What did you touch? Tell me about past and current medical conditions. Tell me about medications you are on, and on through the list. The forest floor absorbed every bit of the fluids coming from my two patients. Ass-squirt also vomited clear fluids. Had we been on a road or in a building, I could have estimated the volume of fluids he was losing. The standard large-sized adult holds about six liters of blood. The same as eight bottles of wine. The same as six liter-sized soda bottles. I could see the volume leaving the patient. Without puddles of past efforts, I could not estimate how much he had already given up. With each of his efforts, I estimated that he yielded between a half-liter and three-quarters of a liter of essential body fluids. And the fluids were coming from somewhere. He had long ago given up his breakfast. He was squirting clear fluids from both ends with no evidence of stomach contents, bile, fecal matter, nor undigested food chunks.

We lifted my two patients to the back of the pickup truck. My guy got placed in a plastic stokes basket. My female patient got

The Little Ambulance War of Winchester County

strapped loosely to a backboard. I climbed up. During the drive down the trail, I provided no medical care except to monitor the fluids going in and coming out. My male patient was not very responsive, drifting in the ether between conscious and not conscious.

The drive down the trail afforded me ten minutes to think. The driver did her best push with haste down a mountain trail while not killing me nor my two patients. I had the metal of the truck bed beating my ass with each bump.

At the staging area, crews informed me that additional ambulances were inbound from Trent Valley and Stark EMS. To keep it legal, we would need one provider per patient. Given the mess my two patients were making, each of these two needed their own ambulance.

During the bouncy ride down the hill, I reviewed every chapter in my paramedic and EMT books. I thought through my pathophysiology training and my anatomy training. Poisonings tend to fall into several categories: dry and wet are common distinctions. When poisoning is wet, we have two mnemonics: SLUDGEM and DUMBELLS. SLUDGEM stands for:

Salivation,
Lacrimation—tears,
Urination,
Diaphoresis,
Gastrointestinal Upset,
Emesis—vomiting.

Whereas DUMBELLS stands for:

Diarrhea,
Urination,
Miosis—pinpoint pupils,
Bradycardia—slowed heart rate,
Bronchoconstriction—narrowing of the
breathing pathways,
Excitation—muscular or central nervous
stimulation with twitching or seizures,
Lacrimation—tears,

Lethargy—fatigue,
Salivation.

These are the common symptoms of organophosphate poisoning—classically called nerve agents. These types of nerve agents are commonly found in insecticides, weapons such as sarin and VX gas, and some herbicides.

What was I missing?

Four people from Montreal, Canada decided to hike in the Green Mountain National Forest. They stayed at the same bed-and-breakfast. They drank the same coffee and ate the same food as the other guests. No other guests from the inn called 911 today. If they had, I would likely have known. They were not on farms where someone might discover an herbicide or insecticide. The risk of serin or VX gas in the massive Green Mountain National Forest seemed unlikely. These four friends all ate the same mushrooms.

Back in the City of Cambridge, we would have stacked these people into ambulances as fast as possible then drive these nearly liquid patients to any of the nearby hospitals. In seven minutes, I would have been done. Here in rural Vermont, I was on the trail for five-plus minutes as I examined patients and took histories. The rest of the crew organized the extraction process. It took ten minutes to bounce down the trail to get to trailhead and parking area where exactly one old ambulance stood waiting for four sick people. At fifteen minutes, it took longer to get the patients from the trail to the ambulance than the call would have lasted in Cambridge. Starting from the trailhead parking lot, we still had another hour of hard travel before getting to a hospital. The three nearest hospitals are at least one hour away: east, west, or south. The nearest trauma center would be two hours from here. If I called for a helicopter, I would still have to manage these patients for thirty minutes before they landed.

My gut told me that this was not organophosphate poisoning. I was missing something in the diagnosis. First, nobody had pinpoint pupils. Second, I saw no tears. Third, I did not really see neurological issues: twitching nor seizures. Fourth, I did not see any bronchoconstriction nor breathing difficulties. Were these four points sufficient proof of what the issue was not? On most paramedic rigs, we carry two doses of atropine. EMS folks started carrying two doses after various serin and VX gas attacks all over the globe. These poisons had been used in Japan in the mid-1990s and in the killing of a rival leader in North Korea.

"Is there atropine on that ambulance? Can you bring me the drug kit?" I yelled out to no one or everyone.

I explored another metabolic pathway. During my medic class, I was fascinated to learn of our body's ability to shed poisons through an allergic and immunity response. The body has histamine cells, which become famous each allergy season. People take antihistamines to control symptoms. In class, we discussed histamines causing itching, itchy eyes, and inflammation. It is why cuts to the skin can feel itchy. The cuts rupture mast cells that secrete histamines. Histamines cause local swelling, trigger localized healing responses, and occasionally trigger the sense of itchiness. Some insect bites sometimes trigger histamine releases, which is then followed by swelling and itchiness.

When histamines go crazy and overreact, we get extreme allergic reactions, including anaphylaxis, a possibly fatal condition. Medics and EMTs are taught to recognize anaphylaxis through the systemic swelling of the body and difficulty breathing. Anaphylaxis is always life threatening. It kills in minutes. This is why people carry EpiPens. One or two shots in the thigh save a life by reversing the histamine response. I had known this since my first EMT class at Northeastern University. Back then, the protocol allowed EMTs to *assist* a patient while administering their own epi. The street approach involved recognizing the symptoms, grabbing the nearest EpiPen from anyone, then slamming it into the patient's thigh. We weren't allowed to carry it ourselves. Ahh, rules.

During my paramedic class, I learned of other histamine receptors. During my first EMT class and biology classes, histamines were histamines and all anaphylaxis involved swelling and airway compromise. The best-known histamine receptor is called H1—as in the first histamine receptor. For anyone who has taken Benadryl, you'll know it impacts the sleep-wake cycle, appetite, and has a role in the bronchial tubes. H1 receptors trigger smooth muscle contractions especially in the bronchial tubes. The H1 receptors are closely related to common allergic responses.

There are other lesser-known histamine receptors cleverly named: H2, H3, and H4.

The H2 receptor appears to relate to allergic reactions in the gut. Back in our early days as hunter-gatherers, we explored the world by eating things. We still do that. Certainly, watch any baby or toddler. They touch it, poke it, sniff it, then taste it. H2 receptors, when stimulated, turn our digestive canal into a raging river of fluids. We pump fluids from our cells, blood stream, or anywhere into the gut. We cover the linings with mucus. Our bodies act to immediately flush any toxin from our body. With mucus at the cell walls, parasites and toxins cannot be absorbed. With a constant wash of fluids, the body sends the bad stuff out of every orifice. Patients squirt mucosal-like fluids from their mouths, asses, and even urinary bladder.

It is like using a hose to wash paint from a paint brush. Just keep doing it until it's gone.

It is the classic approach to toxins and pollutants in the environment: "The solution to pollution is dilution." Not really great advice with our modern forever chemicals or when we flush bad stuff into our water systems. The body's processes are the same. The body doesn't care where the toxin goes as long as it is out of the body. Our bodies, via the H2 receptor, dilute and flush toxins, parasites, and perceived bad things.

It was from that lecture onward that I worried each time I had small amounts of mucus coming from my own backside. We don't normally poo mucus. When we do, that mucus is a clue as to something our body did not like. If you have mucus in your poo, you likely also have other histamine responses going on at the same time, such as inflammation.

With the med kit at hand, I evaluated my options. If this is an H2-type allergic reaction, the patient will flush all fluids out, slip into hypovolemic shock, then likely die. If this is a neurotoxin, then I need to provide the antidote in the form of atropine. Originally atropine was derived from plants such as deadly nightshade, Jimson weed, and mandrake. Atropine is used as a cardiac drug. It accelerates the heart rate during slow heart rhythms, bradycardia. Atropine is effective on two common heart blocks. Then occasionally, it can cause the symptoms you think it treats. Atropine can cause the heart rate to slow down. This is called a paradoxical reaction. Every drug has risks.

On the other hand, the aggressive treatment of an allergic reaction is epinephrine. This drug, also called *epi*, is the same as the human hormone adrenaline. Adrenaline is produced by the adrenal glands that are attached to the top of the kidneys. Epi is responsible for the flight-flight, or freeze response we see in humans and other mammals: eyes dilate, palms sweat, heart rate increases, the need to pee and poo decreases, peripheral blood vessels constrict. It is the perfect response when running from a saber tooth tiger.

If this is a neurotoxin, I inject the patient with a plant-based toxin called atropine.

If this is an unusual H2-type anaphylactic reaction, then I inject a medication that is closely related to a human hormone—epi.

I gave the epi.

Within five minutes of the epi injection, the patient stopped squirting liquids. I ran my IVs wide open, filling the patient with fluids as rapidly as I could.

The other patient seems to be more controlled and drying up on her own. I debated the epi and I debated giving a 25-milligram dose of diphenhydramine, the chemical name for Benadryl. I could not remember if Benadryl targeted only the H1 receptors or was broadly effective across all histamine receptors.

There I stood, waiting for my female patient to improve or decline. If she lost more fluids, I decided I would hit her with epi. If she did improve, I would do nothing more than provide replacement fluids.

"Let's go. Let's get this guy loaded. Let's find a driver."

I focused on getting my critical patient to the hospital before the epi wore off.

"What about the other patient? What are you going to do with her?"

"She can take the next ambulance," I said, vectoring my kit and self to the awaiting ambulance.

"You are the only medic down here. Gary's still on the hill."

Shit. I saw the problem. I had initiated care for two patients. Both patients had IVs. I could not leave the other patient in the hands of a basic EMT. That is patient abandonment. I can only turn over care and treatment of the female patient to someone that has the right level of training. Given my debates about atropine and epi and Benadryl, I could not even leave the patient with an advanced EMT. The provider had to be a paramedic, just in case things got bad again. Maybe the patients will both need atropine. Maybe they will both need epi or Benadryl.

"Load them both," I barked.

We loaded her first, strapping her to the bench seat. We loaded him second. His mental process improved significantly during the minutes since I hit him with the epi.

From the back door, I yelled, "Is there any EMT or certified first responder here?" I looked around, "Anyone?"

I tried again, "Does anyone have any medical training? At all?"

Giving up, I said, "Can someone just come with just in case?"

I got one firefighter to climb into the front passenger's seat. And I had one firefighter in the driver's seat. Yes, another violation of the law. This time, two patients, one provider in an ambulance that requires two certified providers. As Aaron would say, "Follow the rules, follow the law, then do what is right."

We bounced down the access road, wending our way towards the paved roads, highways, and hospital.

15 | Suspension

A week.

One week.

I got a pair of living patients to the hospital who were alert, oriented, and improving after going into hypovolemic shock following a reaction to wild mushrooms. We transported them illegally in an ambulance, given we had a crew of one paramedic and two firefighters—one driving, one in the passenger's seat: just in case.

I briefed my brief. I saw this. They reported that. Here were my assumptions. I explored my diagnostic dilemma. I treated. I saw dramatic improvement. Questions? Any questions? No. I left the trauma room as the staff focused on their patient. I made up the ambulance's stretcher, then the ambulance and my makeshift crew returned to the trailhead to find our original vehicles.

A week later, I got a letter with a handwritten envelope. Someone typed the insides, but clearly did not know how to send an American Number 10 envelope through the same printer. Some poor person at the postal sorting facility had to make sure that this handwritten envelope got delivered into my mailbox at the road a quarter of a mile from the house.

The letter opened formally except it had not been printed not on official letterhead. The letter did not have a state seal or an agency logo. It has been typed and formatted by someone who took a high school typing class in the 1980s or searched "formatting letters" on the internet. The return address block identified the State of Vermont, Department of Health, 108 Cherry Street, Burlington VT 05402 as the entity that generated the letter. It had been sent to my home address and my name.

Although the letter said all of the right things, it looked wrong. It felt as if produced by an amateur.

"Your paramedic license has been revoked following an investigation into recent and past infractions of published protocols." The other interesting sentence stated that I had administered epinephrine in a manner inconsistent with Vermont EMS protocols.

Of course, the author wrote more. Any high school teacher would recognize that the additional text served as filler to make the letter appear professional and a page. The sentence stood alone on the page as the only set of words that had meaning and of those words, my eyes only focused on "revoked," "investigation," "recent," "past."

I am a cop's kid. Later in life, I used to joke, we were a two-handcuff family—given my father and I both carried cuffs back in the day. That thing that I loved about my father being a cop was that he was a real hero. I see him as the cop from *Make Way for Ducklings*, a famous picture taken by mother. I have both images: my mother's color photo and the brittle black-and-white version we cut from the front page of *The Boston Globe*. The Captain knew and understood justice. He believed in the natural goodness in most people. Publicly, he said "all people," but we both knew the exceptions too well. Getting arrested by my father helped a few people. He treated people with genuine respect. He offered jobs to nearly anyone in Boston who needed help. The kid who boosted a car and got a job mowing the lawn, painting the fence. My father even hired one old mobster who could barely stand as our butler for a few months. We never had a butler before, nor after. We all pretended that a butler fit into our home as naturally as grape jelly goes with peanut butter.

A state agency investigated an allegation, made a ruling, and executed a sentence without due process. I got tried, convicted, and sentenced in absentia. I got tried, convicted, and sentenced within five working days. Less if you include the time it took to type the letter then post the letter.

I looked. The postmark on the envelope reported White River Junction. Gone were the days when an envelope informed the recipient of the city and postal code of the sender. This letter could have been mailed from anywhere in Vermont or even parts of New Hampshire.

This state agency flexed its judicial power without nodding to the United States Constitution or even the little Vermont constitution which has protections and remedies which had been written in plain simple language. Vermont's Article Four states that every person ought to find a certain remedy for all injuries or wrongs. These rights protect people from the state taking unilateral action. The state, or a state agency, cannot declare: "We don't like you therefore you lose your license."

In one sentence, I lost my paid work with Stark EMS. In one sentence, Trowbridge Rescue lost the chief. In one sentence, the people of Trowbridge would be impacted. Patients would have to wait longer for care.

I promptly decided that this letter had not come from the actual Department of Health, furthermore it had not been reviewed by the Department of Health. Nick Kinney, chair of the local EMS district, signed the letter. In order for the timing to work out, the investigation had to happen locally, if there was an investigation. Oddly, we transported this patient who was squirting fluids from everywhere to a hospital in Massachusetts. It was the closest appropriate facility.

In order for the information about my actions in the woods at the edge of a national forest to make it to the local EMS district within two days meant that someone had hand carried my run report from the office at Langford Ambulance to the district chair or district doctor. Natural processes of paperwork flow would never have caused such an expedited reaction.

I dropped my paperwork at the hospital ER. I also left a copy of the paperwork at the station for Mike Legg to process and submit to insurance companies for payment. Given we ran an illegal crew, I did not worry much about the billing. There is no possibility that an ambulance with two patients and one paramedic gets the bill paid. Given we fell below the state standard for a crew, the call is ineligible for invoicing—unless Mike Legg substitutes one of the unlicensed firefighters for someone else on the paperwork. With a quick lie, the call becomes billable, and the agency yet again commits felony fraud.

Nope. Not here.

The choice of language bothered me too. Typically, when a government agency acts in a quasi-judicial role, they soften the language with the word suspension and promise a prompt investigation. You might see the phrase "suspended pending investigation." The official letter with the official return address stated that my license had been "revoked."

I went to the sofa in my office, closing the door behind me. I had been accused of a crime and sentenced within seven days of a remote rescue call where my actions improved the outcome of the patient. The fluids and epi may have saved his life. The vital signs thirty minutes into the call showed that the patient was in compensatory shock. His blood pressure and heart rate had been rising steadily since my first assessment in the woods. I could only guess at the volume of fluids he lost given it all soaked into the ground. I gave a liter of fluid in an IV that I ran wide open. His first official blood pressure showed me 110 over 70. Obviously, my first unofficial blood pressure had me deeply concerned. I could barely feel a pulse at his wrist. Given Aaron's old rule, that meant that the patient's BP hovered down near 90 systolic—or 90 over nothing. At ten minutes in, I measured a blood pressure of 120 over 90, a value that seemed good. Ten minutes later, his heart rate climbed over one hundred beats per minute and his BP climbed to 146 over 109. That is not a good blood pressure. That blood pressure can indicate an increase with intercranial pressure that may come from illness or head injury. In our case, this blood pressure indicated to me that the patient's body tried to compensate for the loss of liquids by squeezing every blood vessel—a trick called vasoconstriction. Vasoconstriction plus tachycardia, a fast heartbeat, is the body's response to a lack of blood and fluids. It causes hypovolemic shock, a lethal condition.

I closed my eyes, thinking of my father, the Captain. Jesus, for all of the laws that I have broken over the years, now I face charges and I got convicted. I kidnapped a kid from his house, I think it was a boy, I never looked. I handcuffed people and hauled them to hospital before having the paperwork that makes that action legal. I sat with my old partner giving booze and cigarettes to patients who we had been called to help. With the number of people who have died in my care, I explore the claims that I killed them. Did I kill them? Did my actions shorten their lives? Did I misdiagnose something that resulted in someone's death?

I have broken into houses and trespassed while attempting to deliver health care to people—smashing glass. Heck, Aaron and I cuffed and arrested a fellow for assault, and we were never cops. I have threatened and bullied patients. I have lied to patients: sometimes out of kindness; sometimes for my own safety.

Captain, what do I do? I didn't finish the thought before I heard his voice: *Hire a lawyer.* We all know the line: "You have the right to remain silent. Anything you say can and will be used against you in a court of law. You have the right to an attorney. If you cannot afford an attorney, one will be provided to you." I know if I used the words crime, conviction, and trial, I force it to sound criminal. If I violated anything, I violated a state regulation which would be dealt with in an administrative manner. A protocol violation does not even rise to the level of a civil complaint. This is the lowest form of crime. It is so low down on the scales of crimes that people forget that the process of removing a license and causing a person to be fired serves the same impact as a criminal conviction. Laws fall within a structure. At the bottom stands administrative law, then civil law, then criminal law at the top.

I gave a drug within my scope of practice to a patient. That action immediately and profoundly altered the outcome of the patient's health—for the better. I performed the care in the mountains at a trailhead working from the back of a pickup truck on a scoop stretcher. I continued my care, without abandoning a second patient. I performed a professional hand off to doctors and nurses in a trauma room at a small community hospital in Massachusetts, several miles closer than any Vermont hospital.

Someone took a copy of my run report then carried it to the district chair. With a few quick words, a decision was made to revoke my license. The letter informed me that the state EMS director will be notified for further review. There was no investigation.

Step One—hire a lawyer.

I really wanted to call the state office. Find the state director and scream: "What the fuck, you are revoking the license of a paramedic for giving a legal drug in the right conditions to a patient who warranted it. And you are revoking my license without due process?" So many things I wanted to say. So many processes that I need to learn about. For example, I am a longtime member of the EMS district board. There was no board meeting. No notification of a board meeting. I understand that I may not be welcome as an equal participant during the investigation, but if an investigation takes place, then I ought to be interviewed. We skipped that step. We also skipped "normal temporary suspension pending outcome" bullshit too.

The Real Step One—Notify the crew.

I wrote an email to all members of Trowbridge Rescue, informing them that my license had been revoked by the State of Vermont. I texted the core group of Harry, Robby, Regina, Brie, and Al. Which meant that I spent the next hours on the phone. As expected, after talking with Harry, he drove over. After talking with Robby, he drove over. Regina arrived. Al stormed through the kitchen door. After a while, Brie silently leaned on the door frame.

We ate through all of the cheese, apples, summer sausage, and salami I had in the house as we bitched at the world. We had six people discovering conspiracies behind each white pine and beech tree. We wrote our own tragedy with a cast of evil doers: Mike Legg of Langford Ambulance, Nick Kinney the district chair and chief of Stark EMS, Gary Healey and his wife, Gil Horne the former chief of Langford Ambulance, and others. We tossed anyone who was not "us" into the pile of conspirators.

Step Two—sleep.

Step Three—hire a lawyer.

With my radios off, my pager off, and the fuse pulled from my truck's radio, I isolated myself from all 911 calls. Imagine if I go to a car wreck as a plain firefighter and see something I need to treat. I can't treat anyone because my license has been revoked. Then that patient's family sues the town or me because a paramedic on the scene did not provide life-saving care to their loved one. I could not even go to fire calls for the risk of seeing more charges brought against me.

"Sally," I said during my introductory call with a lawyer, "I am holding a letter from the district chair that revoked my paramedic license. I am the volunteer chief of a small service in Trowbridge, and I am paid paramedic for Stark EMS."

"Alex," she tried out my name, "what can I do for you?"

"I think that the state bypassed due process on this."

"Frankly, Alex, they do not have a lot of rules about how to handle this. Three years ago, I represented a paramedic in Burlington who did something. They got suspended then lost their license. We could not find many EMS policies for managing discipline. It seems that the district doctors have a ton of control. Given you work under their authority, if they don't like you then they can decide that you cannot work. The state believes that because the doctors operated under their private license and their own malpractice insurance then the liability rests on the physician's shoulders. The district medical control docs are not employed by the state. The state yielded that authority. Therefore, when an EMT gets in trouble, the discipline comes from the local doc, not the state agency."

"Seriously?"

"Dead serious," she said.

"Wait!" I strove to understand her words but instead I contradicted her. "If a doctor sits on the district board and acts as the district medical control doctor then they are a defacto employee of the state. They must operate under the state's jurisdiction." I muttered and thought another second, digesting this information. "Ok, Sally, so why am I licensed by the State of Vermont? If this is the case, then I am really licensed by Doctor Asshole over there. So, nothing we can do?"

Lawyer Sally said, "I didn't say that. I am telling you that there is little precedent and few administrative laws. You are at their mercy."

In response, I said, "It is a governmental agency revoking my license without due process. The removal of rights and privileges requires due process under both the Vermont and U.S. constitutions, no?"

"Alex," a bit more comfortable with me, "it gets chaotic in these cases. Let me add these cautions to the mix. First, court oversight of state agencies tends to be deferential when considering technical or medical matters. Second, the Vermont Supreme Court interpretations of due process in administrative proceedings are far from clear and often not helpful. Third, those who investigate will be extremely deferential to physicians who volunteer as a district medical officer."

"Sally, that is mighty grim."

"That is reality. You'd have more rights if you robbed a liquor store. Your rights would be enumerated and protected."

Together, Sally Washington and I scoped out a plan of action. "We'll approach this like any administrative or criminal matter, we will request discovery of all related documents. We will request hearings." She then asked a question, likely of herself, "Should we start with the local district? Or do we go directly to the state office?"

"What about the speed and conspiratorial nature of this case?" I asked.

"What do you mean?"

"I provided care inside of the national forest and transported the patient to the nearest hospital which happened to be over-the-line in Mass. Within a day or two, my paperwork had been had delivered to the district chair and district doc in Vermont. Within seven days, my license had been revoked. Someone or something waved an unseen hand to make this all happen."

"Are you saying someone is out to get you?"

"I am not saying that. I am saying that someone got me. This revocation resulted from the deliberate act of one or two people who wanted it to happen. This was not an extraordinary call. And the outcome was positive. People all lived. This is not a case that anyone would read or care about. I gave epi to a patient with anaphylaxis. Symptoms stopped; patient lived. Happy day for all involved. It could have been so much worse. Without any care, or if that guy had been alone in the woods, he would have been a dried-up corpse by lunch time."

"I don't think that has any bearing on the facts of the case. I'll make a few calls on your behalf."

"And get me your letter. I'll sign it and send you money forthwith."

Two days later, I got Sally's engagement letter. I wrote a check, mailing the payment that same day. I wrote a check that would be reimbursed to me by my insurance company. My medical malpractice insurance covers the reasonable costs of protecting my license against claims of malpractice. Sally called saying that the state director of EMS and the district doc described my past practices as "egregious." Per Sally, "the state director and district medical control doctor were non-specific about the cause of their disciplinary action."

Step Four—request a hearing.

Sally and I debated on the best way to request a hearing. The administrative rules within Vermont EMS do not guarantee me a hearing. Sally found the written rules enumerate the state's responsibility. The written rules state that a district medical advisor may halt or restrict the ability of emergency medical personnel given a letter is written with the effective date, the cause, length of action, and exact procedure in question. The district medical advisor is then responsible for developing a corrective action plan for the EMT or paramedic. The administrative rules describe each action with a specific timeline. First, the suspension shall not exceed thirty days. If no further action is taken, the person's rights are restored. Second, the corrective action plan must be provided within five days of the suspension letter. If all goes well, everything returns to normal. Except that the paramedic, meaning me, must now answer yes to every questionnaire: "Has your license ever been revoked, suspended, or had any action that curtails your ability to practice?" This or similar phrasing appears on every license and certification renewal form.

The call happened in early August. The letter of revocation arrived a week later. The lawyer and I took two weeks to research everything, gather paperwork. Regina and Al snuck into the ambulance station to copy all of my paperwork. And I went to the hospital in Mass in uniform to request follow up notes on the patient. By mid-September, I wrote a letter to the district medical advisor requesting a hearing. Sally and I flip-flopped on the letter. I preferred that it come from Lawyer Sally J Washington of Rutland County Vermont. She said that a letter from her may appear as an escalation of the situation. I responded with a sanitized version of "They already fucked up my life." In the end, I wrote the letter.

I wrote the letter because when hiring lawyers, CPAs, and surgeons, heeding their professional advise often yields better results than fighting with them. Sally again identified that the disciplinary process ought to include details and a suspension. The process went off the rails from the first move. I added, "It all went off the rails before the first move."

"Fine."

I won the point. Someone is out to get me. Right, so what. Who cares!

16 | Hearing

Thirty days after I got my letter, I wrote to the district doc asking for an open hearing. I requested specifics about calls related to the revocation, and description of the alleged protocol violations. We still had not yet seen the discovery, charges, or any description of the actions that caused the revocation.

A month later, now mid-October, I got a letter from a nurse stating that the district scheduled a hearing for mid November to discuss recent "certification stipulations" placed on me by the district doc. Adding confusion to the process, the letter had been placed on official hospital letterhead. The logo read: Winchester Memorial Hospital. I forwarded the letter to Lawyer Sally J Washington via email.

We requested an official hearing by a state agency and its representative, the district medical advisor. We got a letter from a nonprofit hospital, not the state agency. The letter communicated the date, time, and location of the hearing. The letter did not clarify events that triggered the revocation. The letter did not refer to the state's action as a revocation. They now adopted the term "certification stipulations," an awkward phrase to say and understand. The phrasing did not align with any aspect of the administrative law I had been reading and the phrasing could not be found in our EMS protocols. The events unfolded as if the district board did not comprehend their own agency's rules. On the good side, Lawyer Sally identified the change of terms as a hint that the first letter and revocation may have overstepped the mark.

Lawyer Sally managed me well enough, as did Harry, Regina, Al, and Robby and all of the others on the crew.

It felt like something had been turned within the squad. Early skirmishes brought us together like a lean fighting team. We bound to each other facing a common enemy, our neighbors and the regional ambulance crew. With this crisis, our team stealthily fanned out, gathering intelligence.

My home office served as a tactical operations center. Normally, my office contains a wingback chair and a series of training aids. Granted, I got the job chief because I had the administrative ability to manage reams of bullshit government paperwork. I earned respect in the role of chief by working closely with people on the squad. People sat with me after tough calls. Some of the calls were ours. Some of the chats discussed calls our members did during other jobs in Vermont or Massachusetts. My advice came cheaply. I listened. I supported. I offered techniques for managing PTSD. I helped people with exams. At most, I could offer, "Been there, done that."

Polite people, civilian people, do not discuss CPR and dismemberment over a lamb roast. "So, you got an *ET* and opened the airway. Nice. Can you pass the salt? Any more potatoes? What did you do next?" That conversation does not happen at a dining table with normal folks. Then there are the health confidentiality laws. In towns as small as this you can't discuss the guy that tumbled from the roof without everyone knowing who the guy is. Except in Trowbridge, we say, "Which one?"

Twice, Trowbridge got the Blue Ribbon for hosting the first gunshot incident of the year.

Brie delivered an intelligence report stating that people in the EMS community now called me a "rogue paramedic." On a cork board, I hung a picture of me in the middle with the label: "Rogue Medic." I also pinned a NREMT-Paramedic sticker. It is round, plastic, and printed in gold, blue and red. The red letters say: Nationally Registered EMT-Paramedic. The shiny, glittery gold served as the background. Navy blue edged the sticker and described the star-of-life logo. That's me: Rogue Medic, Chief of Trowbridge EMS, Alex Flynn. The adult child of Captain Flynn, a career Boston Police officer. He's a happy ghost for me. I think he is laughing at this. Unlike me, Captain Flynn had protection. First, he had loyalty from a strong union and a strong group of cops. Second, he fostered respect from the crooks. Third, *The Boston Globe* loved him and his stories and the accompanying photos. I was in my thirties before I learned that my mother served as the Captain's press agent. The Metro editor would call her on slow days for a story. She reciprocated by feeding pictures to the *Globe* that nobody else could get, such as me doing CPR in a steel frame of a new building. My mother, the sleuth. My mother, the gossip-queen. Her favorite topics of gossip were me and my father—the two people she loved the most.

Brighid presented her next report to me and Harry in my office: The old-time members of Langford Ambulance worked behind the scenes to create new evidence. Regina learned that Gil Horne, former chief of Langford Ambulance, wrote a letter to the district board about me applying an ice pack to a seizure patient. A story about me that I did not know. Per his narrative, this action plus a letter of reprimand caused him and the Langford board to terminate me. In this letter with a newly fabricated story, Gill described his internal debate about filing felony charges related to me practicing medicine without a license. Brighid presented a paper copy of this letter to us.

I wondered if Brie had yet bugged the ambulance office. Or was she sneaking in during the nights to review paperwork and capture digital data from the computer? I did not ask. Neither did Harry. Brie recounted a story of Gil tearing through the records looking for the original call sheet and my termination letter. No sure how she got that information. We accepted the report, pinning yet more information on our cork board.

I smiled, knowing the problem. "Brie, I got booted for using a ring cutter on a finger, not an ice pack on a seizure patient."

"I wondered. I listened but I could not figure out why you would even give an icepack to a guy seizing."

"I don't know that I would. It sounds stupid. Good luck with finding paperwork on a call I never did. During that first short stint with Langford Ambulance, I never did paperwork. And they never gave me a letter of termination. They sat me down in a meeting then said, 'Fuck off, you fuck up.'"

"Oh, a call without paperwork at Langford, that never happens," Brie said.

"Right, never happens. And they never shift the paperwork to add names to make the calls billable."

Harry said, "I heard from my niece that there are two physician assistants in Warrenton Hospital who remember complaining about a case where Alex cared for a man with Alzheimer's who fell off of a ladder."

"Nice try, Harry. I drove. I gave that call to Gary. He did the patient care. Can't hang that one on me."

"But you wrote the notes, and the paperwork has your handwriting."

"Fuck, hang me now. Gary couldn't follow a bright light out of a tunnel. He can barely write. How did he ever become a paramedic? I can't wait an hour for that idiot to finish his paperwork."

"So now your handwriting is on Gary's fuck-up."

"I guess so. But I drove. He was the boss."

"That matters now?"

"I guess not."

Harry continued: "My niece reports that you didn't put a cervical collar on a lady who fell from a park bench."

"Oh, so true. I did not. The rule involves a fall from a standing height. She was seated. She broke her collar bone. Putting a c-collar would have made her pain worse. And she had no neck pain. That's stupid."

"That's what they are hanging on you."

"Harry, how is your niece getting all of this?"

"They all talk. She is an RN in the ER. I have her asking questions and starting conversations."

We all missed the number one warning sign in August. It should have been hoisted like a pair of red-and-black hurricane flags. The rooftop sirens should have blasted. We did not see the storm clouds. We did not see the warning flags or hear the sirens.

The few remaining members of Langford Ambulance elected Gary Healy as chief in September, the same month that Erik Mason moved out of the region to be closer to his new job. Our ally Erik was gone. We should have stopped and asked ourselves, "What is going to happen now?"

During Al's report, he stated that he heard through his sources that Gary Healy announced, "Now that I am president, I am going to get those people at Trowbridge Rescue." Al fiddled with the Glock pistol he carried on his hip. He doesn't normally fiddle with his pistol. It hangs there day after day.

I wondered what went through his mind when he fingered that pistol.

I noted that I touched my dog tags.

We each have our talisman.

A week later, Brie arrived in my office sitting in the client chair. She presented a hang-dog-oh-shit face.

"What?" I asked.

"I got it."

"You got what?"

"It."

"Ok. Show me *it*."

"It is this." She beamed with a smile. She pulled a letter from the thigh pocket of her EMS trousers. She unfolded the copy, smoothing it down on my desk.

I looked at a letter written on letterhead from Winchester Memorial Hospital. It had been drafted by the same nurse who sent me the letter regarding the hearing date. It stated that, "It has come to the attention of the training committee that Trowbridge is working beyond scope." Further, it stated that Alex Flynn has violated the mutual respect and trust between EMS and the population we serve. That my rogue actions have impacted the efficacy of all EMS providers in southern Vermont. "There were serious violations in numerous reports submitted to Langford Rescue that required immediate action."

"Who is this nurse? The name is a little familiar."

"She is Gil Horne's daughter. And she married Gary Healy's cousin."

"She is the daughter of the former chief and the cousin-in-law to the current chief," I restated unnecessarily.

"And she is the newly designated training officer for the EMS district."

"That's a thing, isn't it? And she is an RN in the ER everyday."

"Yes, she is. And she has her EMT-Intermediate as well. She joined Stark EMS while you've been out, in a paid position. She picked up a lot of your shifts."

"I think you found it," I said with a smile.

"I do too."

"Now what? What do we do with this information?" I asked the two of us.

I called Harry from my mobile phone. Brie and I briefed him on the linkage between the services, the hospital, and the district board.

"I know half of the people who meet you, Alex, hate you," Harry said.

"Only half? I'd like to know more about the few that do like me." I tried to make a joke out of an old hurt. The joke fell flat. I sat on the phone in my office with two dear friends who engaged a newly minted spy network to get information. Brie may likely be committing several illegal acts in gathering data.

"Brighid, do you think this is an early draft of the letter we did get?" Harry asked.

"I know it is. Same date. The opening sentences are the same. Someone got her to tone it down and edit."

"What do we do?" I asked again, thinking I may have an answer. I continued, "If we feed this information back, it sounds like children fighting in the school yard. We need a back channel to feed this through."

"Or several," said Harry.

"Or several," I echoed.

"I can give it to the rescue chief in Snelland. She can feed it to the doc," Harry offered.

"I can give it to my lawyer to feed to the state EMS director, the local EMS chair, and maybe the district doc."

Brighid added, "It proves malice. Doesn't it?"

"Shit, the speed between the squirty-guy mushroom call and the revocation letter was proof of malice. Don't you think?" I asked. "I think what I need to do is prepare for my hearing. I'll provide this information and this letter to Lawyer Sally J Washington of Rutland County, Vermont."

The hearing which took place about one-hundred days after the revocation letter seemed anti-climactic. I walked into the room wearing my uniform with my glittery-gold paramedic patch, my eagle rank insignia communicating my role as chief of Trowbridge Rescue. The nurse who scheduled the hearing did not attend. The public hearing, held on behalf of a state agency, was hosted in a conference room at Winchester Memorial Hospital. I walked in followed by Brighid, Harry, Regina, and Robby. We sat facing the district chair and the district doc. I dialed my lawyer, placing the mobile phone on the table.

"On the phone is Lawyer Sally J Washington of Rutland County Vermont. I have hired her to represent me in this case."

The doctor looked at me. "This is a friendly meeting. We're interested in knowing how we got here."

"Good. That is a great question," I said with a smile. The sort of smile that Aaron would know showed a complete lack of sincerity. I think Harry knew that smile too. For others, it looked actually sincere.

"Do you think you need a lawyer?" Nick, district chair and boss of Stark EMS, asked me.

"I got an official letter from the State of Vermont informing me that my paramedic license had been revoked."

"Technically not revoked," the chair corrected. "We modified your scope of practice pending the outcome of this investigation."

I had the letter in the manilla folder sitting on the table next to my phone. I knew that I was right. The letter revoked my license. The action was done on behalf of the people of Vermont.

"I don't want to start on the wrong foot." I sounded apologetic.

"But I have already paid Lawyer Sally J Washington of Rutland County, and this is an open hearing. If you don't mind, we'll keep her on the phone."

"I don't feel comfortable with that," the doc said.

The flush of anger passed quickly. I am either in a quasi-judicial hearing with the state of Vermont after they censored me in a very public manner, or I am in a friendly chat with two guys—an EMS chief and an ER doc. My brain saw this as a quantum dichotomy. It either is or it ain't, can't be both.

I picked up my phone, turned off the speaker. "I am stepping into the hallway."

I closed the conference room door behind me.

"What do you think?" I asked the lawyer.

"Do what they ask."

"That simple."

"That simple."

"Ok. Thanks. I'll brief you later." I hung up the phone. I then hit the record button. I placed the phone upside down in my uniform work shirt. Just under my name is a small chest pocket. Likely once designed for a pack of cigarettes, now the pocket is used to hold a phone. Upside down, the microphone ought to pick up most of the conversation, I hoped.

"Sorry. I hung up the phone. I'll brief her afterwards." I shut up.

I looked at the district chair. My friends in matching uniforms looked at the district chair. The district chair looked at the district medical advisor.

I remained quiet. Harry remained quiet. Brighid remained quiet. Regina remained quiet. Robby confirmed his radio was off and also remained quiet.

Awkwardly, the district chair remained quiet.

A hearing, even a boring administrative hearing in the basement conference room of a small community hospital, should begin with the bang of a gavel or a statement by the chair. And a hearing ought to have a note taker. Instead, we all sat quietly under buzzing fluorescent lights in a conference room across the hall from the pathology lab. Further down the hall was a bathroom and the double-wide doors that opened to the morgue. The morgue doors remain unlabeled. Likely the only unlabeled doors in the entire building. Every cleaning closet, storage room, office, and patient room in the hospital displays a sign—except the morgue.

I let the silence further the awkwardness in the room. I could have broken the ice with any of my questions such as, "Why did you revoke my license? What did I do wrong?" I remained quiet.

The district doc finally spoke. "I guess the key question is the call in August about the patient who you believe had anaphylaxis. And you treated with epi." He continued, "Can you tell me about this call? Start from the beginning."

And I did. In a practiced pace, I related the nature of the call from start to finish. I shared my internal thoughts when I debated neurotoxicity versus an H2-mediated anaphylaxis diagnosis.

The doctor stopped me when I was sitting in the rear of a pick-up truck, riding down the hill with two patients at my feet.

"What do you know about H2-mediated responses?" His face showed some surprise.

I presented a discussion about the differences between H1 and H2 receptors and discussed briefly the other histamine receptors and their various roles in regulating several functions. I discussed the historic importance of H2 histamine response flushing the body of toxins and parasites from our gut. I casually tossed information about *IgE* and mast cells. I added that H2 response increases cellular permeability. Fluids pass from the cells to the interstitial space like a leaky garden hose. I said, "Toxins cannot be absorbed if lining of the gut reversed the miotic pressure. If it forces fluids out, then nothing can get absorbed. This flushing action in conjunction with the slime of mucus prevents parasites from grabbing hold."

"You did not put this in your report." The doctor leaned to the chair next to him. He pulled out a manilla folder. Thumbing through it, he pulled a copy of my hand-written run report. "You have these boxes with sections of your report. Next to C/C, which I believe means 'chief complaint,' you write NVD—acute, severe.

Can you tell me what this means?"

I opened my folder and pulled out my copy.

"NVD—common for nausea, vomiting, and diarrhea."

"Under your respiratory section you wrote: non-labored breathing. No wheezing. RR WNL. Tell me what this means."

"The patient was breathing normally. No wheezing. His RR or respiration rate was within normal limits. So, something between ten and fifteen per minute—between the bouts of vomiting and the horror of squirting liquid mucus out his backside." I felt like he was setting me up for a trap. I did know the protocol doc. You got me to admit that my patient had no problems breathing and yet I treated him for anaphylactic shock.

"Down here you wrote something. I can't really understand." I am certain he just fibbed to me. I looked down at my copy.

In answer, I said, "Eyes 2-3 millimeters, Reactive, Dry. Neuro A&O times three. Good balance. Walking with obvious weakness. Ruled out OP poisoning because no lacrimation, no salivation, and dry skin."

"Why did you jot this down? What were you thinking?"

"As I said, I sat in the back of the pickup. We were all bouncing down the hill towards the trailhead and parking lot. OP means organophosphate. I debated two courses of action."

"What do you know about OP poisoning?"

"What do you mean?"

"Tell me what an OP is? Where would you find it?"

I answered the doctor in significantly more detail than he expected. I named insecticide, nerve agents, serin, VX, and said that it can be in herbicides too. I then prattled off historic cases of nerve agents used in terrorist attacks and murders.

"How do you know all of that?"

"How can I not know it all after 9/11 and the event on this globe during the last two decades? It was rumored that Saddam Hussein wanted to use OP-based toxins on the Kurds in northern Iraq. Since 9/11, every ambulance carries two doses of atropine, the antidote. What I find odd about that is that we are given just enough atropine to treat ourselves but not the patients. When I do a rig check, I identify that it is there, then I remind myself why we carry it."

"Doesn't the protocol require a respiratory distress in the diagnosis of anaphylaxis?"

"It does not," I answered.

The chair looked shocked. I gave him a look back. My mental message was, "Go ahead, ask me." He did not ask me.

I remained quiet. The doc opened his folder. I left mine closed.

"Here is it. Letter A, top of the list 'respiratory distress.'"

"Yes, it is Letter A at the top of the list. I concur."

"Did you see respiratory distress?"

"I did not. As my notes say, no distressed respirations and rate within normal limits."

"Number two on the list is airway compromised/impending airway compromise. Did you see that?"

"No. No respiratory distress." I shut up.

"Wheezing, stridor, swelling of the lips, tongue or any airway structure?"

"No, none."

The doc, in a television courtroom rhythm added, "Widespread hives, itching, swelling, or flushing?"

"None of the above."

"So why give Epi? You did not hit any of the top eight symptoms."

"Because that is not how the protocol is written. Please direct your eyes to the top sentence under Pearls." Working from memory, I said: "Exposure to an allergen suspected or known and hypotension or respiratory compromised or then the rest of the list. The bottom three items on that list are: gastrointestinal symptoms/vomiting, altered mental state, signs of shock. As written, I only need to have either hypotension or respiratory compromise. Either one or the other. I do not need both. See how the 'and' is in bold. I must have exposure and one symptom. I considered the mushroom as the known or suspected allergen." I continued after a brief pause. "I need any one item from the list that follows. The list is preceded with the word 'or' written in all caps and bold literally means any of the below. For example, the Mass protocol says 'one or more' of the following. I think New Hampshire protocols used the phrase 'one or more.' Vermont uses the phrase X and Y then each element of the list is separated by an 'or.'"

I breathed then I continued.

"Anaphylaxis is an uncontrolled autoimmune response. It differentiates from simple allergic reaction because, with anaphylaxis, you have more than one body system involved. With topical exposures or injections such as a bee sting, you stimulate the H1 receptors. These are primarily found in the skin and respiratory tract. Therefore, the crazy response will be in those body systems. With an H2 exposure, like ingesting a food, toxin, or parasite, the H2 systems go nuts. I would not expect a respiratory component as part of the initial reaction."

I spoke without notes.

"You did not have hypotension."

"I do not have blood pressures taken during the hypotensive stages of this process. I would expect to see hypotension at the early stages of shock. This patient had shifted into a compensatory shock. What I saw as a climbing BP was in fact the body's mechanism for keeping blood flowing to the brain, heart, and kidneys. The patient shifted three, four, five, or six liters of fluid from his body. He absolutely had been hypotensive. In my notes, I demonstrated signs of shock. That ticked that box. On the list of 'or this or that or this or that.' I ticked several boxes."

I looked at the doc. I ignored Nick, the district chair.

"I've got to add that since that day, part of my confidence on my diagnosis was the treatment. I gave epi and the patient stopped vomiting and squirting fluids nearly immediately. Had I been wrong, he would have continued declining on me. I wondered if epi would counteract an H2 response. That was not in any book that I read. And I was not very confident that diphenhydramine would work on H2. Something in my head told me Benadryl was more H1 specific.

But I did not have access to documentation to verify."

"And you thought this through in the field. Where were you?"

"We were several miles into the Green Mountain National Forest. I was part of the second wave of rescuers who traveled by ATVs and small trucks."

"Did you call anyone?" the district medical advisor asked.

"No. There was no cell reception. And literally none until we were halfway to the hospital."

"Did you file a failed communications report?"

"No. I have never seen one."

Now the district chair spoke. "You are supposed to file one every time you use a medication without calling a doc first."

"I have not heard of that. It is in the protocol?" I know it is not in the protocol. I have them memorized.

17 | Coup

The squad met at our dining table. We all know the agenda: last meeting minutes, old business, new business, blah… At the second the big hand landed on the twelve and the little hand pointed to six, I said, "Any motions?" The one copy of our minutes scampered around the table. "I make a motion to approve minutes." Harry's voice said: "Second." I came back with "All in favor?" We all heard the less-than-uniform aye spoken from around the table, although I think Regina sang her "aye."

"New Business," I declared. I lifted my letter from the table. The key sentence read: "Per our discussion, your EMS privileges have been reinstated." The letter informed me that I had rescinded my formal request for a hearing which led to the temporary suspension of your district-level privileges. The letter stated that after a three-and-a-half-month suspension and the loss of a paying job, "No disciplinary actions will occur."

This letter revised the prior communications. It appears the letter revised the facts of the case. My license was never revoked. No, it was suspended by the state. Later, I learned my license was never suspended. Instead, my privileges to operate at an advanced level EMT had been temporarily suspended pending review by the state. No, the license was never suspended, just the district medical advisor put a temporary hold on my advance skills.

The letter concluded with the phrase, "I want to thank you for offering to provide paramedics in the region with an educational lecture on acute anaphylaxis."

My father, who claimed that Columbus got himself a holiday because he had a better press agent than Leif Erikson and the Vikings, also commented that "the history that gets written is the history that gets remembered." Nearly four months prior, I wrote

this phrase in my run report. Next to the letters *RX*, meaning
"prescription" or "treatment."

"NS 1.5L WO 18ga in (L)AC. 1 missed IV (L) hand. 0.3mg Epi
(L) shoulder IM deltoid. 3 lead/12 lead. Non-diagnostic for cardiac
dysrhythmias or blocks."

Translated from cryptic hand-written medical shorthand, I stated: I administered 1.5 liters of normal saline via a large bore needle
inside the left elbow. I missed an IV attempt in the left hand. I
injected 0.3 milligrams of epinephrine subcutaneously into the deltoid muscle of the left shoulder. Then I applied a cardiac monitor,
which did not add anything more to the diagnosis.

Four months ago, I gave a tiny dose of a human hormone that
improved the health of a patient. The only other medic on scene
did not have the knowledge, experience, or skills that I had. He
hated me. He seemed to hate our rescue squad. Deciding that he
knew the protocols and medicine better than I, he leveraged his
position as the newly elected chief of Langford Ambulance to sink
me. He pushed his own version of the story into the hands of the
district chair and the district doc. He and his family reinforced the
stories of long-term systemic malpractice on my part and the part
of these volunteers at my kitchen table.

I am not to face disciplinary action as a result of my treatment.
Except, I lost my license, a job, a reputation, and I had to prepare
and present a lecture on what I did right to a bunch of assholes who
knew I was being punished. My punishment was to educate others
on how I was right. I know it was a punishment. The other medics
all know it was a punishment. The district doc insists that it was not
a punishment.

The author of the official record states that I volunteered to
provide this education to my peers. What a fancy! And losing a job
and losing my license. No, I did not have my license revoked. They
did not mean revoked. They meant suspended. Oops, they did not
mean suspended, they meant that my privileges within the district
were undergoing review. I was not to face discipline. We just needed
you to sign this official letter saying you were not being punished

and that you volunteered to teach a class on how to recognize uncommon forms of anaphylaxis.

I must admit I do not remember the moment my scheduled hearing turned into a rescinded request for a hearing. I got a letter stating the when-and-where of my hearing. I showed up for my hearing. Then in the follow-up letter, I learned that I had rescinded my request for a hearing.

The guy with the quill was always the hero.

I did develop a degree of sympathy for the district chair and district doc. They faced a targeted and deliberate assault launched by people with a purpose.

My letter got passed around the table. We all heard muttered version of "bullshit," "what shit," "what-the-fuck," and "fuck-that." Unlike the crew at Langford, the people on Trowbridge Rescue can read.

When the letter got to Brighid, she skimmed it. She had seen it before. She looked around the room, catching the eye of each person. "I got word that the chief of Trent Valley Ambulance joined in the lobbying. He added his voice to the noise amplifying the message that there are 'numerous complaints from numerous services.' This created an echo chamber of numerous complaints from several districts making the matter urgent. These chiefs pressured our district to protect at-risk individuals in our community from rogue providers who willfully operate out of scope. In an email that I got access to, the district chair wrote to the EMS director that 'unfortunate circumstances have clouded the entire situation.'"

I interrupted with my own: "What the fuck?"

A-One, our friend Al, walked into the dining room. He wore a tri-corn hat with the skull and crossbones. He carried a plastic saber and a hooked hand. "Aye, maties. It's time for revenge." The plastic parrot bravely clung to Al's shoulder. Then from a large shopping bag, he dumped a pile of plastic cutlasses, cheesy eye patches, and a few plastic flintlock pistols.

"What are you doin'?" I asked.

"Aye, cap'n. We're raiding."

Regina said, "Rape? Pillage? And burn?"

"Aye," Al growled back.

"Not really my style," I said in my normal flat tone. "I don't think I need to step lower than disgraced medic. I am confident that a pirate raid on a neighboring town will not help me, my reputation, or this squad."

Harry said, "The great American philosopher once nibbled on a carrot while sputtering, *This means war.'*"

"We're taking tactical advice from Bugs Bunny?" I asked.

"It is what we all grew up watching," Harry responded.

"We shouldn't. We've been in enough trouble."

"No. Trouble found us," Al offered.

I wanted to steer the conversation away from war, battles, Bugs Bunny, and movie pirates.

Regina said, "Let's do it."

"Do what?" I asked.

Regina responded, "What if we all join Langford? What if we send in three this month? Then we send in three next month? They vote in three new members. They are desperate. As long as it isn't you, Alex, each of us can be accepted as a member."

"Even you?"

"I am a member," Regina said.

"Seriously?"

"I put the application in again. Yes."

"Are you insane?" I asked her.

"No, I am totally sympathetic with A-One and his rubber parrot. Fuck 'em." Regina continued, "They have six people. We have eight."

I looked around the room. "We are nine."

"We send three. Then we send three more in. Then we'll have the majority voting block. Then they, I mean, we, elect our own leaders."

"As long as you never elected me. If you do, I will kill that agency in a week. This sounds like we are pushing the fight further. Peace comes when you stop fighting," I preached.

"You never picked a fight with anyone," Regina said.

"Not in the recent decade, that's true. Some people just have a thing about me," I said.

"Fuck 'em. We like you." The rest of the table offered their very worst pirate-sounding "aye cap'n" and "aye matey."

Harry banged his knuckle on the wooden tabletop. "I make a motion." He tapped a few more times. "Hey, I am making a motion that we take over Langford Ambulance."

A chorus of seconds rang out.

"No. That's stupid. How does this make us better? Why do we want to run an ambulance service?" I asked.

"Because we can, and we can do it better," Al offered.

I desired to build a team and now I had a team around me.

"Oh, we are taking advice from a guy with an eye patch and a plastic parrot?" I asked of a friend who also sported a gold painted plastic cutlass and a real Colt .45.

"Why?" I asked the room.

"Sorry chief, there is a vote on the table," Harry said in rebellion.

"No, guys, we're in the discussion phase of the motion. I don't get why we would do this. It can't be for revenge. Those fuckers hurt me. They pissed me off. I had been a mess. We can't do this because Alex Flynn's feelings are hurt. No. I refuse."

"So, what do you want, Alex?" Regina asked.

That shut me up. People started talking amongst themselves, which was very distracting. I stood and left the table quietly. Harry followed me into the kitchen. Then we walked a loop into the living room. I closed my eyes, breathed, and thought.

"Do you know how much we need you? Do you know what we would do for you?" Harry said.

"It isn't about me. It is about the people here. The families, and visitors, and neighbors, and everyone."

"So, if not about you, then them? Is that your statement?" Harry asked.

"That's it," I whispered back.

"Then make it about the community. Use your stupidly big brain to solve that problem. Look around you," Harry said.

"Fuck," I sighed.

"No, not me," Harry quipped as I turned.

"Ok, gang. Heard and understood. HUA. So, let's vote. Then let's plan. All those in favor of Harry's motion to take over Langford Ambulance, signify by saying 'ayes.'"

Given the pirate motif established by Al, they growled and barked a series of piratical "ayes." Gone were the boring New England town-meeting style "aye."

"If we do it, we do it right. Let's plan. Why do ambulance services fail? Hey, Brighid, do you mind wheeling my white board in?"

More than half of the people in my dining room also volunteer with Langford Ambulance. A lot of us found jobs as EMTs and medics in the region. I consider myself a professional medic, even though I lost my paying gig at Stark EMS.

"Why do ambulance services fail?" I wrote FAILURE on the white board.

"Insufficient number of certified staff," Regina spoke up.

"Another reason?" I asked.

Robby, who has a growing family, said, "We pay for the training. We pay for the travel. We pay for some of our own equipment. The squads do not get paid for any of it."

"Robby, you are saying that professional medical providers ought to get paid?"

"Yes."

Al carried us in a new direction. "Look at Erik Mason. He tried to come home and make it here. There just isn't an economy. People come here to retire. They vote against jobs and economic growth. Businesses don't survive. You can do logging, landscaping for rich people, farm and go broke, run a store and go broke, work in a store and go broke. You can drive a truck. You need to travel at least an hour or more for jobs. You can't volunteer all night on calls then commute to a real job all day."

The list had three items: people, pay, and economy.

At thirty minutes in, I said, "New business?" deciding to move the agenda forward.

People all looked around.

"Now guys. Let's not publish these meeting minutes on the website, huh? That seems stupid. Meanwhile, let's think about the next steps."

Two weeks later, I had a business proposal typed up. I used economic surveys and statistics from Vermont. We have an aging population, limited manufacturing base, long term population decline in the rural areas such as Winchester County. Surprisingly, of three thousand counties in the United States, Winchester County Vermont ranked poorly in key indicators: income; lower than average growth: age of citizens older; number of new businesses: trends below average.

My decision when drafting a plan on how to run an ambulance service after nearly twenty years of experience spun around one axis. Over and over, I removed ideas. I called my work stupid. I worked for several professional ambulance services. I did several years with Atlantic Ambulance then with services here in Vermont.

Is an ambulance service a business? Or is an ambulance service a critical public safety function?

The answer bifurcated based on postal code. If you live in Metro Boston, a region that hosts seven level-1 trauma centers within a few square kilometers, then you may write a viable business plan. My guys at Atlantic committed fraud everyday of the year. Was it out of necessity or greed? Peter Clifton stole from his employees. That was likely proof that he was a crook. Metro Boston has dozens of professional ambulance services and the City of Boston funds the primary 911 ambulance service with tax dollars. As does the City of New York. A lot of suburban towns provide tax-funded ambulances via their fire departments. With enough nursing homes, care facilities, rehab centers, dialysis centers, and hospitals, private ambulances can scratch out a living. Some of these ambulance businesses also hold contracts with cities and towns to provide emergency ambulance coverage.

Shift postal codes into rural and remote areas, then citizens expect other citizens to volunteer time for training, travel, and 911 calls. I recognized that the unpaid volunteers pay more taxes than the people they are serving. Restated, in my notes, I said, unpaid volunteers give time and money in compensation for taxes that are too low.

On my white board, I pushed the business plan to an extreme level. Like a slide bar on a computer screen or a knob, I dialed volunteer time down to zero. What happens if no citizens volunteer time for training, meetings, and calls?

The answer was that 911 calls go unanswered.

Does the government promise that 911 calls will get answered? Was the government obliged to provide police, fire, and EMS to the citizens? I think that every town in Massachusetts has a professional police force. A paramedic required two years of training typically after having already taken a semester long EMT course. A paramedic certificate was roughly equivalent to a two-year degree: thousands of hours of study and thousands of dollars in fees.

Who pays?

I sat in my office writing a business plan that would be hated by everyone. The operational challenges started with making sure that one EMT and one advanced EMT or paramedic was available at the station every hour of every day. That meant wages, plus benefits, plus retirement programs, plus housing for the crews.

Crews need ambulances. Langford has a new ambulance, but we will need a reserve fund for ambulance purchases every so many years.

Ambulances need medical equipment and medications. Medications tend to expire yearly. Some medications, such as narcotics, require a locked storage vault in the building and in the ambulance.

The cost of running one ambulance for one year was a value that could be calculated. Adjust for inflation and the cost of running one ambulance can be forecasted into the future.

In my business plan, the expense of running an ambulance service became a fixed, known price. People might want to argue over wages. We certainly do at town meeting when discussing teachers and the road crew. In Trowbridge, we still tend to pay teachers below the poverty level. We justify this downward wage pressure by saying we can't afford it. We add a lot of other justifications to the downward wage pressure on the jobs. I argue that when we under-pay teachers, the teachers and their families compensate for some-one else not paying their full share of taxes.

Did ambulance services generate revenue? Medicare, Medicaid, and private insurances did pay for an ambulance trip. The insurance reimbursements tended to fall below operating costs. The revenue from 911 calls does not cover the operating costs. When expenses exceeded revenue, we should expect to fail. We will also fail if we miss calls, have insufficient staffing, or screw up patient care in the field.

My business plan shall force towns to decide if they want an ambulance or not. The government must decide if an ambulance is required or not. The government must decide if every 911 call gets answered or not. It boils down to a simple if-then-else statement you'd find in a computer program or a decision tree: If you want an ambulance, then you must pay for an ambulance. If an ambulance is required by law, then you must pay for an ambulance.

If ambulance, then pay, or else, no ambulance.

Done. QED, *quod erat demonstrandum*.

Thus, I wrote a business plan. If you want or need an ambu-lance, this is the annual cost of owning and operating an ambulance service. If you don't need an ambulance service, then the conversa-tion is over. The rest of the business plan included charts, spread-sheets full of numbers, and the financial projections of a business guaranteed to fail unless funded by taxes. The short answer was that Medicare and Medicaid reimbursements do not cover the true costs of running one ambulance call, especially in rural areas. While Medicare and Medicaid pay fees based on distance traveled, those fees do not apply for the return trip. Typically, it takes as much fuel and time to return from the hospital as it takes to get to the hospital.

The tones dropped for Trowbridge Rescue and Langford Ambulance to respond in Langford. I looked out my office window. It was full dark at five in the afternoon. Snow piled on the win-dow ledge and pelted the glass. I keyed my mic. "Dispatch, 14RC1, acknowledging the call. Delayed response due to blizzard."

I pulled on thin liner socks, then silk thermal underwear top and bottom. I pulled up my EMS uniform trousers. I layered on a linen shirt, then a wool sweater. At the door, I grabbed a reflective yellow winter parka. I pulled my Elmer Fudd hat down over my ears, clipping it under my chin. I pulled my head lamp onto my head. Next, I gloved up. Thin liner gloves with mobile-phone compatible fingers. Then convertible finger-gloves-mittens. Grabbed my nylon over mitts. These I cinched to my forearms.

Langford got toned a second time, meaning that five minutes had passed.

I stumbled towards my truck. Then returned to the mud room. I grabbed my small snowshoes.

In the truck, I started it. I climbed out to clear snow from the windows. I got enough of a hole at the front and both sides to see.

"Dispatch, 14RC1 responding."

It took twenty minutes to drive the unplowed roads. "Dispatch 14RC1 on scene. Any word from an ambulance."

"None. You're the only one we've heard from."

"Understood. Heading in for an assessment."

Inside the snug home, I said, "Hey Phil, how are you tonight? I think we have a real blizzard going on." I saw the intense pain that the patient was in.

"Phil, what is going on?"

"It came out or something." He pointed to his lap and to his urine bag and catheter. His pain level approached the maximum levels. I did not need to ask. He radiated pain.

"Do you have a spare kit?"

"No. The visiting nurse brings one."

"When is she due?"

"About six hours ago?"

"When did this go wrong for you?"

"About eight hours ago. I thought she'd get here."

"I don't think she can. Literally nobody is moving out there. Let me see what I can do." I am not allowed to insert a catheter. I am not allowed to adjust a catheter, although I have been fully trained and passed related exams. I have stood in hospital rooms ordering nurses to install catheters. I have said, "I can't transport that patient without a catheter." When a medic transfers a patient, especially to one of the distant trauma centers, we have multiple IVs running, medications running, and cardiac monitoring. There was no stopping to pee during the ninety-minute or two-hour drive. I ask for a catheter, and the patient gets one. While trained, skilled, and tested on the modality, the state's protocols do not mention urinary catheters thereby informing me that the management of urinary catheters remained out of my scope of practice.

I looked around for Phil's landline phone. I found the number for the regional visiting nurse and hospice service. I got routed to the answering service. We danced the awkward dance. I explained that I am paramedic at a patient's home with a critical issue related to a urinary catheter and I need a call back from a nurse. The call taker explained to me that there is a blizzard and that none of the nurses are available for emergencies. We performed a verbal pas-de-deux about blizzards, emergencies, and availability. The call ended with a meek, "I'll try."

Next, I called medical control at Winchester Memorial Hospital. I got told, "You need to bring him in."

"Right, I need to bring him in. But I don't think I can get him there. I can't get an ambulance. There is a blizzard. And if we do get him there, you'll have to keep him for the night and part of tomorrow until this storm clears."

I explained my training, hoping that my hint would be picked up. Literally, I would have used a ten-mil syringe. I would deflate the little balloon that held the catheter in place. I reset the apparatus, then re-inflate the balloon. Yes, he'll be sore. He may have an infection or bad irritation, but that can be dealt with after the storm. He could, with about two minutes work, pee again. His pain would disappear.

"You need to bring him in."

I called dispatch from my mobile phone. "It is critical that I get this patient to an ER. We need to find a way. Let's start by toning Trowbridge and Langford again."

Within a minute of the tone, I heard Al, A-One, key his mic.

"14RC1, what do you need?"

"I need an ambulance. We have to transport." I spoke directly to him, violating the normal courtesy on that radio network.

"Roger. Headed."

"Town of Trowbridge to Alex." I heard an unfamiliar voice on the fire and EMS radio network.

"Town of Trowbridge, go."

"Alex, Tommy. I am in town truck 1. Tell me what you need."

"Meet me here. Maybe you can lead me to the ambulance station. Al is headed there."

"Ok."

I took the next twenty minutes bundling up my patient. I kitted him with oversized socks, Velcro sneakers. I stacked up coats. I pulled his shower curtain down and took a couple of towels. I lay them on my truck's seat and backed the truck as close to Phil's door as I could get. I attempted to stomp a path to the door. I half-carried, half-escorted Phil to my truck, which was warm and now mildly waterproof. The snow had melted from the windows. Down the road, I saw the happy amber and white lights of a town plow truck.

I returned to the house. I made sure that the heat was on, and the door closed. I turned off the television before Hoss and Little Joe started their new argument.

In my truck, I tuned my portable radio to the town frequency. "Hey, stay on the road, I'll pull in behind you."

"Ok."

I said, "Sorry, Phil, this is going to be rough." I accelerated. I smashed through the snow on the drive and through the berm that Tommy made with his plow.

"Tommy, I am ready." I called out on the radio to the plow driver in front of me.

Tommy started up the road. I hung back just a bit, following the well-lit truck.

"Dispatch 14RC1, en route ambulance station with one in POV." I used the shorthand for personally-owned-vehicle.

"14RC1 to Langford A-1. Stay in the barn. Tommy will plow you out first."

At the station, we three bodily lifted the patient out of my truck and then guided him in through the side door of the ambulance.

"Dispatch, 15A1."

"15A1."

"15A1, en route Winchester Memorial with one."

Tommy led the ambulance to Winchester Memorial Hospital, plowing us through the blizzard.

18 | Agonal Breathing

We campaigned for a joint meeting of two selectboards, bringing the leadership of Langford and Trowbridge together. We failed. Each board sang variations of "we must meet where we meet," and "we must meet when we meet." In fact, each town retains its own sovereignty. They do not make joint decisions. Trowbridge shall do what Trowbridge does. Langford shall do what Langford does. We asked to get on the agenda. For Trowbridge, it was easy. For Langford, Regina had to plea the case. Langford did not want to hear from people who did not pay taxes and vote in town. Most of the new members of Langford Ambulance live in Trowbridge.

As members of Langford Ambulance, we elected Regina chief. I am glad we did. We gave her the authority in that town to present the strongest case.

I presented in front of the Trowbridge board. Regina presented in front the Langford board. I presented on a Tuesday. Regina presented the day following.

Our presentations followed my financial analysis. In retrospect, someone else should have helped craft the message. I understood the numbers, protocols, anatomy, process, and logic. I reduced the ambulance service down to the simplest binary phrasing. I asked: "Is an ambulance necessary? If so, here is the bill." This logic worked well for us. Our crew started driving farther for paying jobs on ambulances. The farther they traveled for shifts, the less they were available for calls in Trowbridge and Langford. If there were full-time paying positions with benefits nearer to home, our folks would benefit. My approach stripped an emotional and historical topic to pure money. I implied to the select board that ran the town, "if you value us and our work, then you must pay us."

Frankly, I did not look at the issue from the board's point of view. I acknowledge that someone else could have found a means of being more persuasive than I.

I failed to understand prior to my presentation that nobody knew that the 911 system and ambulance services had already failed. They were already dead; they just hadn't accepted it yet. I should have, the squad should have, found a means of defining failure, proving failure, and working through the discussions about the ongoing failures. I know that rural volunteer ambulance services were failing because the rescue squad I built started failing too. Al told us that he planned on moving to Warrenton. He could live there cheaper, save money on the gas, and pick up more shifts if he were closer. Al followed Erik Mason out of the hills towards jobs that pay better.

I could not stand in a public meeting stating that the ambulance service routinely commits insurance fraud and violates state law by operating with substandard crews. Since Regina became chief and I was her assistant chief, we had not yet violated the law. It meant that we had responded to 911 calls with an ambulance and a single rescuer. We worked with the patient until another ambulance responded from farther away. Except for the informal tally sheets kept by Trowbridge Rescue members, we could not find accurate data on missed 911 calls, and response times spanning the recent years.

Given I did not, should not, admit to being a party to felonies, I failed to prove that the emergency medical services were failing. The selectboard failed to find a law that required an ambulance service. The selectboard failed to find laws governing the response time of the not-required ambulance. They voted no. There was no reason to change a system that has been working since the 1970s. Every member of the board recalled an anecdote of the ambulance and rescue teams coming.

That was not how failure works. That was not how math works. Three people can tell a story about remembered successes. Someone else tells a story about delays, failed responses, and frustrations. The truth requires larger sample sizes and data more reliable than human memory.

Regina, Al, Harry, Robby, Brighid, and I failed to recognize how the message would be heard by others in town and in the region. "You all want tax-paid jobs with benefits while sitting in an ambulance station watching TV all day." We came across as selfish. I got framed as the chief selfish person. Within a week, my entire history came up for review. The revocation of my license, arguing with police over a dead body and facing an investigation, my Boston arrogance, my over-educated fact-based brain.

When I sat at the cash box on the morning of the fireman's pancake breakfast, Chief Thomas Reed asked me to walk away from the task. He said, "Alex, or whatever you call yourself, we'll be all set without you." Yes, it is advertised as the "fireman's pancake breakfast." The term firefighter rarely gets used by Chief Reed. He doesn't want to.

Dumbly, I looked up and said, "I'll go help Harry in the kitchen."

Thomas Reed replied, "He's all set in the kitchen. We don't need you today." He literally pointed to the door. I walked out, confident that I had just been terminated from the fire company—a not-for-profit volunteer fire agency that depended on free labor.

Robby and Harry both confirmed that I had been fired by the chief. The chief never discussed the situation with the membership. He never asked for a vote. He made the decision. Out I went.

Within the month of our paired selectboard presentations, Regina sat in my wingback chair sipping iced tea. "My shifts got adjusted. And with the kids, they are all in high school now." She sat in my office, announcing that she needed to step away from her duties as chief of Langford Ambulance. "I am resigning," she finally said aloud. "I cannot do it all and I cannot do it for free. I've got too many bills and the kids have too many activities."

"If you leave, then I am chief."

"I think so."

"If you leave then we have lost two members this month. Al told me he was out." I paused, "Ok. I think we all know my promise."

"What promise?"

"The one I made, if I am ever elected chief of Langford Ambulance, I will kill it."

At the next ambulance meeting, Regina resigned her position as chief and promised that we could keep her name on the roster. Like Al and Erik, we had enough paper memberships to look strong. Paper members strengthened the look of the roster. Paper members did not respond to calls at eight o'clock in the morning. Now, we did not have enough people to actually respond. One ambulance run required a minimum of four hours, half of a workday. Fetching the ambulance and getting to the scene takes forty-five minutes to an hour. Extricating the patient from home or scene of a trauma takes another forty-five minutes. Driving to the hospital takes forty-five minutes. Briefing the ER staff, completing the paperwork at the hospital another forty-five minutes. And then we drove home with the ambulance. Best to budget four hours per run. Done quickly, maybe we finished in only three hours.

"Do not vote for me as chief of Langford Ambulance." Those were my last words as the assistant chief.

"I make a motion: We dissolve Langford Ambulance. Any seconds."

The motion got two, including one from Regina.

"All those in favor of dissolving Langford Ambulance, signify by saying 'aye.'"

In a single unanimous vote, the fifty-year-old ambulance service ended. We noted the time and date in our motion with the same solemnity we have all used when hearing the last beat of a heart, the last agonal breath rattling out of a chest. We did not even schedule a second meeting. We wrote the last will and testament that same night. The ambulance, all meds, and all supplies would go to Trent Valley Ambulance. I liked the ambulance that I helped buy. Erik invited me to the selection and procurement committee as an active peace offering. I felt pride for my role in raising the funds and the quality of our purchase. We decided to return the present year's contribution from Langford back to the Langford board. We returned Trowbridge's annual contribution to the Trowbridge selectboard. Meanwhile, we kept the other cash to pay off any remaining bills, then we pledged that the remaining money would follow the ambulance to Trent Valley Rescue.

The following morning, I called dispatch asking them to remove Langford Ambulance from all run cards. They gave me a rash of grief. I did not have the authority to remove Langford Ambulance from the dispatch calls from any town. In a calm voice, I said, "We filed for decertification with the state and by the end of the day, all supplies will be donated away. There is no ambulance."

Those were the facts. With no ambulance and no crew and no license, Langford Ambulance could not respond. It did not matter what the fire chiefs in Langford and Trowbridge believed, wanted, or had written. The facts were the facts.

As summer approached, I started gathering my recertification materials: my refresher course, the certificates from all of the other courses demonstrating a total of forty-eight hours of training. I had my CPR card, my advanced cardiac life support (ACLS), pediatric advanced life support (PALS), protocol exams, and other documents. On the renewal forms, I had to answer the question: Has your license ever been suspended, revoked, or altered since your last renewal?

I imagined Arlo Guthrie's song "Alice's Restaurant." The hapless hero sat on the group W bench with mother rapers and father stabbers. I had been found guilty. By checking yes, I acknowledged that my license had been altered, revoked, or suspended. I would be required to submit the entire case to an unseeing judge. Guthrie sang about the evidence describing it as "twenty seven eight-by-ten color glossy photographs with circles and arrows and a paragraph on the back." Me, I had a letter revoking my license. I had a letter scheduling a hearing. I had a letter saying there was no hearing and no disciplinary action will be taken—except for teaching a class, losing a job, and having no license for three months. I did not know how to answer the question. It seems that something happened to my license therefore I must answer yes. I attached the friendliest and best letter. I scanned the letter than stated I faced no disciplinary action and informed the readers, including me, that I volunteered to teach a class.

I sent that in.

The national registry folks wrote back wanting the entire case file.

The Massachusetts EMS folks wrote back wanting the entire case file.

Vermont wanted my national registry card which I did not have because my status was pending as the national registry people adjudicated my revocation, suspension, and non-disciplinary mess.

I sent them everything. Meanwhile I sat on the figurative Group W bench. My paramedic card expired while under review. My Vermont paramedic card expired while I waited for the national registry card.

Harry announced that he no longer could keep his certification. It took too much time out of his year.

Robby accepted a higher paying job an hour away. With the commute and long hours, he missed the EMT refresher course thus spelling the end to his certification.

When our roster of certified people fell below five, we voted to shutter Trowbridge Rescue. What cash remained went to the Trowbridge selectboard.

We died.

Within a week, Chief Thomas Reed arranged for dispatch to tone the fire company to all medical calls in Trowbridge. Now we have uncertified people responding to medical emergencies. Instead of having the normal safeguards of knowing who is responding to medical calls, we have none. As EMTs and medics, we had undergone training. We had our skills reviewed. We took courses to maintain our professional credentials. We were supposed to have undergone background checks. Vermont desired to protect our most vulnerable citizens from risk or harm by requiring skilled and certified people attend to their needs during emergencies. In Trowbridge, those who held or had held EMS certifications did not respond to medical calls. This aided in avoiding legal jeopardy. While Good Samaritan laws protect civilians, these laws do not protect those who respond to emergencies in a professional capacity or are certified as medical providers. In other words, if a civilian rendered medical aid, they were likely held harmless. If a firefighter responded to a 911 call and rendered medical aid, they fell within the jurisdiction of a professional provider. That was why I carried malpractice insurance.

Guys with red-and-white emergency lights arrived at a medical crisis then render no medical assistance. I regarded that as confusing. How does one not act when there was something to do?

I can't.

That's ok. I was tossed from the fire company thus liberating me from the ethical dilemma. Had I remained in the fire company, I would have to honor the laws that prohibit me from helping medical patients. That's how laws work.

I got my national registry paramedic card in the mail. And I got my Massachusetts paramedic card in the mail. I did not get a Vermont paramedic card. I lost my eligibility for renewal in Vermont because I was no longer affiliated with a Vermont EMS agency. I had been fired from Stark EMS because my license had been revoked. I killed Langford Ambulance because it required too much cost and too much risk to keep open. I was not willing to face felony fraud charges. And Trowbridge Rescue died quietly when most of our active members moved away for better pay and families.

I could have kept the cycle of recruiting, training, and responding. I recognized that I failed at keeping skilled and certified people in Trowbridge. I could not ask them to volunteer unpaid for hundreds of hours per year when better paying jobs existed off of the mountain.

I studied Trowbridge from the outside. The position I once held in town disappeared. The imagery resembles stepping out of a cold mountain lake. When in, the water accepts you. When you move, the water responds with waves. Then when you get out, no hole exists. The lake forgets you. The surface returns to its normal flat state.

I left no ripple on the Town of Trowbridge. I disappeared.

19 | The Egg Man

At the end of my father's career, cops from all over Massachusetts gathered for a send-off. Robert B. Parker played host and provided the keynote address that evening. My father's colleagues presented him with a mahogany shadow box containing rank insignia, starting with patrolman then following him his career to sergeant, lieutenant, and captain. My father bathed in the warmth of the room. He shook hands with everyone. He listened to every job offer with his signature smile and sincerity.

Three days later, he woke next to my mother with no job, no purpose, no office to go to, and no city-owned unmarked police car parked by the door. My mother set an internal alarm. Seven days, she told me. He got seven days. She gave him seven days, then woke him up. Time to get busy again. She had created an LLC. She bought corporate liability insurance and made business cards for him. She talked with everyone at every news station and newspaper. Overnight, my father became a regional security expert on television, in the press, then hired by Harvard University as a lecturer at their Kennedy School of Government.

I got no send-off. No famous author roasted me from a podium in the ballroom of a posh hotel. I got sent off. Instead of pride, I felt shame. Me, I could not sleep. I did not know how to live an adult life without someone paging me, calling me, texting me, toning me about some emergency somewhere. The black fibers of my tinea mentis, the mycelial tendrils of my life, sparked into living color the hour I put my head down on the pillow. Every failure. Every death. Every horror. My mind tugged at these fibers following unrealistic and untrue memories. What if. Could I. If only. The memories flash. The images strike like lightning. With stroboscopic intensity, pictures both real and imagined exploded behind my shuttered eyelids. At midnight with no calls, I rose from bed.

I paced. I thought about a drink, then did not drink. Then like the old men I hauled from homes, apartments, and care facilities, I watched *Adam-12, Bonanza, I Dream of Jeanie, Dragnet* at midnight. I tried classical music and reading. Sleep sometimes visited again.

A week later, I sat on a shrink's sofa learning newer techniques for living with post traumatic stress. Some techniques worked. When I knew that someone may wake me to respond, then I pushed myself to sleep. I knew I'd require another hour after getting home from a call. It took that long to still myself and return to sleep. The day I knew I would never again wake for a 911 call, I could not sleep. There was no reason to sleep because nobody was going to wake me from it.

I cried over the loss of my friends and that everyone in town hated me. I cried because I was a failure. Late in life, as a few grays hairs appeared, I fell off of the magic carpet that soars under successful people. I landed in the loser pile, the refuse pile.

My mother knew my father better than I knew myself. My mother had spent her entire life silently boosting my father's career. She served as an unseen, unrecognized, unknown partner in every promotion and venture. She knew what my father needed. A minute to feel alone, sad, and isolated. Then she gave him an affirmative kick in the ass.

I never planned for after.

My father's retirement lasted seven days. By the fall, he had to prepare a lecture for graduate students. By mid-winter, he served as a paid police procedural consultant to a movie director, a gig created for him following the combined efforts of Boston mystery writers and my mother. He consulted with the MIT police department as they restructured their organization.

I got nothing from no one.

The 911 calls filled a void left by my career. I spent decades going where the government told me to go, doing what they told me to do. I stepped out of that hell for a quiet set of consulting positions that I worked from my Vermont home office. I met clients in Boston, Albany, Manhattan, or DC, then returned home happy to bill my hours. Like a world-class thoroughbred racehorse, I stood alone in a paddock of green grass surrounded by a fence, never to run a race again. The twitch to run remained strong. I maintained total alertness. I waited for the tones to drop telling me to go. The tones that I will not hear again.

I pictured the racehorse destroying the barn. I envisioned myself stomping through the walls of my office and my kitchen, and my own house.

In Cambridge, Bobby Clifton had a plan for the day he won the lottery. He would take his ambulance, Unit 25 with his name lettered in gold, then smash it into a concrete wall. His day two involved less planning. He'd be a rich man with lottery winnings. No plan needed.

I failed to plan for failure. I left myself with nothing. I hung my uniform work shirt in a little used closet. I hung my white uniform shirts with their patches and stories in the same closet. Given I would have no more guests sitting in my lonely office, I moved the client chair to the living room. I turned my desk to the wall. I wiped the whiteboard and put all of the paperwork from both agencies into white banker's boxes.

When my father retired, the Metro section published an article highlighting his career and impact on the City of Boston.

When I presented to the Langford Selectboard after shutting down Langford Ambulance, they called me and Regina thieves. They publicly stated that we stole five thousand dollars from the town. What they wanted was all of the cash from the dead ambulance service. They also wanted the new ambulance from the dead ambulance service. The ambulance service had been named Langford, therefore they believed that the remaining property belonged to Langford.

We did offer the town all of the remaining property. We gave the contributions back to each town. We gave the ambulance and equipment to the ambulance service that absorbed the territory. We collected the last revenue, paid the last bills, then donated the cash to Trent Valley Ambulance. When we were done, nothing remained. And nothing was what the Town of Langford got. They got their five grand, the five grand they contributed for the current year. It seemed like they wanted the cash we refunded to Trowbridge. They also wanted the cash in the account after final invoices were paid.

Given Regina and I did not do that, the selectboard called the two of us thieves. I can't explain the quote in the paper. Regina did not come to that particular meeting. Yet, Regina got mentioned in the local paper. I had become a rogue medic, trashed a service, begged for public money to pay salaries for my friends, and when things did not go my way, I stole the money, shut down an historical entity, and quit. I was the brat who wanted to play ball, then when it went sideways, I took my ball, quitting in a huff.

My analogy of lake water healing up after I stepped to the shore fails. In the eyes of others, I saw a reflection of hurt. In the hearts of others, I felt the broken promises. I acknowledged the growing scar.

I have a life-long friend in Harry Grasser, a man with bear-claw hands. I have friends in Regina and Brighid Doran. And, of course, I had my work.

As the winter holidays approached in November, Harry called me. "Alex, do you mind helping me out? I got a call from the state police."

"Sure, no problem." Put me in coach. I felt eager to go.

"I need to do a welfare check. It is right there near you. You could save me a drive. Do you mind?"

"Hell no." I got a few facts. "Missing brother. No word in days. Normally checks in with family." And I heard, "Georgia." It felt like the basic man-down call from the early days. In rural Vermont, we call them *welfare checks*. Back in the old days as a real medic and member of a real service, I had arrived at houses, burped my siren at an old man mowing a lawn: "You ok?"

"I am fine."

"Do me a solid. Call your brother. He thinks you're dead." I used to toot, driving away. That served as a welfare check. Just like the man-down call, you may find anything at the end of a Vermont driveway.

I pulled on my old EMT uniform trousers—now with a small hole in the crotch where some stitching let go. I put a few purple nitrile gloves in the pockets. I grabbed a flashlight.

I drove with the flow of traffic: no lights; no siren; no chattering radio. I found the driveway.

The car looked dusty with newly fallen leaves on it. I placed my outspread right hand on the trunk leaving four neat fingerprints and one thumb print. As I passed the hood of the car, I touched it—the steel was cold.

I walked to the door. Remembering my training, I stepped to the side of the door. I knocked politely three times. I waited. I knocked the polite way again. I waited. Then with a fist, I pounded on the door. I could see nothing inside the house. The kitchen was obscured by a curtain that hung in the window.

Walking back, I saw my own footprints in the late-fall grass. My feet had folded the grass over. The presence of my footfalls gave sufficient proof for me to believe that nobody had walked these grounds in days.

I returned to the back of the fellow's car. I snapped a picture of the car plus its plate. I forwarded that to Harry. I then snapped a picture of the house, sending that to Harry.

I called Harry. No answer.

I walked to my truck. Sitting in my own front seat, I called Harry again. No answer. I reviewed the nature of the call and the limited information gathered when Harry dispatched me. I drove to Georgia's house.

I parked in front of the yellow farmhouse. I banged on the door. "Georgia, sorry for the interruption. Someone said that you called in a welfare check for a relative?"

The lady looked at me oddly.

"Did you call the state police recently about a family matter?"

"No."

My phone buzzed and vibrated. I looked down at Harry's name.

"Hey, I am getting no answer. I need more instructions. I drove over to Georgia's house to get more information."

"Why did you go there?"

"You said Georgia called."

"No, I never."

"I heard you," I argued with my friend.

"I said the brother called. He is from Georgia."

"Oh fuck," I muttered into the phone. "Georgia. I am being told the phone call came from the state of Georgia."

Without looking back, I jumped into my truck. I sprinted back to the scene with Harry on the phone.

"I guess I need to make entry. But I am nobody. I am a civilian."

"Then I'll deputize you. Raise your right hand."

"Sure," I lied while driving with both hands on the steering wheel of my truck.

"I state-your-name do your best to preserve, protect, and do the thing you do so help you etcetera, blah, blah."

"I, Alex Flynn, do solemnly swear that I will uphold and defend the Constitution of the United States against all enemies, foreign, and domestic; that I will bear true faith and etcetera, etcetera. Blah, blah, blah."

"There you go. All sworn in."

I parked. Walking back across the unkempt lawn, I said, "I am hanging up. I'll turn on my recorder." I wiggled the door, turning the knob aggressively. Then, as trained, I turned around and kicked at the door like a pissed off mule. The door not only flew open but bounced back closed. I opened the now broken door.

"I am in the kitchen. Old food. Musty. No movement." I narrated my way through the room. I found a corpse rolled into the shape of an egg below a recliner. The chair leaned forward. The fellow had collapsed with his shoulders on his knees, his ass firmly planted on his feet. His head rested on the floor. Both arms lay parallel to the folded legs. "I am examining a human body. It appears to be an elderly male. Body temperature is cool. Same temp as the room. He has several obvious signs of death," I spoke for the recorder. With a gloved hand, I reached for the neck. "I am feeling at the carotid for a pulse. The neck appears heavily mottled." Looking at my phone. "I timed one minute. There is no pulse. Rigor appears to be leaving the body. I am going to step out after photographing the scene and the medications."

I stepped out of the room. I pulled the door closed against the broken latch.

"Alex Flynn." I spoke into the mic. I gave my date of birth, the fourteenth of July, and spoke the time and date. With the recording off, I called Harry.

"Harry, call the troopers. I'll hold the scene until they get here."

"Dead, huh?"

"Folded into an egg shape. Seemed peaceful enough. Slumped out of the chair while watching TV."

"Want me to monitor the scene?"

"Thanks for the offer. I have to stay. If you come, then we will have two people here for hours. I am all set."

"I'll call." Harry hung up the phone.

I started my laptop, connected to the internet via my mobile, and got to work. There I sat at the end of a short driveway in the woods of Vermont waiting for the state police to arrive. My duty, my sworn duty if you count the etceteras and blah-blahs, included protecting the *de facto* crime scene from intrusion. I was responsible for the preservation of evidence. I wrote a small log slash run report about the scene. I signed it with name, date of birth, and location.

It was two hours before a VSP cruiser found me on the dead-end road. The trooper felt the same lack of urgency that I did.

I opened the door to my truck. I stepped down. I closed my truck. Then stepped in front. I held my hands away from my body with palms out. The trooper approached, introducing herself.

"Hey, I am Gwen."

"Gwen, Alex."

"We've met, I think."

"Probably."

"What's going on today?"

"You guys asked for a welfare check at this address. There is a corpse rolled up on the floor as if he slid from his recliner."

"Did you call it in?"

"Did I call medical control already?"

"Yes, aren't you an EMT or something?"

"I used to be. No more. I am a citizen."

"But he's dead. You are sure of that."

"I am." I described the setting, my approach. I pulled my written report out of my pocket. "I wrote these notes for you. It has my name, number, and DOB."

"Does it look like foul play?"

I looked past Gwen to the grill of her cruiser. I waggled my head, looking for the telltale red light.

She said, "No, not recording."

"Ok, no signs of struggle. There is an MTWTFSS on the counter with a goodly set of standard American pills: high blood pressure, blood thinners, acid reflux, statins for cholesterol. I'd say he died watching TV then slid to the floor. His recliner caused his torso to fold over his legs. Looked peaceful."

"Fair enough." She wrote a note. "What is an MTWT—whatever?"

"MTWTFSS—one of those countertop pill things to plan the week: Monday, Tuesday, Wednesday…"

"Dooh. Sorry. MTWTFSS. Clever." Gwen continued, "Do you want to help me identify the meds and what they do?"

"I already wrote them down for you. I'd guess he died on Wednesday. His Thursday pills are untouched."

She looked at my paper. "You've done this before."

"I have. And can I go home?"

"You should wait for the detectives," she said half-heartedly.

"I'll tell you what. If you or the detectives arrive at my house, I will answer any questions. Or you can call me, I wrote my mobile number on the paper." I shook Gwen's hand. "Ping me if you need anything."

As I drove down the road, Gwen turned her cruiser around.

She parked exactly as I had parked. The car blocked the drive. The mirrors provided a view behind to the end of the road. And she could sit waiting for the hours it might take for detectives to arrive.

Harry sent me out for another call after the nation shut down for the COVID pandemic. I walked up to a car wreck in a blinding snowstorm. I wore my old yellow reflective parka.

"Hey guys. I am not a cop. Not a firefighter and not a medic. But I got called out to see if you need help?" I snapped a picture of the scene while I walked. Again, I left my fingerprints on the rear of the car.

"Who sent you?"

"Essentially someone dialed 911. The state police called a friend. He called me. I came out. If you guys are all set, I'll cancel the call. If you need something, I'll do what I can to get fire or rescue here."

"We're good."

"Sure?"

"Oh, yeah. We're waiting for a wrecker."

"Do me a favor, hold out your driver licenses? I'll photograph them for the state police then I'll get out of your hair." I took two more pictures and sent them to Harry. We were nearly a year into the global COVID pandemic. Finally, I did not want to be a paramedic. Without a license, I avoided the worst. Checking on this car wreck revealed that for the first time in a couple of years, I recognized joy at not having to respond to hundreds of COVID calls and work with hospitals during this crisis. The COVID crisis harkened back to my early days on ambulances. I was one of the first in Metro Boston to transport an AIDS patient, a rare and mysterious disease that seemed remote from me. Although I credit AIDS for several of the changes in my cities. Granted, developers had wanted to sell expensive properties to rich people, but some part of the clean up involved eradicating the neighborhoods where AIDS existed. By the time I was thirty-five, AIDS had killed several of my friends. No longer a remote disease. My career spanned the decades from AIDS to COVID. Technically, I had given up my license before COVID. Why let a fact interfere with the flow of a story?

I waved goodbye through an open window. I drove home in yet another Vermont snowstorm.

At my desk, I studied the mementos of my life. The ancient clipping of my father leading ducklings had faded to a deep yellow and the newspaper was brittle. I endeavored to protect it. Newsprint belongs around fish, in bird cages, compost for the garden, or in a recycling cube. It just doesn't last for decades. Thankfully, I do have my mother's original photo she took with her Nikon camera. I had that photo professionally framed behind an acid-free matte board and UV filtering glass. There hung his presentation shadow box, lined in velvet, chronicling his career. He had something very real working for the city, a career and duties for which he expressed deep pride. Cops and capos both attended his funeral. Young officers and young offenders who once mowed our lawn stood with bowed heads and children at their own knees. My mother, the mayor, the governor and the state's adjutant general argued over the flag that would grace my father's mahogany casket. The mayor firmly believed that he should be honored with the City of Boston flag. The governor wanted to claim him as his own, requesting that the Massachusetts state flag be draped instead. The state's adjutant general, the senior-most military officer for the state's national guard, said that my father had earned the right to be honored with the stars and stripes of Old Glory. The general knew something more about my father and his career that the others did not. The honor went to the flag of the United States. After the funeral, the folded flag had been presented to my mother. In a fluid movement, she handed me his flag. That flag, folded as it had been folded graveside, sits on a shelf behind me in my office.

I doubt that I shall have that honor. No one will argue about the flag on my casket, or even know if I have earned the privilege.

I have hung the few award certificates I earned in my office. I can look at the 250 dinar note from Iraq pinned to a cork board. I cannot see the one official government medal I earned during my years of invisible service. On that day, I stood listening to the citation. I got photographed holding the medal and the citation. I got photographed shaking the hand of a very senior official. As per custom and law, I returned the medal and citation. Neither may ever leave the building, nor can the photo that captured the event. I did. I walked out of that building. You can see hints of my life all around me, including the secrets. If you really look, you'll see me.

When I built this office for myself, I tried to buy a shoulder patch from Atlantic Ambulance. All modern hints of that service faded like *The Boston Globe* articles that described their shenanigans: extorting patients, submitting fraudulent paperwork to Medicaid, and robbing employees of their pay. I bought the shoulder patch worn by LA County Fire Department paramedics. Sure, I was a kid when that show came out, but without it, I would never have done what I did.

The Egg Man died a peaceful death. Death visited while the old man watched *Bonanza* in his ratty recliner. The image of his death, while strong and clear, had been added to the decades of other images. He was at peace. I forgot his name instantly. Not everybody gets peace. Sometimes, the clicking of twig-like legs strike from the darkness. Even after years, venom stings. The toxins and dark fibers left from unseen scars etched my soul. I believe that I failed to become the hero in my own story. I am another forgotten warrior sitting at the curb yelling at people who walk by without seeing me.

The End

Author's Note

Having grown up watching the same television shows that Alex Flynn watched, I once appreciated the magic of how our 911 system works by helping all in need anytime and anywhere. Shows resolved their plots within forty-two minutes, even those that had been "ripped from the headlines." In Northern New England, we have our versions of the ambulance wars. During 2022 and 2023, *The Brattleboro Reformer*, a local daily newspaper, followed an on-going saga with Rescue Inc, a fifty-year old ambulance service. The saga, when accelerated, resembled the board game *Risk*.

With a roll of the dice, a commercial service bids for the work long performed by a not-for-profit ambulance service. Within twelve months, a for-profit ambulance service in Keene, New Hampshire goes out of business. Rescue Inc announces a move to fill that gap.

A town manager rolled the dice when asking to review the financial affairs of Rescue Inc. The town manager could not have foreseen the impact on the Town of Brattleboro and the towns along the Connecticut River in both New Hampshire and Vermont. A board of directors govern the management of the non-profit ambulance service. After a new president got appointed, his mother later became the board chair. Several members of the board also work for the agency as either paid or unpaid EMS providers. No one can tell if the board works for the president or the president works for the board.

On this same game board, the Vermont State Police shifted their barracks nearly twenty-five miles north, resulting in a changes in how and when the state police respond to issues. Then in another policy shift, the state police informed towns that the town must hire a sheriff to perform patrols. In the rural hill towns, the selectboard pay a sheriff's deputy to patrol for a few hours a month. But the sheriffs will not respond to 911 calls because the sheriff's departments get no state funding. The 911 calls must go to the Vermont State Police. The sheriff's deputies will accept pay for patrolling and take fees from each ticket they write. They will not routinely head to emergency calls because there is no mechanism to pay for fuel, equipment, and labor during these crises.

New England, like other regions of the United States, struggles to define the role of emergency services and define what services are included. Are we promised a response when we call 911 or not? Is every 911 call answered? Is access to an ambulance service a right, a privilege, an obligation of the government, or do ambulances operate with the independent will of corporations?

We do not know. Our collection of 50 or 51 or 54 states and territories answer the question differently. In fact, the answer varies based on postal code and voting precincts.

STOLEN
MOUNTAIN

A Trowbridge Vermont Novel

A Novel by
I. M. AIKEN

—Chapter One Only—

Forthcoming from Flare Books
September 2025

1 | You Belong Here

I am looking at someone else's dream.

I turn my head to watch it roll past me. A fabulous image of a solo skier executing a perfect turn on a perfect white slope below a perfect blue sky.

"You Belong Here."

Once I saw that I belonged there, I could not stop seeing this image. I do assume the "You Belong Here" referred only to the skier carving down the slope and not the city bus that transported the image. I've got nothing against the M22, a blue and green clean-energy bus. I am walking east on Chambers Street, and it, the M22, travels west. Although I do not recognize that photo, that hill, that skier, I think I know that mountain. It is a rare day when we see skies that blue at home. A bit of photo editing in the spirit of marketing.

The next poster I spy had been installed around a trashcan near City Hall at Centre Street. "You belong here." This time, it was a stunning image of a golden-brown fire built for a lord in his manor hall. I scanned the QR code to discover The Branston Club.

The website is the dude version of my own vision for home. The dude version is painted richly with the colors of warm chestnuts, heated maple syrup, October beech leaves, and leather. I could nearly smell the single malt and humidor not shown. I am clearly supposed to want to be there—and not in the trashcan—but on that mountain. Odd place to advertise, I think. The only people using these trashcans are the tourists. Wouldn't it be better to buy ad space in the back seat of a black car service? Or maybe Joe Branston Club did, and I've just not seen ads yet. Not that I use black-car services too often. I like walking.

I like black-car services too. And I have ridden the M22, thank you very much.

Just so you don't think I live in a palatial manor house on a grand hill in small town Vermont, I don't. Well, I do, but not like that. I have herbs hanging to dry from the beams in the kitchen. And we have a wooden drying rack that I can lower from the ceiling. Clothing and towels dry quickly near the brick fireplace in the kitchen. And yes, it does have a 200-year-old bread oven built into the structure and an iron kettle rack. Given I eschew plastic, my kitchen is dominated by ceramics, fiber-based products, wooden tools, and metal. Some busybody might try to say the kitchen resembles a witch's lair. Of course, I am not a witch. The house is a 200-year-old home standing proudly on the shoulder of a gorgeous hill in Trowbridge Vermont. We do watch the morning fog lift from the village below us.

I know you can picture both versions of Vermont—the dude version with cut crystal, amber colored booze, cordovan leather, sumptuous oak, and my non-dude version with lavender and sage hanging from hooks in the ceiling, cotton towels drying near the stove, the smell of fresh bread, wooly sheep grazing out the window. Can't you? You've seen that photo. In the olden days, it was a postcard you bought at the general store next to the maple candy and raspberry jelly that Misses Fuzzy made then wrapped in a square of gingham cloth tied hemp twine. In the modern days, it is the money-shot on social media.

What you can't tell from most selfies in our village is that the church spire is about five degrees off from the vertical and the spine of that roof has the sway of a twenty-year old mare. The fire station sits over the road from the single church we have in town. That fire station, built by volunteer hands nearly sixty years ago, does have vertical sides and square corners. That's good. The fact remains the building is ugly. Just when you want a stunning brick firehouse with a tall square hose tower, you get this cinderblock rectangle finished with cheap T-111 siding tucked into irregular shaped gaps such as the triangle below the roof peak.

Opposite the firehouse stands the one-hundred-and fifty-year-old grange building. It is classically beautiful honoring the best ideas of the Georgian period. Except, it has been neglected since World War II.

Nobody takes selfies in our village.

Ok, the ironic tourist might. The tourist looking for the rich luxury of The Branston Club would regard Trowbridge with impatience and intolerance. They would recognize themselves as lost, out of place, and maybe slipped from time. Who knows what they think? I only hear them yell at me, but that is for later.

The normal tourist visits Trowbridge for three reasons. First, someone showed them a short cut to the ski hills of Southern Vermont, and they don't even know that they traveled through the corner of Trowbridge. Second, they got lost after falling off the two-lane state highway—the punishment for arguing with the GPS mapping on a mobile phone. Then after having fallen from the grid, they cannot get their map to refresh because there is no signal. Or three, people leave their resort, or country BnB, desiring an adventure in the wilds of the other Vermont. Y'know, the Vermont not on social media. The Vermont with trailer homes, grey plywood shacks, and trees growing through abandoned schoolhouses that are rotting in the forest next to neglected roads. Cue the banjos.

This guy, Joe Branston Club guy, sells luxury. He sells exclusivity. He sells premiere spa trips and the world's best black truffles curated by a dog named Pierre in France. The Jamón ibérico and European raw milk cheeses await your arrival. I expect the bathrobes to be plush, warm, and yet made from something exotic such as downy wool of Tibetan yaks harvested by gorgeous women in stunning colorful outfits gentling combing beasts with alpenglow fading on the glaciated Himalayas.

I shouldn't be too critical. I am wearing a hand made suit from London. I tried domestic. The local guys I tried in New York told me I was wrong. "This is the way it is done." Your skirts need to be A-line and not much below the knee, they said to me. I did get a suit made by them, although I returned twice with complaints about the fit of the skirt over my thighs, the tension on the buttons over my breasts, and the tightness of the shirts in my shoulders and up-per arms. Instead, I flew to London a few times. Yes, I got to hear, "Sure, gladly ma'am," in an East London accent.